KAREN ALDOUS enjoys village life on the edge of the North Downs in Kent with easy access to the buzz of London. Not only does she love the passive pleasures of reading and writing but also craves more active pursuits such as walking, cycling and skiing – especially when they involve family, friends, food, and … wine!

Much of Karen's inspiration comes from her travels. The UK, France, Switzerland and USA are just some of the places you'll be transported to in her books, but wherever she goes, new characters invite themselves into 'Karen's World' screaming at her to tell their stories; strong independent women who are capable of directing their own lives but struggle to control them … especially when temptation strikes!

As a member of the Romantic Novelists' Association and The Write Place, Karen feels she owes so much of her success to the love and support of her fellow writers.

You can follow Karen on Twitter at @KarenAldous_

Also by Karen Aldous

Five Ladies Go Skiing

KAREN ALDOUS

ONE PLACE. MANY STORIES

HQ
An imprint of HarperCollins*Publishers* Ltd
1 London Bridge Street
London SE1 9GF

This paperback edition 2018

First published in Great Britain by
HQ, an imprint of HarperCollins*Publishers* Ltd 2018

A catalogue record for this book is available from the British Library.

ISBN: 9780008321093

Typeset by Palimpsest Book Production Ltd, Falkirk, Stirlingshire
Printed and bound in Great Britain by
CPI Group (UK) Ltd, Melksham, SN12 6TR

*To Lynette & Stephen, Christine & Nigel, Sally and Peter
With Love*

MEET THE GIRLS –
Preparing for Switzerland

Ginny

As Ginny stepped out into the dining area, the candlelit festive dining table caught her breath. She shuddered at the sting in the backs of her eyes.

'Oh, it's …' The amber flickering mixed with the sparkle of the decorations toyed with her emotions. They looked almost too cheerful. 'It's gorgeous,' she said, blinking away those brimming tears. Her daughter Rachel and daughter-in-law Clemmie had laid it beautifully, and Ginny's heart swelled at the effort each of her children and in-laws, even the grandchildren, had made on this difficult day: their first Christmas without their father and grandfather. It just didn't feel right to enjoy Christmas without him.

The family waited in silence for her to be seated, watching as she wiped a stray tear from her face and pulled on a band at the back of her head, unleashing her mane of shoulder-length hair that she had tied back before preparing dinner.

'You've all made such an effort. Thank you,' she said smiling at each of them as she nestled in the chair and smoothed her hair. 'OK, let's enjoy,' she added, grateful for their input. Thank goodness Rachel and Ross had helped in the kitchen getting everything into the right serving dishes. The morning had been manic. In fact, the whole week had. It had been a rush trying to fit everything in before her ski trip to Switzerland. The effort involved in getting time off work for a hair appointment, getting to the farm shop for the last-minute veg, fruit and salad, cleaning the house, cooking the meats and prepping in readiness for the family's arrival had all proved to be worth it. She had forgotten just how much Mike used to contribute to helping around the house, particularly at Christmas and family gatherings. He always prepped the veg and was a dab hand at juggling the food around in the fridge so that beers and wine would fit in. They were small things that counted in a big way.

She heaved out a sigh. At least they were all together. She raised her Prosecco-filled glass, first to her daughter Rachel and son Ross who sat either side of her, then to the others.

'Well, shall we ...?' Ginny waited for each of her family to pick up a filled glass or, in the children's case, plastic flutes of lemonade.

'Merry Christmas, Mum,' Rachel cheered in unison with Ross, and Ginny's eyes glistened mirroring theirs, her gaze flicking quickly to their partners and children gathered around the festive-food-filled table.

'Hope you're feeling our cheer, Dad,' Rachel hailed, peering out of the window and up at the grey sky. 'We miss you loads but we'll always cherish our lovely memories. Merry Christmas.'

'Absolutely,' Ginny rushed in after a gulp of the bubbly, trying again to steel herself against the constant burning in the backs of her eyes; but then catching a glimpse of Rachel's lips quivering, a sudden gasp escaped her throat. 'Me ... merry Ch ... Christmas, Mike.' It was only the third time they had all been together since Mike's passing but it wasn't getting any easier.

Ross reached for his mother's wrist, his caring green-grey eyes, so like his father's, misting. 'You OK, Mum?'

Ginny reached for her napkin, holding back sobs as five-year-old Tommy, Rachel's eldest, gazed at her, concerned. 'Yes, yes. I'll be all right. Truly. I knew it would be tough. Our first Christmas without him. I know it's difficult for all of you too.'

'I miss Grandad,' Tommy said. 'He's going to miss me opening my presents.'

A symphony of swallowing and gasping sounds resonated around the table and, like her mother, the petite Rachel grabbed her napkin and wiped her eyes as she turned to her son. 'I know, darling, but he's here in spirit. We just have to deal with the rest.' She turned to the empty chair then back to her son. 'We'll get used to it; we have to. Come on, there's a good boy, get your dinner.'

Ross leaned back, nervously rubbing his four-year-old daughter Amelia's back and faced his mother. 'If you don't mind, Mum,' he said hesitantly, 'I'd like to ring you on Monday, the twenty-eighth, the anniversary. A bit selfish I know, but I just want to know that you're all right.'

'Me too,' Rachel added, gently squeezing her mother's hand.

Fighting yet another lump in her throat, Ginny smiled as she glanced at each of her children. An image of Mike amused her. It was one from years ago when he was teasing Ross's friends that the *Friends* comedy characters were named after his kids. As much as she wondered and tortured herself about what Mike may or may not have done, he was still their children's dad and they had loved him unconditionally and were both coping so well with his loss. The urge to jump up and kiss them both became over-whelming.

'My cherubs, of course, I won't mind. That would be lovely, thank you. Both of you. It's a major step for all of us and if it helps you too, then even better. I remember when my dad died, it took me ages to come to terms with it. Just hearing Louis Armstrong sing "Wonderful World" on the radio would start me off. For some reason I coped with Grandma's passing better. I've read though, that the first anniversary of a beloved's death can be a turning point, so let's hope so. We'll never forget Dad, but we all have to move on.' She blinked at her own words. 'I've been thinking about having some sort of memorial that day, to help.'

Rachel looked aghast. 'Not on your own.'

'No. With the girls.' Ginny clenched her teeth. 'All of us, I'm sure they won't mind. We may need a rest from the skiing by then anyway. That's if I even get on the slopes.' Ginny gave a snort, realising the impression her negativity would give. Her usual self-doubts crept in. 'Oh, please don't let on to the girls, but I'm petrified.'

'Oh, Mum, I thought you were.' Rachel gazed at her mother with concern. 'You know, there's still time to change your mind, although I think it's a perfect distraction, a great idea to challenge yourself as well as have fun with your friends.'

Ginny slid her knife beneath a slice of succulent white turkey and laid it gently onto her plate. 'No. No, I wouldn't – couldn't – let my friends down. They've organised this all on my behalf. I'm really touched that they care so much. So, no. I'm determined to throw myself into it. And, I'm exaggerating. It will be a new challenge, and I'm sure the girls will expect me to organise something to remember Dad. Angie even suggested it at one point. I don't want the trip to be miserable though. Just a toast at a meal or something. I'm not really sure if there will be anywhere suitable, but once we're there, hopefully I'll find a place I think is right and I'll ask the girls. I'm sure they won't mind. Like you, they'll think it fitting that we remember him.'

Ginny flinched as one of the red candles in the centre of the table flickered. She would never get used to losing Mike despite her need to question him. She missed him terribly. And it was incomprehensible that he was taken at just sixty-one. Was it punishment for his misdemeanour? Not that she could ever know anything now. His words would echo, possibly haunt forever, but no explanation would ever be spoken. All she knew was that she needed closure and the determination to stop tormenting herself and wallowing in self-pity.

'Your hair looks really good by the way. I like the new shorter fringe,' Rachel said, brushing her fingers through a spring of Ginny's bouncy highlighted hair. 'You're looking amazingly fit too. You must have worked really hard preparing. You remind me of that … oh, what's her name, the *Sex and the City* woman, er … Kim Cattrall. That's the one. Don't be surprised if you pull on the slopes.'

'Don't be daft. I'm almost sixty not sixteen.' Ginny laughed, but was thankful to be side-tracked from the incessant niggling that festered in her mind. 'But, I'm flattered. Thank you. It's been hard work and I pray that I've done enough to get me through the week. I'm apprehensive about skiing, yes, but I'm really looking forward to having some fun with the girls. The timing's perfect and I'm certainly glad to be away from that office. I was tempted to walk out on Thursday.'

Ginny shook her head and scrunched her nose. 'It's not a nice place to work, but I thought of today, with all of you, and the week away with my all my friends. The break will be the tonic I need. Maybe I'll look at the job differently when I get back.'

Kim

Sheltering from the late afternoon sun under a canvas canopy Kim Anderson drained the last of the tepid tea from her mug, knowing she should get on with her packing. It was naughty to be lazy, naughty and nice and something she rarely did. And why not? The Perth heat was intense and there was nothing more refreshing after a day on her feet at the hospital than a cool dip in the pool and then that priceless slot of the day slumbering for an hour in the shade, gorging on colours and the heady scents of the rose garden before Will, her husband, returned from work.

In fact, today she would savour it that little bit more just because she could. Will would be another two hours. She had suspended Lena, her personal trainer, for two weeks over Christmas and whilst she was away skiing. The break, she envisaged, would give her time to decide if she should actually continue. Although the sessions had produced a body she had always yearned for, it had been gruelling these last few months, so she deserved a treat.

The pile of ironing in the laundry room could lounge for another half hour despite the fact she couldn't wait to seal up her travel bags and be on her way to Europe. So far from Australia, and so much cooler this time of year, but she took comfort and warmth knowing that she would very soon be with Mai, one of her twin daughters, for Christmas Day. Mai was staying with Kim's friend and former colleague, Tandy, in her home by Lake Geneva. After that Kim would meet up with her besties – Ginny, Cathy, Lou and Angie – for a whole week together. And skiing.

The skiing was irrelevant. An excuse. It was time with her old buddies that her heart yearned for. Since the twins left, a wound had opened up inside her. Kim indulged herself among the roses. Her home served as a place for sleeping, eating, storing belongings and washing clothes. Although beautiful, with every consumable imaginable, its heart had been ripped out when Avril and Mai flew off to study in Europe four years ago. It only came alive every Christmas.

After her friend Ginny lost her husband Mike, Ginny had come to stay a month and they spent hours chatting and consuming buckets of wine in the rose garden – Kim's refuge.

Waking from her reverie, Kim entered the building she called home and, as usual, checked the security cameras before climbing the stairs to shower. The gates were secured and there was nothing signalling alarm. After showering, she towelled herself dry and applied a heavy dose of Nivea to soak into her skin, then slipped on a summer shirt and headed back down to the laundry room. Sticking out her tongue at the pile in the basket, she pulled out the ironing board from its cupboard, followed by the iron. Turning the dial to cool, she briefly ran the iron over the new ski-wear she had collected over the last few months. She had washed fleeces, T-shirts, thermals and jeans. Then she realised what a waste of time it all was – they didn't need ironing. As she looked up at the clock, she heard the rattle of Will's keys.

'Have a good day, love?' she asked noticing beads of sweat bubbling on his skin as he slapped his laptop case onto the worktop close to her. He'd only walked from the car.

'Nah, not the best.'

'I don't know why you didn't book a flight and come with me to Switzerland. Or London at least – spend Christmas with Avril.'

Will rolled his eyes. 'She won't want me there; she's all loved up. Anyway, odds on they'll be spending Crimbo with his folks.'

'You think? She hasn't said.' Kim creased her eyebrows, anticipating more information.

Will shrugged, smoothing his greying hair with his fingers. 'Well, I'm flat out over the holidays so it ain't gonna happen. Besides, you'll be with your friends and I know that means a lot to you.' He kissed the back of her neck as if knowing it should soothe any tension about the subject. She had given up trying to persuade him to retire and move back to England. It only upset him and caused rows. He wasn't ready to give up his specialised work with the oncology team in Perth, and understandably so; they were making great headway treating, even curing women with breast cancer. Plans were now in place to set up a one-stop care centre over the next two years. She knew he couldn't bear to abandon the team.

Kim placed the iron down on its safety grid, turning to Will. As she wrapped her hands around the back of his neck, his arms slid around her waist whilst he leaned down to kiss a short tuft of her hair.

His lips brushed hers. 'I must be crazy to let such a beautiful woman out of my sight for twelve days.' He took a step back and eyed her naked body beneath the thin linen shirt. 'Look at you.

7

Girls in their twenties are less lean and toned. God, I wanna eat you!' He pulled her close again and Kim instantly felt his arousal.

'I have things to do and you need a shower,' she said, freeing herself from his embrace.

'All the trouble you go to so that you can ski and see your friends and you can't spare me half an hour of your time.'

Kim sighed, blinking hard, then peering up at him, she said, 'Go, shower and I'll be up in five. God, why don't men have a menopause and lose their drive? You owe me.'

Will smiled and gave her a squeeze. 'Aw, come on, I don't make that many demands.'

Kim tightened her lips, staring at his hand. 'I know, but …' She paused. 'Never mind, no you don't,' she said softly, when what she really wanted to say was: *Be warned. I'm going to be notching up enough credit so that you honour my desires, my yearning to move back to England.* But it would have no effect. Will had made his view very clear, so it would only create an argument.

'Besides, you're not going to see me for nearly two weeks.' He headed for the hall stairs. 'I'll be washed and waiting.'

Switching off the iron, Kim rubbed her forehead. She would never stop loving her husband, but she found herself immensely irritated with his reluctance to discuss their future. The last time she approached him about it, they rowed and didn't speak for days, and since then she'd lost the courage to broach the subject, allowing the issue to fester inside her for fear of upsetting him.

At times her life was an island, floating in a vast and desolate sea. Yes, Will was her dream husband, but he could be stubborn as a mule. Not that she would have noticed it as a young nurse. She was blinded to his faults and blown away when the handsome Dr Will Anderson flirted with her. She'd almost exploded when he had asked her to be his plus-one at the Hospital Christmas Dinner. And, as a partner, he had always been so loving and strong, even through the dark days of their fertility problems. It was that love that kept them strong throughout the long IVF treatments and the longing for a family.

Naturally, there was tension – lots of it at times – but letters to and from her friends had kept her spirits up so she and Will had got through it. And, eventually, the twins had made them complete. Now that the twins had flown the nest and Will was more and more absorbed in his work, she found herself pining. Her only deep friendship since moving to Oz in her mid-twenties was a previous neighbour, Marnie, who nowadays was blessed enough to spend much of her time with her seven grandchildren.

Kim climbed the stairs, aware that Will had probably had his shower. She didn't find intimacy so easy since the menopause had scared off her libido, but Will was very understanding. He did make an effort to get her in the mood first with his caresses. And the acupuncture she'd had helped. If only he comprehended her other needs as readily. Something to distract her from pining. She lifted her chin as she entered the bedroom, seeing Will towelling his lean body after his shower. Again, she would try her best to push her thoughts to the back of her mind.

Cathy

As efficient as always, Cathy Golding had completed her list of morning chores as well as the last of her packing and sat in her book-bulging study to switch on her laptop. She checked her watch: 8.29. She picked up a brazil nut from a small dish and nibbled on it, well on her way to consuming one half of her daily dose of protein and selenium. Outside the window, the grey winter sky and depleted front garden motivated her to get writing to reach the end of her story. She opened the document entitled 'Sally's New Bike', the summer story she was submitting to a woman's magazine. After enduring more than thirty years teaching English Literature and Language to girls at the local secondary school, albeit with much commendation and personal satisfaction, Cathy was finally living her dream.

She craned her neck to check she had closed the door. There was only Anthony, her husband, in the house, but he managed to disrupt her more in a morning than a class of thirty twelve-year-olds ever had in a whole day. As it was Christmas Eve, she needed to finish the story ready for posting before her ski trip to Switzerland on Boxing Day with her closest friends.

Reading the last two paragraphs, Cathy then read the notes underneath and began typing. Each day, before closing a document, she had formed the habit of adding a few brief sentences so that she could instantly pick up the thread next time. And, she found it was always good to note her ideas down, even if a better idea came along later – which they often did. She tapped swiftly on her keyboard, only pausing here and there for thought, but no sooner was she in the zone than she heard the familiar drum of Anthony's slippers on the floorboards outside, then the clack of the handle on the study door. Anthony was never subtle.

His voice boomed, jolting her from the zone. 'Would you like tea?'

Cathy took a deep breath and turned her head. 'Yes, but please, darling, I shouldn't have to keep reminding you. Just bring it, and quietly. If I don't want it, I'll leave it.'

'Yes, sorry again.' Anthony clenched his jaw. 'How's it going?'

'It was going fine. I want to finish, edit and post by lunchtime. I'm cooking the gammon and sausage rolls this afternoon and your last two meals for freezing so I want to get this off.'

Anthony rubbed his thighs sheepishly. 'Right. Anything I can do?'

'All done, I believe.'

'Need any last-minute bits for your trip?'

'No, darling, but thank you for asking.'

'I might meet Terry and the guys in the pub later. What do you think?'

She looked at him in surprise. 'It will be good for you to see the boys,' she said patiently as he padded out the door. 'And, just tea, love, please.' She returned to her keyboard gripping her knuckles, wondering why she felt she had to treat her husband like a child these days. He knew she craved peace and quiet to write. In fact, meeting friends for a Christmas drink would do him good. His friends hadn't yet retired like Anthony had, but it would help him when they did. The last year or so he was like a lost puppy, moping around and interrupting her, trying to please her. Not the wildly energetic man she married at all. Where was her confident Anthony?

Growing up in an emotionally repressed household, she had basked in all the attention that Anthony used to lavish on her. Unlike her parents, he listened, gave her his undivided attention and allowed her to speak her mind. She didn't have to eat the meat on her plate and behave like the perfect daughter to avoid embarrassing him like she did her famous father. Anthony was proud of her whoever she was and never let her think otherwise. Anthony adored the fact that she was well read. He was always proud of the fact that she could meet his demanding clients at functions and events and talk to them on any level. The devotion and energy he had for her, and his clients, was a rare gift and had very likely contributed to making his talent agency extremely successful.

Cathy had been teaching a few months when she met and fell in love with Anthony and it was at a time when her confidence was sagging with her pupils, struggling to get to grips with exerting authority over rebellious teenagers. His support was tremendous. As luck would have it, he was working with a client who was a speech and confidence coach, so it was fortuitous that he was able to relay some tricks. With trial, error and persistence, and a belief in herself, along with her passion for books, she soon delighted in sharing her love of literature and the English language with her pupils. Kids grew to love her lessons and respect grew among her peers and superiors. She threw her soul into her career, her writing ambitions quashed. Even thoughts of having her own family: quashed. But retirement meant she was freed. She could write her stories down.

Ginny and Lou, her closest friends from childhood, had loved hearing her stories. They used to gather in the little summerhouse her father had built, and their encouragement spurred her on to write more. Many were still stored in the attic. And although she didn't get around to writing a great deal whilst teaching, she had continued to read like a girl obsessed whilst remaining close to her friends.

She still giggled to herself when she thought about skiing. She wasn't sporty or outdoorsy at all like Ginny, Lou, Angie and Kim, but was strangely looking forward to the challenge, especially after the effort it had taken to prepare physically. And, crucially, she couldn't wait to spend time with her old friends, particularly Ginny who was still down after losing Mike and the job she loved. Ginny had spent far too much time hiding herself away this last year. Cathy hoped this trip would show her just how much they all loved and cared for her and that their encouragement would help her turn the next corner. Though, naturally, she would take some books and her Kindle for the quieter times or – she shuddered – in case she broke a leg.

Her door rattled again, only gentler. Anthony edged in slowly, carrying a china cup and saucer, and smiling. 'Here you are, beautiful. You'll miss my cuppas when you're away.'

'I will.' Cathy smiled up at his glistening brown eyes. He was still her sweet husband and she did love him dearly, but at times he was a pain. 'Thank you, darling. I don't think tea will be readily available in the mountains.'

'Exactamundo! But I could pop some teabags in your case.'

'Yes, good idea. Thank you, darling.'

'Anything else before I watch Jeremy Kyle?'

'I'm fine, honest,' Cathy said. She jumped up suddenly and

moved over to the bookcase. 'Actually, I came across that sudoku book you were looking for if you've done the crossword.'

Anthony reached out and took the book from her hand. 'Ah, thanks, love. I might do some after Jeremy.'

Cathy sat down, resting her elbows on her desk with her head in her hand. She listened to the door close. 'Right – focus,' she told herself. 'Roll on Boxing Day and Switzerland.'

Angie

Scratching the upper right side of her torso, Angie Ricci raced from her car to her front door. As she opened the door, despite it being the middle of winter, aromas of summer soared up her nose: garlic and lemon infused with fresh herbs. She poked her head into her spacious shiny kitchen and her husband Robbie peered up from the chopping board where evenly sliced juicy tomatoes lay. A grin lit his cheeks.

She pursed her lips and kissed the air. 'Hi, sweet, this is a nice surprise. Smells delish! I'm just going to run upstairs and take off this bra. It's been driving me mad all day.'

'No rush,' Robbie said waving the knife before resuming his task. 'I'll pour you a glass of wine.'

'OK, I'll jump in the shower then.'

Angie dashed up the stairs to her newly fitted bedroom which, with its floor-to-ceiling mirror wardrobes along one wall, reflected twinkling orbs from the other side of the river in the distance. Closer, a light shining from Ginny's home, just down the valley, brought a smile to Angie's face. Not long now and she and her beautiful friends would all be together.

Stripping off an oversized navy fleece, she slipped three edamame beans into her mouth that slid from her pocket onto the bed. They reminded her to pack some of her supply for the journey and the trip. They were difficult to get in the smaller shops even though veggie food was more freely available. Munching, she stripped off her pale blue T-shirt and threw it on the bed too, before removing the offending undergarment. She inspected it before stepping closer to the mirror and raising her arms. Instantly she scowled at the red rash-like swelling on her smooth light brown skin.

'Nasty bra,' she mouthed, reaching for a bottle of moisturising cream on a chest of drawers and pressing the top to release the liquid balm. 'I hope you're not going to aggravate me when I'm skiing,' she moaned to the sore on her torso. As she massaged the cream in, relief surged, soothing her. Had she been at her own health centre on any normal day, she would have had the opportunity to change, but promoting on a stand in a bustling local shopping mall all day on Christmas Eve, alone, it had been impossible. Wiping it so that all the cream disappeared, Angie then removed her leggings, trainers and socks and seeing a long, lean reflection, posed with a pout.

'Looking hot, babe,' she praised, admiring the recent changes. Her body was the best it had ever been, with a sleek tone and definition she had always envied in younger women.

'If only I could notch off twenty years of real time,' she told her reflection. Not that she hadn't always kept herself fit. Since joining the WRENs at eighteen she had trained as a PT instructor. It was the one thing that gave her the identity she craved, being a biracial child in the Fifties. Later, as the UK became more multicultural, she grew proud of her heritage. Unlike her mother, who never felt London had embraced her. Her dear, now departed mother had sailed from Barbados to train as a nurse and met her father at a stall on Greenwich market where he was selling ladies' fashion.

Her father had also passed. She recalled his claim that he was instantly struck by her mother's exotic beauty and didn't care that his neighbours gossiped or crossed the road to avoid them. He was happy, and prejudice had never entered his brain. Angie relished the colour of her skin now and appreciated the fact that its texture remained taut, even on her face, and had aged without too many creases or wrinkles. Many a time compliments had been forthcoming that she could be thirty-something, despite now being sixty-two, a little older than her besties.

After a quick shower, and another soaking of moisturiser, she towel-dried her thick black curls and slipped on one of the over-sized shirts that she left undone at her breasts, before she returned downstairs to the kitchen.

'Sorry,' she said, reaching up to Robbie on tiptoe and pecking him on the lips. 'That bra was grinding under my arms all day. I think I'll just pack my sports bras for skiing.' She perched on one of the stalls at the central island where Robbie had prepared the salad, rubbing her hands together and inhaling the Mediterranean fragrance.

'Haven't you packed yet?' Robbie asked turning to her as he reached in the fridge for the salad dressing he'd prepared.

Angie splayed out her hands in wonder. 'When have I had time to pack?' she asked, spotting a small bottle of nail varnish submerged among satsumas and Granny Smiths.

Rob shook his head from side to side. 'I hope you don't think you're going to pack when everyone's here tomorrow. Danny and Matt will probably tolerate it, but you know Jonty will moan.

'Of course not. I'll do it later. After dinner,' Angie stated. She unscrewed the nail varnish top. 'I've started piling it, ready.'

'You really need to start delegating. You can't do it all.'

'It's not that easy, Rob,' she said, brushing a thin layer of the ruby-red lacquer on to her thumbnail. 'There's nobody at the centre who knows about promoting or marketing. Any more than me anyway.'

Rob flicked his greying thick fringe from his forehead. 'Get a professional in then. Surely it will pay for itself. The rate you're going, you'll run yourself into the ground.'

He made it sound so simple, but marketing personnel were

so expensive. Only in the last few years had the business been turning a good profit and she was squirrelling that extra money away in the hope of buying a little bolthole somewhere warm – a winter hideaway she and Robbie could escape to if ever they had free time.

She watched as Rob tossed sweet potato wedges over on the hot oven tray. 'Anyway, don't lecture me about delegation or managing my time or myself. I manage to work and keep myself in tip-top condition – you've surely no reason to complain. I could certainly give some of those young actresses you watch a run for their money. Anyway, I waited for you last night. Did you watch another film? Horny as a rig worker I was.'

Angie had always been conscious that men would look else-where for gratification; after all, she knew only too well what her father got up to when he took ladies to try on dresses in his van when he worked the markets.

'I fell asleep, I'm sorry. I still need a shower and a shave actu-ally. I was late for work and I've been busy.'

Angie sighed. 'Yes, I can see that. So why are you cooking? I could have popped into M&S or John Lewis for a meal deal.'

Rob shrugged and even blushed slightly. 'I suppose guilt and the fact that you've been on my mind this afternoon as I wrapped your Christmas presents. I left the office a bit earlier to collect one, popped into the Horse and Groom of course, but got back to wrap them before you got home.'

'Ooh, something mega sexy I hope. Yours is.' Angie's black locks bounced with excitement as she imagined a seductive silk negligee coupled with the latest, most wonderful sex toy on the market. Robbie knew how much she liked to try new gadgets. Their sexual connection had been major from the off. He was the first man she had ever met who knew how to please her, as well as being warm and funny.

Ginny and the girls had never really grasped her insatiable appetite for sex, but it had always been a huge part of her and

Rob's relationship. Even after the menopause, Angie persuaded her GP to keep her on HRT just in case her libido faltered. Lately, though, she had found Rob a little forgetful and complaining of being tired; maybe it was his age – he was sixty-four in a month. But he hadn't forgotten her Christmas present. Hopefully things were looking up. 'Eek, I'm so excited. Can't wait until tomorrow. In fact, if we're still waiting for the food to cook, we could fit in a quickie.'

Placing the sweet potatoes back into the oven, Rob swiped his neck with the back of his hand. 'I don't know where you get your energy from, sweetheart, but I'm bushed.'

'Nonsense. You just want me to seduce you, don't you?' she said and, wasting no time, screwed the nail varnish top back on and leapt swiftly from the stool. She sidled up to him and pulled him close, sweeping one arm around his neck and reaching for his crotch with her other hand. 'You are sex on legs, Rob Ricci, and what if we don't get another opportunity before I go away?'

Lou

It was almost two o'clock when Lou Cavendish checked her watch and straightened the last cushion in the show house. She pulled her scarf tighter so that it hugged the back of her neck; it probably wasn't her greatest idea to get her hair cut so short in the winter, but she was certainly pleased with the result and it would be easier to wear a ski helmet. She decided she looked and felt so much younger and Terry, her husband, had approved too, which was unusual. He usually preferred her hair long.

She switched off the lamps and headed to the hall, happy that the house was finally furnished and tweaked ready for the New Year launch. She opened her classic Chanel flap bag, pulled out her Chanel lip gloss, leaned towards the mirror and stroked her lips with the pink-orange tones of Corail Naturel, until they shone. Satisfied, she rolled and smacked her lips before tossing the lip gloss back in the black bag and slipping on her matching ballerina flats. After a final smile at her reflection, she turned off the hall light and rubbed a speck off the switch with her shiny long fingernail.

'OK, done.' She grabbed her winter coat from the hook and brushed the faux-fur collar before sliding it on. At least that was one more thing ticked off her list; now all she had to do was finish her packing and decide what to wear for Christmas Day.

She and Terry weren't cooking a Christmas dinner this year. They had all been invited to her son Ollie's house with his wife Ella and their two girls, as well as her daughter Emma and Emma's partner Joe. Lou was looking forward to not having to rush around like a headless chicken with all the usual pressures of preparing food for Christmas Day and all the mess that came with it. It was Terry's job to tidy after her. Lou hated any kind of housework but still held a passion for her and Terry's property business – building and selling them. Fortunately, show houses didn't get too messy when you employed good cleaners.

Once out and on the road, the traffic was lighter than she had expected for Christmas Eve, so she was soon back in the village, clocking that Ginny's car wasn't in the drive opposite. She parked her Range Rover Evoque beside Terry's big Range Rover. She knew he would still be down the Horse and Groom with Robbie, possibly Anthony if he dared to leave Cathy alone in the house, and Mike's old partner Scott, along with the contractors who often worked on the developments together. They went Thursday nights and every Christmas Eve. Terry and Anthony even wheeled Mike down to the pub last year – to think he was only a day away from entering the hospice. Lou shivered at the thought. Mike's last day at home had been Christmas Day.

After a bite to eat and a much-needed hot cup of tea, she climbed the stairs to one of the spare bedrooms, Emma's old bedroom, where a case lay partially full on the crimson carpet and clothes were scattered across Emma's pink and purple duvet cover. Ski garments were neatly folded, whilst others awaited their fate.

'So, who is travelling to Switzerland with me?' Lou began to pair up some more outfits, wondering what was most suited to après-ski and what accessories to include. Opening a drawer containing several boxes of costume jewellery, she rummaged through for some navy and pearl beads that had matching earrings. With her new haircut she wanted earrings, but she had no idea which box they were in. She found a set of red beads with earrings, which she thought would go splendidly with her charcoal-grey cashmere, and she placed them on the bed. Tugging at the lid of the next box, her eyes brightened, and her heart gave a light flutter. She lifted a gold belcher chain with a half-sovereign and untangled it from a silver one. The gold one, her parents had given her for her eighteenth birthday. The silver chain, now tarnished, with the words 'I Love You,' also in silver, was from her ex, Jimmy Dixon, when she was twenty-one.

Lou bit her lip remembering her first love. They met at university in Sussex. Instantly smitten with each other, their chemistry had been strong. She smiled while picturing him then, his black curls flopped over the most gorgeous sultry brown eyes. He was two years older, drove a sporty Ford Capri, and treated her with the latest records, her first ever cassette player and album cassettes among other gifts.

They were inseparable at university and, once home, Jimmy had even proposed. But according to her parents, it was too soon. She should wait, they said, persuading her to concentrate on her banking career for a few years and encouraging her to travel, explore life. Knowing her mother had never had the same opportunities as herself, she considered it fair advice. And after much heartbreak, all she could do was forget him. That is, until he found her on Facebook a few years ago.

Lou heard the front door slam and, instantly blasted from her trance, threw the jewellery back into the box. Speedily, she searched the other boxes for the navy and white beads and placed them together with the red in a small drawstring bag before tucking them into the case.

'Terry, hi. I'm upstairs finishing my packing,' she shouted, grabbing a polo neck sweater from the bed and arranging it in her case.

She heard the loo flush in the downstairs cloakroom and the thump of Terry's bare feet stomping on the carpet on the stairs. As she stood back up, the alcohol on his breath and his clothes wafted straight to her nostrils as he walked up beside her.

She met his lips and pecked them. 'How was the pub?'

'Mm, downbeat to begin with. Sad, without Mike, but we soon came to the conclusion that Mike wouldn't want us moping. He was our social secretary – we couldn't let him down – so we toasted his memory a few times. Poor sod. I do miss him.'

Lou rubbed her husband's arm. Terry was still very attractive for a man of his age and she cared for him deeply, despite the chemistry between them never matching her and Jimmy's. 'I know, darling. Must be hard. How was Robbie? Did Anthony go?'

Terry shrugged, clasping her hand. 'Both like me – still missing Mike and grateful we're all still alive. What can you do? I just hope it doesn't happen to us yet.'

'I know – poor Ginny. I can't imagine going through what she has. And I didn't think Ant would go today if I'm honest. He's been down. He seems to have missed Mike most.'

'Nah, I don't think it's just Mike he's missing. I think he's getting bored. Maybe retirement makes you like that. Bit worrying, isn't it?'

Lou squeezed Terry's hand and kissed him briefly on the lips again. 'Well, if and when we sell the business and retire next year, I hope we don't get bored. I want to do a variety of things. As well as watching our children prosper and grandchildren grow up, I want to explore new activities, learn new skills, travel and go on adventures with you, and I intend to spend lots of time with my friends, so make sure you do too.'

He hugged her tight. 'I love you so much, Lou Cavendish, and I hope we have many more years together, enjoying our retirement. At least we know we can work together after all these years, so I'm sure we can get through and enjoy our retirement together. So, don't you go doing anything stupid like knocking yourself unconscious on the slopes. Let's just hope nothing happens and we have a ball.'

As predictable and cautious as ever, she thought, pecking him on the lips. 'Absolutely. I love you too, Terry.'

Chapter 1

Ginny

Out of breath, but euphoric, I glanced at Mike sitting on a fluffy white cloud, watching me as I proudly planted the flag from the side of my rucksack into the mountain's snow-capped pinnacle. 'You didn't think I would do it, did you?' I told him expanding my chest.

'Ginny, Ginny, you're dribbling, sweetheart,' a voice encroached on my senses as a force pushed me upright. It was Lou. My consciousness was returning. We were in the back of the hire car. Lou's throaty, some might say seductive voice was giggling. 'You must be dreaming of that man at the airport.'

'I would be if he spoke to me in that sexy accent,' Cathy added mimicking a French accent. I instantly imagined her little nostrils widening and thin lips pouting whilst her sharp blonde bob shimmied.

Forcing my eyes open, I saw Angie lean forward and her hand flip from the steering wheel to tap her backside.

'Me too,' she said. 'He can sit on my luggage any day. He was hot!'

Typical of Angie. I grinned, then with a stretch, I roused myself, wiping saliva from the side of my mouth and realising the four of us were actually en-route to our ski trip. Sadly, I wasn't with Mike at all. Letting my eyelids drop again, I yearned to return to the dream – to the top of that mountain – with Mike; where I wasn't scared, and he was real. Very real. Those sweet eyes smiling. I wanted to yell to the world – Mike's alive.

I rubbed my eyes and peered out of the window, marvelling at majestic snowy peaks. As a lover of maps, I figured we must be in the Swiss Rhône valley. I sized up the mountains dwarfing us on both sides.

'How embarrassing.' I groaned, trying to imagine what I must have looked like slumped in the chair, dribbling.

Lou was quick to defend me. 'Don't worry. You're in good company. I used to do it all the time when I commuted to London.' She stretched out her long legs and wriggled her socked feet to retrieve her designer snow boots from under the passenger seat. 'We're not far now, sweetheart. You might want to get your boots on too.'

'Oh, right, yes.' I sat up, remembering I was on a promise of fun, not just to my lovely friends, but also to my children. Thinking back to yesterday, Christmas Day, I remembered I'd promised myself and my children – Ross and Rachel – that I would embrace this week and use it as a pivot to move forward. They desperately missed their father too, and I was touched by the mature strength they displayed as they voiced their concerns. Mainly about me being on my own in Kent whilst they lived further north, with their families to keep them busy. So, although they would treasure their memories, they agreed they had both weathered the worst, and a memorial would be good, particularly for me. Like me, they felt it was the right time to let Mike go and whilst not forgetting him, I would set my sights forward and immerse myself in something enjoyable.

Not that skiing and fun had ever sat equally on the scales in my brain. Instead of feeling excited like you do going on holiday, I was feeling numb, experiencing that sense you get when you're not in control. Similar to that day Mike refused further chemo. I couldn't say or do anything to change his mind and all strength and hope bled out of me. Cancer controlled us. And, like the chemo that prolonged Mike's life before that, this week-long ski trip, I imagined, would only be a temporary fix. Nothing would bring him back. After this trip, I would return to my empty home, my purposeless job and bleak life without Mike, even if he had betrayed me. And that, I would never know for sure. It was impossible to question him. My only resolve was to break out of this mode of thinking, this bloody endless circle of self-persecution.

My head fell to the side. Beside me, Lou was holding up a compact mirror and cleansing her face with a wipe, whilst I, in my head, was trying to eke out every particle of negativity that was in my brain. I wanted it wiped clean of the torment so that I could apply some new foundation to my life. Thank God I had my friends. Like Ross and Rachel, they were rooting for me to move on. They had my back, tolerated my gloominess, even when I rejected their efforts to take me out when I'd been wallowing. Well, wallow no more, Ginny Watts. I was jolly well going to make sure they knew I loved and appreciated them and show them I was determined to move forward.

I sat up, lengthening my legs, pointing one foot in search of my boots whilst elevating the notes in my voice as I asked Angie, 'So how far now?'

In a motherly fashion, Lou responded with a smile and ran her thumb along the corner of my eye. 'Only a few miles, sweetheart, and we'll be turning off. You were having such a lovely sleep, I didn't want to wake you, but you were in danger of noosing your neck on your seatbelt. You've been nodding since Geneva.'

'Oh, I'm such a party pooper. I'm so sorry,' I said, raising my tone another octave to flame enthusiasm. 'I should text Kim. How long will it take, Angie?'

Kim was our other bestie who had travelled separately from her home in Australia and was already at the resort. To think we thought our start had been an early one from Camfield Bottom in Kent; her journey must have been exhausting. And all for my benefit. My conscience was a supermarket shelf stacked with tins of guilt. My amazing friends had gone to such great efforts, organising this trip for me and leaving their husbands and families over Christmas. I was thrilled when Kim also agreed to come; it had helped me get over the shock of skiing in the Swiss Alps.

Skiing! Something brave and adventurous to set me on my path, they had insisted. We were all hovering around sixty for goodness' sake. My stomach had wrenched at the idea, but they were thinking ahead. It was designed to distract me from the first anniversary of Mike's death and I guess they knew it would be a good time for a fresh start.

Angie checked the clock on the dashboard. 'About twenty minutes now. A few minutes on this road, then we'll be going up and round the mountain.'

Cathy turned her head from the front passenger seat. 'Darling, Kim knows we're on our way. You texted her soon after we landed,' she said in her school ma'am voice, making me feel like one of her pupils.

'I know, Cath, but I'm sure she'll be glad to hear of our progress. She's on her own there, don't forget. Besides, we don't want her forgetting to order our wine,' I pointed out as I fumbled in my bag for my phone. I grabbed it and tapped in my password.

As usual Cathy's silky bob fascinated me as her shoulders shook indignantly. 'Oh, yes of course. Silly me! Absolute necessity. Yes, do text her,' Cathy said.

I smiled. 'Thank you, miss. I will,' I said, starting my message and wondering if Cathy would ever forget she retired from teaching two years ago.

Kim's avatar was at the top of my phone list. I was so looking forward to seeing her again. After Mike's funeral, on a whim, I returned with her to Oz and stayed a whole month. It was lovely being with her at that time even though I kept breaking down. I found her beautiful rose garden wonderfully soothing, and Kim was great, so patient. So generous with her time as we spent hours talking about what I would do and how I would manage living alone in the future. Those ideas soon fell apart, however, when I returned home to my redundancy letter, but she had offered some great suggestions, even the possibility of her moving back to Kent to keep me company, which excited me no end. She just has to work on Will, her husband, who she says isn't ready yet.

I wanted to dance when she rang to say she had organised her flight. She had flown in from Australia and spent two days in Ouchy on Lake Geneva staying with an old nursing friend, Tandy, having arranged for one of her daughters, Mai, currently working in the fashion industry in Milan, to meet her there too.

'I do hope she had a fab time with Tandy and Mai at Christmas,' Lou said, as I was trying to concentrate on my text.

Angie peered at us from her rear-view mirror. 'Yes. Must be difficult leaving Will this time of year. A positive result though – seeing Mai. And, another positive, we'll have a nurse to hand if anything happens,' Angie added, stirring up my fear again. But of course, it was true. A nurse to hand was always beneficial.

'Somewhat comforting,' Cathy said, 'but unlikely that she'll fit a stretcher and a supply of splints and neck braces into her rucksack.' Cathy rattled a small tub that she had pulled from her bag. 'Anyone want an almond?'

'No thank you.' Although laughing at the image with us, Lou covered her ears. 'Bloody hell, can we change the subject?'

I finished my text.

Mission Control. Not long now, my darling Aussie flower. Twenty mins. Just enough time for our wine to breathe in that chilly mountain air. Over. xx

I had to side with Lou. Talk of stretchers and neck braces was the last thing I needed. Without realising, I was gripping my hair.

26

I swear it had thinned this last year with all that had happened. Not only losing Mike and tormenting myself but also returning from Oz to find out my company had made my position redundant after twenty-eight years. It was devastating – as much as, or possibly more than, losing Mike had been. At least I'd been psychologically prepared for Mike's passing. A widow and unemployed in a matter of months. Things had to improve.

I still wasn't convinced that learning to ski at nearly sixty was the right tonic. God only knows what Mike would have said if he'd known. I think he envied Angie and Rob, skiing with the boys. Several times over the years, particularly when Ross and Rachel were younger, he had asked me to go on a skiing holiday. My reaction had always been 'over my dead body'. Why would I waste a week in freezing snow when I could go and lie in gloriously warm sunshine? It was ironic that I was off skiing to get over his dead body!

It wasn't my idea to ski. It would have never hit my radar. It all came about when my friends took me for a spa weekend in the summer. Lou, Cathy, Angie and I went to the stunning Red Fir Manor with striking views of the Kentish Weald countryside. Apparently, they had already discussed a diversionary trip to distract my mind during the difficult period and wished me to have some input on where I go. I on the other hand thought that they should have input as they were so generously paying for and organising the trip. Subsequently, after lots of ridiculous suggestions and laughter, we agreed to disagree and threw caution to the wind; tossing two suggestions each into an empty china cup to decide on our New Year escapist adventure.

My two ideas were more genteel, but adventurous for midwinter, I thought; for instance, cycling in Provence or hiking in the Lake or Peak District. Lou, who like me loves the sun, suggested surfing in Hawaii or Miami. Cathy suggested rock climbing in Sicily or Majorca. That was bad enough. But we passed the task to the waiter, who pulled Angie's idea out. I nearly freaked. Skiing. And mountains. I would have preferred her other option, which was more my cup of tea: horseback riding in the Berber villages and fields of the Atlas Mountains. Not up in the freezing mountains, that in my mind were cold and hostile. Their scale alone evoked a light-headedness in me. When I'd glanced out during our flight, the ocean of rock whipping up waves from the valley floor looked like gigantic monsters circling me, like a pack of wild dogs. I was under no illusion of their ability to intimidate.

As horrified as I was, I carried determination around with me, eager to take on the challenge and stay upbeat. My friends cared enough to think of me. That was fundamental and I couldn't disappoint them. We had, after all, managed to get through so much together, those troubling baby-rearing and parental stages, supporting one another through the deaths of our parents. We could manage a ski holiday surely? And the build-up and prepa-ration Angie had organised had distracted me to some extent. A fitness programme, diet, five dry-ski lessons. Overtly, I was cheering, skiing at sixty with my Flowers, covertly a faker and betrayer. As for Mike, he would be turning in his grave if he knew I was skiing.

Flowers, by the way, was the name that us girls gave ourselves, because we are still girls at heart. We each had two navy sweat-shirts with our own emblem of salmon pink roses. In fact, we had them on now. The idea came about quite accidently when Cathy declared one night that we were Fun-Loving Older Women Embracing life, and we completed it with a Renaissance of Spirit, which is exactly our philosophy.

As Angie focused on the driving and Lou touched up her make-up, I kept the phone clutched in my hand, but then felt my chest lurch in panic. 'Oh, God, I can't remember if I put my thermals in. I remember putting in my big knickers in but …'

'Stop worrying,' chuckled Lou. 'We'll share if we have to. I'm sure we'll have plenty between us.'

Cathy pulled a face. 'Urgh. No. They're not the sort of things I'd want to share. It would be like sharing underwear.'

Lou leant forward and frowned, her hand gripping a steel stem of Cathy's headrest. 'I know you're getting on a bit, Cath, but you know, there's this stuff they have nowadays called washing powder. It washes clothes. You can buy it in these places called shops, which they have even in the mountains. Correct me if I'm wrong, Ang?'

The car shook with laughter. Cath's shoulder blade collided with her ear as she lowered her head. Her tight lips then burst into laughter too.

'Oh, mock me, why don't you. Charming. I suppose I will have this all week. I love you all, my darlings, but I'm sorry. No. I'm not sharing my knickers or thermals with anyone.'

Swiping a tear from her eye, Angie peered at me again through the rear-view mirror. 'There are shops that sell them if you prefer your own, Ginny.'

'Goodness.' Cathy turned to face me. 'Don't we have it easy! I wonder what our grandmothers would make of us. Can you imagine your grandmothers skiing? My granny looked about eighty when I was a little girl. She could have only been in her fifties, forties possibly.'

'Mine too,' Lou said, chuckling, 'but I bet they would share their knickers. A bar of carbolic and a scrubbing brush would soon sort them. Nan skiing, though. Not an image I can conjure.'

'Lucky for us, we don't have to revert to carbolic soap.' Cathy let out a sigh. 'Gosh, what they went through. All for our benefit. Two world wars to secure our future.'

'And the other battles.' I instantly recalled tales my gran told me. 'Old aunt Minnie, not my real aunt, but a close friend of Gran's and my mother's when they were younger, was a militant campaigner for so many rights we all take for granted, like voting, equality, free healthcare, not to mention pensions.'

'It is amazing what they did. So sad they didn't benefit.' Lou's

29

jaw crooked to one side. 'We owe them so much. Imagine travelling back in a time machine, a hundred years. A war. Women pining for dead husbands, sons, brothers and fathers. Housing conditions damp and cramped. No work. Little food. Filthy streets. Not even a bath or toilet! And, unless you had serious money, you would never holiday, let alone go abroad. Poor mites. Wouldn't it be wonderful to go back and thank all those who fought for us? We baby boomers live like royalty in comparison: our own homes, we choose where to live, work where we please, including abroad.'

I clutched my chest. 'Makes you feel guilty, doesn't it, that they didn't reap the rewards. We've been such a blessed generation. I'm so grateful to have been in a position to be near my children, share their lives and to enjoy our grandchildren.' A mix of emotions circled in me. 'And with spare time to have some fun. My one regret is that Mike's gone.'

Angie blew out a large sigh. 'Flowers, please. They did us proud, they led the way; let's be fucking happy.'

Cathy

'Language, Angie.' I scowled sideways disapprovingly as she mouthed a 'sorry'. I folded my arms as the sniggers silenced. Poor Ginny was sinking again.

'So, Ginny, what's the plan for the week?' I asked, attempting a different angle at getting her to talk, thinking I'd posed an open question.

'Skiing,' she answered bluntly.

Oh dear, this wasn't going well. The elephant in the car was enormous. Whilst our foremothers were interesting and commendable, we were simply so backwards in coming forward. I sighed. So much babble when what we really wished to know was how Ginny was feeling, what she was thinking. It had been the hardest thing to prise Ginny open. I wasn't one to pussyfoot around usually but in all honesty, apart from my parents, I'd never dealt the death of someone so close to me. Mike was so young. Only sixty-one. Anthony and I still couldn't believe he has gone. A dear, dear friend who was such a mammoth part of our lives. Like a brother to us both. And Ginny. All we wanted was our friend back, but we didn't know how to unwrap her from her cocoon. And, as far as I knew, she'd refused bereavement counselling or any help after losing her job.

I popped another almond into my mouth to stave off hunger.

In our own ways, we've tried to get Ginny to share her thoughts, and maybe Kim was the only one who'd managed it, having had some success in Australia earlier in the year, but Ginny's been a closed book since. I was never sure how to broach the subject. In fact, not one of us has yet managed to tap into her heart since. Naturally, we've asked but all we got back from Ginny was 'Stop worrying. I'm fine,' when we knew she wasn't.

I was hoping to sit in the back with her on the journey from Geneva, try and have a chat to find out more about what her plans were for the trip, particularly as it was twelve months on and the perfect opportunity now that we were all together. Even if we could discover what she wanted to get out of this week and whether she wanted to have a memorial on the twenty-eighth. It had all been guesswork so far. Communication with her had been sparse these last few months and she shut herself away at home, refusing to socialise even one-to-one. I understood that she might feel it's difficult with couples, but apart from our preparation sessions at the gym, and a weekend at a spa, she hadn't been anywhere but her new workplace. And, frustratingly, any time I rang to say I'd pop in with a bottle of wine, she told me she had things to do or work to finish. It wasn't right.

Hearing her today, she sounded perfectly normal, joining in the conversation, but I wanted nothing more than to hear her open up and talk about everything she'd gone through this year.

We all did. Saying she's fine told us nothing. Even her daughter, Rachel, who I rang with my concerns, said I shouldn't worry; her mum would talk about it when she was ready. Anthony thought along those lines too. Don't press her, Cathy, he told me. But Ginny was like a sister, and it broke my heart that she wouldn't confide in me.

I dug my finger into my little pot again and fished out a crispy chickpea. Then another. 'Do you want some, Ang?' I asked.

'No, I've got my beans and an apple here, thank you.'

I had always confided in Ginny. She was always there for me through the early years when Anthony and I were trying for a family. She probably knew my menstrual cycle better than me at times, despite her busy life with her children. Every month she would turn up with a book or a bottle of wine, or if Mike was at the Rotary Club or pub, she'd insist I go to her instead so that she could put Ross and Rachel – then babies – to bed before we settled down for a chat. We'd sit with our legs curled under us, at either end of her settee. Sometimes Lou, Angie or Kim would join us.

My mobile rang, and I knew it could only be one person.

'Hello, darling.' As expected, it was Anthony.

'I checked and saw that you had landed. Why didn't you ring?'

I sighed. 'Because we haven't arrived yet.'

'I did ask you to call,' Anthony slurred down the phone. It wasn't even lunchtime.

'Darling, you said, and I'll paraphrase, ring me when you get there. We are about twenty minutes, half an hour away yet. It's stunning, lots of mountains and snow. Look, I'll send you a text when we get to the ski resort. Is that OK?'

'OK. Is it snowing?'

'No. No snow and the roads are fine. I'll text you. Bye, darling.'

'I love you.'

'Love you too, darling; bye.'

I fumbled to switch it off.

So, where was I?

Kim and Will had still been in England and they too had been trying, like Anthony and me. It was Kim who suggested I try the new test-tube method, now what we refer to as IVF, as they were considering it. The whole idea horrified me of course. Being a Catholic I could never have conceived that way. It wasn't at all natural, or moral. Anthony respected my faith despite his willingness to provide the cash for the ground-breaking treatment. He was also willing to adopt, seeking out lots of pamphlets about it, but I was convinced I would fall pregnant eventually.

Ginny supported my decisions no matter what, even when Kim argued – a few years after Avril and Mai were born – that her twins had provided her far more joy than any faith could have brought her. Ginny was comforting, despite the joy she had for Kim and Will. 'We all have to do what's right for us, follow our own heart,' she had said. And, I couldn't be bitter with Kim. Her twins were little angels and Anthony and I loved to shower them with kisses and gifts when we saw them, just as we had with Ginny's, Lou's and Angie's children when they were small. Kim so deserved them after having such a difficult family life as a child herself. I was really looking forward to seeing Kim again – much more than I was looking forward to the skiing. Sport had never been my forte.

My phone rang again.

'Is that Anthony again?' Angie asked.

I puffed and picked the damn thing up and switched it off.

'He's probably sat on it again or slid it in his pocket and hit the button. I'll text him when we get there.' I groaned.

Ginny

I jumped suddenly as a head of caramel blonde hair flashed in front of my face.

'Aren't they stunning?' Lou said, leaning across to my side of the car and peering up.

'They look beautiful from here,' I agreed, following her gaze to the halos of light gleaming from the mountaintops against the cobalt sky; but my gut remained apprehensive.

Lou laid a relaxed hand on my wrist. 'I'm sure it'll be great. We'll make sure it is. Maybe our grans are watching over us, making sure we damn well enjoy ourselves. I can't wait to get on that snow.'

Lou was fearless to the point of recklessness and I loved that about her. She was the person you'd want around if a bullet or missile was heading your way. She would try to catch it. Throw herself on top of you, at worst. Unlike me, ever cautious and full of self-doubt. Lou would take to skiing like a bird took to the sky.

I heard the indicator clicking. My heart rate soared as Angie, whose wonderful idea this was, the only skier among us, took the slip road and crossed the motorway towards towering rocks. The road narrowed and inclined steeply. Angie struggled for a low gear to make a sharp turn. Already, we must have been a hundred feet up. My breathing became short as the car climbed, and Angie's expression was one of deep concentration. I closed my eyes. One mistake and we could drop off the edge. Cathy, in the front passenger seat, squealed as we rounded another hairpin and as I opened my eyes, her anxiety glared into mine.

'I feel sick,' she said, shielding her eyes.

'It's always daunting, the last bit, but it's not far now,' Angie tried to assure us while brushing a thicket of black curls from her face with her right hand.

Lou slapped and squeezed my knee, making me lurch forward. 'Yep, this time tomorrow we'll be up there at the top of one of those peaks and ploughing downhill.'

I forced a smile. I didn't want to harass Angie any more than necessary, but I was also beginning to experience nauseous waves and my head was all over the place. *Like my life.* The thought invaded my head. *No. Stop it!* I speedily corrected my brain. Only positive thoughts allowed. That was the promise, the condition, and exactly why the girls had made such an effort; why they had abandoned their husbands and families for the remainder of Christmas and the New Year. They wanted to ensure I escaped my grief, my job redundancy – that had been a big shock so soon after Mike's death too – and that I would be facing my future alone.

I lifted the corners of my mouth. 'We're going to have a blast,' I said. 'We'll soon lose our fear, especially once we have some alcohol inside us.'

Angie turned her head round to look at us. 'That's probably my worst fear. Please don't overdo it. It won't be so bad on the nursery slopes, but you'll have to limit your alcohol when we go on the runs. I don't want any of you stuffed in a bag and lifted off the mountain, nor ski-doodled off.'

I had no idea what ski-doodled was but ... 'We won't,' I squealed, leaning forward in panic and silently urging her to watch the road. The car swung ninety degrees again and somehow my abdomen clambered to catch up. I made the mistake of looking down outside the window. There was barely twenty inches between me and sudden death. We must have been at, I guessed, about two thousand feet up with a sheer drop. I quickly looked up, focusing ahead, attempting to blot out the possible grave scenarios filling my imagination. The car turned again, and instead I was met with steep rock faces reinforced with humungous bolts and draped with relatively skimpy netting. My mind got to work again, fearing gigantic boulders crashing into the car roof.

'Shall we play I-Spy?' I asked, desperate for distraction.

'You can try.' Angie sniggered as we were suddenly submerged into darkness. We all vanished, and I felt relief wash through me. I could do dark. At least we were safe in a tunnel.

'Oh, we won't then,' I added stupidly.

'We must be nearly there by now.' Cathy stated what we were all thinking.

Angie swiped her brow. 'I think we'll see the village at the other end. I don't pay too much attention when I'm in the passenger seat.'

I felt a stab of guilt thinking of poor Angie having to drive us all and listening to our constant gasps and gripes. This was probably a first for her – driving up without Rob and the boys. Ever since their eldest was twelve and had skied with the school, Angie and Rob had taken all three boys on their annual trip to the Alps or Dolomites. They went with a large group stemming from that first school trip. I'd been quite envious but in a different way than Mike had. I'd never had the teeniest inclination to ski, but there was a lovely camaraderie among them, as a family. They all loved it. I figured this trip must be quite daunting for Angie, leading us up instead of Rob leading her.

As we neared the arc of light ahead and felt the anticipation of arrival, my muscles untied themselves and I let my head roll back. I hadn't felt as tense or as wretched since that day almost two years ago when the consultant oncologist sat in front of Mike and I had confirmed Mike was already in stage four of his cancer. Although the tests and waiting were physically draining, mentally, that day, a switch came on, powering my brain with a huge surge of strength. Instantly, I became wired to fight, to stay upbeat. I was going to shore up every bone, every muscle, every cell in his body to keep Mike alive. That was my coping mechanism. To stay strong for him, to research everything about his condition, nourish him with the right foods and attitude, seek out that miracle cure – mend him. Even Will, our medical expert, couldn't do that, however much he tried.

I don't think I'm bitter anymore. I was. Not towards Mike, but the situation. My life for thirty months involved never tiring or wavering but taking time off work to be around during and after the op, nursing, battling the brunt of his anger and bitterness, sitting beside him throughout long hours of chemo, the sickness, the loss of appetite, the hair loss and exhaustion of his once strong body as his immune system weakened. Then the radio-therapy and change of chemo drugs because the first weren't ever going to cure him, just prolong his life, his suffering.

'No more,' he'd said, when the next round of chemo was offered. I remember it well. It was the middle of August, a warm, muggy day that was more overcast than sunny. 'Sorry, love. I really am, but I can't do this anymore.' He could have hit me with a cricket bat and I wouldn't have felt it as much. There was one thing Mike wasn't and that was a pessimist. It was why I was with him in the first place.

Feeling hot with all the twisting and turning of the car. I picked up my water bottle and took a large swig. We'd be there soon.

I switched my mind back to Mike, to the fonder days of our youth. I could picture him now, caramel hair on a side parting, blond hairs on his warm cheeks, eyes that would eat you up. Apparently, he'd seen me before we first met at the school end-of-term disco. He told me he'd watched me play netball at a rally in our nearest town and fell in love with my peachy-skinned face and long blonde pigtails and made up his mind I was one day going to be his wife.

So confident I would be at that disco, he had it all planned. Soon after I arrived with my friends at he approached the DJ, gave him a list of slow songs to play: 'The First Time I Ever Saw Your Face', Roberta Flack; 'Got to Be There', Michael Jackson; 'Have You Seen Her', The Chi-lites; 'Without You', Neilson; 'Let's Stay Together', Al Green – that was how optimistic he was. And how could a girl resist? Michael Watts was striking. This tall, athletic, blond boy leading me, plain little Virginia Matthews, to the dance floor, never to let go, until that day.

I so missed that crypto-energy he supplied. Sadly, I believed we both switched off that muggy August day. Forced to finally face reality. All that was left was to slowly watch the light in his eyes fade along with the breath from his lungs. That was a year ago this week, and the day I found out he had a secret.

'Hurrah,' Angie yelped as she steered the last of the less threatening bends and a cluster of chalets appeared. Beside the road, I read the sign. '*Bienvenue La Tzoumaz.*'

Chapter 2

Kim

Seeing Ginny's name light up on my phone had momentarily jarred me as it had often done of late, since I'd been party to the unwelcome information. There's nothing worse than having to swallow something unsavoury and not being able to handle it. I read the text. Mission control. I liked that. Ginny was right. This would be our headquarters for the next seven days. Aw, and sweet – a subtle reminder to get in the wine. At least Ginny was in good humour. She'd had a tough few years and deserved some serious fun. After some hectic months nursing at the Midland General in Perth, and trying to deal with the issue concerning Ginny, I was seriously in need of fun too and looking forward to seeing and sharing the experience as well as spending time with my old buddies.

The restaurant terrace was filled with skiers. The welcoming smell of Savoyard cheeses filled my nostrils, making my tummy rumble as the memory of the mini cheese fondue I ate last night enthused my taste buds. I'd skipped breakfast after gorging on so many delicious dishes in the hotel restaurant. 'You taste,' the Italian had urged, and had sent out relentless small plates containing cooked meats, pasta, fried aubergines, curried cabbage, shellfish and finally the one course I'd requested, a flavoursome Savoyard fondue. The perfect mountain food as far as I was concerned. My guilty pleasure. Warm, rich and indulgent.

I ignored a whiff of diesel fumes and even the view for a while. I took a sip of my wine and leant back on the chair to let the midday sun wash over my skin. I closed my eyes. Sleep was tempting but I was too excited. Nervous too. I mean, whilst I couldn't wait to see my friends again, meeting Ginny face-to-face, knowing this was the opportunity to tell her what I knew, was terrifying, far worse than confronting Will about moving back to England. Worse even than confronting my drunk and violent father. Confrontation scared me, I've always feared conflict – but losing Ginny scared me more.

At first, I held back from relaying what I'd learned because I didn't think Ginny would cope. She had not long returned from having such a lovely time with me at my home in Perth earlier this year and was still highly emotional after losing Mike; then when I did drum up the courage to tell her, I found out her company had made her redundant and she was desperately seeking work. When I rang, she was so low.

So, as the months went on, hearing from the girls how she had withdrawn, I just couldn't bring myself to do it. And I had to be with her. Her self-esteem had sunk so low. In fact, I then feared that if I told her after all that time, I would lose her friendship. She would hate me. The thought was unbearable. Ginny was special. It was surreal to think that I was going to hurt the one person who had virtually carried me throughout my younger days. A knot tied in my stomach every time I thought about it, and when this trip was organised, and I knew I would see her, I made up my mind that it was my opportunity to sit her down, face-to-face.

Startled by that fact, I opened my eyes, catching sight of my T-shirt. The Flowers, such a great acronym; they would be here soon. I checked the time on my phone and like a meerkat jumped up, with wine in hand, taking a few steps over to where I could see, and peered up the road.

Ginny

Emerging before us were cute wood and stone chalets blanketed in snow, scattering the landscape among modern concrete and newer, wooden high-end chalets, with glass gable walls. Despite the hostility of the roaring grey rocks, I was surprised to see a glowing sunny village populated with traffic and people bustling around with bags, cases or skis. The pretty scene began melting my fears and as we slowed and inched closer, I saw a young family, rosy-cheeked and bursting with vigour and laughter, strolling alongside our car.

'It's so vibrant,' I said, feeling the glare of all the surrounding snow hit my eyes. I pulled down my sunglasses. 'And busy. I can't believe the number of cars that are here.'

Lou looked over with a reassuring glint in her eye before pulling down a pair of Ted Bakers off her head and setting them on her nose. 'Beautiful, isn't it?'

I smiled back.

'Don't worry, you'll barely see any cars tomorrow,' Angie said. 'It's change-over day so they'll all be parked up by tonight. You may get some locals drive up in the morning.'

'It's not what I imagined,' Cathy added, opening her window and blasting the neat line of her bobbed hair. 'I thought we would be in a lonely little hamlet with only chamois for company.'

I raised my arms and stretched out, whacking Lou on the arm. 'Sorry, Lou! Me too. Isn't it strange how you build a picture in your mind – but there's plenty of life here by the look of it.'

'And wine.' Lou's pearly-white teeth beamed at me. 'I can't wait. You look considerably more awake now. You OK?'

41

'Yes. Thank you, again.' I smiled. Lou had asked so many times, and so many times I'd nearly caved in. That was why I found it easier to be on my own at home. I didn't have to answer their questions, deal with the fussing. I didn't want my thoughts and privacy invaded. I was safe and not forced to talk about Mike because I really didn't know who Mike was anymore. Maybe I was afraid that one of them would tell me the truth about him. I don't know that I wanted to hear it. I was safer on my own. I could think and torment myself without being questioned or judged. And no one could judge Mike because his behaviour wasn't up for discussion.

Although, I feared, this week with friends, my emotions could tumble out so easily. And while my friends would understand, what would be the point? We were on holiday. I would only dampen their enthusiasm and they were so fired up, however anxious they were about skiing for the first time – apart from Angie, of course.

And what difference would it make to them if they did know about Mike? It was my problem – why would I put myself through the humiliation? He was gone, and nothing was going to change what he did. I sighed, feeling in desperate need of that wine.

'What is that huge building there?' I asked spotting a monstrous concrete structure with lots of steps.

Angie didn't even look up. 'That's got to be the lift station. That's where we get the gondola, the lift to the top. And just along here on our left we should see Kim. Ah, is that her?'

Kim

A spectacle of hands waving from a car window immediately gave them away. I hurriedly placed my wine on the table beside the other glasses and the two waiting bottles and rushed to the side of the road, waving like a moron. People sitting at the tables

42

must have thought: stupid old woman. Nothing new. I giggled to myself. Will and my girls think that about me too.

I got to the car as it stopped beside the Belleview, and gigantic bees with white teeth gazed back at me from the open windows; my friends in their designer sunglasses, no doubt prescription, like mine. I chortled to myself. Opening Angie's door, then Ginny's behind her, I laughed out loud at our matching Flowers T-shirts.

'Welcome, Flowers!' I steadied Ginny as she clambered out, wriggling her newly worked-out body into operation.

'Aw, great to see you,' I screamed and hugged her. 'You look amazing.'

Ginny fell into my arms. 'Oh my God!' she said, with a wobble. 'Whoa, a bit stiff. You too.' It was good to feel her squeezing me. Her eyes scanned me as she stepped back and added, 'Wow, you've knocked a few years off.'

I smiled, pleased with myself. 'Thanks. Just hope I've done enough.'

'Sorry we couldn't get here earlier. Have you been OK on your own?'

'Ace, but much happier now you're all here,' I said as she stacked my arms with her coat and hand luggage. 'I stayed at La Poste up there. Never eaten so much in my life. The bloke who runs it is Italian and just kept feeding me – every dish in his kitchen I reckon.'

Ginny laughed, took her coat and slipped into it, then threw her tote bag over her head before aligning it on her hip. She appeared relaxed, which undid some tension from the back of my neck. I greeted Cathy and Lou, then Angie, observing they too had worked out and were in good shape. I was happy to see them all again as it had been Mike's funeral when I'd made my last – very brief – visit and it wasn't the best time for a proper get-together. Their excitement at seeing me was quickly forgotten however when Cathy shrieked at the panoramic view from the terrace.

43

'I'll just go and park up,' Angie told me, waving her hand to make sure I'd heard.

I nodded and made my way back to the table. The girls herded behind me and began rejoicing again when they realised our table offered a front-seat spectacle of the valley. Ginny began pouring the red wine into their glasses and handing them around. She topped mine up. 'Great spot, Kim,' she said, joining Cathy by the glass veranda.

'Perfect, this view is to die for and you're a saint, Kim,' Lou said, lifting the other bottle. 'Just what we've all been gasping for. Well, in Ginny's case, dribbling for.'

Ginny turned her head. 'Err … yes. I must have been dreaming of wine in the car.' She turned back to Cathy and the view.

I picked up my refilled glass, my heart content they were finally here despite their distraction. I couldn't blame them. I'd spent the last hour soaking up the exact same beautiful scene. The snow-filled valley was stunning, particularly whilst sipping the sumptuous local wine. I could feel my adrenaline pumping, imagining the week ahead, spending time with them. I took a mouthful of wine as I watched them – that wonderful upbeat cheer and palpable love for one another that I missed so much; it set me wondering what it would take to persuade Will to move back to England. I didn't want to end up at loggerheads with him again, but I didn't think it was unreasonable or selfish to want to discuss it, and at least have a plan in place; whether it was potentially two years or ten years away, I needed to know it would happen.

'Oh, it's gorgeous, Kim,' Ginny said turning to me. 'Not what I envisaged at all. And it's so warm.'

'Couldn't be happier,' I said.

'I know, it's so good to see you. Did you see Mai?'

I squealed. 'Yes, she looks so well, and after her wobbly start at Mantero – totally self-induced, she admits – she's settling in well. She's working with a team on some vintage silk ideas apparently. It all sounds terribly romantic but she's working hard.'

Ginny put her arm around me. 'It's been her dream. I'm so pleased to hear that. And does she like Milan?'

'Yeah, she's finding her way around. Sharing an apartment with an English girl so they're also sharing an Italian tutor. She's pretty conversant but he's helping her on the business terminology. Overall, she's doing great. I really miss her though.'

'Aww, I can imagine. Well, if you want to be in Europe for a few months, you know you are always welcome to stay.'

'Don't tempt me, Ginny!'

I was just about to ask how she was when Cathy called us for a photo. We scuttled across the wall, my mind still whirling.

Will thought I was overly nostalgic for Kent and our friends. Although he got to know them all and their partners when we began our relationships and married life, I couldn't expect him to ever really appreciate how much the girls meant to me, especially Ginny and her family. No explanation could really describe what I felt for the girls, but it was a major obstacle that held Will and I back from setting off for Australia back in the day. It took Will five years and a lot of persuasion to get me there. Of course, I loved him so much I didn't want to deny him the opportunity that called him to Oz, but I did push him to agree to return to Kent at least once a year for a holiday and of course to see our friends. And us girls had made a pact to write often.

Over time, he began to appreciate just how much Ginny, and the others had saved me as a young girl, preventing me from falling into a pit of despair. None of my friends in Australia came anywhere near close to these guys and I cared for them greatly. I was particularly concerned for Ginny right now. I really wanted to be there for her, to repay her, especially now she was on her own.

I was attracted to nursing because I was a natural carer. I liked to help. It probably stemmed from being the oldest child of four and trying to protect my siblings and my mum from the vicious man who was our dad. Before we escaped his wrath and bullying

45

to the safety of Kent, Mum had ended up in hospital for three months with head and neck injuries and we were put into care. Dad was finally arrested. I was only eleven, my sister Paula nine, my brothers, eight and six. The authorities wanted to split us up until, that is, Ginny's mum heard about us. Her friend was a foster carer who took us all in for a few days until our fate was decided, but she already had three children of her own.

Ginny was an only child and her parents' house had two spare bedrooms, so amazingly they agreed to take us in voluntarily until Mum fully recovered in a Kent hospital nearby. Our dad was never told of our whereabouts. I did all I could to help Madeline, Ginny's mum. I took as much responsibility as I could for my siblings. I was so grateful and I loved Ginny and her parents so much for the kindness and love they gave us.

I then helped Mum to move into the house. That was in August. In September, I started at the grammar along with the girls. Fortunately, I could get the bus with them as my stop was just one away further down the village. Mum was so much happier. Like us, she put on some weight, found a local job, although the hours were long. I was always rushing off the bus to collect my sister and brothers from the village school, but I had Ginny's parents' help. Luckily for us, we settled quickly in the village with a fresh start. Naturally, after that, all I ever wanted to do was care for people and ensure they were safe. Particularly Ginny. Even though we lived miles apart, my love and loyalty for Ginny, her family and friends never faltered. I only wished I could have been around physically to help with Mike. And now she was on her own, it would mean so much to me to return home and support her as much as she did me.

I watched as Ginny and Cath continued marvelling at the view. I sidled up to Lou. 'Spectacular, isn't it?'

'Oh, amazing. I love it here already.'

Lowering my voice, I was keen for an update. 'How is Ginny?'

Lou bit her lip and, staring down at her glass, spoke almost in a whisper. 'Oh gosh, who knows with Ginny. Getting there I think. She's not herself though, is she? High one minute, low the next. I can't tell whether it's the thought of skiing or the anniversary that's worrying her. I've asked, but she says she's fine.'

In front of us, Ginny got out her phone and wandered along with Cathy to a low wall to take photographs.

'Mm. I'm worried,' I said, raising my voice a little. 'It must be hard, obviously. Neither of us knows how she feels. How can we? We've not lost a husband. But … has she mentioned anything else?' I asked, digging to find out if Ginny had learned about Mike's infidelity and if she had confided in Lou.

Lou shook her head. 'Not to me, no. Like I said, she says she's fine. Doesn't want to leave home much despite our efforts. Hasn't really opened up to any of us except to say she's lonely but feels she'll get used to it.'

'I'm sure she is. I feel so useless. Hopefully we'll have a chat. I can't help wondering if she is in some sort of denial.'

Lou ran her fingers through her newly styled wispy hair. 'Exactly my thoughts. When Mum and Dad died in that accident in Spain I was the opposite. I needed people around me. These guys were great, and they helped me so much. Ginny was amazing. I get the impression at some point her mask will crack. I think losing her job shook her just as much as Mike's death. More maybe. I suspect she had time to come to terms with Mike's death during the last few months of his life; the redundancy was a jolt she wasn't prepared for at all. And not to tell us for two months. I don't know why she holds everything in.'

Taking a large mouthful of wine, I almost spluttered. 'Me neither – shocking, wasn't it? The irony is, she is amazing with our problems, but not her own. I only heard when Cathy emailed me. And, not wanting to push Ginny about it, I waited, thinking she would be in touch that day, but I rang her the following morning. It's heart-wrenching when our friend is too embarrassed to even tell us. I mean, she had just arrived back from Australia when she received the letter. I would have been straight on the phone to her if it were me. And redundancy is a normal occurrence in this economic climate. It's nothing to be ashamed about – though I guess she'd been there so long, and after Mike's passing, I don't suppose she ever imagined the company would do that to her.'

Lou pulled her collar up around her neck, no doubt acclimatising to the shorter hair, 'I know, we were all surprised at that, but trying to hide it, to have us believe she was just changing jobs, I did wonder what was going through her mind. I think it got worse for her when she began applying for jobs believing doors would be wide open. Being repeatedly turned down, with her experience in marketing, I imagine it ripped her confidence ragged. Sadly, she's not at all happy in her new job. Apparently, there's very little, if any, number crunching or marketing analysis, which she loved in her old job – the stats, the charts. She does like her figures as you know, but the company rely solely on advertising and PR to get their brand out there. Seems a bit odd in this day and age, especially with all the data available. She said she would have normally brought it to their attention, but it's not her place to tell them how to run their company. I can't help wondering if her lack of confidence is affecting her judgement. Either that or her heart just isn't in it.'

I sighed raising my eyebrows. 'Well, at least she's revealing something. Could be her confidence is so frayed.'

'We think so. Cathy, Angie and I have all noticed quite a change in her. I've popped in to see her a few times over the last few months, and she's looked so withdrawn, sounded it too. And I never get to stay long. It's like she's trying to usher you out as soon as you arrive. She doesn't invite you into the lounge. No offer of a drink. Very peculiar. Let's just hope it doesn't prevent her from enjoying this week. Angie and I were chatting the other day about her confidence affecting her skiing. She was nervous on the dry slope. Though Cathy was too.'

I was concerned about Ginny, but a picture of the energetic sporty Ginny I used to know crossed my mind. I guffawed. 'She'll leave us all standing, I'll bet,' I told Lou. 'Well, at least she won't be alone. Four of us can't ski. And I'm sure we'll gee one another along. I'll never forget the strength you girls gave me when I met you.'

Lou squeezed my arm. 'We're all a bit anxious, but until we try it, we'll never know, will we? I can't wait.'

'Lou, you're ace – that bold spirit hasn't left you. I think it was such a great idea to do something totally different. Especially under the circumstances. She and Mike never skied together so she won't have any associated memories. I would never have thought of it had I been there.'

Lou's voice rose again. 'Oh, the weekend at the hotel. You'd have loved it, the building, the grounds, the spa. A band even arrived and played for us. We were up dancing and making fools of ourselves. It was an amazing weekend.' She stroked the side of my head. 'Your hair looks great by the way. Suits you short. I like the gold hues running through it too.'

I ran my fingers through the top of my hair. 'Caramels, darling. I used to love the colour of Jennifer Aniston's hair. Verity, my hairdresser, suggested the shorter style. I told her to stay away from the pixie-wispy blonde otherwise you might think I'm trying to copy yours. Oh, here's Angie,' I said, interrupting myself. 'Sorry, Lou. Let me get you a glass of wine, Ang.'

'So good to see you, Kim,' Ang said cheerfully and peered across the valley. 'This scene never fails to impress me even though I've been coming here for years. It feels good to be back. Sunshine too. Don't know how you got that in your suitcase, Kim!'

'A beauty, isn't it? It folds up nicely with a sheet of tissue,' I said. 'Let's hope it continues for the week.'

The others had returned from their photoshoots and I handed Angie a full wineglass and raised mine with my voice. 'Well, Flowers, here's to a fabulous ski trip. *Santé!*'

'*Santé!*' We all chinked glasses as we gathered around the table, settling in our seats, breathing in the fresh mountain air, sipping sunshine and wine. 'And, Ginny, I hope this week sets you up for a great year ahead,' I added. I smiled to myself; I was in a dream. In a beautiful setting for a whole week with my beautiful friends. I was afraid that if I pinched myself, I might wake up. Finally, together again.

There was one dark cloud, however, that I needed to offload; I had to tell Ginny what I knew about Mike. The trouble was, I didn't know if Ginny knew already. It would be a risk telling her because it might make me feel better, but I didn't know if she would ever forgive me if I admitted to knowing. I just had to hope it wouldn't cost me my friendship.

The girls from Camfield Bottom were still my closest buddies, although they were Ginny's first.

After her parents offered to take our family in the term before we started senior school, Ginny, Lou, Cathy and I were all in top set in the village primary school, so I was fortunate that I fitted in. And staying at Ginny's house was the best thing that had ever happened to my family. I mean, accommodating four of us, trusting us in their home – me, my younger sister Paula and two younger brothers, Ian and Mark. We were treated so well. And even when we were housed in a village council house, in the rougher end of Camfield Bottom, Ginny and her family, and the other girls, remained so friendly; we really gelled. They all had big hearts as well as their little foibles. That was why I loved them.

Ginny and Cathy were comparing photos and showing them to Lou.

'Have you been to the chalet?' Angie asked.

I quickly reached into my pocket and dangled the set of keys. 'No, but I got the keys. Harold had left them with Stefano, the hotel owner.'

'Oh, cool. You've not taken your things there yet then?'

'No. Well, I thought we would go together and besides, I thought you might be hungry.'

Angie rubbed her stomach. 'Mm. You could say that. Actually ...' She pulled out a packet from her pocket and asked, 'Do you want some of these?'

'What are they?' I held out my palm.

'Just my beans. Edamame beans,' Angie said pouring out a small portion of crispy-looking yellow pods. 'Just a snack. They're crunchy, try.'

'Oh, young soya pods, I like them fresh on my salads. They're green.'

'That's it, but full of protein and healthy fats. Just handy to carry when you work out a lot.'

'No doubt good for someone who doesn't eat meat then. You and Cathy are pescatarians, aren't you? I thought you might have changed your thinking now that animal rearing is strictly regulated and monitored.'

Angie frowned, turning up her nose. 'Ew, no. Hormones, antibiotics. Probably worse. Anyway, I still couldn't. It's still like eating a pet to me. No, there's lots of alternative nowadays. I'm a real sucker for the cheeses out here. Can't beat a nutty Swiss Gruyere.' Angie's eyes lit up and she put her packet back in her pocket. 'They do a lovely saffron risotto here actually, but try Gruyere grated over it instead of Parmesan.

'We can eat here,' I said tipping my wine to my lips. 'Might as well enjoy the sunshine and the view, and try something different. That sounds nice. I do enjoy veggie dishes.'

'I'll get the menus,' Angie said.

We didn't know Angie until we were older. She was Ginny's neighbour when Ginny and Mike bought their first house in Greenwich. Will and I were still in London too then. Then we all gradually moved to the village. Will and I were there for four years before we moved to Oz. I've missed them loads. But Oz called Will and had so much to offer. We were still young and looking for adventure. It was a wonderful place to work and bring up the girls, but Camfield Bottom would always be my home.

'How are you feeling about skiing?' Angie asked me as she handed the menus round the table.

'Nervous, but it would be a shame not to as we're here and we've worked ourselves so hard.'

'You've all done brilliantly. Hopefully, you'll all thank me when your legs ache.'

'The girls are jealous their ol' mum is off skiing.'

'The boys are too.' Angie laughed.

'I was blown away when Ginny messaged me asking me to come out to ski. I'd always fancied the idea, but Will has always been more of a water-skier and I admit I've enjoyed that over the years, especially living in Perth and BT – before twins.'

'Yes, I remember.' Angie nodded. 'How are the girls?'

'Well, I've seen Mai, spent yesterday with her. She's thriving in Milan. I've missed them like crazy since they left for uni and their jobs in Europe. I wished I'd extended the trip to Avril in London.'

Angie nodded. 'Yes, that would have been nice.'

I was thirty-eight when they miraculously surprised us. All the medical knowledge between Will and I, the IVF treatments we had gone through, couldn't make it happen; then hey presto, like magic they blessed us with their arrival. One on the thirtieth of April, hence Avril, and Mai, half an hour later on the first of May.

'There's definitely something poignant about the empty-nest syndrome,' Angie went on. 'I'm glad I had my little fitness business to focus on, even though it wasn't turning much profit then.'

'Yes, I need something. I'm hankering to be back in Europe near them and with you guys,' I said. 'I just don't know that Will has any intention of giving up his career to come with me. He is so absorbed in his work, which I understand. I've just got long in the tooth with mine in comparison.'

Angie swooned. 'Aww, I love Will, he's so driven. It's a good quality. Maybe he can find something similar in Europe and teach Rob a thing or two.'

We chuckled.

Will's dedication to his current work and research, and the wellbeing of cancer patients, was admirable, and why I fell in love with him. We were both driven to curing and caring for our own reasons. Of course, I took pity on him when he revealed his motivation to succeed as a cancer specialist. Losing his mother to breast cancer at twelve and recognising he had the power to discover hope for others seemed extremely mature and gallant to me.'

'I know. I should be grateful. And tolerant. It's a great purpose to have.'

'And, why you love him,' Angie added, draining her glass. 'More wine?'

'Yes, and yes please.'

Mine and Will's connection and chemistry had been evident to everyone except me. We were young, and no one was more surprised than me when this attractive new doctor gave me so much attention. Every one of our colleagues noticed his flirting, and even some of the patients did. Apparently, our sexual energy charged the hospital air. Within just two weeks of meeting, we couldn't bear to be apart. We bought our first flat together in London and remained a strong couple.

Until now, that was. As much as I still loved him, things had changed. I had changed. The arguments about when and where we would retire had created a lot of tension. And a couple of months ago, after another heated discussion, I threatened I would return to Europe alone if I had to, telling him he could join me when he was ready. That was a sad moment. A moment I regretted. I hurt him deeply and to be honest, I didn't know how he was still talking to me. Will could have washed his hands of me, so I was grateful for the way he dealt with it.

'At least you're honest,' he'd said. 'And if you need to go, then I can't stop you. I committed five years to this project. Do what you need to do, and I'll join you.' Naturally, guilt ripped into me and I wondered if I could really go without him. The angels must have been looking down on us though. He kissed me and assured me that our love was strong enough to deal with it. I breathed out a sigh of bliss and thanked the angels for my state.

These last few years, I have discovered my spiritual side through doing yoga and meditation. So many patients of mine have trusted their guardian angels, I now find myself doing the same, and as always, I add my gratefulness. I believe Ginny and her mother were mine. It's only since meeting these beautiful Flowers that my life has changed for the better. OK, the blip was the years Will and I waited for the twins, but sometimes, I feared it was too good, and at any second it could all go tits up. But here we were, together, and I was going to enjoy it.

'More wine, anyone?' Angie was asking the girls, seeing their wineglasses drained.

I caught the waiter's attention and he smiled as he came across to our table. I pointed to a bottle on our table. '*Encore le vin rouge, s'il vous plaît?*'

'*Oui.*' He nodded.

'*Carafe d'eau, s'il vous plaît,*' Angie said turning to the waiter, then back to us. 'Phew, not sure if it's the sun or the altitude that is dehydrating me already.'

'Probably all that stress driving and making sure we all got here in one piece,' Ginny said.

Cathy tousled her hair parting, then her crown, making her bob soften her face. She then held out her glass. 'I think you deserve a toast for getting us all here safely. Thank you, Angie. I thoroughly enjoyed the ride from Geneva and along the lake, but that last bit had me gripped in terror, I confess; it was scary. So well done, and cheers to you.'

'Cheers, Angie,' we chorused.

'My pleasure girls.' Angie gave an embarrassed smile. 'All good practice for next time, eh?' Her eyes checked each of us for approval but was met with apprehensive stares. 'OK, we'll take a snow check on that one,' she sniggered. 'It's given me an appetite though. I think it's the perfect time to order lunch.' Her suggestion was met with smiles. 'Then we can go to the lift station to buy our passes ready for the morning.'

Ginny nodded. 'Absolutely.' Then she turned towards the valley, the tension smoothed from her face.

'So lovely to see you happy and full of energy,' I told her, hoping it was true.

'So lovely to be here with you all.' Ginny gazed at me then, squinting her eyes, she sat back in her chair. That jarring feeling shot through me again, making me wonder if she did know about Mike and if she could sense I was hiding something.

Chapter 3

Ginny

With stomachs stuffed of either *saucisse de veau* and *frites* or saffron risotto with Gruyere, we crossed the road to buy our lift passes then made our way to the car to collect our suitcases. Our chat and excitement was heady with far too much red wine, so it was a relief to stretch our legs following the road along part of the village before heading down a narrow icy path towards our chalet while singing 'Walking in a Winter Wonderland'.

Angie stopped us briefly to point the chalet out. It was truly breath-taking, nestled on the hillside that overlooked the valley and surrounded by thick fresh powdery snow with miniature pine trees poking their heads up here and there. It was smaller than I expected but the smell of new wood was as welcoming as the warm air as we entered. The entrance porch was furnished both sides with racks for skis and boots, and ample hanging space for wet ski-wear.

'We'll soon fill this up,' Angie said, kicking off her snow boots.

'It's nearly new, isn't it?' Lou said pushing open the door to the living space.

After removing her boots, Angie followed her, wriggling her

case as she held the door. 'Yes. This is its first season. Harold and Jean-Paul only finished it in October so we're probably first for the ski season.'

Behind Angie, I pulled off my boots and wheeled my case to my other side and waited until Cathy and Kim were in stockinged feet and inside before Kim closed the door.

'Is there an alarm, Ang?'

'No idea, Harold never said.'

Kim rattled the door handle, inspecting the workings inside its structure and counting. 'Oh, at least there's seven locks on here. You'd think they would have a security alarm and cameras.'

'Maybe they don't have any crime here,' Cathy said.

'Seriously.' Kim appeared indignant. 'You can never be too careful.'

We sniggered. 'What are you like!' Angie laughed.

'I know. I know. I can't shake the habit. It comes naturally when you had a father like mine and had to keep looking over your shoulder.'

'Lose it, sweet, he's six foot under now,' Angie said.

Kim shrugged. 'I wish I could.'

Although the sun was now sinking behind the mountains above us, the living space was airy and bright. Flames from the ready-lit log burner gave a warm homely glow.

'This place is beautiful.' Lou ran and flopped onto one of the three olive-coloured loungers. 'Oh, this one is too hard.'

Running across to the next and diving into a pile of faux-fur cushions and soft-looking throws, she closed her eyes. 'This one is too soft.'

We watched and giggled waiting for her to try the last sofa.

'So I'm staying here, Flowers,' she said, wrapping herself in a throw and tucking up her feet.

'Darling girls, this is stunning,' Cathy chimed, flinging herself into one of two winged armchairs and raising her feet to rest on a solid oak coffee table placed on a grey-speckled rug in the centre, a few feet from the log burner. 'So tastefully executed. I will take some photos before it becomes messy,' she said, retrieving her tote bag from the floor and getting out her phone and glasses. 'Lou, I'm afraid you'll have to move.'

'You'll have to move me then. This is sooo comfy.' Lou closed her eyes, stretching back her neck.

'Darling, please?' Cathy pleaded.

'Do I really look that bad?' Lou protested. 'Actually, I've got a better idea. Flowers, come and sit with me, Cathy wants a photo.'

Cathy shook her head, her neat bob rippling. 'You're incorrigible, Lou Cavendish. If you were my pupil, you would be in detention.'

'Ms Golding, if I was your pupil, you would have kicked me out the first day for swearing,' Lou retorted.

'Absolutely, darling,' Cathy tittered, 'now close in.'

We all sniggered at their banter. I ran over and sat next to Lou. Kim and Angie hugged into us.

Cathy snapped away with her phone. 'OK. So, I'll take one or two and then you will all stand behind me. Deal?'

We looked at one another and laughed. 'Yes, miss.' It felt great to have some fun with them again.

Cathy widened her mouth to demonstrate. 'Cheese.'

'*Fromage*,' Lou and Angie sang together loving to wind Cathy up.

Cathy slowly took three shots whilst we fixed our grins. 'Thank you.' Then we dispersed.

Lou, Kim, Angie and I padded behind Cathy to the other side. A long wooden staircase ran up to the next floor and a long solid oak dining table almost matched the wood on the floor.

'Oh, look at this. More wine,' I said, pointing to three bottles of wine, a box of chocolates and a box of biscuits in between two tall ornate candlesticks. 'We've landed in heaven. Let's find some glasses. Forget the skiing. I could just stay cosied up here all week.'

'Me too,' Kim agreed. 'Did you say we're here a week or a month?'

'Wouldn't it be lovely to stay here a month, six maybe?' I said. 'All of us.'

The silence in the room was deafening as we dreamed.

'And look at that kitchen area,' Angie said, staring wide-eyed in the last corner. 'Oh, Lou, your Terry would love that. Look it's perfect for entertaining and this could be a model for your Cosy Cottages.'

'Yes, if we could build cottages square, this layout would be great. And, I'd just love to stay a month or six,' Lou said, then pausing, twisted her mouth. I sensed something was on her mind. 'Well, nothing's settled, but if Terry and I sell the business, which we've been talking about doing this year, maybe these things are possible. I know it's a leap, but we're seriously thinking of retiring, so you could come travelling with us, Ginny. We could come back here. Spring and summer here must be lovely too.'

'Oh no, sweetheart, you will want to spend time together,' I said, knowing how the romance of it all had become so consuming for me and Mike. We'd had it all planned. It was something I'd often thought about this *last* year. Before his cancer, we were excited to be at that age where we could start thinking about semi-retiring at least. We'd spoken about long weekends away and country walks one day in the week. That excitement had naturally left me. This was the bit I was dreading: spending my last days on my own. And playing gooseberry to another couple on holiday wasn't my idea of fun, grateful to Lou though I was.

'You're kidding. I've already told him he's out the house three days a week – golf, fishing, voluntary work, whatever he decides – as I will be filling my days. There's so many things I want to do and that includes spending time with my Flowers.'

Cathy padded over and took a photo of the kitchen. 'Best thing I ever did, clock up enough years to claim my teacher's pension. Travelling is amazing. Anthony and I have met so many interesting people. Bit exhausting at times, but I'd skulk off and do my writing or read my book leaving Anthony to chat to his heart's content. He and Mike would talk to anyone, wouldn't they?' She turned to me.

I nodded in agreement. 'Yes, the village gossip and my social secretary,' I added as Angie stepped beside me and I felt a light comforting touch on my arm. 'It's fine,' I told her. I didn't mind talking about Mike. I thought I should do it more. Cathy was just thinking aloud, that was all, and I liked that he was mentioned in conversation. But, the thought of travelling alone or with a bunch of strangers scared me. I pinched the skin on my forehead. 'Ah, wineglasses, that's what I came here for.' I remembered the glasses and trundled across the kitchen to search the cupboards. 'Anyway, I'd prefer to work until I'm ninety, even if it's part-time. I couldn't imagine being at home on my own for the next thirty years. That's if I have thirty years, of course. Besides, financially it could be a struggle. We drained our savings and the proceeds of the sale of Mike's business when he couldn't work. I've only got half a pension from Cashmere Cosmetics, as I hadn't worked there long enough for a full pension.'

'You'll be able to top it up with state pension when you're sixty-six though, sweet,' Lou said.

'Yes, but I'd rather work to keep busy.' I gathered five large wineglasses by their stems.

With her black eyes following me back to the breakfast bar, Angie still appeared concerned. 'I know you don't really talk about Cashmere, but have you heard from any of your friends there?'

I sighed. 'Mm, yes. Alex, one of the PAs who I got on with. She rings occasionally, but she has three teenagers keeping her busy. She says it's not the same with Lucy steering my marketing ship.' I grinned at Alex's analogy. 'Apparently, the team don't have much confidence in her. I think Alex is just being kind. It's early days and she'll find her feet. I know, I employed her.'

Angie squeezed my shoulders and kissed my hair. 'Aww, that's a noble thing to say, and demonstrates your professional attitude – that's a positive strength. I'm sure underneath you're cursing for having trained her so well.'

'Lucy's a very bright girl. She'll have her own style of managing and directing the team forward.'

Cathy picked up a clean tea towel and a supposedly cleaned glass and inserted her hand to polish it. 'I think you dealt with it extremely well, considering. I just wish you could have told us sooner.'

A 'yes' echoed around the kitchen.

'Plain and simple. I was devastated and … ashamed,' I admitted, taking a deep breath and staring at Cathy's busy hands. 'I can't really explain why I didn't tell you all immediately. I could barely believe it. It didn't sink in for a while and for some mad reason, I thought if I got another job straight away, I could pretend I had been looking to change anyway.' I shrugged. 'Utterly mad, wasn't it? I suppose it felt like a personal attack, particularly so close to Mike's death. I know I had to take a lot of time off when Mike was ill, but I got the impression they were sympathetic and understood. They paid me for the compassionate leave too. That notice was a bolt from the blue, especially when I'd just returned from my lovely trip to Australia. I was just beginning to cope. Now I wish I had abandoned them earlier and spent more time with Mike.'

'That's not surprising,' Angie said, throwing her arm back around my shoulder and lightly squeezing the top of my arm. 'I would be bitter. I'm so glad you can talk about it now though.' Angie scanned the room. 'We all are.'

Lou struck the marble kitchen top with her hand. 'Absolutely! What are friends for if we can't share our troubles? Gosh, we've almost spent our entire lives together; there's no reason why we shouldn't be able to say what's on our minds. Sweetheart, you can't bottle things up like this. You should trust us by now.'

Fighting off a lump in my throat, I swallowed and leant forward to grab a bottle of wine. 'I know, and I do. I trust you all immensely. And, going forward I will. It was such a shock and … I don't know why … my job was part of me, and …'

'And, it's understandable, sweet,' Lou said assuring me. 'Our identity is a major part of us. Had you found something similar immediately, you may have accepted it sooner and been able to deal with it. No doubt, rejections from the other companies and having to settle on a job you weren't happy with was the crux of your reluctance. The self-doubt soon creeps in.'

Angie gave me another squeeze. 'It's not important now. What's important is that you're moving forward. And, maybe the right job still out there for you.'

'Yes, it's in the past now. I'll keep looking.' I lifted the wine bottle. 'Shall we have a look upstairs before we open this?'

'Yeah, sure; if it's done out anything like this, it'll be fab,' Kim said, heading for the stairs with Lou and Cathy. 'Oh, we have to put our names into a hat, don't we? To find out where we're sleeping.'

'We can do that after,' Lou said, disappearing up the stairs. I placed the bottle down and felt a tap on my arm.

'Can I have a word?' Angie beckoned me. 'Bring the wine; I'll get two glasses.' I followed her to the dining table. She unscrewed one of the bottles of red wine and began to pour as she sat down, so I sat opposite trying to ignore the squeals of delight upstairs.

'Ginny, I thought I'd mention it now, as I hope to bring you some cheer to start your holiday. I know you're not happy with your job so I thought it worth mentioning – I will be needing someone with … Look, how would you fancy working in the fitness and nutrition industry? I'm thinking of getting a marketing professional, but you'd be great. Not full-time to begin with – three days a week. Possibly more later.'

I glared at her as if she had gone mad. Angie had built up quite an empire over the last few years after several years working her butt off to get it to its current size. I was sure she didn't need my help. I was wary of working with close friends, too.

She handed me one of the glasses of wine. 'It would be a new role. I've never had what I consider a top professional marketing person but thinking about it, we could both benefit from your expertise. The business can afford it now. Naturally, I currently keep an eye on what my competitors are doing, but the industry is becoming so large and competitive that maybe your scientific or methodical approach, whatever you call it, could help give us the edge.'

Clutching my chest, I was touched and felt very honoured that Angie thought me capable of taking on such a risky role. I gulped a mouthful of wine. 'Angie, you're so lovely. I'm really flattered. It's incredibly thoughtful of you, and that's such a great offer, it really is. And working part-time. But you're my friend and I couldn't bear to ruin that friendship.'

'My dear Ginny, you would have control, I promise.'

'Oh, you are adorable, and I'm tempted, but ...'

Angie grimaced. 'Look, you don't have to answer me now. You'll want time to think about it. What I will say is that I would totally trust your judgement. Cashmere Cosmetics is a very successful company and I've no doubt you've been very much a part of that. Whether I employ you or you'd rather work freelance as a consultant, it's up to you but I believe Fit & Nourished are at that stage where we need expertise. I'd much rather have someone I could trust.'

'And Rob, what would he think about employing a friend?'

Angie frowned then puckered her lips, giving a mischievous pout. 'It was him who suggested I get professional help. It was only the other day when I came back exhausted. But it's my business, honey – Rob is only allowed to come in to tell us to turn the computers off and on when they go wrong.'

We both sniggered, and I imagined Rob rolling his eyes as Angie told him to take a hike if he interfered.

'No really, he would approve. And he does get involved to

some extent. He does all my IT. He could help you with designing your own software if you need something bespoke. You will have your own office. We can share an assistant for now. I know you'll cost, but like I say, it will benefit us both, so you'll be worth it. Promise me you'll think about it.'

Elated, I ran around the table to her chair and wrapped my arms around her neck. 'The offer sounds amazing. Thank you for thinking of me. You're a treasure. I will give it some serious thought,' I told her, but tempting as it was, I couldn't bear to lose a friendship because we had disagreed over a business decision. I squeezed Angie's arm and smiled. 'I promise. I'm flattered. Can I let you know after the holiday?'

'Of course.'

'Well, for now, there's a lot of excitement up there; let's go and see what all the fuss is about upstairs.'

The voices grew louder with screams and lots of shouting as we climbed the stairs. They were like kids at a soft-play party. When Angie and I walked into the front bedroom Lou was spread-eagled across one of the two queen-sized beds and Kim was throwing half-sized furry cushions across the beds with Cathy.

Lou scraped her hair off her face and knelt up. 'Come and play Piggy in the Middle with us. It's fun,' she urged.

'Wow, this is gorgeous,' I said, ignoring Lou, knocked out by the dramatic effect. Again, oak was floor to ceiling but with flecks of a richer brown running through it. Both beds were draped in full-size faux-fur throws in the shades of mountain wolves: browns, greys, whites. It was full-on luxury and faux-fur rugs felt soft and warm under my feet as I glided through to the en-suite bathroom. Instantly I wanted to soak myself in bubbles as I peered at a free-standing roll-top bath that took centre stage, nestled in the oak that matched the bedroom, whilst his and hers marble sinks sank into oak cabinets suspended under full-width mirrors with a huge shower enclosure glistening in marble and chrome to the other side.

'Just stunning,' I said. 'You often complained about ski accommodation being poky. This is not what I'd call poky.'

Angie gasped beside me. 'That was when we first went. Standards have changed. I think we've struck gold with this though. I know it's not particularly large, not when you see some chalets out here, but I'm sure it should be double the price Harold has charged us.'

A breathless Lou whirled in. 'A real gem, Angie. It's beautiful. And let's thank our lucky stars, eh?'

'I should say – just beautiful,' I agreed, heading across the landing. Apart from the shades of soft furnishings, the second bedroom mirrored the first. 'OK, my beautiful Flowers, you need nourishment – time for wine,' I said, dancing towards the stairs. 'And to sort out our rooms.'

As we drank our wine, admiring more and more detail in the chalet, Cathy pulled down her glasses from the top of her head and wrote our names on four Post-it Notes, which she had found in a kitchen drawer, folded them and put them in a mug before shaking it and holding it out to me.

'OK. Pick out two, darling,' she said.

'Why me?'

Cathy lowered her head and peered at me in her teacher-like manner over her specs. 'Because, my darling, we decided on you and because the two you choose will share with you. Unless you just want to share with one?'

'I'm happy with whatever you Flowers have arranged,' I said, feeling special and picking out the first piece of paper.

'Drumroll,' Angie said, then proceeded to create weird 'brrrhl' sounds with her tongue.

We rolled our eyes at each other as we burst into laughter.

'OK,' I squealed, opening it. 'First to share with me is …' I paused to create a bit of drama like they did on TV shows '… is our amazing Aussie Flower, Kim.' I clapped, and Kim clapped with me then leaned forward for a high five.

'I'm stoked. That's ace,' she said slapping my hand harder than I was expecting.

'Right, and for our next roommate,' I continued, tipping up the mug and shaking it again before picking the next. Lou was gritting her teeth as she looked at me. 'Drumroll please?'

We looked at Angie and she obliged with a longer 'brrrhl.'

'Our next roommate,' I said opening the next, 'is … our marvellous motivator, Angie.'

'Yes,' Angie screamed, wiping her lips with the back of her hand.

'High five,' I squealed, slapping her palm. Then I asked, 'So, Lou, Cath, which room would you like: front or back?'

They looked at one another. 'Are we worried?' Lou said, shrugging.

'Darlings, they both have a bath and beds.' Cathy laughed. And instinctively I knew they would offer me the room with the valley view.

'You take the front,' Lou said, 'we'll take the back.'

'No, no my exquisite Flowers—' I shook my finger '—the special treatment stops now. I've really appreciated everything you've done, your compassion, you've all been so amazing to organise all this and be here for me, but please, no more singling me out, or treading on eggshells just because Mike passed away or because I was made redundant. We're here to have fun. You're on holiday too and I want you all to just let it go. You two have the front so you have the view – I know how much you love it, Cath,' I said, glancing at her. 'Besides, we'll have an excuse to visit you in your room.'

Again, they exchanged glances. 'If you're sure,' Cathy said. 'Kim, Angie?'

They both nodded, and Kim added, 'We're with Ginny. Absolutely sure. There's the veranda downstairs and I'm sure the view of the village will be interesting.'

'Thanks, Flowers,' Lou said tilting her head whilst her eyebrows furrowed, her hair still skewwhiff. 'I'll put the music on whilst we unpack and then pop up to the supermarket for some bubbly.'

'I'll come with you,' I said. 'Then we can get ready for our, erm … pre-ski après-ski.'

For the second time that day, my spirits lifted. The chalet was a dream and even though we were tired, the voltage in the room was high.

Chapter 4

Kim

My face was looking pasty with the Aussie suntan already fading. I pouted at the full-width bathroom mirror, smacking my lips before placing my Rose Petal lipstick back in my make-up bag that sat on the shiny glass ledge. 'Right, I'm ready,' I said, switching off the light.

In the bedroom I saw that Ginny was pulling a second red stripy sock up her calf. 'Ooh, sexy mama,' I teased.

'A bit whacky, but I'm feeling in a whacky mood.'

'That's what I like to hear, my beaut,' I said pouring the last of the Fendant white, the Swiss wine Ginny and I bought in the village supermarket, into our glasses.

Lou popped her head around the door, accompanied by a small knock. 'OK to come in?'

'Of course, but there's no more wine, I'm afraid,' I said pulling a sad face.

Lou raised a bottle in her hand. 'Luckily I just topped mine and Cathy's up, so you can finish this,' she said, showing us a quarter-full bottle in one hand and a full glass in the other. She looked at Angie straightening the fur throw on her bed and putting her make-up bag onto the wooden bedside table.

'Oh, this bed looks so inviting right now,' Angie said as she gave it another swipe to iron out a crease.

Lou placed the wine bottle on the table. 'Not you as well, Ang. I've left Cathy fussing and tidying. You'll only mess it up when you get in it later.'

I had to laugh at Angie's face as she glared at Lou. If looks could kill.

Lou quickly changed the subject. 'Does anyone want to share a fondue tonight? They always smell so nice.'

'Cathy might. I quite fancy that tarti-thingy,' Ginny said, standing up and looking lovely apart from her bright, stripy feet. The grey cable-knitted sweater really suited her.

'Tartiflette', Angie said. 'Mm, I love it! Well, the veggie version. So naughty. Potatoes, cheese, cream, onion all mixed up – just divine. Will and the boys like the traditional with bacon. Oh, not sure what to have now but considering what we had for lunch, my belly is rumbling. Shall we get going?'

I took a big gulp of wine, almost smelling the cheese. 'Yes, let's. I'm famished too.' Checking my watch, I was surprised at the time. 'Do you know it's seven-thirty already?'

'No. Deary me. Are you ready in there, Cath?' Angie shouted.

Ginny got a woolly hat from her wardrobe that matched her sweater and peered across the landing and then mouthed back to us. 'She's on the phone.'

Ten minutes later, parched but reluctant to open more wine and tummies rumbling for food, we climbed the icy path up to the road and along and towards the square we needed to cross to La Poste, the restaurant I ate at last night. Ginny walked beside me whilst the others followed.

Ginny looked up at the navy sky. 'So pretty here, isn't it? Look, a full moon. Lots of stars. And over there, the long shadows of the tall trees on the snow.'

I craned my neck to see, following the moonlight then immediately above us saw the hundreds of tiny twinkling stars.

'Kim, look there, what are those lights? They're moving,' she said, pointing to the middle of the mountains.

'Oh yes, they are moving. No idea. Mountain ghosts?' It came out of my mouth before my brain engaged.

Ginny pursed her lips. 'Hmm. You never know. Maybe it's Mike driving up and down furious that I'm skiing.'

'No. What – social animal Mike? Don't be silly. He'd want you to be out enjoying life. Wouldn't you, if it was the other way around?'

Ginny twisted her mouth, pausing the conversation. 'Of course I would. Maybe he's having a bad day up there.'

We sniggered but I could see Ginny's eyes glistening. I patted her arm. 'Sorry, Gin, I hope it's not upsetting you.'

She sniffed. 'No, not at all, not upset, it's just I get little bursts of sadness that well me up suddenly. It happens now and again.'

We were here to cheer her up, but it was good she was opening up. Since she had stayed with me in Australia, where she had space and a chance to let out her grief and tears, she hadn't given much emotion away over the telephone. 'Do you still get angry or emotional – that it happened to you and Mike, I mean?'

I watched her as she stared down at the frosty pavement. 'I curse him all the time for leaving me on my own. Things – just simple things we used to do – like walks in the park, through the trees, driving down to the coast for lunch, jumping on a train to London to the theatre. I miss them. I was thinking the other day, when I was Christmas shopping. He used to love picking out the kiddie presents. He had a knack for knowing what they'd like.'

I put my arm around her, squeezing her into my chest as we walked. 'Oh, my beautiful friend, my amazing Pommie flower, you don't know how much I'd love to be around to help you. I would be angry too.'

I wanted to cry. How I yearned to be able to help her through all this. She had changed my life for the better and I wanted so much to repay her.

Ginny kissed my cheek. 'I'm going to be fine, really. It's just that sixty-one was way too young for him to go. I was bitter because he was a healthy, fit man with children and grandchildren and he did nothing particularly indulgent like smoking, taking drugs or even drinking that much. Beer with the boys a few days a week. A beer before dinner and wine with dinner. Not excessive, is it? I know he wasn't an angel, but he didn't deserve cancer.'

I threaded my arm through hers. 'I know, chook, such a waste. So unfair, isn't it?'

'It is. I miss him terribly,' Ginny said softly, then she straightened her back and lifted her chin. 'But I'll get there. I am getting there. Especially with you lovely Flowers spoiling me. Mike would appreciate the support you've all given me too. And how much you all care. As I do.'

'He was awesome,' I said, leaning against her, and snuggling close. Ginny was right, he would be demonstrably thankful. He loved nothing better than to rally everyone together in or out of crisis. Mike was the golden boy. Good-looking, athletic, clever, and one of those people who could strike up a conversation with anyone and win their respect. He reminded me of Don Johnson playing 'Sonny' in *Miami Vice* – particularly in the summer months when his skin browned and the sun splashed his hair with honey tones. I could understand why my younger sister Paula had a crush on him. After all, we probably all had a crush on him really. But he only ever had eyes for Ginny.

When he was sixteen – and Ginny, Lou, Cathy and I were fourteen – I remember Paula, barely pubescent, just twelve, blabbering because Mike had asked Ginny out on a date. Infatuation was putting it mildly. She would hang around outside Mitcham's, our local youth club, a couple of nights a week, then monthly at one of the school discos we all went to, usually with her friend Lorna. The pair of them resembled clowns, made up in frosted powder blue eye shadow, clumpy mascara, slapped-on rouge, in their mini-skirts, like a pair of groupies stalking a rock god. It was highly embarrassing. I wanted to disown her as much then as I do now.

I found myself repeatedly apologising to Mike and Ginny. Fortunately for me, they tolerated my silly sister. But even when Mike, along with most of us, told her she was wasting her time, our words fell on deaf ears. She didn't understand humiliation. Getting his attention was enough for her. He was very patient, considering. As was Ginny.

* * *

As soon as Ginny and I walked into the restaurant, we were greeted by a wave from Stefano, the owner who must have recognised me.

'*Bonsoir*, Stefano.' I waved back and looked around the room. It was heaving. The waiters rushing back and forth.

Ginny shrugged beside me. 'Will we get a table here?' she asked, reading my thoughts. 'Such a lovely place.' Her gaze circled the room. 'It's just how I imagined an Alpine restaurant.'

Ginny was right: it had a traditional authenticity that brought a warmth and charm to its big exterior structure. Wood everywhere with cottage-style windows, which although double-glazed, blended in as you would imagine the originals had done. They were dressed in tied-back red check curtains and café nets. On the sills were modern pewter figurines of climbers or skiers, whilst gracing the walls were framed photographs of bygone years, as well as of visitors to the restaurant and Stefano's expeditions. And the silky worn flagstone floor added to its history and solidity, bearing the weight of built-in wooden benches and long banquet tables now filled with Savoyard delights for its hungry diners.

'Bonsoir, ladies.' Stefano came towards us. 'I have table in ten minutes.' He pointed to the only circular table, which nestled comfortably in the front corner. 'Come.' He raised his arm as if he was going for a swim, beckoning us to follow. As we reached one side of the bar, he called to his barman who promptly supplied him with a bottle of red wine and Stefano took a corkscrew from his pocket, popped the bottle open and placed it on a very small table close to the bar. 'On the house. I get glasses,' he said, racing back to the bar and at the same time giving a friendly wave to a group leaving a side entrance.

'Oh, shit,' Lou said suddenly, scuffling to stand on the other side of me and ducking to make her taller frame smaller.

Stefano brushed between us with five small wineglasses clutched between his fingers and, twisting his hand, he placed them steadily on the table. 'Enjoy the Gamay. I call you soon,' he said, dashing off.

'What is it?' I asked Lou, curious.

She squinted her eyes and moved her head side to side. 'Oh, I'm not sure, no. I thought it was someone … don't worry, gone anyway.'

Of course, I was curious. Why would she try to hide from someone? My attention was soon diverted as Cathy launched a glass into my hand.

Cathy

Lou was acting strange, but I didn't feel in the right frame of mind to ask. I was still fuming. I had urged the others to walk on ahead so that they couldn't hear my conversation with Anthony. He was being obnoxious, and he'd obviously been drinking and was in a loudly argumentative mood. I had hoped he would ring once or twice maybe in the middle of the week, since I had texted him to let him know we had arrived safely, but no. And he wasn't just fussing and making sure I was comfortable – he wanted to know what we were doing, so I had spent the ten minutes itemising our plans, which hadn't placated him. It had done the opposite, in fact.

'Please don't drink too much,' he slurred in my ear. 'I expect there are a lot of guys out there in groups, away from their wives and families.'

I sighed again steeling my patience. 'I expect there are, love, but I'm here with the girls, so don't worry. We are only eating. Besides, there aren't going to be too many men looking to chat up sixty-year-old women.'

'Men are men, Cath. They'll prey on anything that ...'

'For goodness' sake, Anthony, you're beginning to sound like some possessive teenager. Now then. That's enough. I won't speak to you if you're going to behave like a child.' I ground my teeth hoping Lou and Angie hadn't heard me raise my voice. His tone was terribly embarrassing. His suggestion, however, got me wondering. 'And anyway, how often have you jollied off to far-flung places? Is it what you would do? Are you suggesting you prey on women?' I asked, clawing my fingers into my neck.

'Don't be daft, Cath, of course not. I've watched men though. I know what they're like.'

I rolled my eyes. 'Well, let me assure you, I'll jolly well stay clear of any letches. Now, I'm almost at the restaurant. Stop worrying and remember why I'm here. I'll call you if I have any concerns, OK? Look after yourself, darling.' I fumbled for the button quick. I wanted him to leave me in peace. Why was it always about him? I never pestered him when he was away.

Furious with him, I upped my pace to catch up with the girls. Yes, I expected him to call me to let me know he had arrived safely when he went away, but I trusted him, always. We were lucky that our bond remained close despite not having children. And even when us Flowers had been away before, say Greece, which was our favourite, 'Shirley Valentine' holiday we called it – minus the gorgeous Costas of course – Anthony always seemed fine. He had never acted like this, calling me and verbalising his insecurities. And, all the years we've been ballroom dancing together, a pastime we stumbled across whilst our friends stayed home caring for their children, there were times when we were instructed to tango, waltz or rumba with another partner and I had never known Anthony to show signs of jealousy.

I failed to understand why I was feeling guilty. He understood the purpose of the week was to concentrate my time on Ginny, and the skiing. He knows I'm worried about them both, but he hasn't even asked. Not that there was much to tell him yet, but I would have thought that would be his first concern.

I couldn't admit it to the Flowers, but I'd been petrified since day one. It was only when our darling Angie promised to get us physically and mentally prepared that I thought: Cathy Golding, you can do this! A bloody hard slog, but I managed, and no one was more surprised than me when I eventually conquered the dry slope. It was a truth universally acknowledged among us Flowers, that sport had never been my forte! 'Floppy Doll,' Ginny and Lou used to call me! I didn't mind.

I knew five lessons on the dry slope would never prepare me for ice. Ice was enemy number one! Ever since I slipped in the playground when I was about ten and cracked my head open, I've feared ice. Knocking myself unconscious and being rushed to hospital was a huge drama and not one I would want to relive. Just walking in the resort and down that chalet path sent the adrenaline pumping, but I managed to hold it together – not that Anthony is bothered.

Wasn't it ridiculous that we couldn't admit our weaknesses to anyone, partners included? These past few months with Anthony, if I was honest, I couldn't wait to get away from him. It sounded dreadful, but I was at a loss as to what to do. I loved him dearly, but I couldn't honestly say that I liked him. God forgive! But I couldn't admit that to him. Neither could I admit it to my friends. I would feel terribly disloyal to Anthony and he wouldn't want anyone to interfere in our marriage.

I supposed I should confront him with it. It couldn't continue.

At least I had a husband alive to confront. Poor Ginny didn't even have Mike's shoulder to cry on when she was made redundant. Opening up about her redundancy earlier was a major step forward for her. Usually she'd just tell you what she was doing, rarely how she was feeling. You would think people coped better as they got older, but it seemed new challenges would spring up and surprise you. Anthony and ice were currently mine!

Reaching La Poste, lagging a little behind the girls, I was ready to scream and would have hugged that Stefano guy, if he had stayed still long enough, for getting us the wine so fast. That first glass lasted me all of two seconds. I handed the girls theirs and refilled mine.

Lou gave a roar as I put the bottle on the small table and spun round. 'Steady on, ol' girl,' she said. 'Is Anthony OK?'

'Yes, fine, darling,' I lied. Clearly she knew who I was talking to. 'How's Terry?'

'Ditto, when I left anyway. Glad to be rid of me I think. Ha!' she sniggered. Kim sidled up to us as Lou continued. 'No, he's got his returns he's focusing on this week and a meeting with the architects. No doubt he'll look at the weather and organise a round or two of golf.'

I smiled. 'Good. At least he's keeping busy.' I glanced at Kim, noticing the beautiful colour of her pink lipstick and how it suited her. 'How was Will when you left?'

'Oh, ace! Thanks.' She raised her eyebrows. 'In fact, I don't know why I'm saying that. He was ironing before he dropped me to the airport, which is a rare sight.'

Lou almost choked on her wine. 'Good on him. And you, sweetie. You've got him well trained. Terry wouldn't know an ironing board if it hit him in the face.'

Laughing, Kim shook her head. 'Aww no, he's working this week, so staying organised I expect. Our cleaner normally does it but she's on holidays. What about Ant?'

'I was just saying to Lou, he's fine. A bit lost but he has his sudoku and his Netflix. Seems to enjoy watching series to reading books at the moment.'

'I think men prefer TV,' Lou replied, playing with long navy beads. 'I can't remember the last time Terry read a book.'

Kim sipped more wine. 'If they're anything like Will nowadays, they just want to get home and switch off from work. They forget our feet are tired too.'

'Luckily for me, Anthony insists on treating me like a princess still, keeping me fed and watered all day while I write,' I stated with an air of satisfaction.

'Sounds a dream!' Kim swooned wiping her brow with her hand. 'I wish Will would retire, hon.'

I forced a smile. Oh, I was such a fraud. It wasn't particularly comforting to hear my friends' husbands were happy working when I knew Anthony was idle and bored. I was betraying myself. Maybe he was a bit hasty giving up his business so soon. Retirement doesn't suit everybody. Why couldn't I just tell my friends the truth?

I breathed a sigh of relief seeing Stefano return to us.

'I now have table, ladies,' he said swiping off beads of sweat from his forehead.

Ginny

I couldn't stop smiling as we waded behind Stefano through the sea of tables back to the front corner of the restaurant on the one round table. The energy from the room and its diners was bubbling through me. And if this was what après-ski was all about, I would return without the skis.

As soon as we were seated, Stefano took our drink order, which was a cool bottle of bubbly in keeping with the mood.

'Can we see the menu?' I asked, licking my lips at the delicious thought of fondue or tartiflette, which been on my mind all day.

'Ladies,' Stefano said in his broken Italian. 'I will do for you, the best menu for the best price.'

We Flowers turned to one another with a shrug and a giggle. 'OK, when in Switzerland …' I said scanning my friends for any disapproval. 'We have two pescatarians though,' I told him, knowing Cathy and Angie would balk if they saw an ounce of animal flesh on their plates.

'Is OK, fish?' asked the enthusiastic grey-haired Stefano.

Angie and Cathy nodded. 'Yes.'

'Is good.' He waved and was gone.

Minutes later, an older waiter who introduced himself as Jean-Bernard placed a bucket with the bottle of Champagne sunk into ice.

Stefano was close behind with flutes. 'Ladies, it is my pleasure to invite you to see kitchen and chef.'

We jumped up, thrilled and honoured to be asked, and waded to the back of the room again following behind Stefano. We passed the little table and the bar, and then through a doorway of streaming chains. On entering, I was amazed at the space. It was filled with stainless steel benches, large sinks, ovens, gas-burning stoves being attended by young men in lengthy white aprons and chef hats; then I spotted a rosy-cheeked, portly-bellied man in the same attire but also wearing a hearty broad grin.

Stefano walked us over to meet Francesco, his Italian chef. Poor man – like Stefano he was beaded in sweat as he shook all our hands. Stefano reported their story. Thirty-seven years ago, he and Francesco came from the same mountain village in northern Italy, fired with passion for food, seeking a good opportunity. With his savings, Stefano bought the hotel with the restaurant and separate bar beneath and together they formed their business and raised families here. Pride shone in their faces as they introduced their staff and the food being prepared and we thanked each of them for the wonderful welcoming tour.

'What a lovely story,' Kim said as we got back to our table and edged around the round bench back to our places.

'They certainly know how to make you feel welcome,' I said as a waiter poured our bubbly into flutes, and as soon as they all were all filled, I raised my flute. 'And you, my beautiful Flowers, have certainly put heart and soul into this trip, making me feel so cherished. So, a thank you from the bottom of my heart, and a toast to you all for being such amazing friends. *Santé!*' I chinked all their flutes.

'*Santé,*' they echoed, with beaming smiles, before thirstily swallowing it down.

Angie leaned across and kissed my cheek. 'And, our pleasure from the bottom of our hearts; everyone's effort has been tremendous.'

A flutter I hadn't felt for ages flapped in my belly and I was keen to keep up this joyous momentum. 'And, whilst we're all together, and not to put a downer on this evening, because I feel it should be more of a celebration …' I felt all eyes on me, but it was important. 'I'd like to do a memorial lunch for Mike on Monday.'

Beside me, Kim thrust her arm across my shoulder and pulled me to her chest. 'That's a brilliant idea, Ginny.'

'Yes,' they all chanted in agreement.

Cathy put down her glass flute. 'I did wonder if you were going to do something. I said as much to Anthony. He thought we should if you didn't.'

'Aww, bless him.' I sighed as a stab of guilt sliced through me. 'I think Anthony and the boys would have loved to have been part of it.'

'No, darling, you mustn't worry about the boys,' Cathy pleaded. 'You're here with us and it's about you and, to some extent, closure. It's that first milestone and very significant. So, where were you thinking of?'

I shut my eyes and, clenching my teeth, gave a shrug. 'Oh, well

I haven't thought about that yet. Somewhere beautiful, I think. Maybe Angie can help me there. But I'll come back to you on that. Let's enjoy our evening. I think this is our food coming.'

Lucien, the younger of the waiters, was indeed bringing the first course: lavaret, he told us. Whitefish from Lac Léman cooked with roast cabbage, mushroom teriyaki and truffled mayonnaise. It was delicious.

Small taster dishes then arrived one after the other, as fast as the waiters could carry them. Didier, another waiter, introduced himself, fetching out beautifully pan-fried scallops with a caramelised crust and a tasty splotch of pea and mint puree. These were followed by a creamy pasta enriched with fresh herbs, spinach and finely chopped lardons, which Cathy actually picked out one by one, so the pasta must have been special. She wouldn't touch meat on the basis her parents had always made her eat it. She can be quite a rebel on the quiet. Whereas Angie just couldn't bear eating an animal, even as a child.

We decided on Gamay wine to accompany our dinner but with so much focus on the food, not much was drunk at that point.

I lay my hand over my bulging stomach. 'Mike would have adored this. Such a shame there's so much. I'm not going to need skis tomorrow, I might just roll down,' I said as Lucien delivered a succulent veal escalope with creamy mash for us carnivores next.

Cathy screwed up her nose at the freshly pan-fried trout in front of her. 'Seriously, we can't physically eat all this. Who wants mine?' She tossed a plate of bean stew to one side.

'We should have brought a doggie bag. It looks divine but quite where I'm going to fit it all in, I've no idea.' Angie grimaced.

Lou cut into hers. 'It would be criminal to leave it. Perhaps we can take it slower. Wash it down with wine.'

'Totally agree,' I said, as I cut the veal into small manageable pieces and sat back with my glass allowing the light-bodied Gamay to slide down my throat, before tackling any more.

Clearly Stefano and Francesco's passion for food hadn't waned over the years, assuming they were older than us. It was evident that sourcing and creating delicious food for their customers kept their relationship dynamic. As Stefano had proudly announced in the kitchen, they used the finest produce the seasons provided.

To my stomach's relief, only ice cream followed the savoury dishes but that didn't stop me feeding it with lots more wine, including three flutes of Prosecco which, along with the vibrant atmosphere and the wine we'd already had, soon went to my head. By then the music had started, and although there wasn't a dancefloor as such, as soon as the first chords of Abba's 'Super Trouper' came on, we leaped from our seats and into the aisle.

With my friends around me, I let the music pulsate through me as I swayed and let it take me, chords hitting chords of memories of happier times with Mike, with our friends. The music we shared, at concerts, parties, garden parties, balls, even in our homes, dancing, just having a blast. I was lifted to another world, singing the words and giggling with the girls, eagerly anticipating the next track, Abba or not. We danced to Queen, Bowie, T. Rex, Donna Summer, Bee Gees, all familiar Seventies tracks, then The Rolling stones, Chuck Berry, Bill Hayley and the Comets, The Supremes, fast, Sixties rock and roll, then back to Abba and 'Dancing Queen'.

I lost myself deep in the moment, ignoring tears burning the back of my eyes, letting the cocktail of grief and joy stream onto my cheeks. I must have been aware of the energy lifting in the room too, as others took to the floor and … tables. Up I climbed, first on an empty chair, then up onto a table, still in my boots, with others on a cleared long solid-wood table; Kim behind me, Abba urging me. Angie followed. I boogied with complete strangers, high and crazy, whirling and … feeling winds of change, possibly living again as though the cracks in my broken heart were binding back together.

Feeling as jubilant as I did, I could have danced all night, but the music faded, and thirst and exhaustion were taking over. Angie and Kim assisted me down and back to the table where Lou had organised water already. She also mentioned something about indigestion, clutching her tummy whilst twisting, chatting with Cathy to three guys on the next table. I remained standing, still wide awake and buzzing.

After two glasses of cool water, I calmed and began chatting with a couple of ladies who were a part of a large group we had danced with, discovering they had their own chalets or apartments and got back here at every opportunity. Everyone was so friendly. I spoke to another Kent couple, a young family from Surrey and a group of five girls from London – like us, only thirty years younger! They were a lively mix and great fun. Nipping to the loo I also discovered a whole other room leading off the main restaurant, with parties of Danish guests who were staying in the accommodation above.

I think I'm safe in saying we all embraced our first après-ski experience, particularly dancing the night away to Abba, Queen and Sixties rock and roll, and thinking it hilarious telling all and sundry we were Flowers on the Piste!

Chapter 5

Ginny

I woke early the following morning, having visited the bathroom three times already. My head throbbed as I watched the bedside clock flick down the minutes. I was afraid to move in case I woke Kim or Angie. I guzzled down the remainder of my water and two more paracetamols then lay back down. As much as I adored the fun and dancing last night, I was wobbling now. What I really needed was diazepam to get me up and out on that mountain and through my first skiing lesson. Unfortunately, all the chemist offered me last week was a small bottle of Bach's Rescue Remedy.

'It'll work wonders. Just spray as directed before you go out and carry it with you,' the assistant in the chemist had told me handing me a tiny bottle.

'Oh, you'd best give me twenty of those,' I'd replied in jest, but purchased four.

I turned onto my side and sat up, tapping off the alarm, which had finally gone off, and clasping the side of my head. I looked over at Angie and Kim who were snoozing, so I thought it might be a good time to nip into the shower, hoping it would wash away the hangover. It had been a wonderful evening and just the tonic I needed after such a shite couple of years. Now all I had to do was get rid of this hangover and get out onto those slopes.

The lovely warm shower hadn't dissipated my nervous energy and I tiptoed as quietly as I could back into the bedroom, tightening my towel and trying not to wake the others. Placing my pyjamas onto the bed, I bent down to the cabinet and opened my undies bag in the drawer. I've never been one for properly unpacking. At once my gaze met my thermals. I shrieked.

'Oh, thank God. Fantastic!' Looking round, I quickly covered my mouth with my hand and pulled out the rolled-up thermals.

'What the hell's going on?' Kim sat upright in a panic and immediately squinted her eyes. 'You OK, chook?'

'I'm sorry, I got excited. I have them.' I let the bundle unfurl as I held them up. 'My thermals. One pair at least.'

'That's ace,' Kim said, probably wondering what all the fuss was about.

'I thought I'd forgotten them,' I said, updating her. 'Sorry to wake you. I couldn't sleep so I got in the shower.' I didn't mention the times I'd been back and forth to the loo.

'No worries, I probably need to get up anyway,' she said giving a yawn.

'It's only seven-thirty.'

'Oh. I'm awake now anyway, honey. I think. My head feels like someone's got inside and sand-blasted it.' Kim grabbed her water glass and then realising it was empty, slammed it down again. 'Pfft. Sorry, my vision isn't operational yet this morning.' She reached for her glasses.

I saw Angie's body jolt and she stirred into consciousness.

Kim combed her fingers through her short tresses and threw back her duvet. 'I'll go and get some more water. Would you like some? I'll make coffee while I'm down there too and get something for my head.'

Angie stretched out and groaned. 'I'll have coffee, too. If you don't mind. And paracetamol if you have some please, Nurse. I don't know why I didn't pack any.'

'I've brought a couple of packs,' I said opening my drawer to retrieve one. 'Help yourselves.'

'No worries but thanks,' Kim said padding to the door. 'I've some in my first-aid kit in one of the kitchen cupboards.' She turned to us scratching her brow. 'I just have to remember which one.'

Angie chortled half-heartedly, heaving herself up then pulling back unruly black curls. She snatched a band from the bedside cabinet and tied a simple bun on the back of her head. 'Our reliable Nurse Kimmy. prepared as ever.' She then sucked in her cheeks. 'Though, I should have known better. That was one excessive night. Ooh, ah!' She creaked her neck, grabbing the front of her head as she got to her feet. 'Oh God, it's Sunday. I've got to get you all your skis and to your lesson.'

'Angie, we have almost two hours. I couldn't sleep. Don't panic.

'Oh, but there's sure to be queues this morning.'

* * *

Half an hour later, we managed to get downstairs in various states of recovery. As Angie suggested when we had shopped for our ski-gear, we wore our thermals or a lounge suit, otherwise we would bake like potatoes. Angie often came out with snippets of advice when we grouped for our ski trip. I remembered thinking in that instance, *she doesn't realise what a cold-bod I am*, but she'd been right, the chalet was incredibly warm. Sexy I wasn't, but I was comfortable.

Lou and Cathy joined us in the kitchen also poisoned by alcohol and appearing faded with a light shade of green around the gills. After an uncoordinated attempt at making coffee with

85

the new state-of-the-art coffee machine, and serving croissants Lou and I had bought in the supermarket, we gathered at the table and collectively empathised in silence.

Ten minutes later, Angie rose like a rocket had shot up her back end. 'Right, my beauties. We've got to collect our skis and boots, so—' she looked at her watch '—twenty minutes to get dressed and in the boot room.' By that I assumed she meant the large entrance with all the shelves, and like frightened five-year-olds meeting their scary teacher for the first time, we jarred to attention checking phones and watches. 'Don't forget ski socks, helmets, gloves, snoods or scarves, ski passes, goggles, sunglasses,' she continued. 'And phones and money. Carry as little as possible,' she finished. Then added. 'I'll wash up quickly.'

Mentally trying to absorb the list, we scuttled from the table and back to our rooms. I'd tried on every item – the ski pants, the thermals, the T-shirt, the roll-neck, the fluffy fleece, the jacket – individually, as and when I had bought them. As I added the layers, I looked in the mirror. Even allowing for the weight I'd lost, I was the Abominable Snowman. I could barely move and, inside it all, I was quickly melting. Looking at Kim, then Angie, who had taken half as much time as Kim and I to get ready, I could see I wasn't alone. Beads of perspiration were sprouting around their hairlines and alongside their noses.

Angie stuffed all her accessories in her helmet and reminded us again what not to forget before racing out the door panting. 'Sorry, I need air. See you down there.'

I quickly chanted off the checklist once more so that Kim and I could test one another's memory just to make sure nothing was missing, and we waddled off to the stairs, our helmets acting as brimming handbags. Angie came out of Lou and Cathy's room shaking her head. Cathy followed, her helmet crammed too.

'Lou's just putting on the essential lip gloss. Let's go,' Angie said.

'How are you feeling?' Cathy asked us as we trooped down the stairs.

'Like Michelin Man in the outback,' Kim answered blowing out a big sigh. 'I think we ought to fill up with water before we all wilt.'

Cathy nodded. 'Good idea, darling. Maybe some mints too. There's still an oppressive odour of alcohol and garlic hanging in the air. And you, Ginny? Looking forward to getting on those skis?'

I could think of nothing worse at that moment in time but replied with conviction in my voice: 'Can't wait.' But with the mention of alcohol, I was reminded of the one essential item that I'd left in my toiletry bag. I stepped aside. 'Walk on, I've forgotten my Rescue Remedy.'

* * *

Collecting our boots and skis wasn't as easy as I'd imagined. You would think we were auditioning for *X Factor* the way the queue snaked around the square outside the rental shop. Then when we finally reached the front and paid our Swiss Francs, we were delightfully rewarded with yet another queue.

Ushered to one side by a bored-looking young lady dressed in what appeared to be the hire-shop kit – navy trousers and yellow polo shirt – we shuffled obediently to the next counter.

'Jesus, it's getting hot,' I said, removing my ski jacket and hanging it over my arm. One by one the others removed theirs, cheeks flushed. We shuffled along for a further ten minutes before we got to a seating area where a purple-haired woman who must have been in her seventies, along with a young stout lad with long hair, signalled for us to sit on the benches. Swiftly, lifting each foot into a wooden device, they measured our feet and moved on to the next customer, whilst two athletic-looking girls assisting them ran off to rows of high mesh racks and returned with our size. Two other older women moved to our bench asking us our comfort level as we staggered along a short rubber mat in our weighty boots.

'More pitbull than Hush Puppies,' Lou replied as we stood with our boots ready to move on. 'They're pinching my calves.'

One of the women adjusted the front clips and when Lou still complained, she told Lou to remove the boots, pull her socks up to remove any creases and put them back on. This, they said, would ease pressure.

Lou shrugged, helpless.

'We should have done this yesterday; you'll be late for your lesson,' Angie complained, looking at her watch and switching legs in agitation.

'That's much better,' Lou said as she tried walking in the boots again. 'Worth the effort and a few minutes of waiting.' She stared at Angie.

Then, suggesting we leave our boots on, one of the girls directed us to the stairs to join another queue. We followed the queue slowly filing down the stairs, eventually landing in what looked like an enormous industrial cave. Two beefy guys stood behind wide benches, whilst a team of what I can only describe as ants bustled around them, searching, fetching or depositing pairs of skis. Our turn came to hand over a boot to one of the assistants who asked us our weight and height.

I glared at Angie. 'He thinks we've come for a medical check-up.'

Angie grinned then answered. 'I'll go with 155s, and I imagine these four to be the same or 150s,' she told him, then shrugged. 'You'll need to tell them if you know.'

I looked at Angie, bemused.

'They work by weight and height, but you don't want them too long to begin with. I remember getting them crossed a few times when I started out and wishing I'd chosen a smaller length.'

I puffed. Why tell us that? Dread surged through my veins,

triggering the familiar burn at the back of my eyes and throat. I looked down to hide moistening eyes, wishing with all my heart that Mike was with me. I missed how his presence could comfort me. With the panic, I yearned for free hands at least to spritz additional Rescue Remedy onto my tongue. I shouldn't be here. I should be cruising the Caribbean with Mike and soaking up the sun. I tightened my lips, steeling myself.

'Hope you're OK, Gin?' Kim whispered as she handed me my skis and Angie continued overseeing Cathy and Lou's. I clutched them in my right hand, forgetting how heavy skis were, as I shuffled along to collect my poles.

'Darling, I can see you're still struggling,' Cathy continued. 'Shall we sit over on the bench there for a bit?'

Please don't fuss – you'll make me cry. I shook my head, clenched my jaw and gazed down at the rubber matting covering the concrete floor. The boots and skis weighed a tonne and with everything else in my arms, I couldn't decide how I should best carry them. I clamped them together against my waist, clinging to everything and hoping I could manage to get up the stairs.

'This way,' Angie called, and automatically I crooked my neck to see her pointing to a glowing green sign saying 'exit'.

I quickly swung around and collided with Kim. All four of our skis crashed to the ground with everything else and we both collapsed in a heap, legs entwined under the bulk of ski boots. Blurry-eyed, but steeling myself again, I quickly tried to grab the sprawling contents of my helmet before they were trampled on and then I caught sight of Kim. I swear I saw tears in her eyes.

'Are you all right?' I asked, while feeling warm fingers slide into my left hand.

'Embarrassed, but yes. You?'

'Ladies, can I help?' a well-spoken English voice boomed. 'Most people have their skis on before they take a tumble,' he said, unhelpfully.

I glanced up, meeting with kind, smiling eyes. The man who

spoke now gripped my hand with one of his and lifted my elbow with his other. 'Thank you,' I muttered, flustered, trying to lift my feet of clay to balance again. 'Sad, stupid pair aren't we?' I said, wishing the ground would swallow me up. 'We are literally finding our feet with this skiing lark.'

'It isn't easy, especially when you're …'

'… our age,' I finished for him as I found my feet. I was mesmerised and mentally trying to brush myself off. This man's tall presence wasn't aiding my balance. Probably similar in age, maybe a bit younger, his thick hair was adorned with skeins of grey and blond waves falling over a high, barely wrinkled forehead. He held my gaze with hypnotic sparkling eyes. I forced myself to breathe. He reminded me of one of those adventurous heroes you see in films, like Indiana Jones – not excessively handsome but rugged and devilishly sexy.

Instead of helping Kim, I stood there stupidly staring as he stepped aside, lifting her under one arm whilst her other arm was being winched up by an even taller man, though younger I noted, in a bright red all-in-one ski-suit. As his face turned, I saw he was one to definitely attract the girls too with his stunning features and long raven-black hair.

'… when you're starting out. I was actually going to say,' the older man said, returning to me with an easy laugh from a lusciously shaped pair of lips. 'There's lots of us oldies on the slopes, and experienced or not, we all tumble, so don't beat yourself up. You'll get used to all the extra weight and carrying your skis around. Here, let me.' He knelt down, gathering all four skis, which to me appeared identical, while Kim and the other man in the red ski-suit crawled on the floor collecting the contents from her helmet. She handed me one of my gloves, which I hadn't noticed was missing, and I rolled my eyes.

I must have appeared so uncool as I fixated on the older of the two men who held out our skis and peered back at me. 'You may have to get these checked. They're very similar. Are your

shoe sizes the same?' he asked squinting as he inspected the bindings. My head and neck were too busy looking around for his
wife. He must have one here in this crowd, I imagined. Probably
watching me make a complete fool of myself.

The man in the red suit examined them too then promptly
swapped one over and as the older man held them steady in their
pairs, the younger man pointed.

'These two match. This pair is for larger boot,' he said with a
smooth French accent, 'but put them on to check before you
leave.'

Kim blushed as the younger man peered down at her. A little
chemistry there, I thought, watching Kim. I clocked the motif on
his suit too. *Ecole Swiss de Ski & de Snowboard*. He must be a ski
instructor.

'I'll take those. I'm a size bigger than Ginny,' she said, returning
his smile. 'They're Ginny's. Thank you both.' Kim's face brightened. 'We're very grateful.'

'Yes, thank you.' I smiled at both but when I reached out to
take my skis, the older one pulled them back and rattled off
something in French to the other.

Then he pointed his hand and said, 'Move over there out of
the way and we'll check them for you.'

Kim and I scuttled to the side of the room where I spotted a
gap. I placed my helmet and accessories in a space as the two
men followed behind. Angie then appeared too.

'What are you two doing? We're waiting. We need to go. Luckily
the ski instructor isn't out there yet.'

'Are you waiting for Christoff?'

Looking indignant, Angie peered up at the tall man in the red
suit and, in an instant, I saw her jaw drop and her eyes widen.
Swiftly, her face softened and her lips curled. 'Yes, how …?'

'You've found me.'

Amused, Kim and I looked at one another and both scrunched
our noses with a snigger. I saw the older man laughing too. I

explained the events to Angie whilst she gazed gormlessly at Christoff. I placed my skis down on the rubber matting on the floor and gripped her hand. One at a time, I clicked my boots to lock on the bindings. I leaned on her and squeezed her hand but she failed to notice. The older man knelt beside me, causing me to shiver and my cheeks to flare.

'May I?' he asked, holding a hand out towards my knee and looking at me with a flirty glint in his eye.

Blushing and unsure of what he was implying, I answered, 'Go for it, yes. You know what you're doing.' But I was unprepared. As his fingers touched the back of my knee, a part of me stirred that I thought had been buried with Mike. I bit my lip and looked at Kim, trying to deny or hide the pleasure he was inducing. A tiny touch. He tugged at my boot and ski with his other hand. Daring to meet his eyes, I saw him nod his approval.

'They're fine,' he said, then repeated with the other leg. I braced myself the second time, but he clearly had a magic touch as the sensation returned, and his eyes locked on mine again, as if knowing the effect he was having. I don't know if I breathed or for how long I gazed at him, but I felt the tug and release, then two snaps as my boots were released from the bindings.

My lips twitched, and I found my voice. 'Thank you, you're very kind,' was all I could say.

Leaning on Christoff, Kim nodded her approval as he checked hers. Angie licked her lips and asked, 'All OK?'

Satisfied, Christoff looked up and signalled with his thumb. 'Good. So now we go,' he said, pushing down the back of his bindings and rising slowly, giving Kim the opportunity to release her hand from his shoulder. He then strode off to a pillar where he grabbed his skis.

'Thank you, again,' I said to the older man, securing my skis, helmet and poles in my arms again.

'You're welcome. Ginny and ...?'

'Kim,' I told him, realising we hadn't thought to introduce

ourselves or exchange names. Tightening my skis and poles towards my chest, haphazardly in my nervous stupor, I shook his hand.

'Neil,' he said. 'Lovely meeting you both. It's a been a pleasure.'

'For me too,' I said, thinking: if only he knew.

Chapter 6

Kim

Those guys were ace, absolute diamonds. After shaking Neil's hand, I thanked him and Christoff for helping us. Their help was above and beyond expectations and the experience had even distracted my mind from my first ski, not to mention the churning in my stomach from our heavy night. I wasn't feeling my best. We'd got quite carried away at La Poste with our drinking and dancing, and clearly we'd all forgotten about the skiing. It was worth it though to see Ginny really letting her hair down. Something she hadn't done for years. And, watching Ginny with Neil just now was quite endearing. She was blushing. I saw her face turn scarlet a few times.

'Wasn't that man sweet?' I said to Ginny as we straggled behind the girls and the tall handsome Christoff up a steep path.

Her face glowed again. She must have noticed the way he'd looked at her. 'Very.' Ginny smiled coyly. 'Though not as sweet as Christoff, I believe. I saw that look between you.'

'Oh Jeezuz, no way. One man is plenty enough for me, thank you. I think he could lead Angie astray though, by the look on her face.' We chuckled. 'But seriously, don't you think you two had a spark? I mean, it looked that way from where I was standing.'

Ginny's eyes lit up. 'He's certainly attractive and a proper gent; in fact, they both were. I mean who does that nowadays? Not only did they stop and pick us up but then to check our skis. Everyone else was rushing around in a panic,' she said, panting for breath like me, trying to get to grips with the hefty boots and weighty skis.

'Exactamundo, hon, incredible. Such gents. I still maintain that Neil may have had an ulterior motive though – the way he was ogling you. Christoff … I reckon he's a player.'

Ginny blinked hard and dropped her head. 'Anyway, I'm grateful whatever their motives. I was in such a panic.' Her voice wobbled, and she paused. It struck me that talking about the men may possibly have made her think of Mike. She continued. 'I was hot, and there was so much to remember. Thank God for Angie getting us organised this morning, especially after last night. My head has stopped thumping, but I'm still groggy.'

This wasn't the time to pursue my confession, but I was keen to know what was on her mind. I couldn't even guess. Was it that she had found a man attractive and felt guilty, or that I mentioned Christoff was a player?

Angie took charge the minute we left the ski-hire shop to join Lou and Cathy outside, making sure we all still had our essentials; snoods and scarves tucked in, ski passes in the right place, preferably inside our inside jacket pockets, our goggles on our helmets, our gloves clipped to our jackets, sunglasses on, skis and poles in one hand to help us when we walked. I struggled trying to keep up with her and I swear I saw Ginny's eyes well up. Christoff kindly helped lift our skis onto our shoulders. At least we had the benefit of their experience to get us going. Although, I doubted it would have made any difference if either had warned us about the hill to the nursery slope, which I guessed would be the challenge every morning.

'Were you flapping there?' Ginny asked me.

'I was,' I admitted. 'It was all too much at once, wasn't it? Trying to hold it all. Perhaps if I, well we, weren't so hungover it would have been easier.' I stopped, catching my breath. I'm not sure if it was the thin mountain air, or that my fitness level was not what I'd imagined. We had only walked about twenty-five metres and not only were my legs feeling like jelly, but I was steaming as well. I could barely see for the mist on my sunglasses.

Ginny stopped beside me, grappling for air, shades steamed up too, so it was a relief to see the others ahead lowering their skis and resting on them as Angie shuffled them to one side. We moved to the side as skiers and snowboarders began striding between us. They walked with such ease, though I did notice many hadn't clipped their boots up, nor fastened their jackets. I zipped mine open feeling some light relief as the cool air hit my chest.

'I noticed you had a wobble too,' I told Ginny, unsure why. It was like I was willing her to talk to me. Open up. But I was well aware of the consequences – so why? 'I saw your eyes well up.'

She bit her lip. 'Oh, Kimmy, sorry. I've been like a wet lettuce. I don't know why. It's been a year I know, but it randomly happens, especially when I'm stressed. It's like I'm expecting him to be beside me to take control.'

'Aw, don't apologise. I don't blame you. He was your safety net I guess. I suspect it's natural. Just talk if you want to. I'm here right beside you. And the other Flowers are too.' I juggled my skis freeing up my hand and rubbing her arm, almost praying I wouldn't be forced to tell her now. 'You mustn't feel alone, Ginny, ever. I'm your friend, your safety net, and I've known you long enough that I'm not going to judge you. Don't be afraid to share whatever is going on in your head.'

She pursed her lips, looking at me as close friends do. 'I love you, Kimmy. I should … I will … try to share, I mean. I admit, the skiing scares me but no doubt it does you and the others too.'

She tilted her head for a second then stood tall. 'But, we're here together, which is rare, and I want to make the most of it. I'm going up there and going to throw everything I have at it and have a bloody great time. I mean, just look at all these people. There must be something damn sexy about this sport that drives them.'

'Bloody right. Well said that, Flower. Me too.' I instantly felt awash with enthusiasm and affectionately slapped her shoulder and gave her a wide beam. 'Good girl. Love the spirit and love you. Let's get going, shall we. We will conquer this!' And grabbing our skis, we lumbered them onto our shoulders and marched determinedly onwards and definitely upwards.

By the time we reached a wide opening, basically a huge open field blanketed in snow between buildings and a steep bank, I wanted to drop. My chest was screaming as my lungs wheezed to breathe. I bent forwards, backwards, any way I could to inhale air into my lungs. I was soaked. At least two pints of perspiration must have spouted from my skin and into the fibres of my clothes. Regaining some sort of consciousness, I focused on Ginny, standing over her skis gripping her hips. Lou was flat out on the snow whilst Cathy stripped off her jacket and helmet and bent beside Lou, who was unzipping hers too.

What a sorry state we were in. I almost laughed to myself at our insanity, our folly – but then felt a little euphoria for what we had accomplished. A few minutes later though, I was fine and grateful I had worked hard on my fitness. The climb up was hard work, but it got the old heart racing and that buzz you get from a good workout was firing me up.

As I looked up, I saw Christoff virtually floating down the nursery slope towards us with what looked like several small bottles of water in his hands.

'You star!' I cheered, as he held them out and, after helping myself, I passed them around. 'Thank you.' I was gulping mine down when I clapped eyes on the lift and almost choked, horrified to see it didn't have seats. Just a pole with a disc on the bottom.

Christoff, sipping his water with ladylike dignity, must have followed my vision as I watched a group of five- or six-year-olds master the moving button-lift easier than a knife and fork.

He chuckled. 'You next. Watch and learn.'

'You can do it,' Ginny said to me, squirting Rescue Remedy into her mouth. 'It's not too difficult. We used one of these on the dry slope. I only fell off twice but that was because I panicked. Just stay calm and you'll be fine. There's a man there to help too.'

I suddenly shivered with anticipation. 'Yes, you've had some practice runs, haven't you? You're all a step ahead of me.' I had seriously considered a trip to the dry ski slope but decided against it as no one at home wanted to come along. What if I broke a leg or an ankle and couldn't get home? I knew it was feeble but you always heard the bad things. Besides, I'd spent a lot of time on water-skis. Not quite the same, but my balance must have been decent, surely? And my knees were used to the squatting. There couldn't be that much difference, could there?

Angie brushed my arm as she called the others over. 'Here you go, my Flowers. I think Christoff is ready to begin your lesson.' She glanced towards Christoff with what looked like a sultry pout. 'I'll stay around in case you need any help.'

Christoff raised his palm. 'It's OK. You ski.' Did he want her out from under his feet?

Angie twitched with, I detected, a little indignation. 'Well, I might just watch for a bit,' she said, stepping aside as Christoff came forward. 'Enjoy, my Flowers,' she said poling her way across to a small bench. We gave her a wave as she turned. I couldn't help but feel sympathetic; after all, she had put in so much time to organise this and being the only one who could ski meant she didn't have anyone to ski with.

Once we were all zipped up with helmets and gloves on, Christoff marched with ease, beckoning us with his arm to follow to an area beside the lift. We circled him as he asked our names and what skiing experience we'd had. I was the only one who hadn't been on the lift or dry slope before, so I gazed at him trying to take everything in as he briefed us. He demonstrated the snowplough and how to brake, where we should hold our sticks, how we sidewalk upwards, and all about staying safe. I hadn't realised there was so much to it and whilst he continued, demonstrating how to use the button-lift, I couldn't help feeling a tad bad for not visiting a dry slope and priming myself as the others had. I was now going to hold them all up.

I blinked, hearing Christoff instructing us to put on our skis. He took our poles and piled them beside the lift shed. We were all shaking in our boots whilst he clicked into his skis and slid expertly through the electronic lift-pass machine to the stack of poles on the frame of the lift. The lift man shook his hand and positioned himself opposite him.

Christoff took one of the wiggly poles and pulled it. 'You have plenty of time. You are in control. Pull it down firmly. Place the button between your thighs. Feel yourself being pulled and hold on. Keep the skis a few inches apart and let it take you. That's it.'

We watched him go up a few feet, then he let go and slid down. 'So, who's first?'

I hung back. In fact, we all stared at him for what seemed like ages, then together Lou and Ginny said: 'I'll go first.'

Ginny slid her skis on and grabbed a rail, shuffling her skis until she reached the poles. She followed Christoff's instructions with precision and set off up the hill. Lou followed, sliding slightly as the pole heaved her.

'I'll go next if that's OK?' I said to Cathy.

'Please do, darling,' she said with a chuckle. 'I'm in no, rush believe me.'

Putting one ski forward and shifting slowly, I suddenly slid speedily into the bar. 'Whooo! OK. Calm.' I talked to myself, shuffling forward as I'd seen the others do. I took the pole and as I pushed it down, it seemed to want to wrench me off my feet; so I let go, my skis sliding forward leaving me and my bum on the snow. Christoff scooped me up under my arm and I was quickly back up but noticed a queue of people. Many of them kids.

Christoff took a pole. 'Firm pull.' He demonstrated.

I closed my fists and repeated, 'Firm pull, right.'

This time I took control of the pole, determined not to be bullied by it, and wedged it between my legs, allowing it to turn slightly, then waited, gripping it tightly with both hands. I felt a jolt and began travelling up. 'I'm on,' I squealed my skis starting to wander to one side.

'Straighten up,' Christoff called, so I dug down in my boots to steer the skis straight.

I was on my way to my first ever ski. 'Yee.' I dared to take one hand off to wave at Ginny and Lou who had reached the top. Slowly it trundled, literally lifting my spirits as it glided uphill. Gripping tight, I twisted my neck to see Cathy behind me and Christoff's red suit behind her. I felt a bump and panicked but couldn't look down. I had a feeling it would all go wrong if I did. I kept my skis and eyes ahead. Gradually the line became shorter and tugged me up a bank and before I could think, I heard a clonk and realised the wire was circling round and back down. *This is where I needed to get off.*

In a panic I pushed the pole, quickly bending my knees to release it. I squealed as my leg jerked and a ski shot forward. Control went from me completely as I felt my body lurch forward. I threw my hands out to balance, but instead of standing, found my legs had straightened and I was sliding forward, my hands gathering snow as I gripped it, trying to slow myself down. I stopped but had somehow spun and found myself in a down-ward-facing-dog position. A very inelegant yoga pose! I looked between my legs. Ginny and Lou were busting their sides whilst

100

presumably side-stepping upwards on their skis to rescue me, but then I felt my feet slipping away … *Shit!*

'Help.' The skis slid backwards taking me down. I clawed at the ice with no better idea of what I should do. Should I throw myself to one side? I saw Cathy behind me, steadying herself from the propulsion. I could knock her over too.

'Out the way!' I screamed then heard the thud of skis bashing the ice and saw Christoff speeding towards me. Swiftly, he stooped beside me, grabbed me under my arm and hauled me upright. Again. I wrenched down my jacket, regaining composure. 'So that's how not to do it,' I said, checking I still had everything in place and straightening my goggles on my helmet. 'Phew, thanks,' I gasped, feeling such a fool with Ginny and Lou still bellowing infectious laughter. I found myself joining them as I pictured what I must have looked like.

Ginny

I hadn't belly-laughed like that for years, but Kim was still in one piece, thank goodness. It was a great feeling, me on snow at the top of a ski slope without falling over – yet! A miracle. We all made it, despite Kim's stunt. Great entertainment though. It was spectacularly hilarious, and I couldn't help but giggle every time the picture zoomed in my mind's eye. I wish I'd had my phone out and caught her on camera. It would be a big hit on YouTube. And Christoff must have known every muscle on her arm by now what with that earlier catch too.

Thankfully, Christoff spoke very good English. I was worried we would end up having an instructor we couldn't understand. He was also great eye-candy. I knew I was past all that, but he had those addictively bright eyes, attentive with silky long lashes. They had a way of making you feel he's interested, even though you knew you were old enough to be his mother. And his stature and the way he just seemed to be there when you needed him brought me huge comfort. A modern-day knight in shiny red armour.

With the drama over, Christoff lined us up in a row across the top of the slope. The first thing he demonstrated was forming a triangle with our skis. So far so good, as we had at least got to this stage on the dry slope, but then he demonstrated the plough and the most important part – to remember how to stop. Our first exercise was to snowplough down to markers zigzagging across the slope he pointed to and then push our heels down in the inside of the ski to slow down, then stop. He demonstrated the move three times, making it look extremely easy. But this was ice, not dry tufts, and being faced with a long slippery slope, we were all edging cautiously barely moving, let alone slowing and stopping.

It was Lou who mastered it first. I knew she would. She just threw herself into it. Ploughed stopped, ploughed stopped, then again to the bottom. Then Kim. Kim who had never had any ski lessons as we had on the dry slope. We watched her confidently let herself slide with her knees nicely bent, then come slightly upright; then she let her knees bend again as she brought the backs of her skis out and slowed steadily then stopped. We held our breaths as she wobbled a little, but then she just seemed to relax and did it again.

'Very good,' Christoff said and we clapped as Lou and Kim made her their way back to the lift, which Kim was probably dreading. I didn't have time to watch her. I was trying to focus but I was so proud of them. After several attempts at leaning forward, and visualising myself gliding down with the same grace, I went next. I allowed myself to slide just as Lou and Kim had, keeping my skis in their lovely triangle as I ploughed, but then I felt a wobble and next thing, I sped up. I was going too fast to think about pushing out the backs of my skis. I automatically leaned back, which was what you shouldn't do, and the skis steered themselves to the other side of the slope.

I threw myself onto the snow. Christoff was there in no time and hauled me up, my legs shaking and skis crossing, then I started to slide down as he let go. He took hold of my arm again.

'Lean your downhill foot in,' he said showing me with his ski. 'Put the weight on the inside of your ski and lean up the mountain. Weight on the edge of your skis is like your brakes.'

I followed instructions. In fact, I knew this from my previous lessons, but the fixation that the snow is slippery compared to the matting on dry slopes wouldn't leave my head, and we all know logic escapes when you panic. Mine did, anyway.

'Good try. Now, go across there and do the same only this time, follow me and do as I do.'

It was so simple following his moves. I didn't even think about it, I just did it. I smirked as I reached the bottom. 'Yes,' I cried. I couldn't wait to get back up the lift and do it again – on my own.

'Well done,' Christoff said as we reached the lift. I glowed inside and out, my fears beginning to melt away as I was dragged back up by the lift. I watched as Lou reached mid-point, concentrating hard but ploughing again beautifully. I saw Cathy ploughing towards the lift, cautiously as I had done, her stance stiffly upright and eyes fixed to a spot. Kim was at the top, mentally psyching herself up, before leaning forward for the push-off. At my next attempt, I held my breath but set off again with more confidence, even making a lovely wide turn as I willed myself to keep going.

We did this repeatedly for the next hour or so, just following a trail, practising, getting used to the snow. Tumbling and getting up. Ploughing again. It was fun.

Christoff gathered us once more together at the top. 'Well done, ladies. After lunch, I recommend you return here for further practice. You're doing very well. For those who want to try, I have an exercise. It is to "Pat the Dog". We immediately giggled. 'I will show you.'

We watched as he ploughed to the side and lowered his knees at the turn to pat an imaginary dog. 'Inside ski. Here,' he said. He turned again, doing the same on the other side. Then side-stepped back up to us.

'You have one go now, but you can practise later too.'

My tummy was rumbling at this point and I was feeling tired, but as we were heading back to the village for lunch very soon, I gave it my best shot.

Between us we ploughed down, creating some interesting variations of 'Pat the Dog', which took some knee work, but I figured we had the afternoon to practise. For now, I was looking forward to walking down to the restaurant, resting my weary legs and sampling some more of the mouth-watering mountain food.

We met Angie at the bottom, who – chewing on her usual edamame beans – wiped her hand on her ski pants and clapped. 'I'm so impressed; you've all done so well,' she told us. 'And provided me with great entertainment.' She winked at us, her eyes rolling towards Christoff.

We proudly removed our skis while discussing our jaunt and gathering our poles as we heaved the skis again to our shoulders. We then headed for the Belleview in the hope of finding a table outside. The sunny Belleview terrace was heaving, but Cathy thought she spotted a party leaving. I was chatting to Lou as we stood waiting, but I could tell she was distracted; judging by her expression something or someone had disturbed her, and she was hobbling around me as if trying to hide. She then pointed to La Poste.

'Actually,' she said, looking over in the direction of the restaurant, 'I'm sure Stefano will have outside tables. Let's go down to the terrace there. We'll still have a view.'

Cathy was insistent. 'No, look – they're doing coats up.'

'I'm going up here,' Lou said and strode off rudely.

I shrugged at the others and followed Lou. 'This isn't like you. What's up?'

'Nothing. Oh, too much drink last night probably. But I'm hungry and we could wait forever.'

I was unconvinced but beckoned the others to follow.

Lou was brushing me off. She's normally so easy-going and that reaction was uncharacteristically bad-mannered. I'm sure the girls thought it too. I just couldn't understand why. Fortunately, she had found a table in a great spot. I sat beside her. The sun pulsed down on the La Poste terrace and although it wasn't sheltered by glass like the Belleview, the temperature was surprisingly pleasant considering it was the end of December and there was still a terrific outlook. I removed my helmet and gloves, instantly feeling cool air on the back of my neck, so I pulled up my snood.

I was just about to ask Lou what was wrong again when Didier, the waiter we had met the night before, came over to us with menus. We ordered water and wine and he told us he would return to take our choices for lunch. Peering around, I spotted Neil, my knight in shining armour this morning, over at another table. He saw me at the same time. I politely waved, trying not to blush. He was with a group of men, some in similar suits to Christoff. He had obviously been out on the slopes going by his ruddy cheeks. He waved back and gave me a warm smile. That was a man who looked after himself. I liked that about him, and his kind eyes. Kim spotted him too and waved.

I nudged Lou with my elbow. 'So, are you going to tell me why you didn't want to stop at the Belleview?'

'It's better here, don't you think?'

Angie leant across the other side. 'I have to say, I was surprised. It's not like you to be uptight, Lou. But you're right. It's lovely. And, look, there's Christoff. I have to say I'm jealous you Flowers got him as an instructor. I was tempted to join you. I've seen him here before. He's really hot.'

105

'He is,' Cathy said. 'That man he's just sat next to isn't bad either.'

Lou and I turned. 'That's Neil,' Kim said. 'He's the one who rescued Ginny in the hire shop. Really sweet, wasn't he, Ginny?'

Trying to appear nonchalant, I smiled. 'He was … is.'

'That's why you chose this place isn't it, Lou,' Angie heckled. 'You saw Christoff heading here.'

Lou held up her hands. 'OK. You've got me. So now you can all thank me for the eye-candy,' she said, seemingly glad for an excuse. She opened her lip gloss.

I left it at that, watching Didier pour wine into our glasses. I picked up the carafe of water and filled each tumbler. After opting for hot tomato and basil soup with crusty bread for lunch and a cheeseboard between us to follow, we launched into chatter about our first attempt at proper snow skiing, comparing notes and variations of the incidents and highlights of the morning, the Swiss wine swimming down our throats too easily.

Didier returned with a large tray, a kettle of steaming soup along with warm bowls and a basket with the crusty loaf already sliced.

'More wine, Flowers?' Cathy asked as she drip-fed her empty glass and held up the bottle for Didier. '*Encore le vin?*'

It was a silly question, wasn't it? But with five of us it only equated to two small glasses each. Swiss glasses are much smaller than the ones we're used to at home. The soup was delicious and filling. I was so chilled sitting there. I leant back on my chair feeling the radiating winter sunshine on my skin whilst the girls enthused and of course embellished their stories. It was so lovely to be with them and after the morning on the nursery slope my view of skiing was changing, and my appreciation of their choice and effort deepened. Closing my eyes, I floated off.

The closest I'd been to a mountain was in the Lake District. Mike and I used to take the children when they were young. We walked for hours of course, but they loved to play around edge

106

of Derwent Water in the late sunshine when we hired a little cottage close to Keswick. It was a warm sunny day like this when Mike and I sat out on the terrace overlooking the lake as Ross and Rachel played – throwing stones across the top of the water, honing their skills to skim and bounce them. Mike and I watched, sitting on an antiquated red sofa with our feet up on a box he made as a stool. His hand covered mine as we sat awash with contentment. I adored those shared golden moments.

Thoughts of Mike and the anniversary in two days drifted in. My mind churned as it often did with memories and questions. How this time last year he was in the hospice, in and out of consciousness, delirious with drugs and not making any sense. He was muttering all sorts, some familiar things, like that he'd left his blue suit in the car, that tea was nice, or work-related stuff, like I can't get to the wires, give me a torch or I shouldn't have sent Brian on that job. Everyday stuff. But still gnawing at me are the less familiar things, like saying 'I didn't mean to hurt you,' then 'Sorry, love, it's the only time I've ever been unfaithful.'

'What? When?' I'd asked, my heart stopping and my stomach tumbling. That hurt. Still hurts. To this day I've no answer. I searched his phone, his contact books, paperwork. Anything I thought would offer a clue. Asking him, of course, was fruitless. Nothing I said made sense to him either. I tried not to dwell on it. Tried. Tried and tried. But it was hard to ignore something like that. I heard Kim's voice calling.

We'd forgotten about the arduous climb as we headed back up to the nursery slope after our cheese and a third bottle of wine. Yes, the Swiss cheeses and crackers soaked it up perfectly. The Gruyere in particular; its solid texture and nutty flavour was just divine. And possibly the one good reason why subsequent exertion is a must. It seemed a shame to leave our sunny lunch spot as we'd discovered the nursery slope was cooler now, shaded by the mountain.

Without Christoff there, Angie joined us insisting she would lead us down. Once we'd ploughed down, practising our 'Pat the Dogs' and falling on our backsides, we were soon warmed up. I was pleased that Cathy was quickly gaining confidence. I knew she was as apprehensive as I was, if not more so, and like me, she seemed to be having fun. I was finding it surprisingly rewarding as well as challenging. I knew I was ploughing, but I felt I was really skiing. I might not have been be parallel skiing yet and didn't feel brave enough to tackle the bigger slopes, but I couldn't help feeling I should have given it a go when Mike had asked me years ago.

After an hour, Angie suggested we save our poor old legs for our lessons the following day. Lou and Kim, both fitter and sportier than Cath and I, protested.

'Oh, no, not yet. I'm really enjoying myself,' Lou moaned.

'Me too. Just another half hour,' Kim urged Angie.

But, to be honest, my thighs and calves were beginning to resemble a rugby player's. At least, that's how they felt.

Angie shrugged, digging one of her poles into the snow. 'By all means, stay. It's not for me to tell you what to do. I'd happily carry on, but I know you'll regret it tomorrow. You'll overdo it and your legs will tire, believe me.'

Lou and Kim glanced at one another, Lou expressing a defiant pout and Kim feigning a sad face.

'She's probably right,' Kim told her. 'My thighs are screaming.'

I let out a sigh, grateful I wasn't the only one in pain, and decided to back Angie.

'I need to go back to the chalet for a hot bath. Hopefully soothe these hard-worked muscles in some Radox and have a snooze.' I rubbed my knees. 'Après-ski will have to wait.'

'Sounds like a sensible plan to me, darling girls,' Cathy agreed. 'Rest now. Go out about seven. We're sure to be hungry later after all the energy we've expelled.'

I wanted to poke Lou in the ribs as I observed the defeated sulk on her face, but I didn't dare reach with my skis on. 'Come on, Lulu,' I teased. 'We've earned some of that yummy Swiss chocolate that's in the fridge.'

Her eyes brightened. 'Oh, you're right,' she said making me titter. 'I can sacrifice the skiing for chocolate. And, I don't fancy going to the bar again.'

I pondered this, curious. Something was niggling her.

Chapter 7

Cathy

I couldn't believe it. I had just had a lovely hot soak in the bath, a little read, wandered down the stairs to join the girls for a warm mug of tea and a bit of chocolate, and was looking forward to burying my head back in my book when my phone rang. Anthony's name lit up. I stared as it rang for several seconds. I wished the battery was dead or that I'd left it upstairs out of earshot.

'Hello, darling,' I said, uncurling my weary legs and making my way to the stairs. 'Hold on, I'm just going upstairs so that I don't disturb everyone.'

As I climbed the stairs, I wasn't sure that I could cope with another round of moaning and questions. It was draining me. And, to my knowledge, none of the others were receiving constant phone calls.

'How are you?' I asked as I closed the bedroom door.

'Missing you like mad, my cherub, and eager to know how your first day skiing went?' Anthony said, sounding chirpier at least.

I walked over to the French doors, looking at the view. 'I miss

110

you too, darling and the skiing went much better than I anticipated.'

'That's good.'

'Yes, I'm a little bit slower than the others, but I'd rather that
than break something,' I admitted. 'Kim was very funny going
up the lift, actually. She slid whilst she was trying to stand and
get her balance, but our ski instructor is very strong and caught
her.'

'Sounds dangerous.'

'Not at all, the snow is very forgiving, and the slope isn't too
steep.'

There was a pause. 'So, how old is this strong instructor?'
Anthony asked.

I opened one of the doors to let in some air. 'Put it this way,
I'm probably old enough to be his mother so don't go there. What
have you been doing?' I asked before I got the full interrogation.

'I was just interested, that's all. You'll have to send me over
some photos.'

'Darling, I'm trying to focus on the skiing. I'm not likely to
get my phone out whilst I'm on the snow. Maybe when I feel
more confident. Anyway, have you been busy?'

'I went online and found the live webcam. I looked for you.
The village looks nice.'

'I doubt the webcam is on the nursery slope, but yes the village
is lovely, and the people are friendly.'

'How was your meal last night?'

'Oh, it was beautiful, and so much of it. I think about six or
seven courses. Ginny really seemed to be enjoying herself for
once. We had a lovely evening, dancing too.'

'Who were you dancing with?' I heard him slurping his drink.

'Well, the girls of course. You know how we all love Abba.'

'Sounds like you're all having a rave.'

'We're just having a bit of fun, darling, and making sure Ginny
enjoys her week. So, will I get an answer to my question?'

'Well, there's not much fun here to report. I did the crossword, sudoku. Walked along to the shop for another paper. Didn't meet anyone unless you count grouchy Gingerman walking his dog as someone. I went on the internet as I said, looking at the webcam there. Do you know there are more divorces in the over-sixties than any other age group nowadays?'

I coughed. 'Really! What newspaper was that, darling? Are there lots of divorce lawyer ads?'

'It was on the internet.'

'So the article had lawyer ads? Darling, you shouldn't believe everything you read. Besides, if marriages are failing after sixty, maybe it says something about the length of marriage now we're living longer. Men and women wanting to do their own thing.'

He took another slurp. 'Is that what you think?'

'Women are more independent now, don't you think? They have their own means. I don't know, darling, you've read more about it than me. What does it say?'

'You have your own means, cherub, but you're not thinking of divorce, are you?'

I wasn't, but Anthony's paranoia was beginning to make me. It wasn't the time to discuss this. If I was to upset him with my thoughts currently, I could open Pandora's box. 'Anthony, I'm missing you, like I said. Stop fretting and find something to do. Haven't you got a book you can read? I fear your brain is idling and you need to occupy it rather than sit and worry.'

I stepped outside onto the wooden balcony; the cool air was refreshing.

Anthony continued. 'Do you know that you're becoming more selfish? I know you don't care about me anymore. You never spend time with me. You're always locking yourself away and ignoring me like I'm a pesky child.'

My free hand reached for my mouth, my fingers pressing on my lips. What was he saying? I tried to swallow the lump in my throat, but it wouldn't shift. I couldn't speak. I listened. First I heard him gulp, then he raised his voice.

'Well? It's true, isn't it?'

My voice rose. 'You don't know what you're saying. You're drunk, Anthony.'

'You don't know what to say because it's true, Cath.'

The anger inside me grew and I spoke louder. 'Just because I'm writing doesn't equate to ignoring you. Anthony, I talk to you when you come in even if I'm working.'

'You do, Cath; that's only because I make the effort to come and talk to you. When do you come and talk to me? I wouldn't see you all day if I didn't come in to your study. Bring you tea, lunch. Don't you understand that I want your company, your attention?'

'Then why choose now to talk to me about it? Why haven't you spoken to me before? We could have discussed it before I came away. You want to ruin my week? Well, you won't. You are the one who is selfish. Just because I'm married to you, it doesn't mean to say I have to entertain you. What if I was working full-time at the school still? You would have to find something to do.'

'I only retired because you wanted me to. You wanted to travel, remember? You wanted us to travel together and do things together, Cath. Now you want to shut yourself away and I'm left with nothing.'

Tears burst out of me as I recollected his enthusiasm. 'You told me you wanted to retire too. In fact, you wanted to travel, do voluntary work and pursue building log cabins or sheds or some-thing – build yourself a workshop at the back of the garden whilst you were doing a carpentry course,' I reminded him, wiping my eyes. 'We were down in Whitstable for the day with Ginny, Mike, Lou and Terry, and we were all talking about what we would do when we sold up or retired, and you were buzzing with excite-ment. They all heard you. And me. I said I was going to pursue

113

my writing. You can't blame me for your own failings. I've never stopped you doing what you want to do. If you choose to sit around bored, that's not my problem.' I found myself calming, satisfied that I'd managed to hold my emotions together as I'd conveyed my argument.

'Once, very convenient,' he retorted.

'Anthony, this conversation can wait. I'm sorry you're not happy but I'm not going to continue now. It's not the time nor the place. We'll speak some more when I'm home.'

'I expect you're going out on another jolly then.'

I sighed heavily. 'Hardly going to be jolly now you've spoiled my mood. I'm going. Bye, Anthony. Speak when I'm home.'

After pressing my thumb on the phone, I threw it on the bed and then myself, hurt and angry. I couldn't solve Anthony's problem, and neither would he with drink. I certainly hadn't realised his frustration but to release it on me now, while I was in Switzerland … He was the one being selfish.

Kim

I was sitting in the lounge with my feet up reading another of Liane Moriarty's books on my Kindle. I'd read one on the flight over from Oz, *The Husband's Secret*, and was so enjoying *Big Little Lies*, when someone's ringtone shrilled through me.

'Who's calling her now?' I asked Lou as Cathy reached the top of the stairs and closed the door to her room. 'She was on it for ages last night. Must be costing someone a fortune.'

'Anthony, I think. I presume. I don't know,' Lou said, shrugging as she put down her paperback. 'Maybe he's missing her.'

Angie snorted from behind a magazine. 'He seems a different man since he's retired and been back from travelling. He spent so many years mollycoddling celebrity clients that now he's mollycoddling Cathy. I don't think he's coping without her there.'

'Yes, she's finding it all a bit intense,' Lou sighed. 'It was all right last year when they spent most of it travelling but she's struggled having him at home full-time, particularly when she's trying to write. She took her laptop up to the village library in the summer. I don't know what she'll do if it closes. Sit in one of the village pubs, I suspect.'

Tucking my socked feet on to the sofa, I switched off my Kindle and remembered Cathy saying that she was writing short stories and had even had one published. She said she had also started a sort of *Eat Pray Love* type novel. About a woman going off to far-off destinations to find herself. I was keen to know where her writing would take her. Living in Australia meant I couldn't keep up with everything that the Flowers get up to. It was a great opportunity to catch up now though. 'Doesn't Anthony have a hobby?'

Lou twisted her mouth and shook her head. 'Cathy says he's up each day at six, has read *The Times* and completed the crossword by nine then spends his days fussing around her before his four o'clock nap. Other than that, he cleans their cars once a week.'

'Not much fun, is it?' I said, getting back to my Kindle, then jumped. At first, I thought I saw a marmot out of the corner of my eye, and almost freaked, then I saw it was Ginny coming down the stairs in grey fluffy slippers and dressing gown, her eyes heavy from a sleep. 'Who is Cathy talking to? She sounds upset.'

'Hmm.' I lowered my Kindle onto my lap again. 'We were just wondering. We thought it might be Anthony.'

Ginny slouched into an armchair. 'Something's up. I hope nothing awful has happened.'

'Probably Anthony missing her? Home alone, he can't deal with her being away,' Angie said.

Ginny glanced at Lou with a grimace. 'I don't think he would make a big issue of it. Though you don't know, do you. He has been acting strange. I heard her crying and shouting. Well, I think that's what I heard.'

'Yes, we could hear it too,' Lou said looking concerned.

Ginny put her finger on her lips and spoke softly. 'Shush. Probably best we wait. Let her volunteer.'

I wanted to say, a problem shared ... blah blah, and that we're all to be trusted. From experience I knew people often wanted to talk about the things that were worrying them. Jeez, some of the things that my patients told me weren't for the faint-hearted, some bent over where they've carried a burden for so long, so I've witnessed first-hand the relief and transformation some of them have gone through and, typically, that was when they found their best solutions.

Having said that, I was as guilty as the next person, not confronting Will anymore about moving back to England or saying anything to Ginny about Mike. I hated hurting people unnecessarily. It wasn't in my nature. The thing was, Will understood I wanted to be nearer to Avril and Mai, but I worried that if he was to discover that I want to help Ginny get through her grief, repay her for the help she's given me in the past, it may create further tension between us. He would naturally feel I was putting Ginny before him. And telling Ginny about Mike, which I do have to face this week, would have so many possible damaging consequences for our friendship. Again, she would question my loyalty, and losing Ginny and all my friends would devastate me. Did that make me a hypocrite?

Munching on a bean, Angie picked up her phone and swiped it. 'It's six-thirty-five,' she said and ran her tongue over her teeth. 'We should be getting ready to go out to dinner.'

'With all that crunching I'm surprised you're hungry, Ang. Let's wait 'til Cathy's finished,' Lou said. 'I don't want to disturb her.' She glanced over at the kitchen. 'Why don't we have a glass of wine? There's still a bottle and a half on the breakfast bar. We can also decide where to go.'

By half seven we were all glammed up and ready, having opted for Les Fougeres, another restaurant in the village. Despite make-up and her hair half-covering her face, I noticed Cathy's bloodshot eyes, glaringly obvious evidence she had been crying, when she and Lou came down to the lounge last. I wasn't sure if she had said anything to Lou, but we each smiled stiffly. The elephant in the room. Like me, were my friends masking their own problems in order to help Ginny through this week?

I brushed Cathy's shoulder. 'You OK?' I asked, feeling we were all being ridiculous. 'Is Anthony all right?'

Cathy forced a smile. 'Yes. Absolutely fine. I'm famished though.'

I sighed. Whatever it was, she wasn't sharing. 'Good, so am I and no doubt everyone else. Let's go eat.'

It was easy to smile back at Cathy but behind those eyes I detected sorrow and that widening of the lips didn't convince me. Same as Lou earlier, hiding something. Instinctively I knew that she wasn't prepared to tell me. Sometimes you just knew when your friends were circumventing. What were they afraid to admit? Me included. Why didn't I have the faith to trust them with the secret I harboured? I looked over at Ginny cheerfully chatting to Ang, looking relaxed and happy, probably for the first time in months, possibly years. Was I going to risk destroying her recovery too, even before it had properly begun?

Chapter 8

Ginny

Les Fougeres restaurant was busy, though not as rammed as La Poste the previous evening. But, like La Poste, the warmth and atmosphere were welcoming. Les Fougeres was a traditional-style chalet from the outside but sat happily with its more contemporary interior with larger windows and higher ceilings. As we shuffled in we received a brief wave and a smile from a barman standing at a renovated wood-panelled bar to our right with matching wooden tables and less cramped seating. Fewer benches, more chairs and a warm glow from a flickering fire.

A tall lady with bright mahogany hair eyed us for several seconds before picking up a wad of padded leatherette menus from a restored tall dresser and approaching us. She appeared quite scary.

'*Bonsoir, Madam. Une table pour cinq personnes, s'il vous plaît?*' Lou said, ever the brazen one.

'Ah, you English?'

'Yes.'

'Yes, welcome. Come with me,' she said clutching the menus with both hands and racing off with jumbo strides as she led us to a table. 'What would you like to drink? The wine menu is on the table or I can get you beers or ...'

'Do you have Gamay?' Angie asked.

'Of course, we have Gamay,' the woman said, gaping at us with a disgruntled expression that we should dare suggest she didn't. 'Five glasses?'

'Yes please,' I said. 'And a carafe of water. Please.'

'Yes. OK.' She handed out the menus as abruptly as she spoke and then turned to the side and pointed to a chalkboard. 'We have specials on the board there if you want more choice. The venison is favourite here. Sergio, my husband, does the best venison in the canton. You will not be disappointed,' she said before strutting off to the bar.

We gazed at one another and tittered quietly, and I felt a sense of relief because we had an excuse to speak again. I think we were all waiting for Cathy to break the silence on the walk down.

'That's a pretty bold statement. Poor Sergio, I wonder if he knows he does the best venison for miles around,' Lou said dryly, which made us all cackle.

'I imagine he's afraid to argue with her,' I said.

'Maybe it's all he's good at!' Angie added crumbling at her own joke but stirring up more laughter. Even from Cathy.

Rubbing her hands, Cathy's shoulders melted back into her chair. She picked up a menu. 'I wonder if Sergio looks like Ken. An older version naturally. She reminds me of my old Barbie when I put cochineal in her hair – all legs and boobs.'

Laughter echoed around the table.

'Aw, I remember her. Yes, that hair,' I squealed at Cathy, picturing the image of her childhood doll. 'That poor Barbie doll, you were so mean. I was into Sindy. I had three, and a Paul. Remember Paul? My three Sindys had to share him. Seems sinister now, doesn't it? God, we were so innocent.'

Lou tapped my arm, her eyes gleaming. 'Yes. What a great childhood though. I'm not sure girls have that now. We used to bring them over to yours, didn't we? Cathy and me. We used to take them up to your bedroom, or in your playhouse. I remember leaving my Sindy in your playhouse. Penny, her name was. I couldn't sleep all night worrying she would get cold or eaten by your dog. I had two Tressys, too. Do you remember the Tressy clothes? I loved the Tressy clothes. And the hair that grew, though never went back in! My blonde Tressy was called Debbie – and Barbara, no Barb, was my brunette.'

Cathy smiled heartily. 'Yes, what magical times we had with our Sindys and Tressys. My mother didn't take to Barbie because she was American, but I bought one eventually, out of my own pocket money, just out of spite. She was the new posh girl in my class. I would always line her up with all my other dolls as one of my pupils, but she was my class monitor. She was so good, in fact, I got her a boyfriend. Ken.'

'Sweet memories,' Angie agreed. 'I suppose I was with you in spirit even if I was living in Greenwich at the time. I only had Sindy and Tressy. Barbie didn't have Sindy's class. And I was out in the park most of the time. Probably too old to be seen playing with dollies by then.'

'I agree, Sindy had class and definitely my favourite,' I said trying to remember when my parents bought Kim's sister a Barbie for her ninth birthday. 'But Barbie did become increasingly popular. Probably because of all the advertising and accessories we started to see on TV.' I turned to Angie. 'Would you have lost your street cred then, Ang?'

Angie began. 'Er, yeah! I'm two years older than you girls, don't forget. I did an extra year at school to resit … my maths … so when I … Bonsoir, Christoff.'

I cranked my head round to follow her gaze. I'd lost her attention as our ski instructor and two others marched in, followed closely by Neil, who looked straight at me and smiled. I felt a little flutter coiling in my stomach and smiled back, sure I was blushing. He was just being friendly, I realised, but was surprised that my body reacted as it did. The tall waitress returned, poised with her notebook

I reopened the menu whilst the men took seats at the other end of our long table. 'Anyway, we need to choose what we are having for dinner,' I said, glad that Christoff was attracting the girls' attention enough that they hadn't noticed or commented on my blush. I scanned the menu. 'Actually, I quite fancy the venison in the wild mushroom and truffle sauce, especially if it's the best in the canton.'

Angie and Cathy glanced at each other, sucking lemons in disgust.

Lou and Kim agreed on the special venison whilst Cathy and Angie opted for a roast aubergine baked with Gorgonzola. I looked along the table where Angie was now shuffling up to Christoff whilst the other guys took their seats.

'If you want a recommendation, the venison here is superb,' Neil said as he took off his jacket and placed it on the back of his chair. I found myself staring as he pulled down a burgundy cashmere sweater over his dark navy jeans.

'That's good to hear. Thank you, we thought we'd try it,' I said, feeling embarrassed again and reaching for my phone in my pocket. I switched on my roaming.

Kim

The tall woman took our order and I wasn't sure if Ginny was still flustered and seeking distraction or was on Google looking at images of Sindy dolls, touched by the nostalgia of our conversation and talk of childhood days, like I was. I suspected the former, but when Ginny mentioned her Sindys I was immediately transported back to when she took me up to her bedroom that first day I arrived at her home. We were both eleven, but still enjoyed playing with dolls.

121

I'd gasped as I walked in. It was the biggest bedroom I had ever seen, with small, paned, cottage-style windows on two walls draped with pink gingham pelmets and curtains. It was the sort of image I had only ever seen in films or posh magazines at my doctor's. The clean white walls were decorated with lots of pink-framed pictures and matching shelves, which made it look so pretty and feminine. And, the toys – so beautifully arranged around the room and on tidy shelves.

I was envious, of course, what little girl wouldn't be witnessing all this material wealth, but I realised Ginny must have been so loved and cherished by her parents that they cared enough to provide it all. I kept making ooh, ah and wow sounds; I was so overwhelmed. She had everything I could ever dream of. Everything any little girl could dream of. Gold-edged white bedroom furniture, a whole double bed to herself with bright fresh pink and white linen, fluffy cushions, lamps on her bedside table, soft pink sheepskin rugs, a white desk with a large round pot filled with felt-tip pens, a little notebook wrapped in pale pink tissue paper, a white bookshelf with rows of Enid Blyton titles, and then, I remembered letting out another gasp, the tall Sindy house. Three Sindy dolls and Paul. All the furniture lovingly positioned and to one side, stables and horses in fenced paddocks with saddles, reins brushes. Everything a girl could possibly wish for. It seemed I'd drifted into another world. She even had a Sindy wardrobe filled with every outfit for Sindy and Paul.

'There's a lot of pictures of Sindy on here, look,' Ginny said now, turning her mobile around.

I leaned over to see her phone. 'Oh, wow, brings back memories. Such happy days, Gin.'

'You were like a new toy to me,' Ginny said. 'A full-time playmate arriving was pretty cool.'

'Yes, we were all jealous,' Lou said, fiddling with her nails.

Cathy threw her chin up. 'You speak for yourself. I wasn't. Kim loved being showered with all my old books.'

'Mine were always in better condition than yours.' Lou beamed.

'Darling, that's because you didn't bloody read them.'

Ginny peered up momentarily from her phone. 'Now, now, girls,' she said, sounding like their mother.

She always liked to keep the equilibrium. Barely a mean bone in her body, Ginny's generosity rarely faltered. I never once got the impression she was spoiled. Paula and I played for hours in her room over the months we were there. Even the boys, my two little brothers. Although her dad wasted little time in whisking my brothers along to the toy shop in the town to buy Lego and Meccano sets along with model aeroplanes. I think it excited him as much my brothers to shop and spend time with one another, building all sorts.

I don't recall my dad doing anything like that with any of us. Just those few months at Ginny's showed us what being a normal family meant. I think we took that to our new home with us and their example helped us reorder our lives. Not so much financially, as Mum could never earn that sort of income and provide as much materially, but our house became a loving home for the first time.

Still staring at the phone, I heard the rustle of an apron and a young waitress beside me. 'Gamay?' she said. I snatched a look. She was petite and smiley with short black-dyed hair and brought a tray with large carafes of both wine and water with tumblers and wineglasses. She set the glasses by our placemats and poured both drinks. My eyes returned to the photos.

Ginny looked up from her phone and caught me staring but I was miles away. 'I'm amazed that there are so many of these dolls still around,' she said. 'We gave all mine to charity, but I remember thinking it would have been lovely to have kept them for my Rachel to play with when she was younger.' She closed her phone and her lips curled up. 'I have such fond memories of when we used to play dolls in my room. I know you weren't there that long, but it was nice to feel what it would be like to have sisters and brothers around. I used to pretend you were my sister.'

My eyes instantly stung. 'You've never told me that before.'

'No. I haven't thought of it for ages.' Her mouth twitched as she stared at the table. 'I suppose being on your own again makes you appreciate what you had. It's surprising how much time you can fill thinking about the past. I seem to have done a lot lately. Mike, Ross and Rachel. You girls. How the years have whizzed by.'

I watched as she breathed out a large sigh. I wanted to go around the table and hug her. 'Well, as long as we're on this earth, you'll have us. Your Flowers.'

'I know, I don't know what I would have done without you all.'

I blinked back tears. 'I miss you all so much, especially now the girls have grown up. Since Mike's funeral and you coming to Oz, I've thought more and more about what old age means to me and where I want to be. Fit and well obviously, but I long to be near you guys. The thing is, most of our friends in Oz are really Will's friends – doctors and their wives, partners. The girlfriends I have in Australia are not what I call my real friends. I have Nealy next door, and Marnie who you've met, but we don't have the strong bond and the kind of relationship us girls have.'

Ginny winced, concern in her eyes. 'I get where you're coming from. I sympathise. It's not an easy position to be in.'

'Tell me about it. I'd retire tomorrow. My plan is to move back as soon as I can … or we can, I should say. I wish Will wasn't so in love with his work. I'm ready to say goodbye to mine. Take my money and return to my bestie Pommie friends and have some fun.'

Cathy clapped her hands. 'That would be amazing. And the twins are this way, so other than Will's mindset, there's nothing to hold you there. You'd both have good pensions.'

'Wouldn't it be great to all get together more?' Lou added.

'Exactly,' I said and peered up to see the tall waitress with several small plates of salad balancing on her arms. 'I don't think anyone ordered a starter,' I told her, seeing Christoff signalling with his bushy eyebrows and nodding.

Ignoring me, she continued placing the plates on the tablemats. 'Everyone has a starter,' she said laying the last one in front of me. 'Sergio insists. The vegetable is good for the digestive system.'

Put in my place, I grimaced as the others around the table laughed. 'Ace. Well, in that case, I'm sure we can manage a small salad.' It was a mix of lettuce, cabbage and carrot with vinaigrette.

Christoff waited until the woman was out of earshot. 'You learn not to argue with Katja. Her bark is worse than bite. In there, is a warm heart.'

Like me, Ginny, Lou, Cathy and Angie snorted with their faces down and returned their attention to their salads. We were just like kids again, I thought.

'I like this village, everyone wants to feed you,' Lou said. I couldn't disagree.

Although the salad was basic, the venison was lovely; a tad salty for my taste but rich and something different too. Even the men, who had been served after us, had finished theirs before Cathy had finished. She slowly chomped away on her cheese-covered aubergine. Angie ordered another bottle of Gamay from Katja, which was delivered with two additional bottles by the younger waitress.

'A gift from Christoff, Tom, Florian and Neil,' she said in a broken accent, which may have been West Slavic. I wasn't sure. We each gazed at one another, grinning, and then thanked our wine donors. This place only got better and better, I thought as I filled glasses around the whole table, inviting the men to draw their chairs closer. It was only fair we shared it as the men had so generously funded it. The wine flowed as we chatted, getting to know our instructor and his friends. Angie seemed to be getting closer and flirtier with Christoff and I spotted her squeezing his knee.

I spoke to Florian, another instructor who, already balding, had a young-boyish wide face but attentive eyes. He told me he was forty-one and proudly boasted about his wife and children who lived in the valley below. His family photos brought a smile to my face; seeing his children riding their bikes, prompted fond memories of our family photos of the twins cycling. I was also interested to see his pretty wife, smiling with dark bushy hair, busy he told me, not only with the children, but also with working several days a week in her family furniture business. He preferred to be outdoors fencing and farming their land in the summer and here in the village with his retired mother weekdays in the winter. At seventy-two, she still loved to ski, he said with an endearing roll of his eyes.

Tom, who I guessed was a few years older than Florian, also lived in the valley with his family and worked as an instructor, so they travelled up together and shared costs. Tom had skied at Olympic level for Switzerland several years ago with Christoff, before Christoff married the village beauty. They had all skied since childhood. Hearing this, Tom tuned into the conversation and stopped talking to Neil. Ginny, Lou and Cathy joined us as both instructors keenly relayed stories of their skiing and country.

Neil sat quietly, listening. Several times I caught him staring at Ginny, but I also observed Ginny snatching glimpses at him, admiring his mature good looks too, no doubt. I then got excited as I watched Neil stand up and lift his chair to the end of the table to sit beside her. Christoff kindly passed his wineglass down as Neil began chatting.

How marvellous would that be, I thought to myself: for Ginny to fall in love again. Ginny was still beautiful inside and out and it would be crazy for her not to find happiness again. For one, she was looking super-hot for someone almost sixty. Not that she ever let herself go. But as I'd found, Angie's diet and fitness programme that she had designed for us all, which she very kindly included me in – sending me emails and videos, the aerobic workouts, muscle building with weights and lots of squats – has added so much more definition to us all. Not to mention all the health benefits.

I'd been really impressed, though not surprised. Angie had such a big heart and worked very hard to make the best of this trip, organising it and making sure we were properly prepared. She even monitored our progress, motivating us to make sure our bodies were in the best condition to ski, plus advising us on all the right clothes to bring. Fitness had been her life and it showed. Even she looked fitter than ever.

Watching her inch up to the younger and fitter Christoff, you would never guess there was over twenty years between them. He was clearly excited by her and, gauging by their closeness and body language, there was no doubt both were getting rather hot under the collar. I wasn't the only one noticing either; Cathy and Lou were staring too. Christoff, who I now knew was married, was overtly flirting too. I wasn't sure how far Angie would go. I mean, did she flirt with the guys at her gym? Surely not on this scale. Unless, and I thought back to my and Will's arguments lately, there was friction in her marriage. Rob was a lovely man but knowing that long ago he affectionately called her the 'nymph' and how much effort she puts into keeping herself looking young, maybe they were struggling to find mutual ground. Surely I wasn't the only one finding it uncomfortable to watch though. I felt compelled to intervene and sidled up beside her. A proper killjoy perhaps but, I supposed, one illicit affair among my friends was one too many for me to cope with.

'Angie, Flower,' I said, 'shouldn't we be headed back? We have an early start tomorrow, remember.'

Peering at her watch, Angie shook her head. 'A little early yet – it's only ten. Relax, Kim.'

I peered at Lou who showed a look of disapproval too.

How could I relax?

127

Chapter 9

Ginny

Several times I'd felt Neil staring my way and I couldn't help wondering if he was a womaniser. It was nice that he came over to chat though. He had a quiet reserve about him I liked, and I was fascinated by his sparkling intelligent eyes, the way his strong brows and full hairline shaped his rugged face as he answered the question I had posed. How long had he been skiing? Which led to another – why did he like skiing here? He leaned forward placing his elbow on the table, and began rubbing his chin. I wondered if I had entered a personal zone and was half expecting a flippant answer.

His lips tightened. 'My wife and I had been skiing in Verbier about twelve years ago.' He shook his head. 'Might be more. We had been to several different resorts in Europe. But we skied over here with friends one day. We enjoyed the snow this side because it's north facing and less crowded. But, more implicitly, we got to know the people. Stefano and Francesco since I've known them, have that inexplicable but uncanny way to draw people. They feed you, attend to you, make you feel special, but never crowd you and always introduce you to people they know. We felt so welcomed

128

and special, and that's it really – we returned every year, often two or three times. Locals and expats became our friends – Stefano, his wife Sylvia, and Francesco, his chef and friend from Italy. Sergio and Katja, Christoff, Tom, Florian, plus many of the residents here, part-time mainly, some Dutch, French, English, Swiss. It has a great ambience and community feel compared to Verbier.' He paused, looking into his drink. 'It just happened.'

It explained why he was so friendly with the instructors, but I didn't say that. Instead I said, 'My first impression is that everybody is so friendly.'

He then bit his bottom lip as if he was struggling and continued looking into his wine. Then he briefly wrinkled his eyes as his gaze met mine.

'When Cheryl died, I sold our house and downsized to a cottage in Surrey. It gave me no solace, sitting in it alone, so I bought an apartment here too.' He glanced down again, twirling his glass around for several seconds then lifted his head again, his brows rising as he met mine. 'It was the best I could come up with to be honest. There was nothing left but a void. That was six years ago. This week, actually. I retired from my job five years ago, so ever since, I've spent the winter seasons here and I return in summer to celebrate Swiss National Day on the first of August. I stay a few days then drive on from here to the lakes in Italy or south to the Italian or French Rivieras for a few months. It beats sitting at home.' He let out a sigh and shook his head. 'Well, that was a long-winded answer, wasn't it? Well, enough about me. How did you land here?'

As I was imagining this lost soul driving passenger-less around exotic parts of Europe, I flinched at his question. 'My friends. A twist of fate. I lost my husband a year ago.'

His eyes widened. 'I'm so sorry,' he said.

I bit my bottom lip to steady it. 'Angie skis here. She and her family have come here for several years, so as she was the only one of us who had skied before, we left it to her to organise. Like I said, I'm impressed.'

'I thought she looked familiar,' he said. 'A bold decision too. For you newbies, I mean. Not many, how should I say, older people, take up skiing.'

I laughed. 'Funny, isn't it, and it wasn't something I would have chosen, that's for sure. I would have preferred a week in the desert! Until today that is.' I sipped the last drop of wine in my glass and was suddenly aware of the shift in my outlook in just a few hours and wanting to share it with my friends, I peered around. Cathy sat quietly beside Lou, munching olives, listening but appearing a little drained. Something was bothering her, and I didn't like to pry. Angie was grinning from ear to ear, eagerly hanging on to every word of Christoff's flattery and Kim peered at Angie frequently as she spoke to the other two instructors.

'Here, let me top that up,' Neil said, retrieving my attention.

'Thank you,' I said, holding the stem of the small glass between my fingers as I felt his eyes on me. 'Stupid I know, but I'd convinced myself I wouldn't like skiing or mountains. I'd always shied away from them, supposing them to be cold, hostile beasts. This has been anything but. It's sunny and welcoming and I even relished the skiing.'

Neil ran his fingers along the neckline of his cashmere sweater, pinching it here and there as if feeling the heat. 'That's great. It shows you've prepared and are willing to try. In my view, it pays to maintain an open mind. My mental block was deep water, but after kicking my own arse and booking a few diving lessons, I went on to do a PADI course.'

'Wow.'

He gave a lopsided smile, which then dropped. 'Losing Cheryl took a long time to accept but after a while my perspective changed. I don't know how long it was … a year, eighteen months, but it was the point after her death when the penny dropped. I couldn't bring her back however much I grieved, and I had to sort myself out; I had to work at it. That realisation hit me that life is too short. A cliché I know, and, for another cliché, I found the more I put in the more I got out.' Neil's eyes shone as he quickly corrected himself. 'Get out. It gets easier, as I'm sure you probably find; it took a lot of effort to put my coat on and walk out the door.'

I nodded, scooping a piece of my hair around my ear as the similarities rang inside my head. 'So true,' I agreed thinking of the numerous times I had talked myself out of doing things. The temptation each day to take a left instead of a right at a junction on my way to Angie's gym. Making silly excuses to avoid social events with my friends because they were in their couples, even to my daughter Rachel when I couldn't face the long drive alone on the motorway to Oxford, I had feigned a stomach bug. 'Maybe I should take all this on board,' I said to Neil, lifting a smile to meet sincere sensitivity in his eyes and taking comfort. Neil had experienced what I had and could empathise.

It was at that point my attention was alerted to Kim shuffling right up beside Angie.

'Shouldn't we be getting back, Angie?' Kim asked.

I looked at the clock on the wall, which told me it was ten past ten, but as tired as I was after lacking sleep, I was happy chatting to Neil. There was an ease about him. I felt we had something in common; our departed spouses were a given, but there was more. And, I had to be honest though it made me feel a little guilty, as it wasn't even a year since Mike's passing, but I found Neil very attractive. But then, should I feel guilty when I suspected Mike had been cheating on me? I shuddered. I still couldn't face that notion.

Cathy

'One more glass of wine, ladies,' Neil rose to his feet and, after attracting Katja's attention, pointed his finger to one of the bottles of Gamay on the table, then signalled with a finger and his thumb for two bottles. As though checking for protest, he raised his brows as he scanned the group. He was clearly enjoying his chat with Ginny, and vice versa. Ginny was looking relaxed and it would be a shame to break up their little soiree.

Kim didn't appear so relaxed. She sat back in her chair, her mouth twisting. I guessed she was finding Christoff and Angie's behaviour a little awkward too, as I was. Christoff was encouraging Angie and I suppose I had to admit, maybe Anthony was right. Some men did prey on women, even older women. Although it's not out of character for Angie. She does revel in men's attention. I've seen her and Anthony flirt together at times when we're out, and she flirts with Mike and Terry too, but it's all very innocent and harmless. Well, I believe it is. Maybe Kim is anxious Angie is overexcited. She doesn't get to see it much.

'Yes, I'm rather tired too,' I said, feeling drained from my earlier tête-à-tête with Anthony and noticing Lou yawning, but as Katja arrived beside Neil with two more bottles of Gamay, we both shrugged and gave one another a thin-lipped smile.

'Thank you, Neil. That's very kind,' I said.

Kim blew out a sigh, 'Yes thanks, Neil. Last one and we'll head back. It's becoming very hot in here.'

'Yes,' Lou and I agreed. Lou fanned her face and took her lip gloss from her pocket and unscrewed it. 'Really hot,' she moaned, adding gloss to her lips.

Kim tapped Angie's arm. 'Last one, beautiful, and we should go.'

Angie held out her empty glass and made the widest grin. 'Yes, my Flowers, I know. Just this one.' She leaned towards Lou and I and said softly, 'I don't like to break up the party.' She jolted her head towards Ginny and Neil. 'So good to see her happily engrossed. I'm excited. Jealous but excited. Oh, how much greener the grass looks when you're married. I'm thinking I should make sun while the hay shines!' Angie peered back towards Christoff who had disappeared.

132

'Make hay while the sun shines,' I corrected her.

'Yes, that one,' Angie said, distracted by the sudden absence of Christoff. 'Where did he go?'

Lou shrugged. 'To the loo?'

'Which is exactly where I need to go,' Neil added as he finished pouring wine and sauntered in the same direction. Ginny shuffled her chair closer.

Kim gave Angie a prod. 'And there's no making hay, you saucy minx.'

'I agree,' I said tilting forward and cupping my chin with both hands so that Tom and Florian couldn't hear. 'You have a perfectly wonderful, sexy man at home.'

Angie took a slug of her wine, slammed down her glass and leaning forward, said in a low voice, 'I might shock you here, Flowers, but I must tell you that man is worth considering having an affair with, or a fling. I don't want baggage, just a fling.'

'Angie!' I think we all screamed at once, but my jaw was hanging.

Angie gave her Tina Turner stomp. 'What? I mean, Rob and I are good, we still have sex, but it's been so long since I've been with anyone else. I've kept myself in good shape; I'd just like to go out and shag for the thrill. Preferably with someone like Christoff. God, he's so horny.'

'Either you're drunk or you've overdosed on those bloody beans you keep eating, Ang. Don't be so stupid,' Kim wailed.

'Exactly,' Ginny said. 'You're getting carried away. The alcohol has probably gone to your head. It's gone to mine.'

'So, it won't hurt. It's good that you're relaxing. And I love that you and Neil get on; he seems really nice.' Flicking her head to check behind her, Angie wasn't to be swayed. 'But come on, Flowers, be honest, how many of you wouldn't want to try someone new?'

I grabbed my chest. Anthony and I were having our problems, but this was a different realm. Angie was contemplating being unfaithful! Surely she was drunk! I accepted that flirting might be a bit of fun, but to risk hurting Rob and the children and everything they have together … My skin prickled. She had to be drunk.

I had always felt compassion for Angie. Although she was Ginny's friend first, and we were in our early twenties when we met, we hit it off from the start because we were both pescatarian and most people scoffed at you back then for having such an affliction. But sharing my oddness with Angie was liberating and when we saw each other more, we soon discovered we had something else in common – neither of us particularly got on with our parents. We discovered we both felt unloved as children and had craved affection.

We still hadn't worked out if our refusing to eat certain foods was a kind of rebellion, but we'd fought the same battle. I refused to eat meat because my parents insisted. She vowed she just couldn't abide the thought of eating a beautiful creature. But she had grown up resenting being mixed race, and she admitted to me she craved her father's attention. I do wonder if I felt the same way. She told me about her parents. Her mother was an immigrant from the Caribbean who had devoted her life to nursing in London. Angie believed she was naive to her father's behaviour. He was a bit of a wide boy and womaniser. Angie had even witnessed him going into his van with women when he sold dresses at the markets.

Perhaps something that had happened recently has triggered her behaviour now. Who knew what went on behind closed doors? She hadn't mentioned anything that Rob might have done though.

Admittedly, we hadn't been dealt an evil father like Kim, but we constantly moaned about our parents and about how selfish and materialistic they were, clearly for different reasons but the result was the same; we felt emotionally starved. We were grateful, don't get me wrong. We understood they worked hard and provided us with the security of lovely homes and possessions, but I remembered just wanting my dad to talk to me rather than at me, to listen to what my day was like or what I thought about a poem or a novel. Same with my mother, she never seemed to make time for me, her daughter, and only a little more for her son.

And we observed over the years that neither of us had any affection for them like Ginny and Lou had for their parents, and Kim did for her mother. I thought my dad had his head up his arse at times. He had a certain amount of fame working in TV. It was a news programme, and everything revolved around his job and his reputation. He drummed it into me very early that I was to be good and never humiliate him. My mother, a typical obedient housewife, suffered the same fate, though thrived on organising charity and WI events rather than spending time with her children. I wondered if it was her escape, her coping mechanism. Like me with my reading. But they made sure we were disciplined. I had often heard her boasting that my brother and I were shining examples of well-behaved children.

So, like the perfect daughter, I followed the rules, believing this was normal, curtailing my anger and frustrations, basically supressing my emotions and seeking comfort at the library, gorging on novels. Angie coped too, sought a new family. She joined the WRENS as soon as she was able and strove to reinvent herself.

I found Anthony and thank goodness. The best thing that ever happened to me, surprisingly. Even at the tender age of twenty-four he had successfully built up two major artists in the music world, attracting further high-profile clients to his list. He brought me out of my shell by showering me with attention. His affection and confidence gave me strength I had never imagined. I had been teaching a year then, and we bought our first place together within months of meeting.

I hadn't told anyone about my inner struggles before Angie, not even Ginny and Lou. Angie and I had shared and mutually respected our inner gripes. So, knowing her, she's been feeling uptight and I have no doubt the alcohol was responsible for her outburst. Though the thought of airing my dirty laundry, even to my friends, made my skin crawl.

'Darling girl, I agree with Kim. You've had far too much wine,' I said with a bright smile. 'And I'm sure you don't mean it. Besides, if you felt so strongly that you would risk everything for one night of sex, I firmly believe you would leave Rob before you'd ever consider something like that. You know it wouldn't be fair to him or the boys. And what would they think of their mother?'

'Oh, Cath,' Angie said. 'I can always rely on your moralistic compass to quash my dreams, but Christoff is so ...'

Seeing Christoff and Neil returning to their seats, I quickly changed the subject. 'Anyway, I have a few books with me you could borrow. I'm sure they will keep your mind occupied whilst you're here.'

Angie peered up at Christoff and raised a raucous laugh. 'Oh, Cathy, don't worry. My mind entertains itself. I think it has much more fun than any book I could read. You are a sweetheart though,' she said, picking up her glass.

Ginny

Poor Cathy, she looked hurt, but it showed how much she cared. She must have felt Angie was mocking her about her books and thinking they provided all the answers. But Cathy was right: Angie needed distraction if she was contemplating such risks with or without alcohol.

Neil jolted me from my reverie. 'I thought I'd ask your friend Angie if she would like to ski with me. I saw her sitting on her own at the bottom of the nursery slope earlier.'

In an instant I felt deflated, wondering if I had read him wrong. Had Neil preferred Angie? I forced a smile nonetheless and encouraged him. 'That's so sweet of you. I'm sure she would love some company,' I said. 'Skiing,' I added. 'She's been skiing for years, so would appreciate a ski buddy, I'm sure. She certainly doesn't need lessons or to sit watching us.'

Kim rose to her feet and clapped. 'OK, my Pommie Flowers,' she said, nudging Angie, 'we need water and bed.'

'OK, let me finish this.' Angie drained the last of her wine and rolled her eyes.

'Neil wants a word,' I said, catching her eye.

'We're off, apparently,' she groaned, sliding an arm into her jacket. Her reluctance to leave Christoff was branded on her face. I looked at my watch, and saw it was now ten-thirty. That wasn't unreasonable.

Neil stood up. 'I was just saying to Ginny that I'm sure you're keen to support your friends learning to ski, but would you like to take the lift up with me and ski in the morning, whilst these ladies are having their lesson?'

She hesitated for a moment and, glancing back at Christoff, said, 'Erm, yesh. I suppose I could,' then pressing her nose in angst with her finger, continued, 'yesh, that would be great, Neil. Shall I meet you outside where we meet Christoff?'

'Perfect,' he replied. 'See you all in the morning.'

I chuckled to myself inside. It was clear her opportunity to ogle our instructor was compromised. I was just glad that she wasn't hitting on Neil.

After saying our goodnights to our band of minders, for they were ubiquitous and alert to our welfare, we headed out into the freezing air and along crystalline tarmac for the short walk to our path. Lou and Cathy trod gently ahead. Kim followed. I waited for Angie to step in front of me.

'Wah, shhlit,' Angie slurred as her foot slid onto the steep icy track. I just managed to catch her arm as I found my footing. 'Not my night tonight, ish it?' she said.

'It was fun though,' I said, meaning it.

'Yesh, it was. I was watching you. You and Neil were getting along great guns. He sheems really keen. What d'you think?'

'I like him, we had a lovely chat. And, because he's a widower, he knows what it's like to be on his own.'

Angie hiccupped. 'I think there'sh a bit more going on there. I r ... reckon he's really into you.'

I pressed my feet tightly against the ground. 'Oh no. It's too soon for anything romantic.'

'Jeesh, I'd jump at the chance. You must be tempted? You're a free agent now.'

'It doesn't mean I'm mentally prepared. In fact, I would still feel disloyal to Mike.'

''Til death though. You'll not be doing anything wrong. Go for it if you like him. You're still young and gorgeous. And, whatever they all say, I still don't see any real harm in a little indiscretion.'

It was sad, and I felt wounded to hear her confess to wanting a fling, especially with Christoff who was married too. Surely, she wouldn't dare. My thoughts jumped to Mike's words. Even a fling would break a heart.

Kim turned her head, looking straight at me and scowling. It seemed she was still rattled by Angie's awry thinking. I saw her wobble and I reached out.

'Kim,' I shrieked as she grabbed my hand and lurched forward into the snow. I slumped beside her and screeched as the thumping weight of Angie crashed on top of me.

'Friggin great, girls!' Kim muttered lifting her mouth, which was full of snow. 'We need to find our feet, don't we?'

Cathy and Lou scrambled back up laughing, pulling at Angie's arm whilst attempting to support one another.

'Yep, we sure do,' I said, shifting my frozen cheek up from the ice. 'In more ways than one.' I laughed but, in fact, I was beginning to gather hope that I would find my feet. I was actually beginning to recognise the old Ginny, the one who loved to be around her friends coiling with laughter. The Ginny who was confident in her decisions both domestically and in her work. The Ginny who loved her children.

Of course, I was capable of driving or catching a train to see my children. How did I ever believe otherwise? I was still that person, Ginny Watts. Proudly independent-minded and spirited. Being here, away from the house and the god-awful job, with my gorgeous, caring friends had brought me back. Angie had expressed enough faith in me to employ me, a lovely man was making me feel special again and, surprisingly, I was attracted to him too. This trip was ruffling my tired, trodden feathers.

Of course there was life after Mike. Mike had never consumed my life as much as he had these last three years, so the possibility that he may or may not have had an affair had paralysed my thinking. If I let that go I might stand a chance. I had found my feet and they were strong. What I hadn't realised was that I had to restore my feathers. Get them strong enough to fly. A wave of anticipation washed over me. 'I'm going to work on my feathers,' I said with a snigger.

'Oh, Gin, that's hilarious, you're drunk too,' Lou roared. 'So, you have wings now?'

'I do,' I said. 'They're a bit bent and out of shape, but …'

Kim then burst into a snigger. 'What are we like? I mean, sixty-year-old women, pissed as old farts, falling about in the snow. What would our children think?'

I breathed with relief as Cathy and Lou hauled Angie off me. 'No doubt they'd walk straight past us, deny any knowledge of us,' I mused with a chuckle. 'Ross would, for sure.'

Angie staggered back onto her feet, scraping snow off her trousers. 'I don't mean to sound ungrateful, girls, but it would have added more drama if we'd have been rescued by the guys.'

Kim rolled on her side, curling up her legs and feet to stand. 'You're obsessed, Ang. We need to get you neutered.'

'Too late for that,' Angie said, laughing.

'She's jesting, Ang,' I said, not sure Kim meant to sound so curt. I was more concerned about finding a spot to grip my foot onto, but I found myself giggling too.

'Are you two OK?' Lou asked, reaching her hand out to Kim and appearing more anxious for us than herself. 'Sorry, I was looking down to prevent myself slipping over. You could have slid all the way down.'

'We're fine, no great damage done,' Kim said.

Angie hurled out her hand and pulled me upright, steadying me. She then brushed off my jacket, which was glittering with grains of freezing snow 'Well, you two do seem to have had a problem with those plates of meat of late,' she said using the cockney rhyming slang for feet to refer to our fall in the ski shop. Although Angie was brought up in Greenwich, she was born in Stepney, an area close enough to hear the Bow Bells had they not been destroyed. You can take a girl out of London, but you can't take London out of a girl. 'I'll have some explaining to do if I send you all home with broken limbs,' she added.

'And we'll have some explaining to do if we send you home to Rob, knowing you've been unfaithful,' Kim retorted sharply. 'Tell me you didn't mean that?'

'Ouch,' Angie shrieked.

'Of course she didn't,' Cathy said defensively. 'She's had too much wine, that's all.'

Angie turned and trod carefully, leading us soberly back down the path as we filed again behind her. 'And yes, actually, I did mean it. Sorry if it's caused offence, my dears, but it's such a powerful urge. 'Scuse the pun,' she sniggered. 'It's my age. I'm worried death is creeping up, I don't know. I can't bear the thought that my body won't be appreciated by any man ever again. I thought my friendsh might understand. Naturally, I wouldn't want to hurt Rob and I would need to be discreet.'

The laughter subsided. What was she saying? For a start, shouting about it was hardly discreet. Neither was committing the offence in a ski resort she and Rob frequented. My annoyance was keeping me gripped to the ground. She was brazenly risking destruction to her and Rob's relationship. Over forty years together – and their family. Three boys, their wives, and seven grandchildren. I couldn't let her do that. Just a trickle of words from Mike's mouth had devastated me.

Kim

I'd seen it happen so many times at home in Oz. Doctors and nurses, porters and nurses, doctors and patients, nurses and patients, even a doctor and an auxiliary. Not to mention, my sister Paula! Hussy. I could never forgive her. Or Mike. Even if Ginny ever discovered the truth, which I suspect she hasn't as I'm certain she would disown me, I don't want anything more to do with my sister.

As for Angie, I'm saddened she could take Rob for granted like that. I know she loves him to pieces. He is a super guy, and over the years, she's relayed so many stories, even admitting they had inherited money. He has supported her so much with the children and her business venture, which took several years to turn a profit, not to mention their beautiful home and the exotic annual holidays, including their annual family skiing trips. Just as my hero, Will, now a professor and doctor at the forefront of research in Perth, has provided for and supported me, Rob – a humble nurse – has been good to Angie. She couldn't let him down now. She has so much to be grateful for. All of us do, in fact. And we do remind ourselves how lucky we are.

Like me, Angie grew up on a London council estate and couldn't believe her good fortune when she met Rob. His family were not only loaded, but he had a good job as a computer programmer in the Seventies and had already bought his own Victorian house in Greenwich when she met him. I hadn't known her at that point but got to know her when Ginny and Mike moved next door to them and we were all invited to their beautiful wedding.

Angie proudly publicises her rags to riches story and our humble background is something that bonds us. I thought Angie would know better. What is it that possesses someone with such love and comfort to deliberately destroy all her family's lives? It made me think that I should be less selfish and think more about Will. Five years seems a long time to wait before we move back to Kent, but maybe I should be more flexible.

Kicking off our boots in the entrance, I circled Angie as she tucked her boots under the rack. I held back my rage until the others were through the door. 'I can't believe you would stoop so low, Ang.'

She spun around scowling, the Velcro from the bottom of her jacket catching on the sleeve of my boucle jumper.

'Don't tell me you've never considered it?' she said, tugging at my sleeve as I pinched the fabric to stop it unthreading.

'No. Why would I? I value my husband and family too much. If I felt I needed another man I would leave him first.'

'I value mine, but I don't believe you,' she said, wrenching the jacket from my arm and balancing herself. 'Surely you must fantasise?'

Thumping the front door, I turned the key. 'Fantasy is something different. And no, actually. I don't fantasise about sex these days. My bloody menopause put paid to that pleasure.'

Angie looked at me with her nose screwed up. 'What? Nothing?'

'No,' I admitted sheepishly. 'My libido is what is known as MIA – missing in action.' I was now on my soapbox. Will and I have had this discussion so many times. Who knew where these statistics come from, but apparently nearly half the female population are mourning their libidos. I found this out when I did my own research when learning to cope with mental health as a nurse. I've read so many articles and books as I missed feeling sexy. Will and I have had to try new strategies in our approach – which basically means he doesn't pressure me and I have time to switch off and relax. Luckily Will is a darling and has the patience of a saint, and we worked at it.'

I grinned at Angie. 'There's no magic Viagra for women. I guess we girls will have to invent our own. But Will and I work at it and have come through it stronger. You and Rob could do the same,' I told her. It sounded brutal but worth it to make her see. In my research, I discovered not so many couples have the same success at finding a solution.

Although libido loss wasn't Angie's problem at all, I didn't want her to fall foul in her relationship. Not Angie and Rob. Not without trying. I thought of my sister. Two failed marriages. Her determination to trap Mike. Ginny being hurt. Paula didn't want just a fling.

I rested my hands on my hips, watching Cathy come down the stairs while texting on her phone.

'Angie,' I pleaded. 'You're in the business of female wellbeing. There's heaps of books, online information, experts out there. I'm sure there's a solution that will suit you both. There's probably more possibilities than someone in my situation. Or, you could try distraction: something else to occupy your mind. Why not put all that extra energy into running for a charity, for example, or learning a new skill, volunteering perhaps? It's healthier than destroying a marriage, your family.'

'Hear, hear,' Cathy muttered and then peered up through her spectacles at Angie before tucking one leg under her bottom and sinking into the sofa. 'Rob's a keeper.'

'But that's the point. I don't want to ruin what I have.' She sighed heavily, looking bruised. She opened the glass-fronted cupboard. 'I … I shouldn't have said anything.'

As she grabbed two tall tumblers from the cupboard, I wrapped an arm around her shoulders. 'Angie, you're right to say something. It's an issue you clearly need to sort out in your mind. Just

143

think about what we're saying before you jump into a pit of regret.' I gave her a squeeze and released her.

'Thanks, Kim, I really appreciate that you care.' She ran the cold tap and, glancing at Cathy with a forced smile, I let my tension subside. At least I'd said my piece. I just had to pray she would take it on board.

Angie held out one of the tumblers for me to take. 'Thanks,' I said.

'Do you want a glass of water, Cathy? Where are the others?'

Cathy tapped away on her phone. 'Er … yes please. Oh, bugger. I … Oh, Anthony. Hang on.' Cathy swiped the phone. 'I can talk to him later.'

'You stay there,' Angie said, placing the water on a table beside her. 'I'll get another glass and I'm off to bed.'

'Me too,' I said glaring an agreeing acknowledgement at Angie. Cathy was keen to talk to Anthony again with some privacy.

'Something weird is going on there,' Angie whispered when we got to the landing.

'Hmm,' I said, pausing at our door equally curious. 'Hope they're OK?' I tapped lightly on the door. 'You decent, Ginny?' I asked, slowly opening the door. Ginny was wrapped in her duvet fast asleep. 'Oh, bless her,' I whispered to Angie, glad to see one of us untroubled. 'She's worn out.'

'That's good. She'll have a difficult day to face tomorrow with the memorial.'

Chapter 10

Ginny

The following morning, after a lovely long sleep, I had the table all set long before any of the Flowers opened their eyes. I sneaked quietly out to the supermarket for bread, meats, cheese and orange juice and was emptying a large pot of Greek yoghurt into a bowl and placing it beside the jar of honey when I heard footsteps on the stairs.

'Wow,' I heard. It was Lou and Cathy. 'This looks amazing,' Lou said, casting her eyes over the spread. 'Mm, delish.'

Cathy hovered. 'Anything I can do before I sit down, darling?'

'No, all done, I think, thank you,' I told her.

'Wow, someone's been busy,' Angie said, padding towards the table and not looking as awake as the rest of us. She inhaled deeply to take in the smells. 'Hmm, cheese.'

I picked up the teapot and began to pour. 'Is Kim awake?'

'Yes, just coming down,' Angie said, leaning over the table to pinch a cornichon from a glass dish. 'Yum.'

'Yes, my Pommie friends, I'm here.' Kim came rushing down the stairs. 'Oh, Gin, it looks beautiful – and roses. Is this for Mike?'

'Sort of.' I put on my best smile, steeling myself to keep my emotions strong. 'I thought it would be nice to start Memorial Day with a taster. Tea this morning, my Flowers. It was Mike's favourite breakfast beverage,' I said, handing the filled cups and saucers out, 'but so you know, I'm setting the tone for the day and for the future. The first anniversary is going to be my first stepping stone, so it's important for me to … hmm, what's the word I'm looking for … mark the occasion. Yes, I think it's mark.'

I swallowed hard, taking a moment. 'The point is, I'm now more determined than ever to move on with my life without Mike,' I said, putting down the teapot and placing my hand over my heart, trying to stop myself from spluttering. It was going to be a happy day. 'Naturally, I'll keep our memories tucked here, tightly in my heart, as I'm sure you will, but as well as a memorial, I thought it fitting to use today to commit myself to my future.'

'Well, good for you. And of course, that's a lovely idea,' Kim said sniffing and drying her eyes.

I looked at Lou as she swallowed and pinched her nose. I could see the moist rims of her eyes as she spoke. 'That sounds perfect, Ginny. We had been dreading today as we'd racked our brains trying to come up with something. It had to be personal to you, so I love that you've worked that detail out yourself. We'd be delighted to share it with you, sweetheart.'

Behind her glasses frames, Cathy's make-up was smeared. She lifted her cup. 'Perfect, darling. To Mike and our new Ginny.'

Angie's chin and lower lip wobbled as she raised her cup of tea, pronouncing, 'Yes, a double celebration: here's to Mike and your new beginnings.'

'Thank you, love, and cheers, my beautiful friends.' I wept as those trapped tears of mine unleashed. My mind seeing Mike take his last breaths before he lay still. In an instant I was surrounded, wrapped and hugged and squeezed and injected with love from my devoted and caring friends, all of whom I loved so much. I let the tears roll down my face because I knew they wouldn't go away, not for some time, but I was ready, I had all the love I needed, the support, everything and more. I would not let them or myself down. Through my blurred vision, I peered at Angie and my contorted voice whispered, 'Is there a restaurant that sits at the top of a mountain?'

She kissed my cheek. 'Absolutely, gorgeous girl, I know the perfect place,' and instantly their love surged into me again lifting me more than the music had a few nights ago. It was the longest hug that would stay with me forever. A tender moment I would treasure where love swathed our souls and silence was all we needed to absorb it.

We feasted like kings and after, with the mood set for the day, we raced to our rooms. Once dressed and reminded of equipment, we put on our boots, gathered our skis and met Christoff and Neil. Angie immediately gave Christoff her lusty smile, making him blush. Neil glowed, said a warm 'Good morning' and blew air kisses to us all, then quickly caught Angie's attention and left with her up to the main lift station. I watched them depart and couldn't help feeling a stab of jealousy. I had enjoyed talking to Neil last night but today I wanted nothing to distract me. I wanted to clearly focus on this special day.

Christoff clicked his boots, gave us a wide smile and then pursed his lips. 'OK. Have you all got everything?'

Satisfied with our nods he led us up the path to the nursery slope and we filed up the button lift without drama. We were getting used to the heat generated by walking and as the sun was hiding behind mist this morning, it was certainly more comfortable. We spent the morning, practising our 'pat the dog' first, which I found soon loosened the tightness in my knees. Then Christoff gave us another exercise where we had to lift one of our skis as we traversed the slope, put it down as we arced the turn, and change legs to traverse the other way. Among us, we had several wobbles and falls, but I felt my balance improving

147

and my snowploughs were becoming much smoother with more movement in my ankles.

We agreed when we gathered at the top of the slope that the walk up was a good warm-up and the exercise helped us control our skis better. Even Cath was glowing with confidence as I waited for her to come down after me. Our morning was fun, and with just a few falls, Christoff said we were doing well. We headed off with him to meet Angie at the lift station, excited about our progress, and I couldn't wait to see where we were going for Mike's memorial lunch.

I told Christoff our plans. 'I'm hoping it has a beautiful view, and now the sun is out, it would be lovely to sit in the warm,' I said as we reached the lift station, looking around for Angie.

Christoff, hearing this, cleared his throat. 'Take the gondola to the top. There's a good restaurant just as you get out of the lift with stunning views. You can then get back in the gondola and come directly back down.'

'Ah, that sounds like the place Angie has in mind.' I beamed. 'Sounds perfect. Thank you. I would ask you to join us, but I'd like this occasion to remain private.'

'Of course. Leave your skis over there against the wall,' he said.

Our eyes followed his finger to a wall at the bottom of the lift steps.

Christoff waved his palm. 'Maybe I'll see you later,' he said with a wave. 'Enjoy.'

At that moment, Angie rushed up beside us and leaned forward to watch Christoff go, then unburdened her shoulders as she released her skis, announcing excitedly, 'That was amazing. Neil and I went down the face, off-piste, and the snow was incredible.'

Neil walked up behind her. 'It was great fun, Angie, thank you for skiing with me this morning. Are you happy to ski with me tomorrow?'

'You bet.'

I searched Neil's face for some acknowledgement and wasn't

disappointed. His eyes and teeth shone my way. 'I hope it's the right etiquette to wish you a lovely afternoon, Ginny. I hope the memorial goes well.'

'Thank you, that's so kind,' I replied appreciating his thoughtfulness. Angie must have informed him.

'Ready for lunch, sweetheart?' Lou asked snapping me out of my trance and possibly thinking the same as myself – how thoughtful Neil was. Lou inserted her skis beside Angie's, albeit with less grace, and we placed ours around them.

'Are you ready? We're going up the gondola to the restaurant at the top.'

I slipped off my helmet and threw in my gloves. 'Yes, so ready, Flowers. Christoff recommended it for the views, too.'

'Great minds eh? Excellent. Let's go,' Angie said.

* * *

My legs were like jelly by the time we'd walked up the stairs. And that was without the skis. It was surprisingly uncrowded considering how full the resort was but then lunch, like après-ski, was a major stop for a refuel after a morning of spent energy. I was grateful and keen to eat too. The building that housed the gondola lift was a huge concrete and steel structure with Perspex windows on the steps but cavernous and dark at the top with high ceilings to accommodate the large steel structure for the steel ropes carrying the gondolas. We entered the electronic lift-pass turnstiles, which beeped and released steel turnstiles as it picked up the sensors and information on each of our photo passes. The rubber matting did little to absorb the melting snow from our boots but softened the sound of the boots banging on the concrete and the clanking of each gondola as they shot into the terminal, and out again carrying passengers.

Angie stopped behind another crowd in front and glanced at us. 'Are we all here?' She seemed satisfied, then said, 'Just follow me in. One car will hold all of us, and it won't race away, so don't panic.'

I had to admit, they did look rather daunting with small double doors that rapidly snapped open and shut. I didn't fancy getting myself caught in one. I sat between Lou and Cath waiting for the doors to slam, which they did finally, and then the car whizzed us out to daylight at lightning speed, then clanked and eased, elevating us slowly. Cath squealed and held onto my hand. As it climbed, following a trail of virtually virgin snow, I looked out marvelling at some of the tiny old chalets that littered the hillside, each nestled comfortably in their blanket of snow.

'How beautiful,' I said.

'It is a winter wonderland, isn't it? They are so cute, those little chalets,' Cathy said. 'I don't know how you would access them though. There are no tracks to these – look.'

Several were submerged without car access.

Angie leaned forward. 'You'll notice the skidoos. Owners park them up outside when they're there. Or they just ski in and out from the lifts during the day. There are a few small chairlifts still, which provide access and allow them to ski down.'

'So, they can't go out of a night?' Lou questioned.

'Not really, no. Not without a skidoo to transport them. Unless they're fit enough to walk back up.'

Kim let out a laugh. 'That snow would be up to your waist, I reckon. Can you imagine walking down and not knowing there's a ledge? You'd literally drown in all that snow.'

'Scary,' Cath said.

Peering out, I watched the village spread before us across the horizon. An abundance of snow-covered roofs. Small chalets, large, old and modern and the very big ones housing several apartments. Beyond, the valley widened, the high snow-covered mountains now facing us in the distance, their faces blanketed in white then rock and forests fighting for space. A tiny village now almost a speckle in the distance. The car rose above the path

150

between the trees widening my vista, enabling me to see around: a chairlift, smaller, older – a two-man chairlift, Angie relayed. Then a long stretch of a tree-lined piste edged intermittently with red-coloured sticks.

It reminded me of watching the Winter Olympics. Skiers swishing under me, their bodies swaying from side to side, making it look so simple. How lovely it would have been to have started skiing as a child. And, there they were, kids no more than five or six leisurely cruising behind each other; fearless. Groups of skiers stood to one side, some sitting in the snow, families, also snowboarders arching their backs, then crashing, parking to catch their breath.

I craned my neck to look at a cluster of stone buildings surrounded by a sunny, decked terrace to my left. It was crammed with diners seated on long bench seats at food-filled tables, a queue trailing from a small window, deck chairs filled with ski-suited bodies, sunning white skins whilst gripping mugs of beer or glasses of wine. I could almost breathe the atmosphere. An invisible energy charged the air and my skin tingled with excitement. I longed to taste more of this place and sample the delicious cuisine of the restaurant whose aroma wafted up to our car. My mouth was watering.

As we passed the face of the mountain with people bouncing as they traversed the moguls of snow, threads of self-doubt wrangled in my stomach. There was no way I was ever going to get to grips with all this. Peering up, I could see the flat ledge at the top and the monstrous lift station.

Angie threw out her arm. 'This is what Neil and I skied this morning. The snow is gorgeous, not too deep and so powdery smooth. Perfect conditions.'

'It looks lovely,' Lou said. 'Can't wait to get out on these slopes. Christoff said we may be able to come up to ski a blue tomorrow.'

'Well, let me tell you now—' Angie glared and pointed '—that is not a blue.'

A knot of exhilaration released inside me. Peering around myself, I could see there were so many different pistes. More than I ever imagined.

Kim peeked out the glass behind me. 'Is that the lift station?'

'Yes,' Angie said securing her gloves in her helmet. 'Again, once the doors open, don't panic, you have time to step out as it goes around.'

We filed out of our travelling carriage without panic or injury, thank goodness, and followed Angie dodging through the traffic of skiers bustling through a narrow pass from slope to slope. I looked up.

'Phwoar,' I shrieked, slapping my chest with my hand, breathless. A landscape of stark white against the cobalt blue of the horizon greeted us and introduced us to ever more spectacular views of the other side, making me instinctively reach for my phone to capture the mountain scene showered and glistening in sunshine. Cathy and Lou snapped away too whilst Kim and Angie wandered towards the restaurant. A familiar mix of cheese and *vin chaud* burrowed into my nostrils as I traipsed behind, casting my focus on the dazzling sunny terrace encased in glass. I scanned the tables, searching for a spot.

'I think the people on that table there are about to leave,' I just about heard Angie say amongst the clamber of our wet ski boots on the wooden deck. She turned around and Lou and Cathy were now beside me. 'I'll grab it whilst you guys go in and get what you want. It's self-service. Pick up drinks and glasses at the beginning and look out for the specials.'

'Do you know what you want to eat? I'll get yours,' I told Angie. 'I'll get a couple of bottles of wine too.'

Angie licked her lips and peered into the air. 'I'll have rösti – the veggie version. You might want to ask if they have their rösti Valaisanne today? It's a dish Rob always eats here.'

'What is the rösti Valai ... sanne?' I asked, keen to try the regional food.

Angie's eyes brightened. 'It is the local version of a rösti – so the rösti, I think, is grated potatoes and bacon mixed and pan-fried in duck fat, then topped with Raclette cheese. Sometimes Rob has it with Gruyere. He loves it, though. It's not altogether the healthiest option.' Angie grinned. 'But you can justify over-indulgence when you're skiing.'

By the time we returned with our trays of Gamay wine and röstis – we had all decided to overindulge in the dish; Cathy managed to grab the last two vegetarian versions for Angie and herself – Angie had managed to secure a fabulous table. It was positioned in a snug corner of the terrace with the best panoramic views over Verbier as well as the reflection of the soft glistening snow. Angie and Christoff had been right: it was perfect, despite missing the personal touch of a waiter. Cathy and I sat in prime seats, Angie at the end, then Lou and Kim arrived just after us, looking at me devilishly.

Lou flashed a bottle of Champagne in front of me. 'I thought as it's to be a celebration of your new start as well, it was appropriate. Hope you don't mind, sweetheart?'

Kim placed her tray down on which she had five Champagne flutes circled on one side.

A lump in my throat hampered my speech. 'Oh, Flowers.' I swallowed. 'You are the best. You think of everything. Thank you.'

Lou unleashed the cork and as she began pouring, asked, 'So, tell us, Ginny, what's your most memorable moment with Mike?'

I laughed. 'I can't tell you that!'

The girls laughed too, and Angie retorted, 'OK, we don't need to know about your orgasms, maybe I should rephrase the question.'

'No, I've got one.' I was giggling before I could tell them. 'It has to be his proposal. He would have killed me for telling you, but he booked a steakhouse in London. That was probably as posh as we got then, as you know. Well, you all know this bit. Anyway, what you don't know is that when he nervously got down on one knee, and when I say nervous, I mean nervous, like the day of your wedding nervous, Mike was so nervous that he kept going backwards and forwards to the loo. I guessed he must have got the squits! So, he was on one knee, just about to open the box with my engagement ring in it. And he ran off. Gone. He left me staring after him and the other people in the restaurant staring at me.'

The girls were bracing their lips with their hands.

'He was gone for ages.' I giggled again, and I think the girls were now guessing. 'So, when he came back, he got down on one knee again, and ...' I could hardly speak for giggling '... even though it was navy velvet, I could see the box was soaking wet, even the inside.' The girls and I chorused with: 'He'd dropped it in his ...' We couldn't finish but their faces screwed up, and our bellies were aching with laughter.

I wasn't sure anyone really enjoyed their rösti after that, but the Champagne was going down very well as each of the Flowers had a story they recalled with fondness.

Lou sniggered. 'Oh, he was such a sweetheart – that time he rescued me after I locked myself out. Some of you will have heard it. Embarrassing. It was a Saturday morning, Terry was working, and I opened the door for a delivery and it slammed shut, so with just my dressing gown on and soaking wet hair, I remembered I'd left the back door open. In desperation, I hurled myself over the shrubs but my dressing gown, which was towelling got tangled in a holly bush. I was trying to untangle myself for a about an hour, and luckily Mike came around to collect an electrical unit that Terry wanted him to fit. So anyway I shouted out and he jumped over. I mean, his face was a picture; he was killing himself laughing. Anyway, he tried, but couldn't untangle it, so bless him, he took off his T-shirt, turned around whilst I took off the gown and I ran in to get dressed. When I returned he'd unpicked it all from the holly. He could have left it, Gin, but he was so lovely.'

I cupped my mouth to swallow down the emotions. It had been a while since I had heard the story, and it had never made me tearful before. Quite the opposite, in fact.

'You make him sound like an angel, Lou,' I told her.

'He is, sorry was, a darling – nothing was too much trouble for Mike,' Cathy started with a grimace. 'I remember him helping me when my old Golf broke down one day. Anthony was working, and this was pre-mobile phone days, so I had to find a phone box. Mum and Dad were away, so on the off-chance, I rang Mike. He was home, thank goodness. I told him what happened and where I was, and he said to wait ten minutes and he'd find me. I'd been on a development day over at Mead Green, and as you know the Camfield Road can get quite busy around five. Anyway, true to his word, he was ten minutes. I saw his car coming towards me in my side mirror, jumped out the car, and waved, but whoosh – I stood speechless staring after him He drove straight past. Completely ignored me, even though I was waving like Nora Batty with paddles directing a Boeing 747.'

Cathy's palms flew out in front of her as she demonstrated, her hair bobbing. We roared with laughter again, imagining the scene.

'Well, funny now, but I was worried. What if he'd forgotten? It was beginning to get dark.' Indignantly, Cathy scratched the back of her shiny bob while her eyes surveyed the table waiting for us to settle down. 'Fortunately, a few minutes later, I saw his car heading back and Mike pulling across the road towards me – his face sheepish. He was so apologetic. He said he must have been daydreaming or on autopilot. Anyhow, there was me thinking he would just take me home.' Cathy's lips tightened as she raised her skinny arm and punched the air. 'But Mike being Mike, he tinkered about with plugs, wires, tubes, whatever it is us girls just wouldn't go near unless it involved a useful aid to detox our bodies, and within ten, the darling man had my old car chugging again. And that was so typical of Mike; that's what

155

made him so endearing. He always went that extra mile. We will miss him terribly. I know Anthony is still struggling with the loss too.'

Cathy rubbed my arm. 'And the boys just adored him. He was their social secretary, and ours when it was a group event. So sad, I'm not sure Anthony will ever get over it.'

A curtain of silence rustled the air as each of us wittingly or unwittingly lowered our eyes in private angst. I heard Kim sigh and then she forced a smile. She said she couldn't recall anything as amusing, but she could offer a memory that was special.

With a swoon, she tilted her head. 'Oh, Ginny, I think you know what it is – you probably all do.' She winked at me. 'My main recollection of Mike's big heart is when he brought you to Oz only a week after the twins were born.' She clutched her chest. 'I mean, it was fricken fantastic, total surprise for both of us, wasn't it?'

My stomach bubbled, and I craned my head as I caught her hand and squeezed it. 'Aw, surprise is an understatement. I almost wet myself with excitement when I looked up to check the flight number at Heathrow. How can I ever forget that! I jumped on Mike there and then. God knows what people thought! What a devious pair! Diverting us by planning to come when the babies were a few months old – and then all the scheming. Not just with Will! My boss, Mum and Dad, Ross and Rachel. They were all in on it! And you two!' I glared at Cathy and Lou, whose faces were streaming. I wasn't sure if they were tears of joy or sadness.

'That was Mike though – always had something up his sleeve.' Kim chuckled. 'It demonstrates how thoughtful he was. I'd love to have seen your face when he asked you to check that departure board.'

'We all would,' Lou sniggered as she topped up our flutes.

I released my hand from Kim and cradled my arms as though holding a tiny baby. 'Ha ha! And your face when I crept in. When you were sitting in the armchair breastfeeding one of them –

156

anyone would have thought that I'd screamed "Fire". Your eyes. And you were shaking. Poor Avril. I'm surprised she hasn't been traumatised for life.'

Kim clutched my cheeks and pressed them affectionately between her fingers. 'You won't believe how much I needed you there then. You de-traumatised me for life, for sure. Or rather, Mike should take the credit. Booking it, organising it. Will for his part. I was super lucky to have you guys. Nothing could have prepared me for twins! Let's raise our glasses to Mike.'

I stood, taming a strand of hair as it whipped across my face. I peered around at my friends, their loving faces flushed from the wind and wine against the cloudless cobalt sky. Skies and sunshine like this always reminded me of Oz. And that trip was special. I was the real Ginny then. The dutiful wife and mother but loving it. I remember the timing wasn't the best. Ross was in the middle of his A levels and Rachel just about to sit her GCSEs. It was the first time Mike and I had left the children to go on a holiday and whilst I worried, it was exciting. It was like our youth had returned; we were young and free again for the first time in nearly twenty years.

We spent much of the plane journey dreaming of romantic locations we could visit on our own once the kids didn't need feeding and taxiing around. It was the start of the time I began to feel like a woman again instead of just a frantic mum. Like Mike and I had found ourselves again, a rekindled fire warmed between us, which I welcomed. Ironically – and I know they had yearned for a family for so long – Kim was just beginning to feel like a mum. I was so thrilled for her and Will – finally blessed with two beautiful girls. The moment I saw them all together was simply magic. I was so grateful to Mike for making it all happen. I loved him so much.

Lifting my flute to theirs, I cheered, 'To Mike and my life that was.' I blinked away a tear as I gazed across snowy peaks on the horizon knowing I had to accept that segment of my life was over. Not missing – I just had to replace it. How, I was yet to work out, but I would be eternally grateful that my Flowers had brought me here, shared this mountain and momentous occasion with me. Feeling as if I was deadheading a rose bush, willing new growth, I lifted my glass again. 'And now a toast to new shoots. Hopefully, I'm a new bud getting ready to open among her beautiful and already fiercely blooming Flowers.'

Kim chinked my glass. 'And we know you'll be a bud that will open and bloom with a fresh fragrance.'

'To the new Ginny Watts,' my friends cheered, piercing my heart with their warmth.

* * *

We continued with another bottle of Champagne I insisted on paying for, with the addition of various suggestions from the girls of what I could look forward to in the future – even the possibility of a man in my life again, which, had I not come to Switzerland, I would never have envisaged. I would be foolish to think anyone would enter my life so soon, and it wasn't something I needed, but it was flattering to feel that attention from Neil. He had that quiet confidence Mike had possessed, that attentiveness, that endearing energy as well as the ability to ignite that internal flame in me. That was a surprise! It gave me the faith I needed at least that I was still a woman and I didn't have to be simply a widow. It was about perception.

I saw now that if Mike had strayed, it didn't mean that I was unattractive or past my sell-by date. Angie and Christoff were evidence that sexual chemistry had no boundaries. I was entitled to engage in life again and, of course, make the most of my biggest gift right now: the support and love I have here with my friends.

In fact, it was time to lock in all the lovely memories of Mike. It may have been the alcohol, but it just seemed the time was right. I needed to let out those demons. Confide, share, confess, no matter what the correct term is; I hadn't trusted my friends with my inner turmoil and I wanted to put that right. They'd been urging me to let out my grief, so I thought it might help me let go of my husband as well if I detonated the issue circling in my brain. I took a deep breath.

'I don't know if any of you were aware, but I think Mike may have been having an affair.'

Chapter 11

Kim

I felt sick. So, Ginny did know. My insides were burning; my skin on fire. This was my opportunity to come clean. I tried to find the words. Ginny deserved to hear what my sister told me.

I couldn't stop trembling. I had to tell Ginny now. My fear was that she would crack with a big C. One of us would soon. Whatever happened, I knew I would lose my friends.

I took a deep breath. 'I'm so sorry, Gin ...'

Cathy clutched Ginny's shoulder interrupting. 'No, darling, I don't believe that for a minute. What on earth makes you think that?'

'Mike would never have done that to you, my sweet,' Lou said holding her hand to her mouth. 'He idolised you; how did you come to that conclusion?'

Ginny closed her eyes as she bit her top lip and I wasn't sure whether her pride was hurt, or, with all the fuss, it meant she regretted her revelation. I was sure her eyes were watering. My mouth seized. My vocal cords liquefied under the extreme heat I was generating.

Angie broke the silence. 'Did he tell you that or have you discovered something yourself? I can't believe that of Mike.'

Ginny appeared fraught. She gazed at each of us, rubbing her temples. Her eyes bore into mine, making me flinch. She could read me, I was sure. I coughed nervously, feeling I was the guilty party. Except I wasn't. My selfish sister did this to us, I wanted to scream. I yearned to be honest with her, tell her the truth, be that true friend, yet I didn't want to shatter her life. Destroy sweet memories of Mike. Destroy our friendship. I bit my lip. *I know.* That was all I needed to say. And of course, add, *I'm truly sorry, Ginny, but it was my evil manipulating sister who tried to destroy your marriage, your life and our friendship.* I wouldn't tell her I knew ten months ago. I shook my head. It was pounding. This would destroy us. She had a right to know and all I could think of was myself and losing them all.

'What do you know?' I croaked.

'Nothing. Mike's delirious muttering. That he was sorry, he didn't mean to hurt me, it was only once he'd been unfaithful. That's it. There is no other evidence than that. I checked everything: his phone, calls, messages, his pockets, his van, receipts in his wallet, business receipts. I searched through everything.'

'Perhaps he'd been dreaming. Can't the dying have strange hallucinations?' Lou said, and at once they all turned to me.

My dry lips bumbled. 'Y … yes. It happens … all the time,' I said struggling with the words and wishing I could throw myself off the nearest ledge. 'The brain dehydrates, slowly failing. Patients are confused. Not necessarily talking to someone in the room. Some even believe they could be talking to someone already passed.'

Ginny's mouth went crooked. I was digging myself a hole and making this worse for my poor friend. I was in deep and now scared, scared for me, for Ginny. Would I make it worse if I told her? I just didn't know.

Lou interjected, leaning in on her elbow and lurching forward, stroking Ginny's hand. 'There, sweetheart. It was probably just his mind deteriorating and playing tricks.'

Ginny's lips thinned. 'I don't know. I'd have killed him before the cancer if I'd have found out beforehand. And don't you think it's a strange thing to say? It's been whirling in my head and causing me as much stress as losing him and losing my job.'

'Why didn't you tell us before, darling?' Cathy asked, her arm now stretched around Ginny's shoulders. 'You shouldn't have bottled all this up.'

'I didn't want to … I still don't want to believe it, naturally, but I feel betrayed. I can't let it go. I can't help it. It's changed my thinking. I now believe any man will stray given the right opportunity. Any woman, come to that,' she said, her gaze settling on Angie.

'Oh, sweetie. Clearly, I think that. Temptation must be in all of us, but …' Angie shook her head frowning. 'But Mike …? Tough call. Really tough call.'

Ginny gave a sigh and again gazed at me. I tightened my lips agonising over what action to take. I tried to appear genuinely sympathetic, which of course I was.

'Sweetie, I would forget all about it,' I heard Lou say. 'Why make life stressful for yourself? Think logically. You have no evidence. You can't confront him so there is nothing you can do about it. You'll end up tying yourself in knots or making yourself ill when it's likely he was hallucinating. It's even possible you misheard him.'

'Good point, I agree,' Angie said. 'And she's right. You've no reason to be suspicious so what's the point in torturing yourself? You have to move on.'

'That's just it. I'll never know, will I?'

'Well, unless the floozy knocks on your door and admits it to your face, no,' Lou chirped. I sensed she was trying to defuse Ginny's anguish but the image of my sister at Ginny's door made my heart jolt, so I was sure that Ginny didn't need any visual encouragement. Subsequently, however, the girls guffawed, and a light relief washed over me. Maybe I was doing the right thing.

'Darling, if it was me, I'd rather not know,' Cathy said matter-of-factly. 'I certainly wouldn't let it eat away at me. Anthony could have committed the same offence. I wouldn't know. My dear girl, you could have another forty years' innings. Let it go, you might as well enjoy life rather than continue it tormented. And if you had told us this a year ago, just think how much you would have moved on.'

Angie stretched out. 'Exactly, petal, you could have been dating again by now.'

'Well, it's not too late,' Lou chuckled, 'Neil is single, and he certainly has the hots for you. And if I'm not mistaken you're quite taken with him too.'

Ginny pulled a face. 'Oh lovely, you don't think I'm ever going to trust another man now, do you?'

'Don't be ridiculous. Just have some bloody fun. You had a good marriage. Kept to your vows, 'til death do you part and all that,' Lou jibed, squeezing her hand and sitting back. 'Go get him. You're on holiday. You're not marrying him.'

'Yes ...' I clapped watching Lou suddenly freeze. Her mouth gaped and at once her body bolted and twisted in its entirety like a spooked horse. Her back was to me.

I jumped up as fast as I could in my boots and with wobbly legs and squeezed in front of her trying to crouch. Amusement switched to bemusement in an instant. I'd no idea how she moved so fast.

'Lou, what's wrong?' I asked, panic rising in me.

'Nothing. I ... I oh hell!'

'What, what is it?' Angie was now hanging over her.

Ginny and Cathy leant across the table. 'Lulu. What's wrong?' Ginny gasped.

Lou craned her neck, looking conspicuously behind her. 'I'm

OK, honestly. I thought I was going to be sick. But I'm OK. I'm fine.'

I've witnessed some strange behaviour when patients are nauseous, but this was pretty extreme. 'Are you sure that's all it is?'

Lou nodded. 'Yes, I'm sure. Really. I think I'll go back,' she said with her focus on the entrance. 'Now. Excuse me?' she said barging past me. 'I'll wait at the lift.' She rose to her feet, snatched her helmet and gloves from the decking and tore off. Without thinking, I grabbed mine too and funnelled behind her, catching her arm.

Angie trod back out of our way and scooped back her cuff to look at her watch. 'It's time we got back anyway. It's three-forty-five. They close the lift at four.' She shrugged. 'Let's go.'

I checked my watch, too. 'Crikey, over two and a half hours we were there'. With our sun-roasted faces, we staggered back to the lift and all the way down in the lift repeatedly asked Lou if she was all right.

'Stop fussing,' was her constant response. 'I'm fine.' Then she lightened a little. 'If anything, it's my thighs and calves have the screaming abdabs.'

Now we were all on the same page. Our excessive consumption of Champagne and red wine may have affected our stiff, grumbling joints but we conveniently blamed the effort and assiduousness we'd put in during our morning's ski. One thing we all agreed on was that we were not going back on the slopes. Mike's memorial had certainly been memorable for probably all the wrong reasons, but we were dog-tired, and possibly in need of coffee and sleep, so we headed back to the chalet.

I suspect, like the other Flowers, that although my head was spinning and pounding, it was in a good place. As challenging as it was, I congratulated myself for not telling Ginny. I was so tempted. I had been thinking of little else all throughout lunch, even when the joking and laughter got raucous, I'd asked myself, should I? Should I just pull her to the side and tell her?

Then the emotions sank low. The timing wasn't right, not on Memorial Day. And, more to the point, in my heart I couldn't break her just to ease my conscience. Ginny was relaxed and in the best of spirits. Just like her old self. In fact, I would go as far as saying she was nearing closure. Which was good. It was exactly what she needed, and I could have ruined a momentous step. As for Lou, I didn't know what that was all about. That reaction, however, was not one of someone feeling sick.

Cathy

I watched Lou pounce into the corner. I had no idea what was wrong with her. It wasn't like her to be sick or sulky, even with excessive drink. In fact, if it was Ginny, I could understand. Ginny handled today with such dignity, particularly as she had such reservations about Mike. I believed Mike was delirious. He would never have wandered or strayed. Ginny was his life.

For Lou, maybe it was the alcohol. I knew her well. We grew up in the same cul-de-sac, went to school together, went to Brownies, ballet and dancing together. I admit, I avoided sport when she and Ginny played after school, but we have spent so much time together, even our own children are close. Unlike me who has always been rather thin and have permanent colds, Lou was very robust. She had a strong constitution, was rarely unwell, but I wondered if she was struggling with the altitude. We did come higher up today. I'd heard that perfectly healthy people can get sick in the mountains. Even get terrible toothaches. She said she was fine, but knowing Lou, she would put on a brave face. She hated any of us seeing her weak.

'Lou, my darling, have you been feeling like this just today?' I asked her as we climbed out of the swinging car. 'It could be the altitude.'

'I never thought of that, sweet pea. It could be. It's probably

165

the highest I've ever been. Oh, I did go to the mountains in Andorra once when I was working in Spain, but I wasn't queasy.'

Hearing this, our geography guru Ginny stepped beside us. 'The mountains here are higher. Maybe it's a cocktail of A&E.'

Lou glanced at Ginny and then at me, confused. 'What, Accident and Emergency?'

Ginny laughed. 'No. Altitude, Alcohol and emotions!'

Looking even more confused, Lou shrugged and humoured our friend with a roar. 'That definitely sounds like a Spanish cocktail I had. I think you might have a had a glass too much of it too.' She rolled her eyes at Ginny. 'How would I manage without you girlies?'

I remembered Lou running off to Spain. She finished her degree at Sussex and got a job trading for the same stockbrokers in London with her then boyfriend Jimmy. She was even engaged to him, but two months later, Lou called it off. She decided to take her parents' advice and remain single for a few years, date other men and see the world before she settled down. She listened when her mother laid her feelings bare. She claimed that her own generation didn't have the same opportunities as ours, so instead of tying herself down so young, she thought Lou should travel, build a career. There would, her mother told her, be plenty of time for marriage and babies.

Lou reasoned it was sound advice, despite giving up her first love. She respected her parents, unlike me. I used to think mine were such a pair of misguided buffoons and I couldn't wait to escape the iron bars they dug around me, metaphorically speaking of course. No, Lou embraced their wisdom, despite breaking both her and Jimmy's hearts. She was on the next coach to Barcelona and with her knowledge of Spanish, soon found a job with a Spanish property developer selling apartments and villas along the then unspoiled coast. She was considered the best salesgirl.

Her father, being the first customer, was a wealthy London jeweller who bought the first three grand mansions in Sitges, south-west of Barcelona, followed by an off-plan apartment block. He made a killing years later in the Nineties, selling out, and invested in the regeneration of the Barcelona slums – yes, more funds to invest, which I believe went south to building ex-pat housing developments around the Calpe, Javea and Murcia areas.

Moving on, a year into her life in paradise, Lou heard Jimmy was engaged to someone else. Unable to believe he could move on so fast, she blamed her parents for destroying her only chance of happiness and lost interest in her job. Only when her father bribed her to help run his jewellery business in London, along with a pied-à-terre in Chelsea, did she return. And to my knowledge, she never heard from Jimmy again.

In fact, it was only a few months later, soon after she settled into her new flat, and the first night I ever took Anthony to a village pub, the Camfield Arms, to meet the girls, that Lou met Terry, her husband. We were all so relieved. As well as being a looker and a property developer, Terry was good for her. Truly grounded, he lured her back to the village and helped bring back her mojo. The flat rented out, she left her father's company in London, building on Terry's business, enjoying marriage and children, and naturally she has the most stunning house in Camfield Bottom.

She would never admit she was lonely in Chelsea, but it was evident that after moving away, she had gained so much in confidence, and with it the determination to break the spell her parents had on her. She refused to let them influence her decisions again. The tragedy is that her parents were killed in Spain, driving out to their villa about twenty-five years ago. They were younger than we are now. And a chapter Lou has closed.

Trundling off the lift station steps, we collected our skis and headed down further steps to the road.

'Hopefully you'll feel better now you're down, darling,' I told Lou, suddenly hearing the shrill of my phone.

'And get some water into you,' our health guru Angie added, having to raise her voice over the ringing of my phone.

'Aren't you going to answer that?' Lou asked whilst I could see Ginny surveying my jacket trying to work out where the noise was coming from.

With our arms full of skis and poles, I said, 'Darlings, it's probably just Anthony. I'll call him when we get back. We're not far from the chalet now. He'll probably want to know how our lunch went.'

'Tell him hi from me,' Ginny said. 'It's gone so quickly today but thank you for sharing Mike's memorial lunch with me. I've actually enjoyed it.'

'You're welcome, angel,' I said realising we would never have got to do all this if it wasn't for Mike's death. There it was. Such pleasure had come from a tragedy. Was I being insensitive? 'Darling, am I wrong to also want to thank Mike? Our ski trip was only prompted by his misfortune.'

Ginny stepped onto the sun-melted path and dug in a pole. 'No. You're absolutely right, Cathy. We should. Thanks, Mike. You've opened our minds as to what's possible, turning a negative to a positive.' Then she swung her head round. 'I wonder what you'll do when I go?'

'Good Lord.' I smirked, almost tripping behind her. Ginny might eat for England, but she is extremely healthy. 'You will be the last of us to go. You may have to gather a few more friends, darling girl. I tell you what, when I go, you can all swim the channel.' I chuckled to myself. 'Actually, I might suggest Anthony start training for it now.'

Lou was close behind me and I heard her snigger. 'Do you think he's getting a bit porky?'

How could I explain this? It was like my thoughts were seeping from my seams. 'Hmm, yes, he could be fitter, don't you think?'

'Terry could too,' Lou mumbled in agreement. 'I think he spends far more of his time in the golf club than with a golf club.'

It was my turn to smirk, revealing a little more. 'Ha! They are such a cliché aren't they, our men. Why didn't I get a husband who does something amazing with his life? Like Bill Gates? What a way to retire, eh? Travel the world spending all your surplus billions on helping others.'

Ginny stopped in front of me and turned. 'Cathy, my Flower. What's to stop you from doing something amazing? Skiing at sixty is amazing. It doesn't have to be Anthony. When you've written your bestsellers and have all those film companies falling at your feet paying you millions, you could do the same.'

'Oh, I'm really not that deluded.' I sniggered. 'I doubt my version of *Eat Pray Love* is going to spin the world on its axis. It hasn't even reached an agent or publisher yet, let alone been accepted,' I told her, knowing that it probably never would if Anthony kept on interrupting me. 'I think the difference is that the author of said work had actually gone off and lived her epic journey. Mine is all total fiction. My character was still at Shirley Valentine's kitchen table talking to the walls and contemplating striding along the busy Thames Embankment naked. Would she ever do it? No! Did she know what she wanted? No! Sixty-year-old Ursula, my main character, suffers inertia and has more chance of falling pregnant than baring her all along the South Bank. Even her dog switches off to her voice.'

The girls laughed.

'You never know,' Ginny said. 'Sounds like an interesting character to me.'

We reached the chalet and clambered in, my phone bellowing again. Angie, having placed her skis swiftly into the rack, pulled my phone from my pocket.

'Here, sunshine. Your Billy Gates calls.'

I grabbed it but deliberately hit the wrong button. 'Oops.' I needed a moment. A few minutes to steel myself and drum up

169

the energy. It was ironic that this man who came into my life forty-odd years ago with so much confidence and energy had turned so needy and vulnerable. Kicking off my boots I ran up the stairs to my room and poked his name on the screen. Billy Gates, aka Anthony Golding was going to get a very large slice of my mind.

Chapter 12

Ginny

Tired and worse for wear from all that wine, I dumped my skis, jacket and boots as quickly as I could and headed to my bedroom to run a bath. Angie was close behind me eagerly kicking off her socks then unfastening the top of her ski pants.

'Oh, that's better,' she said. 'I'm absolutely stuffed after eating all that rösti. Lovely though it was. I can be such a gannet at times.'

I peeled off my socks and sat down on my bed. 'Nothing to do with the booze then?'

Angie turned sideways to the mirror rubbing her stomach as she stared at it. Her eyes then rose to inspect her skin, and she pinched her cheeks. 'No. Good Lord, look, that's all on my face.'

'You're glowing and beautiful,' I told her. And it was true. Angie had the most youthful skin out of all of us – not a wrinkle or a blemish in sight – and her mixed European and Afro-Caribbean heritage added a natural bronze to her complexion, which I rather envied. An effortless, gorgeous year-round tan – who wouldn't love that? 'I on the other hand could advertise Tizer!' I added seeing my reflection glowing in the mirror across the room.

Angie laughed. 'You do look a bit sunburned.'

'Sundried you mean. Like a shrivelled tomato,' I whined.

'I don't suppose anyone thought to bring after-sun?'

'I doubt it. But, hey ho! Nothing wrong with a bit of winter sun. I've got moisturiser. And, it was such a glorious afternoon. Some lovely memories. And, such a weight lifted from my shoulders. Telling you all my suspicions about Mike was something I should have done earlier. Much earlier. I was so humiliated and hurt – wondering who and why all the time. You Flowers attacked it from a different angle, which made me look at it from a different perspective too.' I got up from the bed and opened my wardrobe door, detaching my dressing gown from its hanger. 'There is little I can do, so I might as well forget it and get on with living.'

'Absolutely!' Angie whipped off her top layers one by one and put on her dressing gown. 'That's great to hear. So, you think it's all been worthwhile?'

'One hundred per cent.'

'And you're enjoying the skiing too?'

'So far, yes. The whole experience is amazing.'

Angie rushed across the room as I tied my dressing gown belt and threw her arms around me. She almost crushed me with those solid arm muscles. 'I'm so thrilled. I really am,' she said, finally allowing me to breathe. 'I was so worried you wouldn't like it – we all were. We have all been worried about you. All that grief. I mean, the last few years have been the pits for you and now we know why you haven't been able to come out of your cocoon.'

'Whoa, I didn't realise. I'm fine, honest. But, Ang, do you really think I should ignore it? Could you? Be honest.'

Angie cupped my face. 'I wouldn't give it the time of day. It was probably delirium, as Kim says. Put your mind and energy to better use, and as Lou said, have some fun. Go on some dates. Just think of all those adventures you can have. You're still young and beautiful. Keep your fitness up, your diet.' She let go of my

172

face and winked before grabbing a towel and heading for her shower. 'And it'll be easy-peasy if you come and work with me.' I grabbed my phone as she left.

* * *

After speaking to both Ross and Rachel, my day felt complete. They were both thrilled to hear their father's memorial was celebrated with a lunch and even more thrilled that I'd declared it pivotal for a fresh start, so despite only having a glass of water to hand, we toasted both.

Bathing in bubbles a little later, whilst Angie got dressed, I thought of what was possible. Angie made the future sound exciting. The possibility of working in the health and fitness environment could certainly be an incentive for me to stay fit. And I could explore options that I could try; activities or adventures I could organise to do alone, rather than relying on my friends, much as I loved them. Covered in bubbles I looked for my towel. I stepped out and crossed the warm granite floor to the upright steel radiator on which I'd left it. I quickly wrapped it around me, the warmth soothing my skin. I towelled off and slipped on my dressing gown, then opened the door.

Angie was still in her dressing gown, when I stepped into the bedroom.

'Nice bath, hon?' she asked.

'Yes, so lovely,' I said, tying up my gown and sitting on the bed to dry off my feet and between my toes.

'It's thinking time for me,' Angie said rubbing thick white cream on her face.

'Me too. And, I have been thinking.'

'Do tell?'

'Oh, it's all mundane stuff.'

'Rubbish it is. Come on, you need to air some of these things, however mundane you think they are.'

173

I continued wiping the towel between my toes. 'I was thinking about the future, me, what to do. Marrying and having the children so young, I got into the habit of letting Mike take charge, making decisions and organising things. I was thinking it was time I got my act together, attacked some of the paperwork, started thinking for myself and stopped burying my head in the sand. Who knows how far I could stretch myself. And I need to decide how would I run my affairs if, and it's a big if, I did meet a man at some point in the future.'

'Of course you will.'

'Regardless, I need to get to grips with managing things independently.'

Angie nodded, and I grinned watching her lips mumble from the tightening facemask. 'I agree.' She stretched her mouth wider. 'I can't imagine what it's like to be in your shoes, but it must be hard to suddenly have to take everything on yourself.'

My stomach lurched at the thought of all the paperwork that had piled up in the last year. Mike told me all the bills were paid by direct debit, so I hadn't even bothered to look at them. Any envelope with a window I tossed on the pile now higher than the box they were stacked in.

'Well, I have to be realistic. There wasn't much money left and what I have left over from my redundancy is for emergencies, such as the boiler or the car breaking down, as well as paying for this trip. Mike did warn me it would get tough. I don't think I've mentioned it, but he sold his electrical business for a relative song.'

'No. Why?'

'So that his business partner could afford to buy him out. But those funds saw him through much of his illness, and the rest went towards his funeral. That was when I was in a well-paid job, though, remember.'

'I don't know how you coped,' Angie said, shrugging her shoulders and lying down on the bed. 'And why you didn't say? We can help.'

Picking up my Nivea cream, I squirted some on my legs and feet. 'I know, but luckily my boss allowed me quite a bit of paid time off, and I was grateful, believe me. It was a shock when he let me go later. Bastard.' I stretched out my soft, shinier leg, and raised the other one, squeezing the cream on it and began to rub.

'Unbelievable!' Ang mumbled.

'My new salary just about keeps me afloat and I was going through the options. Downsize or scrape by until my pension paid out? Selling the house would at least allow me to buy a smaller place with some cash left over. I wouldn't want to leave Camfield Bottom though and leaving our lovely family home would be heart-breaking of course – all those fond memories.' I sighed. 'But maybe a new place would give me some focus as well as releasing some cash. I thought of your job proposal too and think we should discuss it in more detail after this week. There are pros and cons that I need to weigh up.'

'Mm,' Angie said.

'I wish my dad was still alive to chat with. He was good with money and talking through problems.' I finished my foot and second leg and turned to Angie. She was drifting into sleep, bless her. I snuck my feet under the faux-fur throw and lay my head on the pillow, thinking of my parents. I missed them both.

Mum and Dad had me late and had both gone – leaving me the chunk of their will, of course, which soon disappeared. A new kitchen, a new bathroom, plus a few nice holidays. Mike and I passed most of the inheritance on to Ross and Rachel to help them up the property ladder. I was grateful they were comfortable in their lovely homes, even if they were just that little bit too far away. And having friends close by was probably something I had been rather taking for granted. Something else I needed to address. I had avoided them. Each had rung, come to the house, or invited me out – to help me. I hadn't wanted to talk. Not about Mike, my job, what I had to do.

I suddenly heard a shriek, then a loud bang. I shot up from

my relaxed stupor, put on my slippers and waded haphazardly to the top of the stairs.

'What was that? What's happened?'

Kim looked up the stairs from her position on the sofa, her finger over her lips as she spoke softly. 'Shh. It's Cathy. I think she was out on the terrace and has just gone back into her room. She was talking to Anthony.'

'Oh. Oh dear. Not good by the sounds of things,' I said. 'Where's Lou?'

'I'm down here, sweet, waiting to get into the bedroom. I need a bath.' Lou's face appeared seconds later, with a smile.

I leant forward clasping my hand on the smooth chrome rail. 'Well, come and use ours. Angie's gone to sleep.'

'I might have to,' Lou said. 'I'll hang on a few minutes and go in, I think. I need something to change into.'

I sat on a stair halfway down. 'Something must be up. Do you think I should go in?'

Lou shook her head. 'I don't want her to feel embarrassed.'

'That's my worry too,' Kim agreed, twisting her mouth.

I took a deep breath. I didn't want to interfere and embarrass Cathy, but Anthony seemed to be constantly upsetting her. 'After today, I don't think we should be keeping secrets from one another. I feel much better now I've told you about Mike. I'm going to see her.' I got up and ran back up the stairs to Cathy's room and knocked on the door. 'Cathy, are you all right?'

After a short pause, she responded, 'Yes, fine.' Then I heard her tell Anthony that she had to go. 'Come in.'

I opened the door. She was on the bed wearing black thermals. 'I'll call you later.' After pausing she whispered, 'Bye.'

Cathy

I was still staring at my phone when Ginny came in. I poked at the phone, then threw it down beside me on the bed as though it was burning my fingers.

'Sorry, I heard you scream and the door slamming. Are you all right?' Ginny asked.

My hands reached up, covering my face and rubbing my temples; my eyes would give me away. 'Oh, Ginny.' My voice wobbled and I let out a huge gasp and uncovered my eyes. 'Anthony. He's being horrid and don't be sorry. It's a relief to get off the phone.' Tears rolled down my cheeks.

She opened her arms, saying nothing, just held me as I sobbed.

Sniffing, I released myself from her grasp. 'I need to get a tissue,' I said, dashing to the bathroom. I ran the tap, splashed my eyes.

When I returned Ginny was sat on the bed, looking at the clothes and make-up that were strewn across Lou's side of the bed and on the floor. Three half-filled water tumblers paraded on her bedside cabinet. It wasn't surprising Lou had gone through so many cleaners at home.

I blew my nose. My hairline was damp. I swept my hair to one side, the neat bob disarranged. I sighed heavily and sat beside Ginny. 'I can't deal with him. He's acting like an abandoned child.' I sniffed again. 'Apart from asking stupid questions, which are unnecessary because I left clear instructions on every appliance, he's giving me the third degree. He wants to know what time I go out, what time I come in, where I've been, who I've spoken to, who the instructor is, if I've spoken to any other men. It's the Spanish inquisition every time we speak. I've never known him to be so possessive or insecure,' I told her, wiping my eyes. 'Or drunk. He's getting worse. I don't know what to do, Ginny. I think he needs professional help.' I leaned back on my pillow.

Ginny bit her lip. 'Oh, Cath. I agree. It sounds like he does. He isn't coping, is he? But it is difficult, especially while you're in Switzerland, to help him. I don't understand, why would he try and ruin your holiday?' She brushed a tear from my cheek. 'Look, Cathy, he does need help, but *he* needs to see that, recognise it for himself, otherwise he won't help himself. Is there anyone we can ask to go to him in the interim? Terry? Rob? We need to provide some distraction for him. Terry would be easier as he's usually around and easier to contact. Maybe he can take him out for a bike ride or a game of golf. Shall we ask Lou?'

'Oh God, this is so embarrassing,' I said dropping my head into her lap and threading my hands together. 'That's what he needs – distraction. Gin, he constantly follows me around like a lost puppy. He needs something to do. Some purpose.'

Ginny rubbed my back with her hand. 'What does he do now then?' she asked.

'Nothing. Well, unless you count the *Times* crossword each morning as a purpose. Barely anything apart from interrupt me. He doesn't even stay in contact with his old colleagues or clients. He's not the confident Anthony I fell in love with and I'm realistic enough to accept that his ambition and all that reputed Midas touch will dwindle with age, but I don't understand him or what he expected retirement to be. I know it doesn't mean cutting yourself off socially. I mean, I'm a recluse with my writing to some extent, but he was always around people, preoccupied with his job, his world centred around his clients and now I feel as though he has just noticed I exist again. I seem to have become the entire centre of his world, his existence.'

I felt Ginny's hand fold around my shoulders. It was warm and comforting. 'Well, you certainly seem to have identified the problem. That's a good start. Retirement has been a big change for both of you, but don't feel embarrassed to talk about it. I'm your friend. The others too. OK, I admit, I've been a bit slow learning, but believe me when I say that sharing really does help and I wish I'd learned that lesson when I lost my job, but it really does. I was embarrassed, ashamed and didn't tell anyone for ages, but honestly, yesterday after I told you all my suspicions about Mike, I felt two stone lighter. The pride or shame, or whatever it is we drag ourselves down with, is a lead balloon. You can only take so much pressure, then you'll explode.'

I sat up. 'Oh, darling, you're right. I should know all this. Yes, I fear I will explode, but you know me, I don't like airing my dirty laundry in public.'

Ginny shot me a knowing look. 'Oh, Cath, that's me to a tee! I don't know how or why I've let Mike's words fester inside me for so long. It's hideous behaviour for a mature woman. And think about it, how long have we all known each other? Hardly strangers, are we? Neither of us will be off sniggering behind the other's back; we're past all that. And, interestingly, what I discovered was how you all had different views about the issue of Mike possibly having an affair. What you all had to say completely switched around my thinking.'

'It did. How?'

'I was irrational. Totally irrational. What could I do? I've spent the past year feeling humiliated that Mike could be unfaithful to me. Torturing myself as to why he did it, with whom, trying to find clues and answers to those questions, when in fact, I don't even know if he did have an affair. It was all in my head. Like the redundancy, and trying for jobs, I felt useless, past it, ugly, confused, betrayed, constantly telling myself I was on the heap. I can't tell you how much effort it took me to come along to the gym and classes. I now think if only I had told myself there was nothing I could do about it anyway, I might have stopped beating myself up.'

Ginny pulled her shoulders back and clasped her hands in her lap. 'So, don't bottle it up. If Anthony carries on, you could do the same. You'll let the shame build up. You'll possibly begin blaming yourself for his behaviour, looking inwards for answers,

179

trying to work out what you can do to put yourself right; what it needs is objectivity. Outside input. Others will give you a new perspective and have probably already worked out what is happening by the changes in you both.'

I stared at Ginny. 'Oh, darling, that makes so much sense.'

She smiled. 'Believe me, Cathy, I've only just discovered its magical effects. I'm no expert, but I'm giving you my point of view. The benefit of my experience. That's all. You have a lovely husband who loves you dearly; he just needs help.'

I sighed and felt the muscles in my face soften. I held my arms out and embraced her. 'Dearest Ginny, I'm so lucky to have him. And you. I … talking to you, I feel better already. I just don't know what to do. I want my Anthony back. I suppose it makes sense to get help. If this continues, I swear I'd have to leave him to it. I can't live with him like this.' I pulled back, my mouth twisting, wondering where on earth I would start. Then patting my friend, and stepping towards the dressing table, I glanced at myself in the mirror. I had no answers. I attempted to straighten my hair with my fingers. 'Let's go downstairs and tell the others. I do need to share this. Maybe between us we can work out a way forward.'

'That's my girl,' Ginny said and took in a deep breath before opening the door. 'It actually feels really good to be needed. It's been so long since I've helped anyone else. I was so engrossed in my own self-pity, I forgot everyone has their own problems. Let's hope Anthony will accept help or seek it for himself.'

'Well, thank you, darling. I do feel much better,' I told her as we headed down the stairs. 'And, it would be wonderful to have our old Ginny back.'

Lou and Kim were sitting with their feet up reading when we got down the stairs and Angie, her face glowing, was just sitting down with a tea. Ginny went directly to the kitchen to put on some fresh coffee whilst I sheepishly caught the Flowers' attention.

Gathered in the sitting room together, we listened as Cathy opened up to us about Anthony driving her mad since they had retired. I wasn't too surprised to be honest after hearing their arguing on the phone. I was surprised that Anthony was idling so much though. I knew how much energy he put into his business and socialising. I also got the impression that Cathy might be spending too much of her time writing. Perhaps they needed to balance their time better.

I was glad she told us. For their sake and for mine. It was an issue I needed to bring up with Will when I got home. Neither of us wanted to be bored or take up so much time on our own project that we completely ignored each other, which I supposed could happen if I was to come to Europe alone.

We all agreed Cathy needed to discuss it with Anthony though. Maybe Cathy needed to limit her writing time to office hours, or create some flexibility, say three or four days a week, so that she could spend more time with her husband.

Lou was such a star though – she got straight on the phone to Terry, enlisting his help to get Anthony out. Angie messaged Rob too. Between them, they would try get him out of the house. Will wouldn't be much help but could at least ring him for a chat, I suggested, and messaged him. We offered some ideas about trips they could take together, weekends, day trips. I quite enjoyed the exercise and got some great ideas for planning my own retirement. Besides, we were high on cups of coffee, which Ginny refilled from the coffee machine, and on chocolates; yes, we had spent the arvo gorging on the yummy selection of Swiss chocolates left for us by the chalet owner.

My tummy was rumbling again, however, and glancing at the clock, I said, 'Guys, I must go and have my bath. It's a quarter to seven.'

'Gosh, is it really?' Cathy said peering up at the clock. 'Me too.' She stood up from the corner of the sofa, slightly hesitant. 'I'll ring Anthony later otherwise we'll never get out.'

'Good idea,' Lou said and stood up too, tightening the belt on the dressing gown I had lent her. She did eventually get her bath whilst Ginny was talking to Cathy in our room. She then continued. 'And, hopefully by then, Terry will have spoken to him and organised something. Although, didn't they organise a memorial for Mike tonight?'

'Hmm.' Cathy clung to the rail on the stairs and rolled her eyes, her lips curled. 'I think you're right. I was thinking a film at the cinema would be nice, but even the pub with the boys is better than Anthony sitting in on his own, getting drunk and worrying about what I'm doing. Fingers crossed the boys can work their magic. Thank you, my darling Flowers. Anyway, bath, or shower?' she muttered as she cheerfully climbed the stairs. Then as we were still watching, unexpectedly she turned around, lifted her shoulders, stuck out her chest and raised her arm with a pointed finger, just like the poster of Lord Kitchener himself recruiting troops for the Great War.

'My Flowers, "Our Marriage needs you",' she said in a gruff voice. 'With you, Anthony and I can fight this.' Our shrieks pierced the air as we laughed; but when I glimpsed Cathy's face, ironed of its creases and shining back at us, and her posture as she marched up the stairs, it was evident she had also taken the figurative step she needed in order to climb the next. 'Ginny, you were right,' she said, reaching the top. 'Sharing the load and having all your support has been extremely therapeutic. I was beginning to get in such a state. My head is certainly so much clearer now.'

I smiled and saw Ginny's eyes glistening too. Because she had dug down and sourced her own courage today, she'd been able to plunge in to talk to Cath. What a difference in both Flowers, I thought, wishing I too could unearth some inner strength to tell Ginny the truth.

An hour later once dressed we ventured out into the freezing night. The melted snow had quickly iced over, and we trod carefully on our ascent to the road. We were soon warmed and greeted in La Poste by Lucien, the waiter. He showed us to a large booth with bench seats along the walls and sides and, as we ordered our wine, we each quickly ordered a pasta dish before Stefano appeared to fill us with his wonderful but filling eight-course specialities. Stefano found us a few minutes later.

'So, you are enjoying the skiing?'

'Yes,' we all cheered.

'Better than we ever imagined,' Ginny said.

He leant his hands on the centre of the table. Bare forearms revealing dark hairs unlike the thick but fading, greying hair framing his warm and still handsome face. His gaze shifted back and forth along the table before being caught by Angie's beaming smile and usual flirty allure. That irritated me slightly, especially after our little tête-à-tête. I thought she had listened. Flirting with intent with one man was bad enough, but not every man!

'*Magnifico.*' Stefano raised his right hand and pressed his fingers to his thumb and kissed it. 'So, you must come here to celebrate New Year with us. Best price. We have special ten-course dinner menu. Francesco and I plan all year. You have wine, a bottle of Champagne all included.' Stefano lifted his chin, then lowered it again. 'Two for you ladies. And I have excellent band.' He raised his eyebrows and shook his head as if we doubted him. 'They play music you like. You like Abba, yes?'

We nodded.

'They play Abba. They play the rock and roll. They *magnifico*. I squeeze you in. We are full.'

Not quite knowing how he was going to squeeze five of us in, I looked at the girls seeking agreement. Stefano had won us all over and we settled on booking our New Year celebrations. It made sense to have somewhere to go and the atmosphere was always warm and welcoming here. Stefano wore a cheeky, satisfied smile when he brought over his card machine. He really could sell sawdust to a sawmill, I mused to myself as I watched Angie pay our deposit with her card.

A familiar voice, followed by laughter, snared my attention. I waved as Christoff scanned the restaurant. Like homing pigeons, Christoff and Neil strolled the aisle towards us, closely followed by Tom and Florian. I enjoyed their company and I was sure the others did too, particularly Ginny and Angie. Heads turned as our handsome friends squeezed into our booth. Maybe I hadn't realised there was so much space between us girls, but I now understood how Stefano managed to expand his covers. We were closely seated but not uncomfortably so.

From the back of the table, Angie jumped up, just as our wine arrived.

'Sorry, I need the loo,' she said.

Lucien poured red wine into our small glasses and took the boys' orders. Didier, the other waiter we recognised from the previous visit, shouted a '*bonsoir*' and waved from the aisle between the tables on the other side of the central strip. Chatter began as Christoff asked how the memorial lunch went and we relayed details. Angie returned and as I went to step out to let her in, she held up her palm.

'No, I'll pop myself on the edge this end. You don't mind do you, Christoff?' She fluttered her eyelids and swung her behind in next to his, nudging everyone along to my end. She glared straight at me, daring me to say something as I scowled back. In that moment, I decided to ignore her behaviour. It had nothing to do with me. I cared, but the message clearly hadn't sunk in. What could I do?

I turned to Ginny sitting in the corner between Lou and Cathy. She returned a shrug as if signalling her disapproval. It was a shame because it wasn't what the trip was about and Ginny, I'm certain, didn't need undertones of infidelity spoiling her fun. As Angie and Christoff continued their frolicking, Florian, Tom and

Neil shuffled further to our end of the table and the conversation flowed lightly between us.

Florian and Tom told us about their children and how quickly they learned to ski from a young age. Neil's three grandchildren, he told us, also learnt when they were small, and he said how he loved to ski with them and his two children and their partners when they visited him here over the February half-term. The grandchildren, now ten, eight and six were growing fast; he chuckled as he explained the difficulty accommodating them all in his three-bedroomed apartment.

After we had eaten our delicious pasta, Neil suggested we walk along to another bar. The Bellevue or Les Trappeurs. I got the impression he felt uncomfortably stifled next to Christoff and Angie.

'Yes, sounds like a good idea to me,' I said, tempted to add, 'Let's leave these two to get a room,' but I didn't want Angie to do anything of the sort. 'Angie, did you hear Neil? We're going to walk along to The Bellevue or Les Trappeurs,' I shouted above the noise.

She turned. 'Oh, why?'

'Well, it's getting a bit hot in here and I fancy a walk after all that pasta I've managed to stuff down me,' I said.

Neil signalled to Lucien for the bill and the waiter came straight over.

Lucien picked up our pot of bills and was totting them up.

Angie glanced back at Christoff. 'OK. Shall we follow on in a while?'

Christoff shrugged and gazed our way. 'I … think we …'

Again, I scowled as I grabbed my jacket, interrupting Christoff. 'I'd rather we stayed together, Angie.'

'We won't be long, promise. Which one are you going to?' Angie gazed at Neil, then at Christoff.

'I think we go together,' Christoff said, glancing up at me and, I guessed, reading the tension.

185

Neil lifted his jacket from the pile in the corner and shuffled around to put his arm in. 'Bellevue?'

Lou and I nodded. Cathy answered, 'Wherever. I don't mind.'

'OK, Bellevue. We'll be along soon,' Angie said, not attempting to compromise.

Ginny cleared her throat as she zipped up her jacket 'Christoff is coming with us. Grab your coat, Angie.'

Christoff reached behind Neil for his jacket then rose to his feet.

'OK, fine,' Angie groaned with a defeated pout and tossed two twenty Swiss-franc notes to me across the table. 'I don't understand why you all think it's so urgent we go.'

I put the notes I'd collected from the girls and settled with Lucien. Neil paid the men's bill whilst I slipped on my coat. I sidled up to Angie and murmured in her ear. 'Please don't do this. It's not fair on anyone. You know he's married too.'

'No, he isn't actually,' Angie bit back. 'They're separated.'

I wasn't sure how I kept myself from screaming. I murmured back into her ear, firmly, 'But you're not.'

Chapter 13

Ginny

Neil walked beside me, his scent tormenting and enticing my nostrils. Between us a warm pondering silence shielded the biting air as we headed uphill towards the Belleview. Perhaps he sensed I was angry with Angie. Her motives were blatantly obvious to everyone. Why would she risk her marriage like that? Just for a quick shag – probably in a bush or goodness knows where. What had gotten into her? She was a natural flirt, she liked to get attention, even with our other halves, but I'd never seen this side of her before. Dog on heat sprung to mind. Teenage hormones raging.

Was this what Mike was like? Would he have … with Angie? No. I had discounted my friends from the off. I knew, just knew, they would not do that. And in my heart, I knew, neither would Mike. His memorial was propitious; I have accepted his delirium and would do all I could to completely erase his words from my memory. I felt rescued from the torture. Now I – or should I amend that to we, because knowing Angie, she won't listen to just one person – needed to rescue Angie from hers.

Unlike its terrace outside and the stunning views inside, the Belleview was featureless – and less crowded. Tiled floors and large steel windows that were great for a daytime panorama and obliterated most of the wall space. A large group congregated on a long table across the centre of the room, so we aimed for two window tables, which we pushed together. A young waitress stood nearby as we discarded our jackets and settled.

Christoff sat on the bench seat at the back of the table between Florian and Tom with Neil at the end holding the back of a chair for me, inviting me to sit close. Angie sat the other side of me next to Lou. Cathy and Kim at the other end. The waitress took our drinks order and strolled back towards the bar, the conversation resuming at the table on the lack of ambience the bar had compared to La Poste. Angie, still in a sulk, glanced at me. I sighed and shuffled closer, keeping my voice down.

'Why, Ang?' I asked. 'What could possibly drive you to take such a risk with Christoff?'

She lowered her head. 'You only have to look at him to see why.'

'OK, but there must have been other men you've been attracted to but resisted.'

'Yes, but … we're here and Rob won't find out. It's the perfect opportunity.'

I rubbed my brow, my thoughts wandering back to Mike's words. 'Think of Rob and how hurt he would be if he found out. You wouldn't like it if he did it to you. What if it slipped past one of our lips when we're talking about the holiday? It could easily happen.'

Slumping further down her chair as she adjusted the waist on her leggings, Angie whispered, 'My dad always got away with it. My mum never knew.'

'What do you mean?'

She slid her tongue to the side of her mouth. 'My mum, she didn't know my dad shagged women in his van at the markets.'

'Did he?' I gasped in shock but remembered him as being a larger than life figure, quite a charmer. I used to see him at

Greenwich market sometimes on a Saturday, occasionally when Angie and I walked around there. That was where she introduced me to him. In fact, at her wedding, he flirted quite a bit with the female guests too, now I thought about it.

'Yes, I thought you knew,' she said looking up at me.

'No. I had no idea. But that doesn't make it right. Or give you permission to cheat on Rob. And, maybe your mum didn't know or, possibly turned a blind eye if they stayed together. Rob might not be so forgiving. And if you knew, didn't you feel sad or sorry for your mum?'

'Yes, of course I did. I wanted to tell her.'

'Why didn't you?'

Angie shrugged, then stared at her lap. 'I don't know. I got on better with my dad. He was always nice to me. Mum was the strict one. She could be quite a force, my mum, and I couldn't bear the thought that she might throw him out or that he might leave.'

'Didn't you tell him you knew? Hope that he would stop?'

Angie nodded. 'I did. He laughed and said I had a wild imagination. I cried for days. I was only thirteen. I hated other women getting his attention. He was my dad. I swore when I got married that no woman was going to turn my husband's head.'

Now it was all beginning to make sense. Angie's drive to stay young, keep herself fit and beautiful to hold Rob's attention. Her insecurities were likely to have stemmed from the relationship with her father. I squeezed her arm.

'Oh, Ang, Rob thinks you're gorgeous. Any man in this room will vouch for that, the women too. You've got nothing to prove. It's accepting yourself in here,' I said laying a hand on my heart. Angie was clearly driven to stay young for Rob so that his head didn't turn like her father's.

'I know, I read all the articles in the magazines. I think I'm scared of getting old and fat like my mum and not being good enough.'

'Well now, I thought I had the monopoly on not being good enough. I'm waking up to that false belief.' I leaned closer. 'A little secret. Neil has made me feel like a woman again if you know what I mean.'

Angie gave a roar. 'Oh my God, Gin. That's so exciting.'

Kim shouted across: 'What are you two whispering about?'

I cleared my throat and licked my lips addressing the table. 'Well, after today, Flowers, I need your help,' I said boldly. All eyes were on me, but I needed to steer the conversation and it was my attempt at diverting Angie from this latest obsession with sex and Christoff and helping her. 'So as you know I've made the decision to move on but I want to explore possibilities. I know we did this tongue-in-cheek earlier, but as it's the New Year in a few days there's not much time to plan, I wondered if you could offer some serious input. I mean it's a perfect time to make a fresh start, so what can I do to distract my mind from Mike and the misery I've subjected myself to this year?'

'Distraction! He's sitting right next to you, sweetheart,' Angie said. 'It doesn't get easier than that.' There was a mixed reaction of short sharp laughter and an intake of breaths.

Blood immediately rushed to my cheeks, and I couldn't look at Neil. I should have half expected Angie to come out with something like that, but I wasn't prepared for her retort. Nor the tingling that shot through my skin. My attraction to Neil and his demeanour felt so right, but I didn't feel anywhere ready for a relationship. Affair, fling or otherwise. I'd been married for almost forty years, so my relationship with Mike, my soul mate, was only really beginning to exit my psyche.

'Trust you, Ang!' Lou said poking Angie in the side and attempting to lighten my embarrassment. 'I happen to think there's no harm in having a bit of fun if you're comfortable with it. You're a free woman, like I said before. I'm sure Neil is too much of a gentleman to respond to that, but you two do make a lovely couple.'

Neil and I swapped rosy glances. 'You're very kind, thank you,' he said smiling at me and Lou. This wasn't going quite as I'd planned, and my mouth twitched nervously with Neil right beside me. Luckily, three bottles of Gamay and nine glasses arrived at our table, delivered by a young waitress, and that diverted everyone's attention. I watched as Christoff and Neil eyed her curiously as she opened and poured the wine. Mike would always check out a woman, I remembered.

So, as the topic had shifted from my intention, I was about to suggest something more practical that Angie could pursue to distract her from ruining her marriage by chasing Christoff, but Florian rejoined the trail of my original conversation in his beautiful French accent.

'Ginny. When my mother lost my father, she sold their home, our family home in Sion. She found it hard, emotionally, but opened a bar in a nearby tourist village in the valley. It was something she always wanted to do, and although it is very busy, she is happiest there. She made it a successful and profitable business. Is there something similar you have always wanted to do?'

I was just about to respond when Kim clapped her hands then entwined her fingers. 'That's amazing, Florian. I think Ginny should make a list of all the things she's ever wanted to do in life.' She scrunched her nose as she grabbed my fingers. 'Like a bucket list, then narrow it down and see where it takes you.'

'Yes, my darling, think about what excites you,' Cathy added. 'The magazine I subscribe to has articles about women who change course in later years. They turn their lives around and find their purpose in life at fifty, sixty or seventy! You could have some of those to flick through for ideas.'

I nodded. 'Well, isn't that exactly what you've done – started writing, Cathy? It was always a dream when you were teaching, wasn't it? And now you're doing it.'

Neil smiled, raising his eyebrows. 'Good for you, Cathy. Are you published?'

'Just one short story to date,' Cathy said proudly. 'My dream is to write a novel.'

'Well, a great start,' Neil said. 'I gather that's what you're working towards then?'

'Absolutely. I had always known I would write one day, published or not. I find it therapeutic and unlike some that I won't mention, something to look forward to in retirement.' Cathy tittered. It was good that she was making light of her and Anthony's plight.

Kim puffed her cheeks. 'Well, Gin, you know what I want when I retire. I'm desperate to return to England and be closer to the twins and you Flowers. My dream is to come back and keep you company, Ginny, especially now you're on your own. It would be nice to do more together. All of us, even if it's walking in the park,' Kim said.

'We would all love that,' I crooned.

Kim blew me a kiss. 'But for now, have you thought about joining a local evening class, maybe? Learn something new. A language, musical instrument, local history, gardening.' Kim stopped and clasped her hands to her chest. 'Now, there's a challenge. Create your own rose garden. You love sitting in mine and you liked your dad's.'

I stared at Kim, clenching my teeth with apprehension. 'Really! Gosh, a rose garden. But I'm useless in the garden. I can't even tell a plant from a weed.' I was a little stirred though thinking about Dad's and Kim's roses, Dad's veg patch, and I had on a few occasions, helped Mum make up the summer bedding and hanging baskets. 'Hmm, food for thought. I do love making up hanging baskets and planting pots for the patio, so increasing my plant knowledge could be useful. In fact, growing my own veg appeals.'

Angie sat back. 'Yes, growing your own produce would be complimentary to your new health and fitness ethos, and don't forget that job I offered you. Free fitness classes on tap. Updates and monitoring on diet.'

'I have to say, you are really tempting me, Ang. And I've read cultivating-slash-gardening is apparently very good for the soul. I can imagine myself tending vegetables in the garden, watching them grow, fresh herbs, maybe some soft fruits, planting an apple tree.' Ideas rolled over in my brain, but I had started this exercise with Angie in mind. 'You're right, Ang,' I said. 'I wouldn't mind learning more, maybe some wild challenges are what I need.' I bit my lip. 'I'm getting a little carried away, I couldn't possibly cope with all this at once.'

Angie put her wine-free hand on my shoulder. 'Absolutely not, Ginny,' she said with conviction. 'Let me help you. God, you've got my juices flowing to do more too.'

Awash with wonder, I gulped. 'I have?'

I couldn't believe it. Had I unwittingly inspired Angie or was it just a momentary distraction? I had to probe further. 'That would be great, Angie, but what about what you want? Your own challenges?' I asked her.

She removed her hand, placing both her elbows on the table, and focused on the stem of her glass. 'Well, don't get me wrong – you, all of you, have done an amazing job with your diet and fitness, but I'd like to encourage more people. Encourage and educate them about their bodies and nutrition.' She looked upwards staring into the air. 'My dream would be for everyone, with money or not, to listen to their bodies, seek out the best food and exercise for them, form new habits, find what's comfortable for them, employ new, healthier attitudes. Basically, treat their bodies as temples.'

'That's a great ambition,' Christoff said. 'I admire that er … what do you say, vision.'

'Thank you, Christoff,' Angie said blushing, but determination glistened from her eyes. She looked at me and then at Cathy. 'This is where I need help. Marketing my vision. I think a blog on the website would be a great start. All those areas I mentioned, plus recipe ideas from me and readers' suggestions. It would be like having my own online magazine.'

'Sounds amazing,' I said, feeling fired up myself, 'and Cathy and I can help you there. Well, if Cathy agrees – she has the writing skills; I can work the metadata.'

Lou's eyes lit up. 'And I could put your website link on to ours. We have lots of visitors and a monthly newsletter on the site, people seeking inspiration for new homes, a better lifestyle. All ages too. I think it would link in beautifully. I'm confident they would be interested in that type of blog.'

'Wow, girls, what a dynamic force we are. But there is one more thing.' Angie pointed her index finger into the air and waved it, wishing to maintain our attention. 'It's something that's been ambling around my head for a while and is possibly the personal challenge, or diversion that I need.' Angie looked at me. 'It's to go on one of those mountain climbs for charity. For cancer research in honour of Mike.'

I felt a lump in my throat at the same time as my eyes began stinging. 'That's so sweet of you, Ang. It's the perfect diversion.'

'Exactly. Ideally somewhere like Machu Picchu or the Himalayas. I would need to check their website, but I'd look to join a Nordic walking group to train, hopefully altitude training too. Basically, I'd acquire the skills I need to go to somewhere like Nepal to raise money. I would love that.'

'Aw. Take me with you, possum!' Kim begged with a snort. 'I so need you girls.'

Poor Kim. It was evident she needed her friends.

'I wouldn't mind coming with you either, and the Nordic walking course,' Lou enthused. 'I desperately need to keep up my fitness. I feel so much better after our six months of training. And, raising money for charity would be great.'

Here was my opportunity to support her too. 'Mountains have grown on me too, so it sounds as though you have lots of company. That means you're going to keep us all busy as well as yourself, Angie. You will unquestionably have to begin planning this itinerary, our diets and fitness schedules too.'

Angie patted my arm and craned her neck towards me. 'So, mission accomplished, my beautiful friend,' she said tapping the side of her nose.

Joy waded through my veins. 'I really hope so,' I said squeezing her arm. So far, the outcome couldn't have been better.

Cathy then squealed. 'I can't believe I'm saying this, darling, but I think I would benefit too.' Cathy wriggled in her chair. 'With all the writing I've been doing lately, I need to stay active. And think how much we could raise for the cause between us.'

This was music to my ears. 'Cathy, fantastic,' I said, knowing how much she said she had struggled lately sitting for long periods, even with exercise. On the aeroplane, she said her knees had become stiff and painful and she found herself getting up every thirty to forty minutes to do lunges or squats to relieve them.

'Well, use it or lose it, I've come to realise,' Cathy added. 'These recent changes have made such an impact on me and lifestyle. I was on the go and standing as a teacher. I wish I could persuade Anthony to join in too. He needs to increase his activity. He has put on so much weight over the past year.'

'Terry too.' Lou shook her head. 'Yes, he likes his beer and his bread.'

Angie clutched her hands and was almost bouncing in her seat as she bubbled with excitement. 'So this is what I'm getting at. Well, maybe we can set an example. Let's focus on our goals first,' Angie said before she slid into pedagogic mode. 'You see, that's the thing. The guys need to be motivated too. It's not just a message for the young or overweight, it's everyone. As we age, everything begins to slow down. Metabolism, digestive system. We do need to eat less and become more active. You should see some of the changes in clients who come to my clinic.'

She looked directly at Christoff, then Florian, then Tom and Neil. 'These girls are perfect examples.' She held out her arm and took a bow of satisfaction. 'Sorry, I sound such a bore, but I run a holistic health and nutrition centre. We teach new eating habits including nutrition, but the fitness classes make such a difference and I love to see the results. This is my purpose. And I have to create a bigger splash. If only people realised. Weight just falls off after a few weeks. Many of my clients really transform their shape, and even at our age, look amazingly toned – as you can see.' Angie lifted the base of her cashmere sweater, showing the slender silhouette of six-pack through her thermal vest. 'So this is mega exciting; these girls are my inspiration.'

I watched as the men gazed approvingly. Christoff's eyebrows rose at her as she squirmed with pleasure. I just hoped this evening was turning her around in the right direction and not Christoff's.

'Indeed. You all look amazing,' Neil said gazing my way and slapping his hands on his knees and rubbing the tops of his thighs. 'I'd be a blob if I didn't stay active. You go, Ang.'

* * *

The sense of pride I felt for Angie was immense and, feeling the heat rise in my chest, I tried to remain calm; but inside I was feeling anything was possible. It seemed the whole table was ignited with Angie's enthusiasm.

'How do you stay active?' I asked Neil, immediately regretting my phrasing.

He leant on the side of his chair, his eyes smouldering. 'Do you really want to know?' He cackled along with everyone else. 'No, seriously, I know you're too much of a lady to get smutty. When I'm home in the summer months, to keep the pounds off I usually run, swim, play tennis, badminton or golf once or twice a week. I have to say, I do enjoy sport. And don't you think regular exercise keeps your spirits up?'

'That's not all it keeps up,' Angie blurted.

I almost choked on my glass of Gamay. Should I laugh or cry? I knew I couldn't change that love of flirting she had. 'Angie, I honestly don't remember exercise ever lifting my spirits but they're lifting now, just hearing your enthusiasm.' We had spent the last six months running two mornings a week plus slogging it out in the classes or the gym three nights a week, then the compulsory yogalates Saturday morning with Angie, all to get fit for this holiday. After each session I could just about manage to drive home and climb into bed. They were the best nights' sleep I'd had since losing Mike, I admit, but I didn't even have the strength to join the girls for a glass of wine on Thursday evenings after class.

Angie's eyes were ablaze. 'Absolutely, there's nothing better to get the endorphins pumping, as well as the serotonin and dopamine it releases. I find it addictive,' Angie said, high as a kite just talking about it. 'And—' she pouted as she winked at Christoff '—it's probably responsible for my ravenous sex drive.'

I sat back in despair wondering whether Rob was actually coping with Angie's sexual demands on a daily basis. Maybe Rob needed a break!

Kim

The following morning, I woke to find the room unusually dim. Sliding back the duvet I blinked at the clock until my eyes focused. It was a quarter past eight. I tiptoed to the window and peeling back the luxuriant curtain, I discovered why. There was nothing to see but white. White fog and showering snow.

'Wow. I don't think we're going to be skiing today,' I said, throwing back my head and looking over my shoulder to Angie, but the duvet on her side of our bed was still in situ. She wasn't in it. I frowned, looking closer. No, my eyes weren't deceiving me; it hadn't been slept in. Instantly I clutched my chest. *Surely not.* Ginny was stirring.

'Angie's not here,' I shrieked.

She mumbled something.

'Gin. Angie,' I repeated. 'She's not here and her bed is still made.' I felt a rush of bile in my throat. *Stupid, stupid woman.* No, I told myself, letting out a sigh. Maybe she had crashed out on the sofa. 'I'll go down and see if she's there. So, confident that our ski lesson would be cancelled, at least until it eased, I quickly slipped into my dressing gown, and went in search of Angie. I checked the bathroom. Empty. I ran out the door and down the stairs. It was all in darkness. I ran over and pressed the switch to open the curtains and gazed around an empty room. My blood raced. I couldn't believe she had stayed out all night, presumably with Christoff. My head now raged. I ran to the porch, which was still locked, and out to the front door. That too was secure. How could she? I ran back up the stairs.

Ginny was up grappling in the wardrobe for something to wear.

'She's not down there,' I said. 'And, the door is locked. I doubt she would lock it if she had popped out.'

Turning around, I saw Ginny had the dressing gown in her hand and was fumbling to find the arm as she gawped at me. 'Oh, please tell me this isn't happening,' she said. I would have laughed at her misshapen hair had I been able to touch base with my humour, but then her jaw moved again as she stared at the empty side of the bed. 'God, no. Ang, what have you done?' Ginny wrapped the gown around her and covered her mouth. 'She's not in her right mind.'

I sat on the edge of my bed, numbed. 'No. She's …'

Ginny raised a hand to her mouth. 'She wouldn't have gone along to the supermarket, would she? We needed some bits for breakfast.'

My face gnarled. 'No idea, but both doors are locked. I doubt she would have locked both after her. I glanced at her side of the bed. She would not have got up and made that bed either. Why would she?'

198

'Oh, Kim, what do we do? I don't want to believe it,' Ginny said leaning across to check the bedding. The fur throw was ruffled where I had slept but the zillion-thread Egyptian cotton sheets were tightly tucked in place as though waiting for a military inspection. 'And, you're right. That's definitely not her handiwork.'

I covered my eyes. 'You bloody fool, Angie. A whim! You're insane!' I pursed my lips and for the want of something to do said, 'Oh, chook, I'm going to make a coffee. Do you want one? And, I wouldn't rush ...' I rose to my feet and headed for the door. 'There's thick fog and heavy snow falling out there.'

Ginny pulled a face. 'Oh, yuck! So, we can't ski?'

'I doubt it. I'm not sure what happens when it's snowing, or foggy. We won't be able to see where we're going.' I spun around to grab my phone. 'I'll text Angie to find out.'

I left Ginny still dazed from the shock and made my way to the kitchen, filling the water on the espresso machine and switching it on. I unlocked my phone and messaged Angie. It was brief. *Are we skiing this morning?*

Opening the fridge, I was relieved to see we still had cheese, a little salami and ham, but the French stick on the side was rock hard. I found a bread knife and tried to slice it. The crust needed sawing but maybe, I thought, as I got through at an angle, it would toast. I was halfway through sawing through it when I heard the familiar voice.

'Morning.'

I turned around, the bread knife raised in my hand. 'Where have you been?' I said accusingly. Angie came up beside me and I looked her up and down. The pink bunny pyjamas and long fluffy cardigan she was wearing clearly weren't hers.

'Whoa, good morning to you too!'

'Well, your bed was empty and ...'

Lou tottered down the stairs, followed by Ginny.

Angie watched me cutting into the bread. 'No, we didn't get

to bed until about half three. I slept with Lou, so I didn't wake you. Cathy was talking to Anthony when we got back so I was keeping Lou company, then Cathy came down and we sat chatting. With wine, of course. Finished off that white Fendant.'

A wave of relief swept over me. 'Well, thank God for that. I … was worried.' I thought it best not to mention my suspicions and glared at Ginny, hoping she would follow suit. 'So, was Anthony all right? Did Terry take him out?' I popped some of the bread in the toaster and began sawing the loaf again.

Angie peered at Lou. 'Yes. Lou will tell you. He was calmer, apparently. They went bowling. Rob met them there too.'

'Oh! Good. Did they knock any sense into him?' I glanced from one to the other.

Lou slotted a capsule into the coffee machine and placed a mug under it. 'Hmm. It's not something that can be tackled overnight, is it? And we're only getting one perspective. Terry, who unfortunately has never been one of life's great observers, was under the impression that Anthony was totally normal. Terry didn't have a clue what he was supposed to say to him. But he said he did ask how he was getting on without Cath.' Lou gave a shrug. 'And Anthony's response was, fine, he was enjoying the peace and quiet.' I could see she was as perplexed as us as she peered down while filling the fourth mug of coffee.

'In denial, huh. That's not good,' I said raising my voice to be heard over the loud gurgling noise it took to barista coffee. What was wrong with a good old-fashioned kettle and instant?

'Amazing, isn't it? Poor Cathy. Who knows?' Lou said, slotting the final capsule in the coffee machine and pressing yet again. 'Terry and Rob are going to meet him at the Indian tonight and then they're meeting up tomorrow for golf. Fingers crossed they can keep him busy for a few days. Keep him off Cath's back.'

As the coffee appliance silenced, the boom of Cathy's schoolmistress voice bounced into the air. 'My ears are burning, Flowers.'

I glanced up at her as she reached the bottom of the stairs and I greeted her with a smile.

'Well, at least it's not the toast burning,' Lou scoffed, watching me remove two golden brown slices from the toaster. 'You could start buttering that though,' she said to Cathy, and I sensed she was having a dig at Angie who was still leaning over the worktop staring at the bread and the knife in my hands.

'Ah, there's no butter,' I said. 'I couldn't see any anyway.'

'Oh, bugger. I was going to go to the shop yesterday, wasn't I,' Lou said removing the fifth mug and inserting a milk capsule in before beginning the process again. Her eyes veered to the window and, baring her teeth, she shuddered. 'We'll manage without it this morning. I can't face that weather yet.'

'Healthier too,' Angie said, standing upright and stretching out her arms. 'Thanks for all your support last night, girls. I'm so excited and fired up.'

I gave her a hug. 'And, we're one hundred per cent behind you, sweet.'

'Yes,' Lou agreed and switched on the machine and shouted out. 'Oh, Kim, Terry said Paula was at the bowling last night. With a group of lads from her running club or something … Sounds as though she was feeling sorry for herself, he said. Didn't like the fact that we were all here and she was bored at home.' The machine silenced. 'He got the impression she was feeling left out and would have liked to have come skiing with us.'

I felt my stomach twist, hoping she wasn't now preying on Terry, Rob or Anthony. I peered at Cathy who turned to me with a frown. I forced a smile. 'Really? Typical. Probably seeking sympathy. You know what she's like.' I grimaced, extracting more toast from the toaster and trying to think of something, anything to divert the conversation away from my sister. I could think of nothing worse than having her here right now. Not that I had ever encouraged her to come out with me and my friends, for obvious reasons.

It was then I suddenly felt my stomach lurch. Would she tell the boys of her misdemeanours? As far as Paula was concerned, it didn't matter who she hurt. What if she had and it got back to Ginny that I knew? I licked my dry lips. 'So, Ang. Are we skiing this morning?'

Chapter 14

Ginny

As we marched from the chalet, patches of grey-white cloud dented the fog, with a rendering of promising blue hues beneath and the fresh dump of snow adding a further thick layer blanketing the ground and buildings. The village was the epitome of a winter wonderland. I waited for Kim as she dawdled behind, her head down, seemingly distracted.

'Are you all right, sweetheart?' I asked softly, utilising some of the abundant energy that had coiled within me since we'd had Mike's memorial. I was feeling like the younger, carefree Ginny again. Being able to finally open up to my friends had been cathartic and like a daffodil bud, my confidence was beginning to bloom. It was like another school day and us girls were on our way to meet the bus. I wanted to share the sense of liberation and love and see everyone as happy as I was.

Kim heaved her skis onto her shoulder, blowing out a sigh. 'Yes, I'm fine, thanks, but I'd rather the sun was shining. I've added extra layers to brace against the cold, but the light is dismally dim this morning isn't it?'

It was. But in all honesty, I hadn't really taken much notice even though the mountain air gave out that hostile chill. It was our first cold day and it pleased me to know that I wasn't worrying about it. There must have been a seismic shift inside me in the last twenty-four hours. I felt six inches taller. Fog had cleared from my head and with my Flowers' input, ideas about my future were already beginning to bloom. I looked up to the sky and noticed the thick swirl of mist hovering above us.

'Hopefully, the sun will burn through that and it will brighten,' I said.

Just before nine-thirty at the ski-school meeting point, we found Christoff. Angie didn't sidle up to him in her usual flirty manner but blew him a kiss instead.

'Morning all,' she said.

Neil was stood beside him, a pink glow to his cheeks, which suggested he had already been up for a first ski down. When he saw me, his warm eyes creased with a smile. I returned the smile, unable to conceal signs of heat radiating from my complexion as my veins involuntarily pulsated.

I lowered my eyes then glanced back up at Angie who had positioned herself to inspect us one by one, making sure we all had our goggles on our helmets before she set off for the lift with Neil. We then followed Christoff. Although the sky brightened, small white flakes continued to fall on us as we made our way to the nursery slope. At the bottom, Christoff instructed us to warm up by ploughing down a few times with our goggles on to get used to them. We made our way to the button lift, which the attendant was still banging snow from.

Christoff supervised our safe delivery onto the buttons and as I let the pole take me, I watched my skis part the fresh powdery snow and then lifted my head to enjoy the lovely smooth ride. Light flurries of snow whirled onto my face from the cable over-head, showering me with gentle kisses I interpreted as bliss. My numbness was gone.

Reaching the top of the lift, I released the button and carved, floating as I glided, traversing and turning the silky-covered piste. What had I ever feared, I wondered as I ploughed seamlessly down, repeating it several times, my stance steadily improving as I allowed my legs to relax and the skis to slide parallel after each turn. I barely noticed the mist curling down until it smeared my vision.

Christoff called us all and we gathered at the bottom of the slope. He adjusted his woollen beanie hat and removed his goggles from the pocket of his red jacket, placing the goggles over his hat, on his forehead.

'So, I see you are now ready ski on the mountain. We will take the gondola.'

'But we won't be able to see,' I said.

'It may be clear up there, but you have to learn in all conditions, Ginny,' he relayed seriously. 'You never know what to expect. The weather changes very quickly in mountains and you have to ski to get to the safety. I explain when we are up. I show you.'

'Of course.' I nodded, then filed behind as Christoff led us across a narrower path to a steeper slope, which we hadn't attempted before. I ploughed slowly before reaching the entrance to the main lift station. We copied Christoff as he took off his skis and clambered over to the steps. In heavy ski boots and carrying our skis, our loads were remarkably different to our previous ride for lunch. We arrived breathless as we got to the automatic turnstiles at the top of two long flights of steps. I watched other skiers in front of us as they entered the two gates, each with two turnstiles. The side panel flashed and gave a high-pitched bleep before releasing the turnstile and letting them through. I got through without fuss, but I heard Cathy squeal as we walked towards the car. I turned to see her dancing from side to side.

'If anyone's going awry, it's me. Always,' Cathy puffed as she twisted again. We each giggled as the attendant gesticulated to her from our side of the barriers and she fumbled with the pocket on her left breast.

'Put your skis in your other hand,' the attended bellowed over the noise of the rolling gondolas.

Cathy's eyes widened at the same time as her mouth as she realised she had blocked her signal. 'Oh, gosh, I didn't think,' she said switching her skis into her right hand and then she rushed forward as it flashed and bleeped.

'There's so many things to think about,' I assured Cathy knowing she was the one out of all of us who was less physically confident. I guess she imagined herself inferior in anything connected with sport. She was never into PE or games like us. After school or during lunch, whilst Lou, Kim and I were playing netball or hockey or rounders, Cathy preferred to be on a bench or at home with her nose in a book; she was by nature, less athletic. She was our greatest cheerleader, but not one of us could persuade her to take part.

I was surprised when she agreed to train with us at Angie's gym recently. 'You're doing very well actually, Cath. Just remember not to panic. That's the main thing,' I told her. 'We're all learning and I'm sure everything will fall into place. I hope so anyway,' I said, wondering if I was trying to convince myself too and nudging her arm as we scuttled to catch up with the others.

'Fingers crossed,' she said, rushing beside me. 'Thank goodness I got fit before I came. Angie prepared us well, I have to admit.'

'She knows her stuff, doesn't she?' I agreed, and I watched as a group in front of us rushed into a moving car. Christoff then stepped forward to the next car. He tossed his skis into a narrow slot at the front of the gondola then snatched Kim's and Lou's and slid them into the same slot, tapping Lou's arm to jump into the moving car. I lifted mine and slid them into the rear slot, which matched the front, whilst he took Cathy's. Cathy followed Kim into the car and Christoff waited as I climbed in trying my best not to be seen to panic. Christoff then shoved me along the bench before I heard the sound of the doors slamming and the cabin giving a wiggle and whisking us along and up into the brightness of the foggy air.

'Phew, that's fast,' Kim said craning back her neck.

'And no view. Very different to yesterday,' Lou said, scratching her glove on the window and wiping off a patch of condensation.

After a few seconds of silence, I asked Cathy, 'Have you heard from Anthony this morning?'

Cathy

I shook my head. 'No, but when I spoke to him last night, he seemed in a much better mood. I was saying to Lou and Angie last night – well, early hours of this morning – getting the boys to take him out was a terrific idea. He enjoyed the bowling and is looking forward to going again and the other things they've organised. I don't know why he gets himself in such a state when I'm not around. I did chuckle to myself though. I'm not sure if he knows that Terry was prompted.'

'It doesn't really matter if it has given him the kick he needed, does it? The important thing I suppose is for them to keep at it. Even when we're home, he needs to find something,' Ginny said.

'And I'm glad he went. The way he was acting and feeling sorry for himself, I thought he would make some excuse. He's been a nightmare this last year. I think he should have cut down on his hours rather than fully retired. He's not keen on amusing himself. I did suggest he speak to Chester – do you remember him, his business partner?'

Tilting her head, Ginny took a few moments. 'Yes, I do, is he Gordon the founder's son?'

With a nod, I said, 'Yes, that's right. You see, I'm sure he would appreciate Anthony's help a few days a week. I know it was stressful, but Anthony wouldn't have to take on so much as if it were still his business, maybe just a few clients. He loved the work and being around people.'

'Did he ever plan to do anything when he retired? Mike thought about it more than me. He would have loved the opportunity to retire and fulfil his dream of sailing around the Mediterranean. We had promised ourselves after we learned to sail with a flotilla in Greece that we would take further lessons and hire a charter yacht.'

'To travel. And that's probably where he went wrong.' I then corrected myself. 'Or, rather where we went wrong! We did so much that first year, dashing here there and everywhere to see the world in such a short space of time, we couldn't wait to get back home for a rest. Well, I couldn't, even though I was able to read and write anywhere, I wanted to be around my books, have my desk and computer without the hassle of recharging everything. I don't know. We should have paced ourselves and spread the trips out more evenly. We would have had something to look forward to every few months, at least.'

'Why don't you plan a ski trip with him? He's never skied, has he?' Lou suggested.

'Yes, you could teach him!' Kim said, prompting laughter.

I pulled a face. 'That would go down well, wouldn't it? Can you imagine!'

Christoff joined in with the laughter.

We continued suggesting what activities the Flowers could teach the boys only realising we had risen above the fog as we neared the top lift station. I suddenly felt nervous at the prospect of actually skiing on a real ski slope. As the car shuddered, the doors opened and Christoff stepped out and swiftly grabbed at the first skis. Ginny and I grabbed our own and switched apprehensive glances as we trailed the group. Although the sun was still refusing to appear from a murky sky, white peaks paraded luminously as though welcoming us.

Christoff gathered us a few feet from the lift. As I peered

around all I could see was peaks and clouds and several skiers standing in groups to my left on about a thirty-foot square of snow. Some were tightening boots or putting skis on and disappearing over an edge. Watching them made me quiver. How on earth could I ever teach Anthony? He would just bomb down regardless with his confidence. Or would he?

Was that where we were going?

Indeed, Christoff led us towards that very edge and threw down his skis.

Kim squealed first. 'Oh, my God. Look at that.'

'I know, I think we're going down it,' I said shakily as I trudged across to Christoff, wondering if Anthony would now have that same confidence. I tried to think of the last time he showed any great faith in himself like when he used to do diving, or track racing. I couldn't recall a recent incident. Even on our travels, I hadn't seen him dive into a pool. But maybe it was just his age. It disturbed me though, how much he had withdrawn recently – from everything.

As we put on our skis Christoff told us to stay close and take it steady. I was first on with my skis and jostled into position behind him, steeling myself as I watched the others. I couldn't look down, but I witnessed each face pale as they prepared.

'OK. Gently.' Christoff turned for the off and ploughed slowly across the slope. I swallowed, keeping my nerve, and ploughed behind seeing the run was only so wide so there was little room for error. He turned easily watching us and I now had to follow him round or slide off the edge. I felt my heart pounding, my teeth biting my bottom lip, my knees shaking as I turned, digging with my heel as I carved around to stop myself sliding. I was round but I was speeding up.

'Plough,' Christoff commanded.

Blowing out small breaths, I spread my heels out feeling the brakes but then jolted to a stop. 'I can't move,' I said, fearing that if I shifted another inch, I would slide. As I dared to look up, my stomach churned as I noted there was no netting, definitely no fences on the slope. I gripped in the snow with the edges of my skis. My body was half bent and I was aware that Kim was closing in behind.

'Relax and do what you were doing earlier,' she urged. 'Your turns were beautiful.'

'That's not helping,' I said, feeling hot and frozen at once.

'Go,' she said coming closer.

I took a deep breath and brought up my torso slightly, my teeth on edge as I gingerly let my skis go. I slid towards the edge, quickening, my heart stuck in my throat. I heard myself squeal. I was out of control heading for the next turn.

'Wheee! Whoo!' My legs miraculously took me, and I was round but spread-eagled into the widest plough. Carefully, slowly, I brought in my skis, carved, trying not to think about it. I ploughed towards Christoff following his tracks in the smooth snow around the next turn. Mindfully concentrating.

'Aaargh, no, no … aargh …' I then heard Lou telling me not to panic. How could we not panic? We were sliding on a steep mountain. Next, I slid past Ginny – on my side, head first, one ski scraping at the surface, one arm out and a hand desperately seeking a grip.

'Oh, Jeeees,' I shrieked as I headed straight down, my heart tumbling twice as fast.

Luckily, Christoff immediately whooshed into action; like lightning he was kneeling on his skis beside me, tugging my arm and spinning round like an acrobat to catch me. Within seconds, my limbs and body relaxed into the safety of his arms.

'Wow,' Ginny cheered as she passed. 'What a speedy rescue.'

As I breathed, a skier with one ski in her hand, passed it to Christoff, and skied off.

'Keep going,' Christoff instructed, peering up to the others as he lifted me to my feet. I was shaking as I gripped onto his arm with gratitude, my face feeling drained of lustre. Christoff knelt again whilst I clutched his shoulder to get my balance as he placed my loose ski onto the snow parallel with the first. He hammered down the binding with ease, then took my weight as he led my ski boot back in the ski and guided my heel down. I reluctantly let go of him as he slowly rose upright. He took my hand, a patient smile on his face as I composed myself.

'So, you skipped some slope—' he shrugged with mischief on his face '—and the worst is over.'

I giggled with relief, grateful to be alive as I rubbed the sides of my thighs before boldly filing behind Christoff to join the others.

'Well recovered. Are you OK?' Ginny said as I reached her. My knees and thighs now screamed with exertion.

'So scary,' I said. 'I saw my life flashing before me.'

'I can imagine,' Ginny said, covering her mouth. 'And thank God for Christoff. I wouldn't fancy facing Anthony with bad news.'

Thankfully, I found myself calming from the trauma but bruised with fright. What if something had happened to me and I never got to speak to Anthony again – ever? I wept for myself and Anthony as I carved over the smooth and level surface, wishing I could see him. Talk to him. Explain. Tell him I want to understand. One night out with the boys was not going to provide a resolve or bring all the answers. I had to talk to him, tell him I've been so blinded by what I've wanted to do these last few years, that I had barely considered or asked him where he was at. Perhaps he'd just got lost.

I felt a rush of love warm its way through me as I glided, picturing the man I fell in love with, the man that always gave me strength, nurtured me from a shy youth to the woman I had become. I steered warily as we took a right along a wide gently sloping ledge skirting the mountain. But as we rounded, I went suddenly blind. I gasped, taking short sharp breaths.

211

'I'm wrapped, that was awesome,' I said as Lou crept up beside me.

'Me too,' Lou said. 'I feel like a real skier now. We've got down our first real run in one piece. Poor Cath though. That did look frightening. I thought she was going to keep going.'

'I'm in awe. What a hero Christoff is!'

'Amazing. So fast and no panic. Ginny did well too, getting out of the way at that sticky bit.' I glanced up and braked fast. 'Fog.'

Lou braked beside me. 'Where did they go?'

Screwing up my eyes, I could see the large outline of Christoff, beside one of the long blue poles. 'This way,' I said to Lou and skied off towards him.

Christoff acknowledged us and turned, ready to go. Although thick at that last point, the fog thinned as we followed him down. He led us past a chairlift and down another wider slope, which wasn't quite so steep as that last. When we reached the end of a span of open snow, he stopped us by another blue post.

'So, when the fog is heavy, and you can't see, make sure you mentally note the posts. The posts on the right have a red top. The left-side ones are all blue. If you ski from one side to the next, you will be able to stay on the piste, safe. Just take your time. Is that clear?'

Happy we were all nodding in the right places, Christoff turned and we continued the lovely wide blue slope, which was not only cleared of fog but twinkled as the sun shone down. The warmth wrapped me. It was a much larger version of our nursery slope and I felt my heart lift as I sashayed contentedly across, creating fabulously neat turns. In fact, we all looked to be enjoying it and I'd almost forgotten about what I was going to say to Ginny. Whether I should say anything. I was still nervous, more concerned after hearing about Paula. Her being at the bowling was unsettling to say the least. I couldn't trust her not to say anything. And my sister had no scruples when she sought attention. I had to tell Ginny before it was too late. I knew I had to risk my friendship and somehow deal with that, but I felt I owed far more to my friend than my sister.

Reaching the end of the run and going down another smaller, steeper run to reach a path, Christoff led us to a four-man chairlift. As we queued, we watched as skiers positioned themselves after two small turnstiles, shuffling through smaller gates and along a matted platform to where the metal chair scooped them up. I'd been on one similar in Germany, so it didn't seem too intimidating. Cathy, however, was peering at me with apprehension. Ginny was psyching herself, whilst Lou was like an athlete, ready to sprint. We staggered forward as the little gates opened and managed to sit ourselves on as the chair swung around. I then pulled down the protective bar.

'Phew. We did it,' Cathy sighed.

Ginny pinched her nose as she laughed. 'It's one thing after another. I'm amazed I'm doing all this.'

'Aww, but doesn't it feel amazing? That long piste was incredible,' I said.

'I thoroughly enjoyed it,' Ginny answered. 'I really get it now after that. I mean, when you look around and see all the experienced and beautiful skiers serenely skirting around you, you understand the thrill.'

Cathy wriggled her legs. 'I can't believe I'm saying this, but I want to do that again.' She paused. 'Without the fall, of course.'

Lou roared. 'That was pretty spectacular, Cath. I wouldn't mind if you did that again.'

I felt a jab of pain on the side of my head when Cathy's helmet knocked mine as she tilted her head with indignation. 'You're incorrigible, Lulu Cavendish!' she said. Then added dryly, 'I'll have you in detention after lesson.'

'I just wish I'd had a camera running,' Lou added.

As we neared the top of the lift, I sighed. 'Now all we need to do is ski off.'

'Yikes, I'd forgotten about that,' Cathy squeaked. 'OK, Cathy Golding, just don't panic.'

The lift station was getting closer and I watched the one in front. 'Right, lower your skis off the bottom. I'm going to lift the bar,' I said. 'If we all ski forward first, we shouldn't crash.'

I heaved the bar up and sat back, then decided to go forward. The chair rose to the platform and as I saw the little slope, aimed to go straight, but the next thing I knew, we were all in a heap on the ground, bubbling with laughter.

Christoff steered around us as he skied off the chair behind us, the beam of a knowing smile stretching across his face.

'You have not let me down, ladies. You begin so well getting on the chairlift. It was too good,' he said, his accent so endearing, and reaching out his arm to pull Cathy clear from the landing area whilst we tittered, cherishing his irony.

After composing ourselves we ploughed on again, trailing behind Christoff until he stopped us. He described to us what he termed as shushing. This was, he assured us, nothing more than speeding up without turns in order to keep momentum on the uphill parts – bending forward if we needed to streamline ourselves. We filed behind, copying his movement. Speed increasing. I found it exhilarating. The air whooshed past me whilst I imagined the thrill of experienced skiers, like that of a bird, the swooshing and liberating rush of flight. I didn't want this moment to stop. Why hadn't I discovered this sooner? The adrenaline rush was addictive.

We shushed several wide paths behind Christoff and out to a big wide junction where we shushed until he slowed to make long turns, passing a pretty restaurant to yet another chairlift. The turns seemed so much easier even though we were going downhill faster and the slope steeper. This time it was a six-man chairlift – which we all managed to master in our breathless state climbing on, and arrived back to the top by the gondola, without a crash.

Angie was waiting with Neil for us at the bottom of the gondola and, along with Neil, was thrilled as she listened to us babbling about our breakthrough. The consensus was instant. We would skip lunch and go back up to do more skiing. I certainly didn't want to eat or drink, and the girls agreed. Even Cathy. Our enthusiasm was bubbling like Prosecco, but alcohol was the last thing on our minds. All we needed was Angie to guide us on the slopes.

We also invited Neil along, who skied behind us and his encouragement and praise helped tremendously – not to mention his camera skills. He obliged willingly as we handed our phones over to him or Angie for some shots of us skiing.

* * *

After our hard-earned baths and rest, we ventured out to La Poste at seven to finally eat, chatting incessantly about the thrills and spills of the day. Both Cathy and Ginny's confidence was buzzing. It's true to say we were so utterly proud and pleased with ourselves, I didn't want the day to end. I knew Will and the twins were proud of me too as I'd sent them some photos and a short video Angie had shot, and despite the time difference, they had WhatsApped me back with their cheery comments and emojis. Ginny sent some to Rachel and Ross, Lou to Terry and the girls, and Cathy had WhatsApped some to Anthony, though she was still waiting to hear back from him. She seemed really disappointed and more so when she rang and couldn't get hold of him.

I had, however, still been thinking of Ginny and continued battling with my conscience. As I'd warmed my aching muscles in the sumptuous bubbles in the bath, I'd reached a decision. I would tell Ginny about Mike and Paula. As much as I didn't want to hurt her or ruin what was the best time she had had since losing Mike, it was only fair that she heard the truth from me. But not tonight. No. I didn't have the heart. Tonight would be a celebration of our accomplishment and progress. I would selfishly take comfort in sharing with Ginny the magic of our friendship and what we had achieved this week before I shattered her world. I hoped Ginny would appreciate that gesture someday at least. I knew in my heart she wouldn't blame me, but the fact that I'd known for several months and not told her would hurt her tremendously. I needed to tell her privately. Face-to-face and before I returned to Oz and before anyone else did.

As luck would have it, a couple were just leaving our favourite table in La Poste. Our round one in the corner. Stefano was air-kissing his goodbyes and immediately turned to greet us too, sensing by our excitement that we were out to celebrate.

'You have a good day, ladies?'

Ginny beamed with pride, her cheeks glowing. 'Yes, thank you, Stefano. We are celebrating tonight. We are officially skiers.'

'*Magnifico!* So, I bring Champagne?' he said raising his hands. 'And feed you the best menu.'

Disposing of our jackets on the benches behind us, we gazed at one another. 'Heck, it's only money,' I said. 'My treat.'

'No, no,' they started, objections proffered my way.

'Yes, absolutely, yes,' I insisted. 'Tonight, my Flowers, you are my guests and I can't think of anyone better that I want to spend my money or my time on.'

'Are you sure?' Ginny, Lou and Angie said together as they sat down. Then suddenly Lou shot back up again, staring over my shoulder, her body shaking.

'Jimmy,' she voiced huskily to the person behind me.

'Lou, blimey, Lou. Good to see you,' Jimmy barked and bounded around me to take her in his huge arms.

I had only met him twice, years ago when Lou brought him to

216

Kent – once whilst they were still at uni, then at their engagement party in London, but it was obvious this was her ex. The guy she used to be crazy about. The guy she jilted to travel the world.

Jimmy stood to Lou's side. 'Guys, this is Lou. Gray, you must remember her?' He glanced from his mates with a beaming large grin and back to Lou, then at us – briefly. 'Let me get you a drink, babe. God, you still look amazing. Come and have a chat,' he said, grabbing her hand to drag her away.

Lou stood firm, blowing air from her lips as if to appear calm, but I could see her chest rising. 'We can chat here. Besides, there's nothing really to say. How come you're here?'

Locking eyes with her, he took Lou's hand, his broad stature braced, appearing chastened. 'We came on Saturday. I messaged you again several times on Facebook. Why didn't you answer?'

Lou bit her lip then said. 'Jimmy, I made that perfectly clear when I messaged you back. I'm happy in my marriage, I told you I was.'

'I know, I know. I respect that,' he said looking self-conscious as we all stayed rooted to our spots. 'Yeah, but you could have come and met an old friend for a drink, for Christ's sake.'

'But why? I have no wish to get involved with you again.'

Fidgeting with his wrist, aware that we and his mates were surrounding them, he said again, 'Let's just have a quick chat outside, please, babe?'

Lou retrieved her arm. 'No. Whatever you need to say, you can say it here. In fact, I'm with friends and there's nothing else we need to talk about.'

Jimmy looked irritated. 'You still owe me an apology for buggering off to Spain and calling it all off. You couldn't even tell me to my face.'

Lou shook her head. 'I wrote you a full explanation and apology nearly forty years ago. I can say sorry forty times if you really want me to, but get over it. You're clinging to the past. It's not my problem your marriage didn't work out.'

He took her wrist again. 'You were the only one, Lou. You've always been the only one. Andrea never came up to your standard. I mean, what we had was special and you know it.'

Lou folded her arms as he tried to grab her hand. 'Was. Past tense. My feelings are with someone else – the man I married. Jimmy, you have to accept that. I made that clear when you hassled me on Facebook and I can say it again if you didn't understand. There's nothing between us, and I'm here having fun on my holiday so, if you don't mind.'

'Just give me five minutes outside,' Jimmy persisted. 'Lou, don't deny you don't still feel something. I can feel it. Please, five minutes.'

'No, Jimmy. It was nice to see you, but now you should go.' Scratching her head nervously, Lou tried to sidestep him.

Jimmy stepped ahead of her. 'So you didn't deliberately post about this place?'

'I haven't. Why would I? I didn't even know you skied. In fact I didn't know I was coming here until about six months ago.'

'So how would I have found out?'

'No idea! Now, please let me sit down and go.' Lou raised her arm and addressed his friends. 'Take him away from me please.'

Ginny pushed her small frame between them and sat Lou down. 'Please, Jimmy. Lou has finished. You've both made your points clear, so let's leave it there.'

We girls sat back down around the table and, as promised, Stefano had left Champagne on ice in the bucket.

'Sorry, girls, can you give me five?' Lou said rubbing the back of her neck.

Chapter 15

Ginny

I couldn't believe my eyes when I saw Jimmy. Jimmy Dixon. Lou's ex-fiancé! The guy she met at university. I peered around twice to check. Yes, he still had those lovely chocolate eyes; yes, it was definitely the man Lou dumped years ago on her parents' advice – they managed to convince her she was too young!

I was devastated at the time because although we didn't see Lou and Jimmy very often, just by their smiles and affection when they were together, they ignited a room. They were so in love. And there was no doubt he could still turn heads; just a small beer pouch under his shirt, a receded hairline, which was greying, but he was still striking. No wonder Lou looked dazzled, like lightning just struck her! What a shock! I was certain she would still have feelings for him. I knew she regretted her decision, but I wasn't going to stand by and allow him to harass her. She loved Terry too and would never hurt him.

As I watched Jimmy and the three guys march to the other side of the room, I suddenly felt like an excited puppy at seeing Neil heading towards me, his expression wide-eyed.

'Is everything OK?'

'Yes, I think so.'

'Can I have a word? It's private,' he said.

I needed to stay with Lou. 'Can you give me a few minutes? Lou is upset.'

'Of course,' he said. 'Certainly, it can wait. Anything I can do?'

'Well, if trouble starts, there might be.' I swung to face Lou and then turned back to Neil. 'Things seem to be calming down. I'll come and find you shortly.'

Neil squeezed my shoulder and walked off, leaving my skin with a warm tremor.

'Are you OK, sweetheart?' I clutched Lou's arm as she gave me a frazzled stare. 'You might relax and forget after a glass of Champagne,' I said pointing to bottle in the bucket.

Angie immediately removed it from the ice and began to pour.

'I think they're going,' Kim said, gawping out of the window.

Lou let out a sigh. 'God, I hope so. I can't believe he's here. None of you have been in contact with him, have you?'

'No,' came the chorus.

Lou ran a hand down her face. 'I told him years ago we were a no go.'

I patted her hand. 'Yes. You were brave then and I know how much courage that took just now. I could wring out the chemistry that's still here between you.'

'Really? Yes, I felt it. I don't know who I'm trying to kid. That's why I didn't want to see him. I've not seen him since before I broke the engagement off. I thought I was over him. You know I love Terry.' Lou twisted her mouth, blowing out a cheek. 'I have thought about him, I can't deny it. It was, I don't know, about five years ago, soon after I joined Facebook, he got in contact and asked to meet up. I think he'd not long got divorced. He kept messaging and pestering, so I came off Facebook for a while.'

'I wonder how he knew you were here?' Angie enquired, like us, curious. It wasn't a highly commercial resort.

'I wondered that too,' Lou said. 'But I think I know now actually.'

'Oh, good, I like a mystery, solved,' Cathy said.'

Lou chuckled. 'Well, yes. I did go back on Facebook when you were in Australia, Ginny – to follow your updates. Jimmy hadn't got in contact, so I assumed it was safe again. Anyway, Lisa from uni posted a few months ago excited that she was going to ... somewhere skiing in Switzerland, and of course, I put on the thread that I was coming here. I just didn't think because I'd blocked him, but then, it's clear she's friends with him. That's the only time I've mentioned it on there. He's obviously been trolling.'

'Not trolling, darling. He hasn't provoked you there,' Cathy pointed out.

'Well, OK nosing, scouring Facebook, whatever the term is. He's been more subtle. Unless of course he's spoken to Lisa. Who knows? I shall be careful next time ... no. I just won't go on social media.'

I swept back a tuft of hair swirling on Lou's forehead. 'No, don't feel intimidated. You did what you thought was right, sweet. He's gone peacefully, so I think he got the message.'

'I shouldn't have spoken to him in the first place,' Lou said. 'I was a bit shocked, curious maybe, when he first got in contact.'

'Were you tempted to meet him?' Angie asked.

Lou dropped her head for several seconds, then looked up curling her lip. 'Actually, I was. That's awful, isn't it?'

'No,' I would be flattered if an ex got in touch,' Angie roared, grabbing the Champagne bottle and filling our glasses. 'I just didn't have any decent ones that were worth going back for. You were engaged to him, weren't you?'

Lou nodded. 'Yes, I thought the world of him.'

'You don't regret it now though, do you?' I asked.

'Not now.' Lou hunched her shoulders. 'I did for a while, but then I met Terry. And Terry was so much easier to get along with. For all our chemistry, Jimmy was intense. A bit scary at times.

He would never have been a good fit with all you guys like Terry is. And I suspect Jimmy would have been hard work. I mean as in highly possessive. I remember seeing a pic and comment on Facebook from a woman, maybe a friend of his wife's saying that Andrea, his wife, was so much happier now she was out of her cage.'

'Well, beautiful girl,' I said, subconsciously clasping both my hands, 'let's pray he stays out of your hair. By the sounds of it, you had a lucky escape.'

Lou dusted her shoulder with her other hand. 'Yes. Maybe Mum and Dad were shrewder than I thought. At the time it was painful, really hard going through the break-up with him. It does seem they found the right button to push.'

Cathy leaned forward, taking the stem of her full Champagne flute from Angie. 'Indeed, they were, my darling. Very wise. If they had warned you off him, you would have been infinitely more determined to stay with him.'

Lou nodded. 'Gosh, yes. And, thank God they had that insight!' she added dropping her chin as she digested the information. Then, as if analysing Cathy's argument internally, she paused momentarily before lifting her chin back up. Like her senses had jolted, a light beamed from her eyes. 'Well, that wraps that episode up, doesn't it? I can't believe I was even remotely tempted to go back there.'

Angie raised her flute in the air, encouraging us to mirror her. 'So, a double celebration tonight. You can thank your parents you got to travel and meet Terry instead of being trapped in a cage, and we can all claim officially to be skiers, you Flowers now having skied a blue run on a mountain.' She thrust her glass to Lou's. 'So, Flowers, to you. *Santé!*'

'*Santé*.' We chinked glasses. 'And forget him, Lou,' Angie said. 'Let's enjoy our evening.'

Lou stretched out her arms. 'Absolutely. Let's toast to our lovely day. I'm not wasting another thought on that man.'

'Hear, hear!' Kim said picking up a flute the same time as me.

'Here's to great a great day's skiing, my Flowers,' Kim said raising her glass, 'and to many more.'

We cheered as we chinked our Champagne flutes again.

We continued chatting and patting ourselves on the back, when Neil joined us at the table carrying a large beer and another bottle of Champagne. I couldn't believe I'd forgotten about him. He winked as he sat beside me. My insides took a tumble.

'A very well-earned cheers, girls!' he said, raising his beer. 'May I congratulate you on your terrific day. You looked amazing out there on the piste. You have every right to be celebrating. Well done to you all.'

'Thank you, Neil, cheers.' We chinked yet again, triumphantly.

Neil bestowed a sweet smile upon me, meeting my eyes as his glass tapped mine and despite the drama just a few minutes before, I readily lapped it up with my Champagne. 'Cheers,' I said exchanging glances with him, eagerly drinking in his eyes. Like Mike, he was such easy company, more serious, more rugged around the edges, but his energy pulsed in the same way, which gave me comfort. I wasn't sure after being cossetted at home for so long whether this was sobering or not. I'd never had much experience, with men or boys. And I'd barely communicated with the world for an age so how could I tell?

I turned away from him to see Angie and the others still hugging Lou, so whilst the girls nattered, I returned my focus on Neil, aware he had asked to speak to me. He must have seized his opportunity just as I was sifting my thoughts, because he bent towards me. He spoke softly, with his fingers entwined together. His fresh scent was becoming familiar.

'I hope you don't think this forward. I just wondered if you would like to come out with me tomorrow night, or Thursday?' He flashed a glance at the girls. 'Just the two of us, I mean.'

Slapping my chest, I wasn't surprised my fingers pounded along with my heart. Was he really asking me on a date? It must have been forty-five years, maybe forty-six, I couldn't remember. My mind whirled as I peered down at Neil's hands; his fingers were wriggling, possibly with nerves. I bit my lip, thinking of Mike. Wondering whether he would think me disloyal. That, and I felt like a shy teenager. I wasn't sure I was ready for any of this. Neil lightly touched my wrist, and I looked up to him, my skin reacting with a tepid shiver. He must have sensed my unease.

'Look,' he continued softly. 'I've never asked anyone since … well, since my wife Cheryl died.' I saw pain in his eyes as I studied him. 'I feel you should know that. And your loss is more recent, so I will understand.'

'A year,' I said fanning myself with my hand. I didn't really know what was considered recent in terms of dating. I hadn't thought about it.

'I would hate to make you feel uncomfortable, so please don't feel you have to answer me now. Maybe you are like me and need some adjusting. Time, I mean. Don't rush. You can let me know in the morning.'

I drew a breath, the girls' words ringing in my ears. 'No. I mean, yes. Why not?' I told Neil. Go have fun, Angie and Lou had said. 'I think I'd like that,' I added, surprising myself but knowing we couldn't go far. The girls would be close. 'Thank you, I'd like to come out with you.' My tongue felt like it was tying itself in knots. 'I'm sure the girls won't mind as long as I tell them where I'm going. Will we go far?'

Neil sat back and squeezed my fingers, relief washing over his face. 'Well, I'm chuffed. Thank you. I feel honoured that you've agreed. I had Ma Maison in mind – a smaller restaurant just along the road. It would be perfect. It's quieter and the food is delicious.'

The excitement in his eyes was enchanting and his expression considerably more relaxed. If he'd waited all this evening just for a refusal, I was syre sure he would have been equally charming. Whether he was telling the truth about not asking anyone since his wife passed wasn't terribly important. Over the few days I'd known him, he had been the perfect gentleman. There was no reason in my mind to doubt him. Besides, as Angie pointed out, I was a free woman, and on holiday. Near enough to the chalet to get home too, if I became uncomfortable. Mike was never coming back. Why shouldn't I have a little flutter, live a bit again?

I scooped my hand through the top of my hair. 'Sounds perfect. So, shall we say tomorrow?'

'I couldn't be happier. Tomorrow night it is,' he said, tapping his thighs with his palms. 'I'll book now and come along to your chalet at seven tomorrow if that's OK?'

'Lovely, Neil. I'll looking forward to it.'

'Me too,' he said looking pleased, and considerably less nervous. He drew his hands up from his legs clasping the bottom of his jacket. 'Right, I'm off to meet the guys at the Trappeurs for dinner. We might walk back up later; if not, I'll probably see you in the morning.'

I smiled back at those iridescent eyes surrounded by creases. As we glanced at the girls, they all cheered and clapped.

'Yay, go you two,' Angie roared, her eyes sharp.

'Woo, woo!' Lou cheered rolling her fist.

Kim leaned forward raising her right hand at me and instinctively, I raised mine. We smacked them together. 'High five, Ginny our blossoming Flower,' she boomed then smacked Neil's hand. 'High five, Neil,' she hailed.

He blushed. 'Thank you, ladies. Being so engrossed, it didn't occur to me you were all in earshot.

Cathy swirled her hair where her bob met her ear. 'Yes, we heard; well, the end of your conversation, and what a wonderful end to a perfect day. Nothing like a bit of romance to provide a happy ending. I think I could use some of this material for my novel. And Anthony will be so delighted for you. I can't wait to tell him.'

'Oh sweetheart, we haven't started yet!' Lou snorted. 'Let the

Champagne flow. This is special, Gin. Terry will be pleased for you too. My shout.'

'See you tomorrow, ladies.' Neil made his exit as we continued with our celebrations. Inside, I was still stunned, nervously shaking at my spontaneous decision, aware that, had he asked me the same question a day or two ago, I would never have consented. Maybe I was getting carried away in the moment, but it was done. I was going on a date.

Lucien, the waiter, brought out our first course. A mouth-watering light salad with a mustard dressing and a plated selection of charcuterie. Lou ordered another bottle of fizz as the conversation naturally led to Neil.

'So, where is Prince Charming carrying you off to tomorrow?' Angie asked, wiggling her eyebrows up and down seductively. She did look the image of Tina Turner tonight with her curls let wildly loose.

'The restaurant's a short walk that way.' I pointed. 'Ma Maison, it's called.'

'I know it. Fabulous. You'll love it. It's very Swiss,' Angie cheered.

Lou hugged herself. 'Ooh, sounds very romantic.'

'He's such a sweetie,' Kim said. 'You seem to get on really well.'

Licking my lips, I admitted, 'I'm so nervous. I know he's really easy to talk to and talking to him is like talking to an old friend, but now we're going on a proper date, I'm quite scared.'

'Aw, hon. Try not to overthink it,' Kim said, her slight Aussie drawl getting stronger with alcohol. 'It's going to be no different than talking to him here. It's not like you're going on a date with a total stranger. He's a lovely guy, and it must be quite exciting. You like him, right?'

I blushed, pinching the nobble of my nose. 'No disrespect to Mike, but I do. Not that I'm thinking anything more than holiday romance here, and even then—' I looked around me and whispered '—I don't think I could ... you know?'

'Shag, darling, the word is shag,' Angie blared bluntly rolling

226

up her sleeves. 'Clearly I know because that's all I've wanted to do since we've been here. I say go for it!'

I screwed up my nose. 'I couldn't.' I was so not ready for sex. 'Baby steps, I think.'

Kim agreed. 'Absolutely, go with the flow.'

Our next course arrived. It was a small dish of pasta ravioli drizzled in oil and sprinkled with fresh herbs.

'This is delicious,' Lou said swirling it around her mouth.

'Mm, very,' I agreed with my mouth full.

Cathy finished a mouthful, pointing her fork in the air. 'If you really like him, why not—' she lowered her voice '—shag him?'

I shook my head. 'One, I don't feel ready and two, I don't want to get myself in too deep. What happens if I really fall for him? Or possibly worse, hate myself for doing it and regret it for the rest of my life.'

'Oh, Jeez. Opportunity knocks, and she shuts the 'effin door!' Angie sprawled her arms on the table, almost knocking over the ice bucket. 'It's a bit of fun. No one is going to get hurt. You're a grown woman. A widow. No sex for God knows how long. Let yourself go, sweetie.'

I furrowed my brows. 'Any more Champagne anyone?' I asked, grabbing the bottle and topping up. However hard I tried I couldn't separate the old Ginny from the new. I was still Ginny Watts – wife and mother living in our family home in Camfield Bottom. Who was the single Ginny?

Next in front of us, Lucien placed a tiny sorbet.

'I happen to agree,' said Kim. 'Take it for what it is – a bit of fun.'

'But, from what he says, he hasn't been … or rather he says he hasn't asked anyone out since he lost his wife. He may not even want to.'

Angie winced and burst into laughter. 'You make me laugh, Ginny. If he's got a pair of bollocks, believe me, he wants it. All men want to do is fuck your brains out.'

'Angie, don't be so crude,' Lou said crossly. 'You'll put Ginny off. Darling, don't listen.'

Instantly my humour sharpened. I was never square. We all burst into boisterous laughter.

I was wiping the tears rolling down my face when Stefano appeared with another chilled bottle of Champagne and in his other hand a large ceramic dish of curried red cabbage, which he expertly placed down. Then, as he unleashed the next cork, Francesco the chef arrived with a delivery of a huge platter of large butter-fried steaks and crispy noisette potatoes, positioning it in the middle, whilst Lucien removed the cute little empty sorbet pots and replaced them with scorching plates.

'Enjoy ladies,' Stefan said, and Francesco nodded shyly before they turned to go. It all looked so beautifully cooked. I saw Cathy glance at Ang.

I picked up my knife and fork and dug my fork into the nearest steak realising there were five. Cathy and Angie were missing their pescatarian options. There was no way these girls would tuck into a steak.

'Oh, Stefan does know, doesn't he?' I asked, feeling confident we had told him.

'I'm sure he does,' Cathy affirmed. 'They'll be here separately; they usually are.'

I wasn't so sure. 'Lucien, can you check Stefan has two veggie options?' I asked.

Stefano appeared several minutes later with an iron pan sizzling with something alien to me.

'I sorry. I fuck up, ladies,' he said placing down the pan on the table. 'Salmon for you ladies.'

More giggles spouted from our mouths. 'Ooh, salmon,' I raved, recognising it among the beansprouts and quinoa. 'Looks lovely, I wondered what that was.'

The Champagne was beginning to make us giddy. Lou was pouring it down her throat like it was just about to go on rations.

'Yummy. Looks amazing,' Angie said as she and Cathy tucked in.

'So, getting back to you and Neil. You go and do what's right for you,' Kim said. 'We only want to see you happy and enjoying yourself.'

'How old is he by the way?' Lou slurred.

'No idea,' I said as I shrugged. 'Can't be much deviation from us. Possibly a bit younger.'

'Fifty-seven, I asked him,' Angie said chomping on her salmon. 'He was only married for ten years before his wife died, but they'd been together about twenty-five. Apparently, Cheryl was a divorcee, and her husband wouldn't divorce her or something. I'm sure he'll fill you in on the details. He'll definitely fill you in.'

Cathy's hand went to her mouth as they sniggered. I was beginning to tire of the jokes and smutty comments. They were wearing thin and I guessed I was becoming apprehensive.

The finale arrived – a succulent mango cheesecake with a miniature pot of crème brûlée beside it. I felt we were being treated like royalty. The food and service exquisite, attentive, and I began to wonder if Neil's plans for the following evening at Ma Maison could deliver food as fine.

Resting our palates, we opted for our favourite red Gamay to finish. Then it was time for the pièce de résistance: Lou's thoughts or, more precisely, what exactly had happened on Facebook. I was sure the others were as eager as I was to know about the previous contact with Jimmy, despite the fact that, even after meeting him for the first time tonight since their break-up, she seemed to have closed the chapter.

I peered across to her, her cheeks glowing compared to earlier. 'So, Lou, tell me to mind my own business, but I'm curious. What tempted you to respond when Jimmy first messaged you?'

Lou licked her lips as she finished her mouthful of steak. 'Mm, that's so juicy. Oh, embarrassing but, yes, I'm sure you're all gagging to know.' Lou proffered a drunken laugh as Lucien poured more bubbles into her glass. 'How shall I put this ... just to excuse ... no, that's the wrong word, erm ... let's say admit I suppose. I'm not sure what I'm trying to say, because those bubbles have frothed my brain, but anyway, stupid as it sounds, I was keen to see Jimmy again.' Her voice quickened. 'I thought, just the once. You know me – act first, ask questions later.'

'Yup. I thought I was crazy,' Angie said.

Lou's face turned stern, as she rolled her eyes at Angie. 'Oh, I'm not proud. God no. Far from it. I would never have hidden it if I wasn't ashamed. And there aren't many things I wouldn't own up to. As you know.' She hiccupped, and our sniggers must have infected her as she sniggered too. She hiccupped again, shaking her head with a giggle. 'Anyway, to say I was surprised is an understatement when I heard from him after so long. And I wrote back admitting that I did regret my decision, and I put that I missed him terribly whilst I was in Spain. Hmm. Yes, it was the worst thing I could have told him, because it only encouraged him. He was going to come to Kent. Gosh, when I think how I could have ruined everything.' She put down her knife. 'Then, about two hours later, when I'd calmed down a bit, I wrote and told him no. I was wrong. That what I said was in the past. I was truly happy with Terry and wouldn't betray him. Ever.'

Cathy sighed. 'Oh, darling.'

'No, not oh, darling,' Lou continued. 'I was wrong. I'd been a bit pissed off with Terry at the time. When I say pissed off, I mean it was more like I was in a rut. You know when life is a bit humdrum and there are lots of pressures, work pressures. Terry was on the site a lot when we were building at Rye, annoying me with this and that, getting tetchy when I kept on at him about the snagging. Said he had to now prioritise the new site, Rye could wait. I was livid. Clients want their new home finished, looking perfect; they don't want to wait. And, in my head was: there's not going to be a next site for me. I've had enough. The thought of the next thirty years or so with Terry wasn't thrilling.'

Lou waved a drunken hand. 'You know what I mean. Anyway, Jimmy appeared, I had said it, rather admitted it, even wrote saying how pissed off I was,' she hiccupped, 'so when I messaged him back again, of course he wasn't going to accept that. I'd fed him the bait.'

I cupped the side of my neck as I leaned forward. 'We all have those shit moments, off days, weeks. Jimmy obviously caught you on a low.'

'Yes, he was probably a tonic and sounded exciting,' Angie agreed.

Lou scratched the back of her neck. 'Oh, he did, believe me. But then I couldn't get rid of him. I got piles of messages, promising me the earth, offering me anything I wanted if I left Terry. He would look after me, he said. He has a house in southern Spain he said we could live in, but I could choose anywhere I wished to be. He could buy me anything my heart desired. He has his own jet! I could shop in any city, anytime.'

'Urgh, slime bucket,' Angie slurred, feigning sticking her fingers down her throat. 'Why would you want a jet when Terry has a very nice van?'

Our laughter roared through the room.

Lou looked at Angie with tears streaming down her face. 'My thoughts exactly. Ha ha! Do you remember that advert years ago, some soap I think it was, where that couple are in a bath in their luxury plane, looking out of the window and she says, "Bermuda looks nice, darling," and the plane takes an immediate dive towards it?'

'Yes! I remember. Wowzer, what are you missing, Lou?' Kim said wide-eyed as we glared back at her. 'Was it Imperial Leather?'

Lou shrugged. 'Something like that, I don't remember but sounds about right – I don't think I realised what a slippery character Jimmy was.'

Cathy sniggered. 'Maybe that's why his wife left him – she got bored of splashing into resorts, naked.'

Again, we laughed, the infectious giggling probably irritating other diners. I couldn't help but think of Mike and what state of mind he was in to deceive me. But I had to stop. I've moved on, I told myself.

Lou composed herself, wriggling into the back of her chair. 'I've never told Terry. But now you know, I hope we can keep it between us. I'm just so glad I saw sense.'

Kim cleared her throat, wiping her eyes. 'Of course, Lou. That's what friends do. And, what is clear is your instinct. You knew in your heart what you wanted. That was key. But, don't think you're alone in getting frustrated with Terry. Will irritates me no end at times.'

'Goodness me, if I had a penny for each time Anthony annoyed me, I'd give Bill Gates a run for his money. I thought it was just Anthony. It's quite a relief to hear you've got grumpy old men too.'

Listening to the girls, I totally empathised. However much I loved Mike, he could still drive me to despair. We regularly came to loggerheads because he would finish his day before me. He was often home by four and it made me cross when he couldn't take ten minutes of his time even to run the vacuum cleaner round or peel the vegetables for dinner. Men didn't seem to have that initiative around the house. Mike never spotted anything out of place or anything that needed picking up from the floor or taking upstairs. It was no wonder we women nagged. They needed constant reminding. I could understand that frustration Lou was feeling. I wondered now if Mike felt it about me. What is it we women don't see?

'Lou. Don't beat yourself up; you bravely told him straight tonight. No messing, no flustering, no flapping,' I added.

'Oh, absolutely,' Lou agreed ruffling her collar. 'It was a fleeting moment of flattery, I think. No, I'm certain of that now.' She smiled. 'I was stupid to encourage him. Well, it's been quite a week for confessions, hasn't it? Anyone else got any?'

Still curious about what she had actually said to him, I stretched my legs, stating my claim: 'I've told you mine, Flowers. It was such a release, too. And these revelations are providing some great entertainment, don't you think?'

'They are,' Lou said.

'Hmm.' Angie grimaced, half amused, staring distractedly into space. 'I'm definitely fired up,' she claimed, lacking conviction. She may have followed my thoughts but I got the impression her energy was waning, her bodily temple protesting at the toxicity of the alcohol.

'Oh, we'll be keeping an eye on you, sweetheart,' Lou said curling her tongue in her cheek. 'And, believe me, you'd have only regretted it.'

We chuckled, nodding in agreement.

Angie narrowed her eyes accusingly. 'I still don't know how I'm managing to contain myself. That man is so horny, but I'm trying my best. I'll convert that lust to lustre for change. I've so much buzzing in my head now that it's imploding.'

'That must be all our fitness programmes and diets you're organising,' I said.

'So much to do and think about. But that's a project for when we're home. I've half a week yet! I'll just have to steer clear of Christoff.'

'Well, in the meantime, borrow Cath's vibrator – just make sure you clean it after.' Lou thrust her finger at Cathy.

We each screamed, turning heads.

Cathy's face was aghast. 'I don't have a vibrator.'

'Oh, come on, Cath,' Lou jibed. 'We know you aren't talking to Anthony all that time alone in the room. Christ, we know you miss him, but don't be greedy, let someone else have some fun.'

Again, our raucous laughter shrilled through the room.

'With all your mess in there, I'd never find it if I had one,' Cathy hit back.

'*Touché, mon ami!* Anyway, Kim. You're keeping quiet. What have you got to confess?'

As the focus had moved on now from Lou to Kim, I repositioned myself, facing Kim, waiting as she studied the table, tapping her lips with her finger. I sensed she was trying to think of something. Or not.

Chapter 16

Kim

As Ginny stared at me, the sound of my accelerated heartbeat drummed in my ears. Was she able to read me? I wanted to swallow the lump in my throat but feared I'd give myself away. Instead, I rolled my head back, throwing my chin in the air. My head screamed at me to tell the truth, but I couldn't. I couldn't pop Ginny's rapturous bubble. Not yet. She was the happiest she'd been for a long time and she had the date to look forward to. It made every sense to lie. I felt all eyes boring into me as I searched the blurred depths of my brain to reach a snippet of alternative material.

Lou lifted her glass to her lips. 'There has to be something.' I sensed their impatience and felt myself crumbling.

I thrust my head forward, my brows furrowing under the weight. 'I really can't think of anything,' I blurted out. 'You all know my past, about my family, my background. Other than that, you're aware I was the most boring dedicated student, super eager to get good grades and do my mother proud. I never did drugs, unless given by a doctor. I met Will when I was a virgin. You know about the years of heartache, not able to conceive. IVF.

Then getting two angels together. Hats off for finding the strength to fight the temptation though, Lou – and Ang.' I looked at Lou, crossing my legs as I sat back, the topics of infidelity and temptation rolling around my conscience. I couldn't look at Ginny. But suddenly a little ovary of an idea released.

'Oh, actually, there is something. One crazy notion I had. Yup, mega embarrassing.' I cringed, then laughed. 'It was years ago when Will and I were trying. I suppose we'd been at it for about four or five years and we'd already been to see the specialist and gone through three IVF programs. I was desperate I suppose – the maternal bug that eats away at you, or at me at least.'

'Well, come on, spit it out, Kim,' Angie said; in fact, all of them were sitting forward as though waiting to snatch the first word.

I rubbed the sides of my legs feeling sweat in my palms. 'It sounds so idiotic but at the time I was desperate.' I heaved in a breath. 'I asked a guy to impregnate me,' I admitted. My eyes scanned for evidence of horror. And, if raised eyebrows and dropped jaws were evidence, I had it.

'Oh wow! Who was he?' Cathy asked.

I continued. 'We were still in Sydney then. I needed something to get me out. Spending time with horses was something I missed from when I used to go along with Ginny and Lou. So, I found somewhere to ride; a place called Centennial Park close to the city. It was a huge park but sometimes a group of us would go along to a wild spot, called Hidden Valley. It's about an hour north of the city with forest trails, creek crossings, et cetera. Anyway, Tom – this guy in the group – was single, great company and we got on really well, in that brother-stroke-sisterly way. He used to drive us to Hidden Valley, and sometimes if there were more of the group joining us and someone else drove, I got in with Tom and it was just the two of us. We spoke about things, his girlfriends, his family, my family, Will and my longing for a baby. He knew the background. Sympathised but was never forthcoming or encouraging me to ask him. This was totally me! And, for some crazy reason one day, I thought it would be a good idea to ask him if he would father my child. No commitment. Just do the deed and Will would be the father. Safe to say, after his flat no, our friendship hit the floor. It was awful. I couldn't face him again. It was a painful journey returning to Sydney that day. He was pretty disgusted, and the silence as we drove back was elephantine.'

'I'm sure he understood you were desperate,' Ginny said. 'But maybe he took offence because he fancied you himself.'

I grimaced. 'Unlikely – I don't think I was his type. He wasn't mine, but he was intelligent and had nice features close enough to Will's that I thought I could get away with it. But, yes, he understood or said he did. I think he was more shocked that I'd even consider it.' I then sneered. 'He said I'd watched too many movies and it wasn't like that in the real world.'

'You poor love,' Cathy sighed.

'Silly woman, you mean. Like I said, those were desperate times and I suppose I was grappling for a scrap of hope.'

Lou swiped her brow. 'I can imagine. I was pulling my hair out after just a few months. Luckily, I fell after about eight. I completely get it though. That maternal instinct takes over your life, doesn't it?' she said and reached her hand out to mine. She folded it under leaving her thumb to caress the top. 'I don't think we realised the extent of what you were going through, sweetheart. I'm sorry we couldn't be with you during those dark days.'

'I chose to move to Oz. With Will, of course. We were young and had our future to look forward to. New jobs, new horizons. I missed you all so much though, especially then.' I felt myself choking up. 'And now. Now the girls are grown, and in Europe, I so wish I could up sticks and come home.'

'You will, sweetie,' Ginny said, wrapping her arm around my shoulder.

Immediately, I burst into tears. 'Please don't,' I said pulling away from Ginny. 'You'll make me worse and I … I don't deserve it. Really.'

'Don't be so bloody ridiculous.' Ginny's eyes spilled with tears too. 'You're the next best thing I have to a sister. I was heartbroken when you left. You're welcome to come home anytime. Crikey, I don't need all that space.'

I wanted to scream: *You wouldn't be saying that if you knew how much my sister and I had betrayed you.*

Lou reached her arm out again, catching my fingers. 'Will needs a bit more persuasion, that's all. Why don't you visit us more often or lengthen your stays here? He'll soon get the hint.'

'Maybe.' I lowered my head. 'I sometimes think he should have married his job instead of me.' I sniffed, wiping my eyes. It slipped out. That statement was unnecessary. Will meant everything to me still, and I didn't need to betray him. Cathy picked up a clean serviette and thrust it in front of me. I unfolded it and blew my nose. I didn't deserve this attention and I certainly didn't wish my friends to think I was feeling sorry for myself. 'Honestly, I'm fine. I don't know where that came from. I'm just having a moment.'

I blinked a few times urging the tears to stop whilst remembering Will's face the moment Bob, our reproductive endocrinologist, told us we were pregnant. He had become our friend throughout the IVF and offered to do a proper test and a scan shortly after I realised I was late and did a home test. Will thought I was having a phantom. I remember watching Will though. He took my hand and braced himself, tightening his lips, then nibbling them. He looked into my eyes before he turned his gaze back to Bob. I felt his tension run up my arm and as his jaw dropped his wrist flexed. 'Bob, not the time to joke,' was his response to the news. As if Bob would joke – a professional and, increasingly, a dear friend. Bob shrugged nonchalantly. Will then jumped up, twisting my arm with the force. 'There's really a sprog in there?' He patted my belly with his other hand.

Bob held up two fingers. 'Not one but two.' Will turned to me with his mouth open and grabbed my legs, the mass of his arms crushing them as I flew up in the air. 'The egg split. Two embryos. You have identical twins, Will,' Bob confirmed as Will kissed my belly and put me back down on earth. 'Congratulations, Kim,' Bob said planting a celebratory kiss on my cheek. 'Congratulations, Will.' He held out his hand. Will took it, shook it and kissed it. We often refer to that magical moment. And did so after the last big row about Will retiring and us returning home to London. It was always the perfect anecdote to make up. I wiped my eyes again.

This was ridiculous. I fanned my hand in front of my face. Where was all this emotion coming from? I drew in my breath. 'Sorry, sorry. Clearly, I … my heart's telling me something. It's saying time to return and spend time with you all. Have fun times like we've had tonight, this week.' I forced a smile, my guilt spilling into my blood urging release. 'Let's enjoy our evening, Flowers,' I said, fearing this could be the last, the end of a beautiful friendship. Although, it occurred to me, telling Ginny tomorrow wasn't good either. I couldn't ruin her date. I steered the subject in a different direction. 'We could even go and try the late bar downstairs. Is it The Pub, they call it? Is anyone up for that?'

Ginny

A brilliant sunny day greeted us, but we were late meeting Christoff the following morning and feeling extremely delicate, despite rehydrating and taking painkillers. The excited fluttering in my stomach due to anticipating my date didn't help matters. Not that we were terribly late getting back but with the alcohol and all the dancing, not forgetting the skiing, we had pushed ourselves to the limit. We began our uphill slog to the nursery slope. Each of us was quiet, possibly psyching up for our ski or locked in thought. I had thoroughly enjoyed our celebrations, the meal, Champagne, dancing, drunken banter as well as hearing revelations from my friends. So funny when I thought about it. What we hide!

Whilst Lou's incident wasn't exactly carnage, her assertive, deal-with-it attitude was commendable. Giving Jimmy up once was heart-wrenching for her, then going to Spain alone, but to resist him the second time around showed what strong stuff she was made of. In so many ways, I've always admired her brave approach to life. She has always been willing to jump in, try new things and put herself out there. I watched her drive a motorbike over a car once! My heart in my mouth, naturally. But, I've also seen her running into a road to chase a straying child's stroller, saving the child's life. I wished I could be more like that sometimes and I'm not surprised she had a skeleton in her closet. I think she probably has a few more.

And, Kim, bless her. A tough cookie on the outside, but I still loved to mother Kim – wrap a protective coat around her soft centre. But desperate times could make us crazy and called for desperate measures, I supposed. She was human and vulnerable like all of us. I believed she thought it was worth a punt to keep her sanity. It was times like that you needed your friends. Not something I would have done, but then who knew what I might have done in her situation. The maternal drive in women can be incredibly overpowering. My Ross's arrival was sooner than I'd anticipated, just after I'd come off the pill, so I was ill qualified to judge or totally understand. I felt relieved the man refused Kim, if I'm honest. And karma paid her.

That aside, judging from the emotional outburst last night, Kim was clearly feeling alone. That saddened me. It was painful to see her cry. I sensed it when I was there last year; it was evident that Will's focus was on his latest project. Will was a lovely guy, I admired his dedication, his standing in the cancer research field – he was a great doctor. But now the girls were independent and the nest was empty, Kim needed him. And us. I would love Kim to come back to the UK; maybe she could lengthen her stays, for now, until she can persuade Will. I was certainly going to make the most of her company this week.

Again, Christoff recommended we warm up on the nursery slope before skiing over to the gondola to take us back to the blue run we'd skied the previous day. The morning's lesson flew by as we managed two runs down to the two-man chair, our ploughs improving, and I paid particular attention to Christoff's demonstration, working harder to get my skis parallel and my turns neater. I found the turns easier and increased my speed, though I was still careful to stay in control. A skill, Christoff told us, that women seemed to master so much quicker than men – who tended, he told us, to race fearlessly until they crashed!

'You will be safer skiers,' he told us at the end of the lesson when we travelled down in the gondola to meet Angie and Neil.

Florian and Tom were with them as we arrived and so we all made our way across the road to the Belleview for lunch. Angie sat with Cathy without monopolising Christoff's attention for once. Seeing Neil, the butterflies in my tummy began flapping their wings again, but once we had sat down, ordered drinks and lunch, we looked out from the warm terrace and admired the scenery. He pointed out villages and towns in the valley. He indicated dairy farms, fruit growers, winemakers, local industry, smaller engineering businesses, service industries, and explained the commerce and their contribution to the canton and its population. I quickly became absorbed. Neil had got to know the area well and had versed himself well with the local trade.

'There's still a great deal of traditional bargaining that goes on between producers, wine for cheese, fish for meat or fruit – that sort of thing,' he said. 'Makes so much sense.'

I smiled. 'A tradition we seem to have lost in England. That's lovely.'

'I love it here. I'd love to take you along to the lake. Have you been to Lake Léman?'

Shaking my head, I said, 'No. I haven't. And, annoyingly, I was asleep in the car when we drove from the airport, so I didn't see it then either.'

'That's a shame.' Neil's head tilted to one side displaying a small scar just under his chin. He had youthful skin considering his mass of creamy-grey hair and, with weather exposure, his skin was turning golden from the sun.

'I'll make a point of looking out on the way back.'

'And, such a shame you're not staying longer,' he said. 'There's so much here to see. Are you still OK for tonight?'

I didn't hesitate. 'Absolutely, I'm really looking forward to it.'

'Good. I'm glad. No relieved, to be precise. Me too. In fact—' he looked at his watch and briefly rolled his eyes '—I'm afraid I have to go. I'm just going along to get my hair trimmed so …' He picked up his helmet and gloves. 'I'll see you at your chalet at seven.'

After an exhausting afternoon's ski, my legs yearned for some relief, and the long bubbly soak was utter bliss especially with my Kindle and a glass of wine for company. The girls had gone into La Poste for wine and the hope of a slice or two of Stefano's famous freshly baked après-ski pizza – an amazing way to lure customers in if ever I tasted one. They left me to get myself dolled up for my date. Because I forgot to top up my face with sun cream, however, my nose and cheeks steamed in the heat and when I climbed out and saw my face in the mirror, I was horrified. How on earth could I go on a date looking like a clown?

It was ten to seven and, although dressed and ready, as best I could with my make-up anyway, I looked in the mirror as I reached the bottom of the stairs and the beacon on my face was still alight. I poured myself another wine wondering if I should go back up and rummage through the girls' make-up bags. Fortunately, the girls swaggered in from the bar and immediately spotted my problem. Quelle surprise!

'Oh, Jeez, look at you, my Pommie fleur,' Kim slurred trying hard not to laugh and rushing up the stairs. 'I'll get my concealer.'

At that moment I heard the doorbell ring and, after freezing momentarily, I dashed up after her. 'Pl ... please pour Neil a drink,' I yelled as panic caught my breath.

'Oh, quick, he can't see me like this,' I squealed to Kim, hopping behind her as she dove into her make-up bag.

Angie rushed in behind us. 'I might have some too, but I'm sure it will be too dark for your skin tone.'

'This should fix it, honey.' Kim unfurled the beige stick and pressed on my shoulder. 'Sit down on the bed,' she ordered, and leant over tapping the creamy substance lightly on my nose and cheeks. She tapped her finger over the cream and then gently rubbed the skin around my nose, blending, then adding more. She did the same to the roses on my cheeks and stood back. 'Ace. Just a bit more, here.' She laughed. 'Much better. Lucky, we caught you in time. You looked like Truly Scrumptious dressed as a life-size doll. Oh, what was the film?'

'*Chitty Chitty Bang Bang*,' I said. 'Thank God you came back. Are you sure it looks OK?'

She laughed again along with Angie who was scooping back a stray hair from my forehead and feathering the top with her fingers. 'You look gorgeous, sweetheart. Neil won't notice. Promise. But take this with you and when you pop to the ladies', you can top up. It may be warm.'

'Flowers, you are my saviours,' I said getting back on my feet and taking the stick of concealer and sticking it into my jeans pocket.

Angie looked me up and down. 'Beautiful. I love your top, goes lovely with the stone jeans; the cream really suits you—' she giggled again '—especially with a bit of colour.'

I raised my hand to my face. 'Don't. Can you still see it?'

She rocked her head from side to side, pursing her lips. 'No, but you have that sun-kissed glow and it suits you. Really. You look amazing.'

'You do. So go. Have a terrific time.' Kim held out her arms and squeezed me, careful not to crease me.

Angie then swathed her arms around me too. 'Enjoy, beautiful girl,' she said, pulling me close and patting her hand on my back. 'Have as much fun as you can muster – while you can. You won't believe how jealous I am!'

It was my turn to laugh. 'Aww, get real. You're too smart to do anything stupid,' I told Angie as I stepped back from her arms and checked myself in the mirror. Kim had done a terrific job and thankfully, in the panic, my nerves had all but disappeared. 'And remember, focus on keeping us all fit. Especially if we are going to go to Machu Picchu or Nepal.'

'I'm so excited,' Angie squealed, her eyes rolling from me to Kim.

'Angie baby, I'm coming even if it's to keep you out of mischief,' I assured her.

'Me too.' Kim smiled.

She jumped in the air. 'I'm so excited. We definitely need to up our fitness.'

I kissed her cheek as I passed her and headed for the stairs.

Neil, looking dashing in dark navy jeans and a mint green polo shirt, took my hand as I reached the bottom of the stairs. 'Wow,' he said, 'you look lovely. As always, but … simply beautiful.'

I smiled, feeling calm, Kim and Angie circling me as they followed. I felt all eyes on us. 'Thank you, Neil,' I said air-kissing his cheeks the Swiss way; three times. 'You look very smart too. Did the Flowers get you a drink?'

He nodded. 'Indeed, the Flowers have been perfect hosts. I've got a beer and Cathy topped up your wine. One can only hope the food and service is matched at Ma Maison.'

'Oh, you smooth-talker you,' Angie said, affectionately squeezing his arm. She gazed at me and smirked. 'He didn't stop jabbering about you all morning. I couldn't get him back on the slopes after we stopped.'

The room filled with laughter and as Cathy handed me my wine, Lou gave a toast. 'Here's to two wonderful people and to a lovely evening. *Santé!*'

244

'*Santé*,' we cheered.

'And, here's to Angie's fund-raising trek.' I explained to Neil: 'We've pledged to go with Angie to raise money for a cancer charity. Machu Picchu or Nepal, we're hoping.'

'Wow, you ladies get bolder by the minute,' Neil enthused. 'That's five sponsorships I'll have to find – whoa, what's in the cupboard?' We cackled as Neil stepped towards the kitchen in jest, then winked before stepping back and taking my hand. 'Sorry, I wouldn't miss this dinner date for the world. Ready?'

'Indeed, I am.' I smiled back at him.

The girls air-kissed us. 'Think of us scraping around the empty cupboards,' Lou said.

'And don't do anything I wouldn't do,' Angie sniggered.

I would have cried if I hadn't rendered my face with so much make-up. 'I love you, Flowers – you are the best!' Gathering my coat and bag, I swanned out of the chalet feeling like Cinderella.

Chapter 17

Cathy

I couldn't deny that seeing Ginny holding hands with a man other than Mike was a little disconcerting, but it was truly poignant to witness the change in her in just a few days. Her posture, the brightening of her eyes, watching her smile radiate as she strode happily out of the door; I found it so rewarding to watch. This trip had worked wonders already, so all our efforts had paid off, I thought smiling to myself as the door closed.

I bounced out of my reverie and picked up my phone, once again trying to contact Anthony. I was bursting to tell him the news and to have a chat. Again, it went to voicemail. It didn't make sense. After all his calling and pestering me, he was now ignoring me. I cursed myself too for insisting we disconnect the house phone before we went off for the year travelling. We both had mobiles. The internet. What was the point when it didn't get used? I slipped my phone back into my pocket and then it suddenly shrilled into life. Kim said something as I hit the button. I mouthed to her it was Ant before curling up on the sofa.

'Darling, I've been trying to get hold of you; where have you been?'

Anthony captured his breath. 'Sorry, love, I was so busy I forgot to charge my phone yesterday, so it's been here at home whilst I was out at golf all day.'

'Didn't you see my messages?' I asked, quickly screwing up my face. After that petrifying fall, I had decided not to evoke any arguments when I next spoke to him.

'I've just come in the door. So, are you OK?'

'Yes, fine. I …'

'Cath, look,' he interrupted. 'I'm sorry about the other day. I shouldn't have let off steam like that. You were right: it wasn't the right time. I was missing you and feeling sorry for myself.'

'But, darling, I couldn't help feeling that some of what you said was true. It's been on my mind and I'm keen to have a chat with you about it when I get back. There's an element of me that I accept needs addressing. I have been preoccupied with my writing and feel I should spend a bit more time with you. We should do more things together, is what I'm saying.'

'Yes and no, Cathy. Yes, a day or two a week would be great to get out and about. Like we used to. Visit the coast or go for a walk by the river at Hampton Court, or the odd weekend away.'

I gripped the bottom of my fleece as my lips wobbled. 'Oh, Ant darling, that would be lovely, yes, I could manage my writing routine better so that we do more.'

'But, to be honest, I've been in a rut. I was talking to Terry and Rob about it yesterday. I need to do something. I'm not sure I should have fully retired and I'm considering looking around for options. I know I'll need to get my head into gear, maybe start running again—' he paused '—stop drinking so much. But it's stuff I can work on. I love you, Cath.'

I sniffled involuntarily. 'And, I love you too, Anthony.' I composed myself. 'Darling, I had a scary fall which has given me quite a jolt actually.'

'What do you mean a fall? Were you hurt? I'll come and get you, drive over …'

'No, darling, don't panic, it was nothing major or critical, no damage done, just a jolt to my senses more than anything. I slid ...'

'Oh, God, Cath, you be careful. Are you skiing again?'

'Yes, and I did go and ski again after it happened. I'm made of tough stuff, surprisingly, tougher than I imagined. Maybe we could come together next year. Darling, you would love it.'

'It all sounds pretty dangerous to me.'

I chuckled. 'That's what I thought, darling, but really, it's lovely. It's beautiful, the scenery, it's sunny most days, the skiing's hard work on your legs but you find yourself wanting to get to the next level. And the après-ski is just down your street, a fabulous ambience in most of the restaurants and bars. And Ginny is out on a date tonight.'

The silence was deafening. I remained silent too, interested to gauge his reaction, especially as he had worked himself up previously about the behaviour of men away from home. I thought he would be pleased.

'Do you all approve of this man she is out on a date with? Is he married? Do you know where he's taken her? I'm not getting great vibes from this ski trip, Cathy.'

'Darling, don't panic. He's widowed too. He's very nice and Ginny likes him. That's all we need to worry about. She's come a long way this week; it's done her good. And, they're not far away from the chalet. It's only a small village. He's met us all a few times and none of us have any undue concerns. We're just happy the spring is back in her step.'

He cleared his throat. 'Well, as long as she's OK. You don't seem worried. But who knows what an axe-murderer looks like?'

'Darling, we would have used every power possible if we had any doubts, I can assure you. Now, be happy for her. She's entitled to move on with her life any way she pleases.'

248

'Of course, I'm happy for her. Let her know, too.'

'I will, darling, and I'm looking forward to seeing you. We'll have a lovely chat, OK?'

Kim

'Ginny looked so happy,' I said to the girls as she and Neil left, but my heart was still torn – how could I burst that blissful bubble? I turned to Cathy who had just answered her phone.

'She was,' she said and gestured, waving the phone, mouthing it was Ant. She slumped on the sofa.

'Exciting. I'm so jelo,' Angie shouted from the downstairs cloakroom.

I waded across to the kitchen behind Lou who was leaning in the fridge. 'Lou. You can't still be hungry after all that pizza?' I asked.

'No, but I do fancy something sweet. The chocolates are finished and there's only one yoghurt.'

'And the supermarket is now closed,' I told her, glancing at my watch. I pondered for a few seconds. 'Why don't we shower and go out to the Trappeurs? I saw people eating crepes there the other night.'

Lou's eyes popped out almost hitting the ceiling. 'Great idea. Let's.'

Angie came out of the loo. 'What's that?'

Cathy finished her phone call. 'What's going on?'

'Do you fancy crepes? I thought we could shower and go along to Les Trappeurs, have a drink and a crepe.'

Patting her stomach, Cathy puffed out her cheeks. 'I've had more than enough to eat. But feel free to go. Now Anthony's settled a bit, I'd quite enjoy curling up in the bath with my book. I'm exhausted. We haven't stopped all week.'

'Me too,' Angie said. 'I fancy a nice hot bath and listening to some music.'

I glanced at Cathy. 'That was a short call; is Anthony OK?'

'Yes, thank goodness. Getting back some perspective it seems, and possibly tired after being out in the fresh air playing golf.' Cathy gave a little clap accompanied by a wriggle. 'Well done, Terry and Rob. Thank them for me.'

Lou clapped cheerfully too, leaning over the kitchen counter and picking three sachets of hot chocolate out of the dish. 'Fantastic news, sweetheart. I must thank Terry. And look what I've found.' She waved the sachets in the air. 'So, three hot choccies and a yoghurt – who wants the yoghurt?'

Cathy laughed. 'Not you, darling, clearly. I'm happy with the yoghurt,' she said picking up her Kindle and heading for the stairs. 'I will eat it after my bath.'

Angie followed Cathy. 'Could you bring my chocolate up, please, Lou? I'm going to run my bath too.'

Whilst Cathy and Angie disappeared upstairs, Lou and I got cracking, finding the biggest mugs at the rear of a top cupboard to fill with our milky chocolates.

'A quiet night in then?' I said to Lou, half-filling the first mug with milk and putting it in the microwave.

She scrunched her nose. 'I know, sweet. It's criminal when there's so much to do, but it will do us more good than harm, I suspect. It's been quite a rollercoaster this week, hasn't it?'

'It has,' I admitted with a sigh, feeling the angst of the next big dip. I feared that if we sat and chatted, I could very well end up spilling everything out to Lou.

Lou half-filled the next mug with milk, then the next. 'I'm glad all our secrets are out,' she said. 'I'd virtually buried that Jimmy episode. Can't believe he turned up here! But it felt liberating, knowing I have nothing hidden from my friends. His lure at the time was far more excruciating though. I can't believe I was actually contemplating going to see him. Can you imagine?

Terry and the kids would have been devastated. And I love Terry so much.'

I reached out and hugged Lou. 'You followed what was in your beautiful heart, honey,' I said, squeezing her tighter. 'If it feels right, then it is.'

'What would we do without one another?' Lou asked giving me a final squeeze.

I dropped my arms and shuffled back to the microwave and replaced the first mug with the next, pouring the sachet and water in and stirring. 'Impossible to imagine, hon. Here. You have the first choc,' I said passing the chocolate-filled mug to her. 'There must be people who are lonely, castigated for something or other. I doubt anyone can go through life without something damaging them. Your perspective changes as you become older, certainly. I wouldn't dream of doing what I did back then, asking a guy to impregnate me. I must have been mad.'

'Kimmy. Sweetheart. Don't fret about it,' Lou said. 'None of us know what lengths we can be driven to until pushed. It's turned out perfectly. You and Will have two beautiful girls. I have Terry, Emma and Ollie. I just can't imagine living life with another man and having other children or grandchildren. Crazy thought!'

'Poor Ginny. No Mike now.' I watched the mug in the micro-wave turning as my own conscience spiked. I had a vision of Ginny's now happy, smiling face, which then turned distraught. 'Do you think she will marry again?'

Lou leant on the worktop, biting her lip. 'I don't know. She's a grown woman capable of deciding for herself. I would say she would prefer to have a man in her life. It may be a generational thing; we are all used to having men in our lives unlike girls nowadays.'

'Yes, a different world now. Less dependent. Youngsters seem to have financial independence as well as a self-assurance about them that we didn't have. I'm sure they are still self-conscious though despite appearances. Besides, they are so much more self-aware and used to photographing themselves. They post on Instagram, Facebook, Twitter, Chat this and that – their life is on social media. They're informed. Photos and news items are on social media before a newspaper reporter has time to write anything. Such a different world to ours when we were young. Even friends are virtual.'

I put the last mug in the microwave and mixed the second chocolate, my throat tightening as I contemplated the outcome after my conversation with Ginny. 'I really couldn't imagine only having virtual friends. I need my beautiful Flowers.'

'I know, it's crazy how far technology has leapt. From barely a radio in the home a hundred years ago, we're almost beaming one another up.'

'Good ol' *Star Trek*. Decades ahead,' I said. 'All going well, I reckon Ginny and Neil could have virtual dates. They can at least Skype now, can't they?'

Lou laughed. 'Wouldn't be my idea of a date, if you know what I mean!'

My face screwed up. 'Nah! Definitely not. I'll just run this up to Ang.'

We heard the sound of a phone beep. 'That's probably mine,' Lou said, waving her hand. 'Terry said he'd text me when he got home. I'll ring him back in a bit.'

Lou and I drained our mugs of chocolate chatting for another hour before she rang Terry. I left her on the phone and hoped that Angie had finished in the bath.

The stench of nail polish swiped my nostrils as I entered the bedroom. Angie looked up from painting her toenails.

'I wonder how the date's going?' she said.

'Good, hopefully.' I sighed as the anxiety I was trying desperately to contain stirred again. I unclipped my watch, noting the time. It was gone nine. Neil was a gentleman. I figured by the time I'd had a bath, Ginny would be back. We definitely had to talk.

Ginny

Ma Maison was a Christmas card. A verandaed log cabin blanketed in thick snow and nestled in snow on an edge overlooking the distant village of Isérables and its glistening lights, surrounded by a magical navy sky twinkling with luminous stars. I could almost touch it, feel its glitter sprinkling on my tongue.

I'd stopped walking, I realised. 'It's stunning, Neil,' I said, the romance of the vision swelling my heart.

'I thought you'd like it. But it does look exceptionally beautiful tonight,' Neil said, looking up to the stars. 'They've put on a show for you.'

'Ha ha! Well, I'm impressed,' I said, stepping forward while leaning on Neil's arm. Neil had taken my hand the minute we left the chalet, placing it on his arm, and it didn't feel awkward at all. In fact, I felt honoured he felt so comfortable with me.

Inside Ma Maison the first thing my eyes set on was the huge burning logs in the fire. I could hear a gentle crackling as it blazed. The maître d', on seeing us, instantly offered to take our coats and led us over the stone floor to a quiet corner by one of the picture windows. I could see the lights of Isérables in the distance. Small red-checked curtains, tied to the side, framed the view. Like La Poste, the décor was traditional, dark tongue-and-grooved wood flanked the walls with a textured cream surface in between and amber-hued ceramic lamps hung from the ceiling, except our table had a small table lamp that sat on the red-checked cloth.

The maître d' pulled out my chair and waited as I positioned myself before burrowing me into my seat opposite Neil. I then wondered how many times Neil had brought Cheryl here. They had, as he had said, come out to the village regularly.

'Monsieur Jackson, Madame.' He handed us a drinks menu.

'Merci,' Neil said to the maître d'. Then he leaned towards me. 'Do you know what you would like to drink?'

253

'Is there something local you would recommend?'

'I personally like the Dôle, which is the Gamay, Pinot Noir blend or Cornalin, quite similar, slightly fruitier maybe.'

'Dôle sounds perfect,' I said, looking around as Neil ordered. There were two long tables with two families on each. Several tables with three or four dining, a few couples. A pleasant ambience and the staff looked friendly and attentive. I noticed some people melting cheese on a frame, a strange conical hat on top, which the children found amusing.'

'That's Raclette. The racks don't normally look like that though. Have you had it before?'

'No. I had the fondue – that was lovely. Rather heavy, all that cheese and bread. We should have had one between five of us, I think.'

'Yes, it gets tiresome with too much. They do a few specialities here, and you don't have to have cheese. One is the trout, *Truite du Vivier*, and one is steak, the *Tartare coupé au Couteau*. They may still be doing the *Menu Chasse* – hunters' menu – which is the venison. I can ask.'

'No, I had that, up at, oh …' I frowned trying to think of the name of the restaurant.

'You mean at Les Fougeres. Sergio's finest,' Neil said.

'Yes. That's the one.' I laughed. 'Of course, you were there. But I'd like to try the steak.'

'I should warn you the steak is rare. Best quality but not for everyone.'

I shrugged. 'When in Rome …'

'Excellent. I was opting for that too. It is amazing with all the spices. I'm sure you'll love it.'

As we put down our menus, a waiter brought our wine and poured us each a glass. I took a sip eager to try.

'Mm, that's pleasant.'

Neil's eyes glimmered. 'A girl after my own heart. *Magnifico*, as Stefano would say. Can't abide all that fussing with food and drink.'

We ordered mains. I couldn't face a starter too. We then chatted easily, just like the rhythm of the seasons. I told him about my long career and redundancy, the job I now hate but also about possibly working with Angie, the part-time marketing role in her health and fitness centre, which I was becoming increasingly excited about.

Neil told me about his career in the city as a stockbroker. The stress, and burnout, particularly through Cheryl's illness. He carried all the compassion of a man who really cared. He told me how his love of skiing kept him together and his plans to return periodically to Surrey to see his grandchildren before returning for his early summer trip to Lake Como and Lake Garda, before the crowds arrived end of July and August when he would take a slow drive back along the coast, stopping off along the Italian and French Rivieras, meeting up with people he had met before.

'So, you don't mind travelling around on your own?' I asked, sipping more wine.

'I'm rarely on my own. At first, yes it was difficult. But once I got into a routine, I got used to it. Sometimes I had to force myself to make conversation and at times, being a single man, travelling alone, I found it awkward. It can be easy to offend, particularly husbands, but I've learnt how to handle myself now, I think. I make a point of talking to the men first so that they don't think I'm trying to chat their ladies up.' He wrinkled his forehead, taking a mouthful of wine. 'It's true. I rather enjoy chatting to women. I find women cheerful and uncomplicated. That might be from working with men for too long or simply not having to compete, as men often do. Many of the friends I go back and see are couples.' He leant forward. 'No swingers, to my knowledge, you'd be glad to hear.'

I chuckled. 'I'm sure you choose your friends wisely.'

'I like to think so. You certainly do. You're a lovely bunch of Flowers. Go back a long way, I hear.'

I beamed with pride. 'We do. I'm extremely lucky.'

'I lost touch with most of the guys I grew up with. Even those I worked with. I play golf and tennis with some when I'm back in Surrey, but I've been friends with Christoff and Florian for several years now. Tom only started with them last season. But they're great company. Lots of ex-pats from the UK here too who are great fun. It's not so bad when they're out here on their own, but often, they bring family or friends out and I don't like to intrude. Most are out with family or friends this week – being New Year. What are you doing for New Year by the way? Ah, I believe this is our food.'

The colourful plates contained a neat circle of beautifully lean red steak chopped and stacked with what looked like some herbs, oil and pepper, served with sautéed potatoes, a side salad and small pots filled with a selection of spicy sauces.

'This looks adorable,' I said, licking my lips. 'I'm a bit apprehensive about the steak being raw, but, here goes.' I picked up the steak knife and dug into the steak, swirling it into one of the pots and popping it into my mouth. I gazed up at Neil, who was waiting for the verdict. I nodded, savouring the flavours. 'Mm.' I tasted capers, parsley, onion and Tabasco. 'Very good.'

Neil tucked in hungrily and we ate in silence bar a few 'mms'.

I took a sip of wine, which slipped down nicely with the food. 'New Year's Eve, we're going to La Poste. Stefano squeezed us in, which is a bit worrying.'

Keeping his lips firmly closed, I could see Neil was trying not to laugh. He finished his mouthful. 'Sounds like Stefano. He was fully booked by Christmas, so he must like you to be "squeezing" you in. He knows what he's doing. It might be compact but it's worth it. It's a great atmosphere at New Year. He has a band, a disco, food and wine coming out your ears. Dancing on the tables. Then you fall outside to the square, which comes alive with music, and they serve *vin chaud* and the fireworks at midnight. The whole village congregates bringing bottles and glasses of

Champagne, and you'll be kissing all and sundry and wishing them a Happy New Year.'

'Wow! Sounds amazing. Although, I have to confess, I have danced on his tables already.'

'And why not! It is a spectacle and like I say, fantastic atmosphere. This place is addictive, believe me. You'll be back next year. You wait and see.'

Neil finished his last mouthful. 'I hope you come back.'

Even though my cheeks were burning, I still felt myself blush. 'I can't believe how much I've enjoyed it here. I didn't think I would like the mountains or the skiing. It's got better and better.'

I finished my steak and salad, and placed my cutlery on my plate, leaving a few potatoes. 'I thoroughly enjoyed that. Thank you for inviting me out.'

'You're very welcome. I feel honoured you accepted. It's rare to find someone so special.'

I blushed again and couldn't avert my eyes from his. His hunger stared me in the face. Luring me. I thought how easy it would be to lean forward and kiss those lips, lose all control and fall into those arms. Was this meant to be? I fumbled with my glass, draining the last drop. Neil refilled it. The sexual tension was building.

'We can have dessert or coffee?' Neil said, finally.

I clutched my stomach. 'That was ample, thank you. Maybe it's nerves but I've not much of an appetite,' I said and took a larger gulp of wine. I felt I was being tested. I wanted him. I wanted Neil to take me to his and for us to make love. It felt so natural.

'Shall we walk back then?'

I peered at my glass. 'Yes. I'll just pop to the ladies' and finish my wine when I get back.'

'I'll get the bill,' he said.

Flustered, I fanned my top and rose to my feet, grabbing my bag from the back of my chair.

Instinctively, Neil pointed to the sign. 'Just there.' I followed his finger.

After flushing the loo, I opened the door and stood at the wash area. Looking in the mirror, I saw my nose and cheeks were beginning to flare. Kim was a queen. I washed and dried my hands and reached into my pocket, pulling out the concealer. I dabbed the reddest areas and blended the cream into my skin. I then opened my small bag, pulling out my phone to reach my lipstick. I ran the lipstick around my mouth, carefully so as not to smudge, then pursed my lips. I took out the small perfume bottle and sprayed it subtly around my body. I tidied my hair, then adjusted my top.

'OK, you'll do,' I told my reflection.

I placed the small items back in my bag and then picked up my phone. I hadn't checked it for ages, but the blue light flashed. 'Oh,' I said, annoyed that I had to check. Not that anyone was at home to worry about me. Should I tell the girls I might be late? I saw a message from a number I didn't recognise. Maybe it was Christoff or one the boys looking for Neil and his phone hadn't got a signal. I opened the text message.

Ginny,

It's time I came clean with you about my affair with Mike because from what I understand, Kim hasn't told you, and she's known for months, and I know Mike never told you. He told me never to tell you, but I don't see why you should be so cosy and happy going on holidays with my sister and your friends and having a good time when I am the one left miserable. I even heard you met someone there. So quick! That proves you couldn't love Mike as much as me. It will take me years to get over him.

So, this is to let you know we would have met again too if he hadn't got ill with cancer. I hope you feel as hurt as I do. He deserved so much more. He might have lived if I took care of him. He went downhill fast when you looked after him and all that time, you didn't know he loved me. We should have been together. I still really miss him. I've always loved him. I thought I would respect his wishes for you to never find out, but I can't. Why should I? I still cry all the time because I miss him so much, and you blatantly don't care about him like I do. You can't do if you're gallivanting around like an old slut. You and Kim can go to hell along with all your other friends for all I care, and I hope you all rot in hell.

Paula.

I grabbed my throat as if containing the bile. Paula with Mike?

Chapter 18

Kim

I was lying in the bath rehearsing what I was going to say to Ginny. Dread still knotted in my stomach. 'Kim,' I heard Ginny shout. 'Kim, where is she?'

I froze. The sound of her voice shrilled through me, even though she was downstairs. 'Fuck!' I jumped up, and out of the bath grabbing the towel from the radiator rail. I swiped it quickly round my face and wrapped it around me. 'Shit, she knows.' I choked, frozen again. I heard thunderous boots crashing on the wooden stairs as they raced towards me. 'Kim, where the fuck are you? Where's Kim?'

The door flung wide. I met eyes so evil that I knew I would be scarred for life. Ginny was shaking, her coat unfastened. Mascara smeared on her cheeks. Her phone raised in the air in one hand, and small cream-coloured bag tucked under her other arm. 'Is this true? Mike had an affair with Paula and you knew?'

'Yes,' I admitted instantly.

'Why didn't you … you tell me? Why?' she sobbed, waving her phone in anger and tossing her bag on the bed.

'How did you find out?'

'Your darling sister texted me.'

'What does the text say?'

'Does it matter?'

My arm reached out to her. 'Ginny, please.' I swallowed. 'Oh God. Believe me. I was going to tell you tonight. You've been so happy. I ... I couldn't. You ...'

She swiped away my hand. Her voice was fierce. 'Not tonight, this week; why didn't you tell me months ago? Years ago, for all I know?'

My complexion pinking, I saw Cathy and Lou's reflections in the mirror as they crept up to the door.

My lips trembled and buckled as I tried to operate them. Beads of sweat pumped from my skin, the shame oozing from my pores. Why had my sister committed such an evil crime against my friend? And me? And how could I make it better? 'I've known for a few months. I'm so sorry – I wanted to. I was scared. Scared to hurt you, scared I'd lose you.'

'Protect your sister more like.' Ginny's hard scowl hurt me more than her words.

'No, never,' I pleaded. 'Not over you. I thought I was protecting you. You'd not long left me in Australia. You'd just lost your job, on top of losing Mike.' I tried to reach out and comfort her, cradle her like a child.

Ginny balked. 'Huh, I'm supposed to believe that?' Her arm pushed me away, her wild eyes avoiding mine and resting on the door. I could see she was looking to escape.

'OK. Tell me what she told you?' she demanded, twisting her lips and folding her arms as she leant against the wall. 'And, no bullshit, I want to know verbatim.'

I bit my lip, feeling inadequately prepared. I'd seen Ginny get cross with her kids, Mike even, but never with me – but I owed her the truth no matter what. My insides ached with what was to come as well as the consequences. I wanted to sit her down so that I could explain. I wanted to hold her, heal her wounded heart before it shattered. She stood stern, waiting. I breathed deeply and began, my words wobbling.

'It was a couple of days after you left Australia in May. I'd finally got around to ringing and thanking Paula for offering to put Avril up for her job interview in London. I'm sure it was just a token gesture on her part, but she had offered just the same. After thanking her, I asked her what she was doing at Mike's funeral service; thankful of course, that she didn't come along to the wake.'

I licked my lips; saliva was draining from my mouth.

'What she said was: "I loved him. You know I did." I said, "But that was years ago. Surely you've moved on by now?" She laughed. "Not when he loved me too," she said.'

Ginny's eyes and mouth were twitching. Her fingers tapping at points around her face.

I licked the nervousness around my lips again. 'You can imagine, my blood started boiling then. "Oh God, Paula, you're not still deluded, are you?" I asked.' I stopped and cleared my throat. 'She then said, "Actually, Kim, we would have met again, but then he got the cancer."'

I watched Ginny's throat swallow the pain.

Ginny shook her head. 'Carry on.'

I sighed. '"Oh really?" I said, exasperated, at first thinking I would just go along with her fantasy.'

Ginny changed legs, uncrossing them. 'I don't need your commentary. Just the facts.'

I was trembling but continued in Paula's words. '"It was easy," she said. "I dealt with the contracts at Roysons. I contacted Mike's firm. I knew he dealt with the contracts there. Got him to come along to discuss some lucrative jobs over lunch at The Noble Grape. I don't suppose you know, but they converted their stables there, creating some beautiful B&B accommodation. A glass of wine or two and … believe me," she said, "married or not, men don't need much persuasion."'

I sat myself on the bed before I fell and I saw that Ginny's skin was pale. 'My sister was clearly determined to get what she wanted, and I'm ashamed to admit somehow, after all those years chasing Mike, she had finally got her way. Finally trapped him in her web. "You got him drunk," I said.' I had to pause for breath. I then continued, mimicking Paula's voice. '"He was willing. He couldn't get enough of me."'

Ginny blinked, swiping an eye. 'Go on.'

'"You're disgusting. You're making it up. They're my friends, Paula. You'll destroy Ginny. You'll destroy our relationship." I felt sick. I remember thinking she should be sectioned. Then she said. "Ginny destroyed me. They both did."'

'I said to her. "Paula. You destroyed you." I was so angry. Then I asked. "Does Ginny know?" I couldn't bear to think of you struggling with it all. Of losing our friendship. It was hell, insane. I didn't know what to do. I asked again, "Does Ginny know?" It was torture, as though she was enjoying her kick, manipulating me, us. You know Paula thrived on hurting people, just like my ol' man. Neither have a stop button.'

'Well, clearly I didn't know,' Ginny growled, pinching her forehead as she scoured the floor. 'If I had, he wouldn't have died of cancer.' She frowned. 'And I would definitely have lunged at your sister if I'd known. Funeral or not.'

'Ginny, Mike would never have gone back there. That I will never believe. She was fantasising.'

Ginny held up her palm and headed for the door. 'Stop. I don't need to hear any more.'

'She's twisted. Ginny, please, let's talk about this.'

Ginny held on to the door post. Cathy and Lou shuffled themselves closer to the door.

Oh God. I could barely breathe. I knew this would be the result. Ginny would never speak to me now. As I'd recalled it I was even more convinced Paula must have been blackmailing him. Poor Ginny, she looked crushed. I had no idea how to handle it. Lou glanced at Ginny. Cathy stared down at me like a piece of dirt on her shoe and stepped towards Ginny, wrapping her in her arms. Angie stepped into their embrace too.

'I am so sorry, Gin. Paula is selfish, evil. I am so ashamed that she has done this to you.' I tightened the towel around me, clenched the top of it and stepped off the bed towards them. Ginny shifted forward, and I balked at the steeliness of her stare as she leaned closer, and I even inhaled a gust of onion on her breath.

'Evil's the right word. She's the devil incarnate. But who are you, Kim? You are … correction, were my friend. Friends are loyal, and what riles me is you hate your sister, you've always hated her for her twistedness, yet you've defended her just by omitting to tell me.' She let out a cry and my chest heaved. The words 'were my friend' rung in my ears, crushing my soul.

I couldn't contain my tears seeing her so hurt. They fell shamelessly. My lips wobbled. 'Not true, Gin. Of course I didn't defend her. I was …'

'You did. By your choice of action, in my eyes, that's defending her.' Ginny threw down her phone and, flustered by the heat, started ripping off her coat. 'You're the one person I …' Ginny wrenched her arm out of the sleeve and threw the coat to the floor, then swallowed, pinching her nose, as she continued. 'You were the one person I could really trust.' Her shoulders shook violently, her eyes combing for support as she leant against the vanity unit. 'Argh! The slimy slut! I can't believe Mike stooped so low …' Her head shook as she sobbed. 'What a sucker. I hope he's burning in hell.'

How could I explain to her how much I wanted to carry that humiliation for her, spare her the damage and destruction it would cause. 'Ginny, it was wrong of me, but rightly or wrongly, I felt you weren't strong enough at the time and prayed you would never find out … it was a risk … a huge one, knowing what my sister's like, but I thought if I waited … at least until you were in a good place ...' I trailed off, struggling to organise my thoughts, questioning myself, and to keep my voice even. 'I hated that I knew. But, for some reason I thought if I kept it to myself, at least until you'd had time to cope with everything else, I would protect you.'

'But we were even talking about it the other night, when I told you about Mike. You didn't say a word.'

I lowered my head in an effort to bury my shame. 'Yes, I know, I know.' I shrugged, and rubbed the back of my neck where my hair was still wet, then wiped my cheek with the back of my hand. 'I'm not proud of myself, but you were in a happy bubble I couldn't burst. The girls will agree. You've become so much the Ginny we used to know this week. I knew it was wrong of me, but I intended to tell you and coincidentally, I thought the right time would be tonight. To sit you down and explain.'

'Jesus, Kim. If I had proof of my suspicions six months ago, I could have moved on before now. I don't understand your logic.'

I clutched the towel closer to my chest wanting to throw my arms around her. 'But I didn't know you suspected anything then. You only told us the other day. If I had known, then I would have.'

'So, then why didn't you – Monday or yesterday?'

I covered my face with my hand, willing my mind to find the right answer, some sort of perspective. I'd let her down but not in the way she imagined. I didn't know how best to explain. I wasn't getting through to her. I should have planned and rehearsed how I was going to tell her. I may have had some eloquence to my argument. I sensed her impatience growing.

'The time hasn't been right this week, nor then. It was just after I'd discovered you'd lost your job. I was devastated for you, and hearing that so soon after, I was gobsmacked. Stunned. I was at a loss. I couldn't even tell the girls. You were still grieving and shocked at losing your job. I just couldn't bring myself to call you. I didn't tell anyone. Not even Will. I ... I just didn't know what to do. I tried to bury it, I suppose to protect you,' I said watching as Ginny pulled a tissue from a box on the shelf. I grabbed one as well.

She stared at me coldly, sniffing then blowing her nose and throwing the tissue in the bin. 'Well, you certainly protected your sister; handing her the power, even more power to humiliate me.'

'No, you were in such a good place after the memorial, and yesterday, the euphoria of the day's skiing and Neil asking you on a date. Like I said, it was a bubble I didn't want to burst.' I sighed heavily, feeling I was just repeating myself. 'And it's completely selfish of me, I know, but I was scared. I wanted the time to be right as I knew it could ruin our friendship.'

'Well, you got something right,' she said unreasonably, smudging her face with the heel of her hand and promptly collected her bag and coat from the floor, then her phone from the bed. As she stood back up, she turned her back to me. 'It has ruined our friendship. I can't stay in here.' She strutted out the door.

I chased after her. 'Ginny, don't be ridic …'

She turned to me briefly, poison spitting from her eyes. 'Kim. Go console your sister. The witch is clearly heartbroken. You want to protect someone; her need is greater than mine. I'm done with caring about you, about Mike.' Brushing angrily past me, to her bedside table, she gathered up a few items including her pyjamas and headed back out the door.

I stared after her, clawing my face, my fears realised. A huge sob rose in me.

She shrugged. 'She was your friend and you betrayed her; what do you expect?' She snorted and threw bits into a bag. She too padded across to the Cathy and Lou's door. The crash hit me like a bullet shooting me in the head, leaving me bereft and alone. The pit of my heart emptied as I curled on the bed and sobbed. Was what I'd done so terrible? All I did was show compassion for my friend who was already hurting. They'd got me so wrong.

I grabbed another tissue. I'd really screwed up. Perhaps that was an understatement. I lay on top of the bed, stroking the faux-fur throw, the distorted chatter from the other bedroom piercing my ears. I pressed the ache in my breastbone, squeezing it as though I could stop my heart bleeding. There was no plaster to mend this. Ginny was deeply hurt, feeling betrayed. Just like my dad, Paula was so menacing. It was tempting to call her and give her a piece of my mind, but I quickly figured that would be playing directly into her hands. For some reason, she wanted to create havoc between me and my friends so why should I give her the satisfaction of knowing she had succeeded? And, not content that she had managed to lure Mike after all these years, she was also intent on breaking up our long and beautiful friendship. Why? Did she resent us? Hadn't she wounded Ginny enough by seducing her husband?

With a large sigh, I rolled over, hugging my pillow and urging Paula out of my raging head. I needed to concentrate on what was important – to find a resolution and repair my relationship with Ginny and the girls. How was I so stupid? Why didn't I just tell Ginny? How would I ever rebuild that trust? The other girls were right to support her. They wouldn't trust me either. I'd been wrong, and this was my sentence, my worst fear; I'd lost my best friends.

So, what were my options? I could call a taxi, or possibly Tandy and Jean-Pierre in Ouchy; drag them out to fetch me. Or I could wait until first light and get the bus to Isérables and take the cable car down to Mayens-de-Riddes to the station. I sighed. I could even be brazen and burst into their bedroom and insist they listen. The decisions too heavy to weigh up, I uncurled my legs and lay on my back. More than anything, my preference was to stay and calmly talk to Ginny. Press on her my utter remorse. I held my head in my hands, clawing at my hairline.

I couldn't return to Oz without a fight. If the Flowers ignored me for the next three days, at least I would have tried. I resolved to wait until morning; give Ginny the chance to quieten her mind and think straight. Maybe she would figure out my heart really was in the best place. I could pray for a miracle. Surely we couldn't part without coming to some resolve. We were in too deep. Although, quite how I could rebuild trust, I had no idea.

I must have exhausted my brain as the next thing I heard was Angie whispering about me.

'She's asleep.'

'Well, we have to get dressed,' Ginny said, less considerately and scraping around loudly at a drawer. 'So will she if she's skiing.'

I opened my eyes with a glimmer of hope. At least she wasn't expecting me to run off home. A positive. I'd take that. Maybe she had calmed down. Was I clinging to some hope it would be possible to chat and try to mend some bridges?

Ginny sat on her side of the bed, then continued in the same tone. 'Though I'm sure she'd rather go and soothe her sister.'

I felt the twist in my heart.

Ginny

I had barely slept with the anguish going on in my head. The flash of Mike with Paula. Blood had rushed to my head as I had got to the end of the text but then it rushed out as I read it again trying to make sense of it. Bile rose to my throat. I had been rooted to the spot, physically numb, unable to grasp the reality. I read it a third time, which must have been the point at which the repugnant reality hit. I had rushed back to the cubicle and thrown up. It was like I'd stepped into another dimension, or a film set. I was hearing but it wasn't real. It wasn't happening to me.

Wiping streaming eyes, I remembered I kept wittering. 'Mike

wouldn't, surely not, surely not her …' His guilty mumblings rang in my ears. My worst fear had worsened. The bitter taste of disgust had stuck to my tongue. How could he?

I know I had read it right, but I'd had to ask myself if it was a jinx. A cruel hoax. How could he with her? Paula? Of all people! The slut! The bastard. He had cheated. He had actually cheated on me. My Mike with Paula. Vomit had stuck in my throat again as I visualised them. I'd had to lean forward again to release it. My head whirled with poison. She had to be pretty sick in the head if she was so desperate for me to know. But why should I even believe her? Like I had ever done anything to her – or Kim come to that. Kim knew! That fact had stabbed at my heart. Kim had been party to all this! Why the fuck didn't she tell me? My anger had raged to an inferno. I had to get to Kim.

Poor Neil, he had gaped helpless when I had eventually rushed out demanding to leave. Who knew what had been going through his head? I doubt he had known what to do, seeing me in that bedraggled state. Thankfully, gent that he was, he immediately held out my jacket and got me back to the chalet without too many questions. I remembered garbling on to him about it, but how much I had blurted was a blur. And Kim's excuse – shamelessly lame. And why would I believe she had planned to tell me?

As supportive as they were, and I was overwhelmingly grateful that they had all rushed to my aid, I was surprised when Lou and Cathy took Kim's reasons for holding back as quite a reasonable explanation, particularly, they said, since I had already been stricken with grief and had just received shocking news about my job. Though equally, they said they had understood my view – that she might have been covering for Paula. After all, we had agreed, blood is thicker than water. Kim has always been protective of her siblings.

But, it really hurt to think she would betray me to protect her sister rather than inform me. I still can't believe that Mike had not only been unfaithful, but that it had been with Paula! What was he thinking! It still didn't ring true. Paula was a joke. A pitiful joke. And now the whole world and its dog would be laughing at me.

* * *

Kim was sleeping when I entered the room, which meant either she wasn't too upset, or she would have lain awake most of the night like me and become exhausted. Either way, I didn't care. I was still fuming with her. I watched her eyes flicker and I picked up my small hairbrush, side-stepping to the mirror. Her eyes closed again but I heard her sigh and then move her pillow. Peering down at that person I had loved and trusted so much, it crushed me. It was crazy to think she couldn't tell me; that she would let me discover what my dead husband had done in two inches of text from that evil sister of hers. I shuddered. The image of Mike with Paula stuck in my brain still. It had been playing over and over in my mind all night. I shuddered again. The thought of all three of them colluding together. Beyond comprehension!

Angie looked concerned. 'Are you all right, sweetheart?'

I looked round. 'Yes, fine,' I said nodding, but I was at a loss. When I turned back, Kim was sitting herself up slightly. I glanced at her briefly, in disgust. Who was she? I hadn't long lost Mike, and I had lost my job, but surely you would want one of your closest friends to know the truth, particularly with a sister as volatile as hers was; I was surprised Paula hadn't told me before! Why would she wait a year after his death if she was intent on me knowing? Would she have made it up? Who knew? If Mike hadn't uttered those words then I would have questioned her sanity, but it was in her nature to wreak havoc.

Mike was in the wrong. And Kim, why was her loyalty to Paula rather than thinking of me? She had never liked her. That was the why I found it so difficult to accept. I've done nothing but

270

treat her like a sister; well, better than a sister, probably. We've rarely fought. Why would she conceal something so significant to me? That was the betrayal.

And the timing of Paula's revelation. A year on and I was on a date. My first date since Mike. Someone I considered special, too. It had been going so well. Like sitting in the bar any other night, we had got on so well. Neil and I were on the brink of going back to his. I had virtually committed myself and hadn't felt at all uncomfortable about my decision – I wanted to make love to him. How was I to trust any man now?

My head spun. A madness in me throbbed. This wasn't happening. How had Paula known about Neil? How? Had Kim spoken to her, messaged her? Why? Or was it Mike divinely intervening? I shivered. Was his spirit unsettled? Riddled with so much guilt maybe? Or was I overthinking? The bowling. It was possible one of the girls mentioned it to the boys? Lou? Cathy? Umm. I scrunched my face. Angie? The boys had met Paula bowling. My gut spiralled. So, she told the boys, too? Bitterness salivated on my tongue again.

Like Angie, I rummaged for my things and dressed as if Kim wasn't in the room. She didn't attempt to get up, so I wondered if she would stay put. When I woke this morning, the last thing on my mind was skiing, but Angie and Lou persuaded me that sitting around the chalet stewing would be destructive. I saw their point, but I knew my heart wouldn't really be in it. Figuring they were probably right, I had splashed my eyes with freezing water to sting out the haze.

We dressed for our ski lesson as Kim lay there, her eyes opening, then closing. I did feel bad that we had all abandoned her last night, but, as we discussed, they would want to know if their husbands had betrayed them – even if he were dead. They had their own interests to think about too.

Kim turned her head. 'Ginny, can we talk?' she croaked as I sat down on the bed to put on my sun cream. 'Please?'

Feeling uncomfortable, I peered over at Angie who was pulling up her big knickers, which nearly made me laugh. I saw her puff out her cheeks with the squeeze of her pants, then she shrugged one shoulder at me. I didn't want to talk to Kim. I looked back at the contents of my make-up bag sprawled out in the drawer. What could she say that would change anything?

She raised her pillow slightly and cleared her throat, half lying, half sitting.

'Well, I'll tell you anyway as I'm sure you're still angry. Again, I want to emphasise how sorry I am. I'm so sorry that I've hurt you and sorry I made the wrong decision. I promise, my thinking was based on believing I was doing the right thing. I was genuinely protecting you. It wasn't for Paula's benefit at all.' Her voice rose as she looked squarely at me. 'I want to make sure that you know that. I'm bitterly ashamed of my sister. But, there's nothing I can do to reverse the way I handled the situation. I'm sure I've lost your trust as well, but be assured but be assured, you can still trust me, I swear. You still have my loyalty.'

She swallowed hard, blinking away the tears on her wet lashes. 'I only hope one day you can forgive me, Ginny. And you girls.' She glanced at Angie. 'I realise you also feel that I should have told Ginny, or any one of you for that matter. But …' Her hand reached her mouth and she cleared her throat. 'Now I can't undo my mistake, and I couldn't bear not having you as my friends.' She leaned on one side, towards me. 'Ginny, you've been the loveliest person in the world to me. I could never hurt you. Not deliberately, so please trust me. There's not a chance in hell I would have jeopardised everything we have by hurting you. That's exactly the reason I was waiting to tell you when you returned from your date. I can only assume Lou or one of them have told the boys about Neil.'

I watched as she pulled herself up to sitting, knees bent, and scrunched her cover against her chest. The puffiness around her eyes aged her. She sounded genuine, but as I stared, my mind

272

was made up. I couldn't accept the apology or anything she had said. The only truth I'd heard in what she was saying, was that she had made a wrong decision. I chewed on my lip, the difficulty for me being to know whether she was protecting her sister or me.

'That's gracious of you to apologise again, but I don't feel ready to accept it. Sorry, Kim. Your reasons may be sound to you, but I would rather have known.' I struggled for breath and to find anything further to bring about some resolve. 'Kim, I need time to get my head round this. Get up and come skiing. Don't ruin your holiday. It's happened, and we have to deal with it one way or another. Let's be civil, give it time to digest.'

'I appreciate that,' Kim said. 'Honestly, you won't believe how bad I feel.'

She lifted her bedcover and trotted to the bathroom. Angie and I continued to dress in silence, then hearing Kim's electric toothbrush hum, Angie asked.

'Should I let the girls know?'

I stared at her confused, then the penny dropped. 'Good idea. Yes, please,' I said, feeling conspiratorial. 'I'm so mad still. But we were all in shock last night.' I pinched my forehead. 'I still am in fact. I really do need some thinking time, so best we all remain civil. It's only a couple of days.'

Cathy

Lou was bending over the dressing table brushing on foundation cream in the mirror whilst I was pulling up my thick ski socks. We had been scrutinising Kim's argument. Neither of us could adopt a position on whether we would or wouldn't have told Ginny at the time. I think I would have been more inclined to have told her after a few weeks, given her some time to digest the redundancy, but then told her face-to-face whereas Lou felt

273

that she would have struggled to decide a timeframe, but we concurred that telling her face-to-face had to be the way. We began to understand Kim's position even though we were deeply concerned about Ginny.

'Just as she was doing so well too,' I said.

'I know. Bloody Paula. She's always been trouble. Such a contrast to Kim. I feel torn, if I'm honest. I really feel for Ginny but in Kim's position, what would I have done? Knowing Kim, she probably was worried that it would send Ginny over the edge, especially then. And at least she kept it to herself without burdening our consciences. I wouldn't have liked that either. She hadn't told you, had she?'

'No, I didn't have a clue,' Lou said, now flicking her eyes at the mascara brush.

'And what doesn't help by the sound of it,' I rattled on, 'is that Kim was going through her own anxieties with Will about returning home, so, no doubt, she's been trying to deal with it all.'

Lou spun round. 'I know. I can't believe what's been going on. We just don't seem to have time to chat lately. You think life gets simpler as you get older, but with the children, grandchildren, planning for retirement, work, the stress is still there.'

I puffed. 'Ha, bloody retirement's overrated. Mine has been extremely stressful so it doesn't disappear even then,' I said. 'This week has certainly shown the stains in our linen. Many in a good way though. Airing our dirty laundry has helped me and I think we've all discovered what a pain in the arse our other halves can be. Though, I'm sure we are to them at times.'

'Oh, absolutely. And don't forget, when Kim found out, Ginny hadn't long returned from Oz. It's not like Kim could justify spending on a flight over immediately, to tell her. Was it May? Maybe, then, once this trip was booked, in June, maybe she held off so that she could tell her personally?'

With my socks neatly in place, I rose, grabbing my hairbrush.

'It sounds plausible. And, when would have been a good time to say anything this week? Ginny's been cracking her shell and making her way out. I couldn't have risked stamping on it. Oh, I do hope they come to an understanding. Kim wouldn't set out to deliberately deceive her or hurt her. She cares too much and all the history they have … No, it's beginning to make sense.'

'I agree,' Lou said stuffing her make-up back into her make-up bag. 'I doubt her motives were misplaced. Paula's a nasty piece of work. I wouldn't be surprised if Paula threatened Mike. Blackmailed him in some way. It's possible the contracts were quite substantial, and Mike needed them. Or, she just saw an opportunity. She'd always liked Mike.' Lou picked up her hairbrush.' Let's just hope she doesn't try it on with Terry.'

I stood beside her as I finished brushing my hair. 'Or Anthony.'

'Or Rob,' Lou added.

I glared at Lou in the mirror. 'Oh, I've just had a … ew, I feel sick.' I clutched my stomach. 'Lou, I couldn't get hold of Ant last night. Nor all day today. He said his phone died. You don't think?'

Lou stopped brushing, her hand resting on the side of her head. 'No, Cath. No, I'm certain he wouldn't. Wasn't he playing golf with Terry?'

'But it's her. If she can lure Mike, who probably thought her a joke, then who knows what she's capable of.'

Lou held my gaze for several seconds. 'Any of them. Oh God, I hope she hasn't got her claws into …'

Angie stormed into the room and both Lou and I spun around. 'What happened? Is Kim awake?' I asked, still panicked.

'Yes. Well …' Angie drew the door to. 'Kim's apologised again but Ginny's still riled.'

'Oh, this is awkward,' Lou said.

Angie rubbed her thighs and placed her hands on her hips. 'Well, yes, but she has at least said that she won't spoil her holiday. She asked that we all be civilised.'

'Oh, good. But, Ang, we're now worried,' I said. 'Sit down.'

Chapter 19

Kim

When I opened the curtains, thick mist hung outside the window – it was another foggy morning. And, although a little lifted by Ginny's gesture, I was still feeling devastated by her response. Arriving down late for breakfast, I was met with pleasant 'good mornings' but the air inside was icier than out. I was grateful to see Lou had made my coffee and there was a boiled egg and toast on a plate where I usually sat, even though I had to force myself to eat it. My throat and stomach tightened with each gaze that bounced between them back and forth as I rushed to get it down me.

After finishing her breakfast, Angie got to her feet and began gathering and washing the dishes and cups. 'I'll just rinse these, while we wait,' she said. I could barely swallow. I was a criminal without knowing the crime. I wanted to scream at them: *All I did was care.* This behaviour was so unreasonable. Yes, they felt for Ginny – after all, she was the victim in all of this – but still, they knew me well enough to understand surely.

As we marched from the path to the road. Lou held back and walked beside me. She spoke softly but she didn't seem unduly worried if the others heard.

'It's so awkward at the moment, I know, but let's enjoy our skiing and worry about everything else later. Such a shame Paula chose to tell her now. I could kill the bitch. But hopefully, time will figure it out.' She nudged my arm in a friendly, almost soothing way, which took me by surprise.

'I hope so,' I said shaking my head. 'Nothing I say will convince you of my sincerity, but I won't give up.'

Lou's mouth twisted. 'Good. I'm not sure that I wouldn't have done the same. I told Ginny that too. Let's just see how she feels in a few days.'

I nodded. It would have to suffice, and I could only pray things improved before we left. I would hate to return to Oz leaving it like this.

As we reached Christoff, Angie gave him her usual three air kisses, but showed considerable constraint, whilst Ginny walked directly over to Neil. She shuffled around the other side of him to create some distance between us and I could hear her as she began to apologise. Neil gave her a hug, telling her he was glad she was back out ready to ski this morning. She peered over at me and lowered her head, saying something inaudible to my ears.

Christoff, however, soon rounded us up, informing us we would be going straight up on the gondola and back to the blue run again to keep working on our parallel turns. Although the atmosphere was uncomfortable travelling up in the gondola, once we were under instruction with Christoff, and the sun burned through the fog, I began to feel more relaxed. We managed to get five runs in the two-hour lesson and I felt my skis carving easier and more confidently with each run. Apart from a few minor falls, we all did well and Christoff promised that for our last day tomorrow, Friday, and New Year's Eve, he would take us over to the Tournelle slopes, which were gentle reds. He said he had every confidence in us, but we would have to ski a steeper part to get there. He added that that was going to be our new challenge. I was so excited. I never imagined myself skiing a red run on my first week.

'Excellent,' I squealed, grinning around me, Ginny dropping her smile as I caught her eyes, which tore at my heart. I could see the others bubbling at the prospect.

'Why don't we carry on skiing now and have a later lunch?' Lou said. 'I'll ring Angie to meet us up here.' She peered round for our approval.

'Sounds good to me,' I said.

Cathy put her hand up. 'Me too.'

'I'll see you ladies later then,' Christoff said and skied off with a courteous wave.

'Yes, me too,' Ginny said, then frowned. 'I'd be interested to know why Christoff doesn't let us ski all the way down.'

'Apparently,' Lou said, removing her helmet, and tousling the top of her hair, which had flattened, 'Angie said it gets steep and narrow at the bottom, so no doubt Christoff doesn't want us scared. Although, she said there's another run, but it's very long, and I think she said you have to get a bus if you want to avoid the last horrible bit.' She pulled out her phone. 'I'll text Angie.'

Ginny sucked in her cheeks. 'Ooh, maybe he'll take us all the way down tomorrow after we've done Tournelle.'

'I'm not sure I'd want to yet. Steep and narrow isn't a good combination, is it?' Cathy said.

I scratched my lip with my glove. 'That little bit we ski at the end of the blue is tricky enough for me. But maybe he'll see how we get on.'

'True,' Ginny agreed, and however brief her reply, I was heartened that I had got a response from her.

Lou tucked her phone back in her pocket saying she had organised for Angie to meet us. Angie and Neil were apparently just getting on the six-man chair. We decided as we were close to the restaurant, we would make use of the ladies' cloakroom. Ginny actually spoke to me again as I heard her in the next cubicle to me.

278

'Kim, do you have any loo roll or tissue you could pass? This one has run out and I don't have any tissues in my pocket.'

I know it was an emergency, but again, I was comforted that she had asked.

Angie and Neil were out by the lift when we returned to our meeting spot. The sky had clouded a little, but the light was still OK as we continued to perfect our parallels and turns. I remembered Christoff's encouraging comments as I skied easily across the slope and prepared for what Christoff called my neat 'smooth' turns.

I was elated, and the sun penetrated through for a while bringing patches of sapphire sky and white summits back into view, the smooth snow beneath me glistening. As my confidence grew, I paralleled across the slopes, daring to ski that little bit faster, the adrenaline pumping in my veins. It was magical. We were on our third run down, and the cloud began closing in. The light became flatter, which meant the definition of the snow topography was making it increasingly difficult to read the contours.

Angie was leading, and I was behind Lou with Cathy and Ginny following me, Neil at the rear. We were just at the bottom of our lovely blue run, the trickier bit heading down to the three-man chair where it met another run. I'm not sure exactly what happened next, but as I neared a turn, a huge thud with a scream bellowed in my ears followed by a heavy scraping in the snow. Next, I saw a body whoosh through the air. Limbs spread, skis crossing. Then, just missing me, a snowboarder hurled face down in front of me. I lost balance, my speed increasing, my heart lurching as I realised it was Ginny crumpled over by the edge of the slope, but then, to my horror I saw her body slide, spinning faster towards a child. Her skis trailed behind as they tumbled, then came off. She missed the child, but her body sped on nearing the edge. I was hurling uncontrollably towards her crossing the slope, powerless. Then I heard a roar.

'Stupid bitch! Out the …'

Ooph! I felt a huge thud. I was in the air.

Cathy

'No, no …' Motionless, I held my breath watching as they disappeared. Ginny and Kim gone. I could barely breathe. It happened so fast. I stood frozen. Ginny had spun off the edge and Kim had been pushed or knocked by a guy into the air and all I saw was her body flying over the edge of the slope after Ginny. I tried to push myself forward but was too shaky.

'Oh, God. They must be …!' Panic tore through me. 'Oh God.' I couldn't bear to think. *Stupid woman, get over*. Neil was at the edge in seconds, spraying a jet of snow as his skis turned and stopped sharply. He stooped, picking something up and leaned forward for any sight of them. He then skied along a little further, scanning below. He turned towards me as he whipped his phone out from his jacket, tapping vigorously with a drained expression on his face as he held it to his ear. This didn't look good.

My emotions surged. I whimpered, terrified for them both. Neil began speaking in French as I waited for two skiers to pass, my throat and eyes stinging. Unrooting my feet, I urged my skis slowly over to him. Other skiers were beginning to congregate around us. Lou and Angie, oblivious, had skied on ahead, towards the chairlift. I stood helplessly looking at the steep crevice below. I wanted to retch. What could I possibly do to help instead of standing here as a snivelling wreck?

Neil handed me a phone as he clicked off his skis and trod cautiously nearer the cambered ledge, scanning the depths below like he was figuring ways to climb down. I shuffled closer and clicked off my skis too, thinking he must be calling the mountain rescue. I ripped off my gloves, went to unclip my helmet, but figured it wasn't the best idea. My vision blurring, I looked at the phone recognising the cover as Kim's. It must have fallen out of her jacket. With trembling hands, my fingers tapped the screen and it lit up. It was an older version of mine without any security. I scrolled down her contacts and rung Ginny's phone. It went to voicemail. I tried again in hope she would pick up.

'Please be all right, Ginny,' I snivelled. 'Answer, but don't rush,' I mumbled to myself.

Neil finished his conversation.

'The mountain rescue team are on their way. You OK?' he asked, trembling with worry.

I nodded. 'I'm so scared for them. Ginny's not answering.' I blew out a sigh, trying to keep my composure whilst inside I was feeling hysterical. 'Damn!' I cried, trying to think. I rang Ginny again, guessing she might have to struggle to reach her phone. I was worried she could be unconscious. Even with a helmet, she could have injured her head the speed she was spinning at. God, I prayed they would be safe. It rung again for what seemed like forever before it reached voicemail. I left a message to say Neil was above her and he'd rung the services. She could ring me on Kim's phone. I paused. Then my voice broke. 'Stay safe, Ginny darling. Please be safe.' I then texted the same, then WhatsApped, just covering every communication channel I could think of. The tears now streamed down my face.

Neil put an arm around my shoulder. 'Let's just pray they've landed on snow. I can't see how far it goes down.'

Instinctively I pressed Ginny's call button again. 'I don't know. She may be trying to get her phone or reach safety. It could be off. I don't know. Please, God, please let her be OK.' It was then I realised the other two were probably still waiting at the lift. I said to Neil, 'I'll try and get hold of Angie or Lou.

Ginny

The melody on my mobile stirred me. The tune was 'The Rose' and I immediately thought of Kim. In a dreamlike state I was sitting in her rose garden so full of vibrant colour; pale and vibrant pinks, velvety mauves, brilliant whites as luminous as snow. I blinked several times, the skin on the left side of my face numb, my lashes wet. I could see particles of ice on my nose and cheek and the realisation dawned. I was alone, amid crushing silence and an intermittent electronic rendition of 'The Rose'. Surrounding me were snow-filled gorges, trees, slices and ledges of rock.

Flat on my stomach, I crushed some ice with my right hand as I pushed against it, feeling a sharpness in my spine. My left arm was dangling. I rolled towards it, almost instinctively checking for any numbness. As my eyes hit the clouds, the stark light singed my sight. My goggles had gone. The tune started again, and I remembered setting 'The Rose' tone to Kim's ring on my settings whilst we were sitting in her garden. It was the prompt I loved to hear. I would go to my laptop to talk on Skype. It played over and over but I lay listening, thinking of the heady scents and the sunshine.

I was afraid to move in case I damaged my back. It stung. One leg was painful too. The phone in my pocket stopped. In the silence in between I heard something. A whimpering. It wasn't far away but it was becoming louder. I craned my neck glimpsing a silver-grey-coloured ski boot and the bottom of the leg of a black pair of ski pants. That position didn't look good. My heart raced to a panic. I had fallen. The person whose leg I saw must have fallen too. I should get to them.

'Shh – ouch,' I whispered, trying to manoeuvre my torso gently to locate internal muscles to find out what was working. I then wondered if I was just bruised. At least I had sensation in my back, despite the pain. Peering down at the dangling leg, I looked at the deep crevice of snow below me, wondering if I would be able to throw myself into it. Would I sink into it, slide off it? I then wondered if I should talk to the person. Would they try to move, making them fall?

Horror gripped my throat. Then bile. My mind flashed to puking in the toilet. Mike, Paula. An image that had plagued me all morning. They were laughing and having sex in my bed. Mine and Mike's marital bed. They were naked, sweating and laughing. His eyes meeting hers. His touch on her skin. The bile turned to vomit, projectile gushing from my mouth then running down the ledge. The pungent odour wafted up my nose.

'Hel ... hello.' It was little more than a whisper, but I was sure I recognised that voice.

'Kim? Is that you?' Instinctively I called, almost gargling in my own vomit, but my phone buzzed and vibrated into my chest. Kim's signature jingle followed. She was trying to message me. Could it be her on the ledge above me? If only I could reach my phone. I peered at the deep pile of snow again, and wriggled slightly, easing my torso forward. My jaw dropped, my lungs snatching my breath as I gasped. I was on some pinnacle, I realised. I then heard a pant and saw the leg jerk and kick out. Then I felt another buzz in my chest.'

'Stay completely still,' I muffled to the boot. 'I'll try and reach you. I'm not far.'

'No ... no, stay still,' the voice whimpered with obvious pain, and I was now sure it was Kim.

'Kim, where are you hurt?' I asked. My phone rang again so I couldn't hear her answer. I tried again to reach inside my pocket. She must have rung the rescue services if she had rung me. Lost for ideas, I knew I had to move and try to reach her. My pride might have been hurt but Kim's survival was more pressing. And who knew who else was knocked. I could only hope that Neil was still on the piste and would know what to do. He was behind us. I wriggled my muscles, sure I was in once piece. My toes wriggled OK, my knees. I felt a bruise on my left thigh, and although I felt pain in my spine, there was movement in my muscles. Surely, I'd be able to get to her.

I thought of Kim, her crazy decision to ask a strange man to impregnate her. A desperate time in her life, driving her to take such a risk. Was the choice she claimed she made to protect me just as desperate? Did she feel she would risk sending me over the edge then? Revealing Paula's confession. Had I not had my own suspicions, I might not have believed her anyway. Should I even now? Paula is an evil minx.

I reached into my lungs for breath. This was the time to take a risk and I had to keep perspective – this wasn't just about me. This was life and death; no stronger purpose.

I stared at the spot I needed to be, then mentally, I took that leap. Then physically, I rolled off the ledge towards my aim. My heart filling my mouth, I tried to tuck myself into the pile of snow. I sank several feet. My body was wedged but seemed to be in working order, pain shooting through my back. I had to pray the snow would hold me as I clambered out the pit of snow and, leaning into it on my hands and knees, focusing just ahead, I steadily traversed it, clinging to its bulk.

My phone began playing 'The Rose' again but weirdly it soothed me. Kim was with me. The snow was sticky, surface chunks sliding and falling. 'Oh, shit, what have I done?' I groaned quietly with fear, praying I hadn't panicked her, or sparked an avalanche. I had to get up to her now. I knew she was above me and to my right, but I feared looking up in case I lost balance. I also feared looking down.

The tune from my phone stopped. 'Don't move,' I breathed soothingly as my heart thumped. I'd never been so scared, clinging for dear life, but somehow, I knew I had to be brave. I reached the trunk of a tree and forced every ounce of strength in me to stand. I kicked my boots into the snow, sinking with each step

284

until I reached something solid. Rock. I stepped onto a mound and above it saw a crag I could possibly grip. I reached out my hand and swung my body to reach it. Finding strength from I don't know where, I lifted myself onto a ledge. My top half was up. I had to get the rest of me up.

'Stay there,' I heard Kim say, but my instincts told me I had to act quickly.

'Shh …' And with an almighty haul, I was up. Immediately I saw the hood of her ski jacket hooked to a thin branch, one leg angled awkwardly on another. One false move and … I couldn't think. The distance, her weight, my balance.

'Gin, please.' Her voice sounded clearer. 'Leave me. It's too risky.'

I stood and viewed the scene. Looking just at Kim, not down, I considered if I could possibly grab her legs and pull her weight, so we landed over on the patch of snow below us.

'A helicopter will come,' she insisted.

I gripped my cheeks, praying. *Faith, Ginny.* I weighed up scenarios. Could I carry her? If I left her on that thread and a helicopter arrived, would she panic and move? Would the helicopter get close enough to blow her off?

My insides churned. I looked up to her face. A tense mouth and a bobble of a nose was the only flesh I could see. Her helmet and goggles covered the rest. I couldn't let her fall. I needed to protect her. My phone began its Rose chorus again and its presence prompted me to action.

'Kim, be brave,' I said. 'When I lean forward, I'm going to twist and take hold of your legs. All I want you to do is lean towards me and … hug me. Is that OK?'

I steadied my legs, hip distance apart.

'Gin, no!' she said. 'You'll fall.'

'Have faith,' I said, gripping a flag of rock and leaning forward, praying her hood would let her come to me. I reached out with my arms like I was taking a dive and braced myself. I lunged, twisting my body towards the patch of snow several feet below, then grabbing her legs as tight as I could, I screamed. 'Lean.' Her dead weight lunged on to me one side of my shoulders, one gloved hand punching my neck, squeezing hard. Our bulk hurled down. I prayed.

In the deep quarry of snow, I reached for breath. Kim's groin was in my face. To my relief, Kim began wriggling, she began to unfurl, and I manoeuvred where I could in the space, so she could lift her buried head. As she came up for air, I helped her straighten, her helmet knocking mine. We were in semi-darkness, our bodies creating quite a trench. She lifted her goggles on to her helmet.

'Words fail me,' she sighed.

'We're alive and in one piece,' I replied. 'Can you reach out?' I ask, her boots crushing my thighs.

'I think so. We'll both have to try and stand.' Kim positioned a boot between my legs and pushed herself against me to wrench herself up. As she worked her other foot in, I wriggled my body up and got to my feet, lifting her as she scrambled higher and climbed out.

'Ooh, bright,' she said, clutching her stomach and perching her bum on the edge of the hole then, reaching with both hands, hauled to help me up.

On the surface, I realised our plight as the snow below us fell away. We patted and firmed the sides of the snow hole, hoping it would sustain our weight, still in survival mode. The sound of rotary blades in the distance broke the silence.

'Sounds like our rescuers,' Kim said.

I sat beside her and instantly felt a squeeze of my arm.

'You OK?' she asked.

'Just a bit bruised. What about you?'

'Shaken and a bit sore from being winded, unsurprisingly. How can I ever thank you?' she said.

I gripped her gloved hand on my arm. 'You would have done the same.'

'You're kidding – I don't have that spunk. That was phenomenal. And it's not the first time you've rescued me. Sweet, I owe you big time. You saved my life.' Kim suddenly shook and let out a cry. Whipping away her hand, she buried her face. 'Ginny, I'm so sorry about Paula and Mike. I thought I was doing the right thing. You know I love you as much as my own daughters. I would never deliberately hurt you.'

Tears sprang out as I choked. 'If I'm honest, Kim, I'm not sure if I was angrier with you than with Mike and Paula. I thought you had my back. Would you have told me if it wasn't Paula?'

'No.' Kim looked up at me. 'My decision was based purely on protecting you and what you were already coping with. I suppose what I'm saying is that in hindsight, yes it was right to tell you, even over the phone, or Skype, but on top of everything else you had going on, it seemed cruel. Can't you see that? As a friend, it seemed the right decision to me. I wanted to save you the hurt like you saved me all those years ago, and today.' She smiled, touching my arm again. 'I don't know how differently I can say it to help you understand and forgive me.'

'I wish I could,' I said meeting her tear-filled eyes. 'I mean, just now, seeing you in danger, wondering what could have happened to you; evidently, I care about you. Mysterious when I think about it and how hurt I feel, but what I did was instinctive. It's clearly putting things into perspective. You do still mean a lot to me. Mike's fling, affair, call it what you will, I would have dealt with it mentally. It might still be a scar, but like mine, your life is precious, finite. Will; the girls. I could never forgive myself if I didn't try to get you off that tiny branch.' I inhaled, peering up at the sight of the helicopter, the noise increasing. 'Kim, I need time. I can't just let it go. I know I was grieving, possibly running low on esteem but I need to absorb and analyse it. You of all people know what I'm like.'

'I do. And this is exactly what I feared. Your rejection. I couldn't bear not being part of your life, especially now without Mike.'

I raised my voice. 'Well, honesty and loyalty is the price you pay for love and friendship, Kim. You can't avoid conflict in life. The world is not this utopian fluffy cloud where you can wrap everyone up in cotton wool. I'm not saying knowing about them would have got me through, but hearing Mike *was* unfaithful was my biggest fear, the one thing I dreaded. Especially discovering it was with someone like Paula. I couldn't bear the humiliation. Your love and support would have got me through.'

The loud clatter of the helicopter was now above us. A wind whipped around us. I put my arm around Kim's shoulder and hers gathered at my waist. We huddled tightly, tucking our hoods around our heads, keeping them snug, together, safe, a wave of hands to the pilot before he ascended again, and the figure of our welcome rescuer appeared and winched us up to the safety of the helicopter.

Chapter 20

Cathy

Terrified didn't even begin to describe my state as I saw the helicopter approaching. What on earth would they find?

'Please, please God, let them be OK,' I begged, again. I must have prayed more in the last twenty-five minutes than I had in my lifetime, and for a practising Catholic, that is a lot of prayer. I watched the helicopter as it whirled above us. Swiftly, a figure winched its way down as another gripped the wire from the craft in an effort to control the swaying and spinning as it disappeared just yards from where we stood. Although time seemed to slow as the thump of my chest raced, within minutes I spotted Kim's jacket emerge from the depths; harnessed, she rotated steadily while ascending.

'No stretcher at least,' I sighed to Neil, Angie and Lou, now beside me.

The girls had got the lift back up and skied down to us after receiving my text.

Lou was chewing her lip, staring ahead as the wire inched its way up. 'Well, that's Kim. Let's hope by some miracle Ginny follows. Presumably the medic is with her.'

'Gosh, poor darlings,' I whimpered. 'Just the hoist will be enough to send them into shock.'

Angie wrapped her arm around me. 'Let's not panic. Maybe the fact that Kim's hoist was so quick to come up is a positive sign.'

'That's true,' Lou said, tapping her chin and puffing her cheeks.

I gazed at Neil watching the wire with high intensity; his cheeks still appeared hollow. Kim was up and in the helicopter to safety and he sucked his bottom lip.

Several minutes later, we spotted Ginny being hoisted with the medic on a longer wire just below her. Thankfully, she was secured in the harness and, like Kim, she appeared to be in one piece and looking around as the helicopter winched her up to safety. I let out an almighty sigh and heard the others around me do the same. A mix of exasperation and apprehension.

'Phew, what a relief neither are on a stretcher,' Neil repeated as the winch climbed. I spun around opening my arms.

'Thank God, they're safe,' I said as we embraced, hugging Neil along with Angie and Lou. I must have squeezed Kim's phone too as I pulled it from my pocket. It was ringing Ginny again.

'Whoops!' I went to cancel but Ginny declined. Either the rescue services had switched it off or she must have been sick of me ringing, I surmised, tucking my phone back into my pocket. She hadn't answered one call, and I was desperate to see for myself Ginny and Kim were well. Just because they weren't on a stretcher didn't mean they weren't hurt. Especially after a fall like that. I looked at Neil, noticing the colour returning to his complexion.

'I wonder where the rescue services take them to.'

'I'll call and find out,' he said, bending to pick up Ginny and Kim's skis from the snow and slid each pair together. 'Can you take these, Angie?' He handed her all the poles, then slipped his boots into his own skis, prompting us to do the same, and then he held a pair of skis in each hand. 'They'll probably take them to Sion or Martigny I imagine. If we get on the lift and back to the top, I'll ring from there. We'll get the lift back down. They should have got there by then. I'm not sure what happened to that boarder who took Ginny out. Not that I care. I was more concerned for her.'

'Is that what happened?' Angie asked trying to make sense of it all. 'Clearly we didn't hear anything. Neither Lou nor I saw anything. We didn't realise something was wrong until you texted; we were waiting at the lift.'

Neil pointed to the spot. 'Yeah, just there. I saw him. Totally out of control. Big guy, slammed into her back and sent her flying, then Kim went. I didn't see what happened there. Just saw her in the air. Neither stood a chance.'

I shuddered wondering how I was going to ski again; in fact, if any of us would want to ever ski again. I couldn't make a fuss though – not after all that. Following Angie down as we skied to the chairlift, I felt my body still shaking. Gazing at Lou in front of me, I knew she was unnerved too. The worry on her face as she curved cautiously and carefully across with glances as though to check no boarders were hurling towards her. I found myself instinctively doing the same. Thankfully we reached the four-man chair.

Once through the barriers, Neil clambered through with all the skis. 'You girls go ahead on one chair; I'll need to put the skis across my lap.'

'I don't know if I can carry on skiing,' I said as we sat on the chairlift together and pulled down the safety bar. 'In all honesty, I imagined both of them would be dead.'

Lou groaned. 'I know. I felt sick. Lucky though. They must have landed on snow. Thank God! I understand what you mean though. It certainly brings it home how easily and quickly accidents can happen.' Her lips began to wobble. 'Every time I hear one of those boarders behind me, that heavy scraping noise, as though they're coming at you unable to steer, it makes me freeze. Poor things, I expect they'll be scarred for life.' Lou let her emotions flow and she immediately set me off again. I sniffed, and I put my arm around her shoulder feeling the tears sting the backs of my eyes.

'It's the shock coming out, I think.' Angie quivered, trying to contain the emotion.

Lou nodded. 'And I'll be honest, my initial reaction was to blame Kim. I thought maybe Ginny had lost concentration and slipped after her ordeal last night. I thought she must have been beside herself thinking about Mike betraying her, poor love.'

I swallowed hard. Of course, the exact same thing had been going through my mind. 'It must have been quite a blow, Kim letting her down like that as well as Mike. She's not in a good place …'

'Maybe it did contribute,' Lou said, dabbing her eyes and seemingly wrestling with her own juxtaposition. 'Maybe she should have told her earlier. Obviously, in Ginny's eyes she was wrong,' she said clenching her jaw, steeling control. 'But who knows. If it felt right at the time, then … I'll just be happy that they're both in one piece.'

I released my arm and dug into my pocket for a tissue. 'Me too. It's all academic when something like this happens though, isn't it.? Although it's nice to think we could be totally honest with one another, there are things that you hold off until the timing is better. You don't think they're important, but they can be to others.' I blew my nose watching Angie in deep thought. I continued. 'It's human nature. We strive for an easy, peaceful life. Anthony, for example, I've wanted to confront him for ages about his idling, but I put it off hoping he would work it out for himself. I think I just conveniently fooled myself that I would raise the subject at a time when I thought he was in a better mood, or sober at least, so that we could discuss it. It didn't occur to me he wasn't coping. That's pretty worrying, but I was so focused on what I wanted.'

'Whoa, I have to put my hand up too. Oh, Cath, you're not

the first, and won't be the last,' Angie added. 'This holiday has certainly had its merits. Don't you think it's been good for us to listen to one another's issues and hear what others have to say about our own?'

'Oh absolutely,' I agreed.

'Yes, it has,' Lou said.

'I hope so anyway,' I said, 'And since we spoke this morning, my mind keeps conjuring up an image of Paula's tentacles stretching out to seduce Anthony.'

Shaking her head, Angie grinned. 'No. Don't torment yourself. Paula always had a thing for Mike. I wouldn't even be surprised if it was some sort of revenge.'

'Yes, good point, but, Cathy, I think Anthony craves your attention, not that slut's,' Lou reasoned. 'They were playing golf and I'm sure his mind is on more important things.'

'You're probably right. I'm actually looking forward to talking to him. I only spoke to him briefly about it. Amazingly, something's shifted. I think Terry and Rob must have jack-knifed his thinking. He says he's considering some options. So, fingers crossed. Like you girls suggested, it would do him good to go and see his old business partner. Look at returning part-time. Maybe business mentoring would suit him.' I frowned. 'I do wonder why we don't confront things.'

We neared the top of the chairlift. 'At least you've opened the can and can discuss it when you're home,' Lou said, lifting her feet off the bottom bar. 'And we'll have to pray Ginny understands Kim's motives in time. She's had several nasty shocks to deal with.'

I pushed up the top bar and prepared to ski off as we reached the top of the lift. It was there I froze. Angie must have felt the tension as I felt a gloved hand on mine. 'Cathy, you'll be fine. Just remember that Ginny and Kim's was a one-off, a freak accident.'

Virtually shushing around the mountain towards the six-man, we slowed as we reached the steeper downhill slopes, taking them with care. Scrambling off at the top of the lift, Angie helped Neil place all the skis in the rack and he took out his phone.

'You ladies go and get a stiff drink while I make the call. You've earned it.'

* * *

Accompanied by Angie, Neil drove down the mountain to the hospital in Martigny where, the rescue services informed him, they had been lifted to. Lou and I went back to the chalet to change and after a text from Angie to let us know Ginny and Kim were bruised but should be released in an hour or two, we sat outside on Stefano's terrace at La Poste, comforted in that knowledge at least. We ordered wine, which Lucien brought out to us, and Stefano followed with a large plate of consoling Margherita pizza.

He told us he had heard about the incident as we gorged on our delicious cheesy slices and hoped Kim and Ginny would be fit for the evening celebrations. He also added that it was a blessing the weather had brightened as it kept the après-ski crowd out from under his feet whilst he and his staff were setting up the tables for the New Year feast. Even as darkness descended, and the chilly evening air nipped, we sat, patiently, guessing the shape of the vehicle headlights and hoping the next would be Neil's Range Rover.

Ginny

I was alive. Still very much shaky and in shock, but it was such a huge relief to be alive, nothing missing, nothing broken, and safe, in the hospital. The rescuer on the mountain and the doctor in the helicopter were brilliant. The medic asked questions and checked out our injuries as soon as we were up inside the helicopter and unclipped. The medic was able to assess to some extent our capacity to move but needed to check us thoroughly. They insisted we be X-rayed for any internal damage at the hospital in case of any bleeding or injuries.

My body ached, particularly my back, but I think it was the impact of the boarder hitting me rather than the fall. And although one side of my body felt bruised – from my head to my lower leg – I knew how a broken bone felt and I didn't have any of that excruciating pain I had experienced when I broke a bone playing netball as a teen. From the moment we arrived at the hospital, the staff were amazing; their English excellent as they questioned and examined us, whizzing us both in turn off to X-ray and to the MRI scanner.

Kim was still being scanned when the nurse brought me a welcome coffee. I was resting on the bed reflecting, my eyes drooping, tired but my mind highly active. In a flash my life could have ended. It took some comprehension. A few inches over, I would have plummeted to my death for sure. And Kim's hood, hanging by a thread. How that branch hadn't snapped, I don't know.

'Tsch!' I sipped at the hot coffee and quickly placed it down. My stomach churned just thinking about the up-draught that the helicopter had created and how easily it could have blown her off that branch. We had both been extremely lucky. And this week had meant so much. I had been pretty unmotivated over the last year – and naturally upset by the revelations last night and of course today's incident – but this week had undoubtedly begun to alter my mood. I no longer felt like someone had bitten a large chunk out of me.

'Yuck, it's all so reminiscent of those IVF days,' Kim said, bringing me out of my reverie as the nurse walked her back to the bed next to me. 'All the prodding and scans.'

I smiled. 'I'll bet.'

'I don't suppose it's much fun for you either,' Kim said flattening out her cover. 'All that time you spent with Mike with his chemo, sitting around in waiting rooms, the hours waiting for the drip to do its stuff, putting him to bed afterwards, clearing up the sick.'

'At least I had Google and forums I could read and ask other people questions on. And Will, of course. I don't suppose you had any of that back then when you had IVF.'

Kim shook her head. 'No, nothing like that at all. There were a few of us who used to chat and compare notes at the clinic, relaying our cycles, how many follicles, how many eggs, the number, the size, the quality. Several of the regulars I saw fed you their data. Most beat me to it, though. We were all at different stages so the last thing you did was remain friends and listen to all their pregnancy and birthing stories.'

'Hmm, true.' I tested my coffee again, and this time swallowed. 'But then nowadays, reading forums and all the info about the type and number of cancer treatments people go through, success or not, I imagine it's like the IVF forums today. Yes, I got the occasional good luck, or sorry to hear, but you don't get the type of support you need emotionally when you're up and down on that rollercoaster.'

'No. Exactly. It's just a comparison ...' Kim paused '... well, because these people aren't your friends. They can't offer that shoulder to cry on, the hug, even the ear at the end of a phone. In fact, they'd think you pretty square if you were to list the number of breakdowns from the hopes and the disappointments you go through emotionally.'

'You get on with it if it's important to you though, don't you?' I widened my eyes.

'Like you did earlier, you mean. Saving my life. I'm eternally grateful, Gin. A friendship like yours is irreplaceable. I will stop talking about the other stuff though. Let it be and give you some space.'

I downed the last of my coffee and sat back, running my fingers through my hair. Kim's eyes were on me as she nervously smoothed her blanket again.

'Is there anything else you haven't told me? Have you heard from Paula since?' I asked.

'No. I haven't even tried to speak to her. I don't even want to speak to her. I want nothing to do with her. I told her that.'

'So, why was she so keen to let me know? Did she not say?'

'I wish I knew. I'm guessing it's her skewed means of attention-seeking or she's seeking some sort of satisfaction. Revenge maybe? She was at the bowling so if the boys told her where we were, they could have unwittingly evoked her jealousy. She wouldn't have known we were skiing from me. She could have been upset because she wasn't asked. Maybe she resents us going away together and enjoying ourselves. Or, she's trying to break up *our* relationship.' Kim blew out a sigh. 'Now that wouldn't surprise me.'

My face twisted. Paula had got her way with Mike. And I was damned if I was going to let her destroy any other part of me, or Kim. I still had nagging doubts about Kim's loyalty, however.

'I just don't know,' I said lowering my head.

'Ginny, I knew it could potentially ruin our friendship, and I was scared, but that wasn't my main motivation. Like I told you. I genuinely worried about your frame of mind. I'm so ashamed of what she's done, especially after all you and your family have done for me and mine.'

I looked up at Kim, scowling. 'I still can't help thinking you were protecting her. It's instinctive for a sister, surely?'

Kim raised her hands and her chin, looking up to the ceiling. 'Ginny, no. No. Not where you are concerned. Not at all.' She turned to me. 'OK. I could have rung you and risked our friendship then, but by not telling you, I've risked our friendship anyway. I've lost your trust. I've fucked up completely.' She clutched her forehead. 'In fact, thinking about it, I was damned if I did and damned if I didn't.'

297

'Well, she's got her desired result. She got Mike and got us where she wants us. Broken.'

'She did, and I'm sure she'll be satisfied that I've lost my best friend.' Kim's voice wobbled. 'I'll wait for the doctor out there,' she said, sliding off the bed and gathering her things.

'No, Kim. Stay there.' I pointed to the pillow. 'It's something I have to get over. I have to learn to trust you. I want to believe you.'

I gave her a reassuring nod and smiled as she stood staring at me. 'I'm sure you'll still need time, but I really hope so,' she said, wiping away a teardrop.'

'Anyway, we've drifted. I wasn't referring to the rescue, I was referring to the fact that I haven't coped well because I hadn't let you in, you or any of my friends. I shut you all out convincing myself I was getting on with it. There was a dose of pride involved of course. I thought that it was important to just get on with my grief, and not to burden anyone. I know now that I made a wrong choice. I really do need my friends. This week has shown me that.'

Kim jumped on the bed and folded her legs towards me. 'I hope I'm still considered one of your friends. If I'd had my way, I would have flown back and told you sooner – told you face-to-face so at least I knew that I could be there for you and help you through it.'

My eyes moistened. 'I believe that. But you'd just done the trip for the funeral. I wouldn't have exp …' The penny dropped. '… So the friction with you and Will?'

Kim leant forward on her hands. 'He doesn't know about Mike. I promise. I couldn't tell him especially knowing how much he cared for Mike and helped him with his treatment. No, I wanted to discuss it with you. I wanted to come over and see you. Paula could have been lying for all I knew, but when you told us what Mike had said, it fitted her story.'

I sighed heavily. 'I don't know why I couldn't tell anyone. Embarrassment? Humiliation? I didn't want it public.'

'Ginny, it makes sense that you've buried your head in the sand, but I wish I could have come. Oh God, Will thought I was being over-dramatic wanting to fly back so soon. He had had enough of me nagging him about retiring so it probably made him dig his heels in further. He's been so stubborn. We had the biggest row. It sent us backwards rather – to those intense days going through the infertility, the IVF. And of course, I wanted to come on the ski trip too, but the reality is, I could have made such a difference.'

I immediately slid off my bed and hugged my friend. 'Oh, Kimmy, you can't carry this debt you feel for me around with you. Will needs you more than me and I would never expect you to leave Australia for my benefit.'

Kim played with a strand of my hair as I leaned back, sitting sideways on her bed. 'I've been feeling really sorry for myself since the twins left,' she admitted. 'I need a purpose. I feel there's only Will holding me back. I want to spend time with you and be able to see the girls.'

'I know, I understand,' I assured her. 'Urgh, and yes, I hated the empty nest too, but at least the Flowers have been close by for me – although I've been too stupid to see it of late. I've wasted so much time dwelling on Mike, the bitterness. Not to mention all those evil thoughts I'd created in my head wondering who the hell Mike was likely to have an affair with. I discounted Paula merely by the fact that Mike thought her a joke. I doubt she would have made the whole thing up. It's quite possible she is capable, but I'm wondering now if she had some other motive.'

My eyes felt heavy and my pondering brain was becoming exhausted by more questions I couldn't answer. I let my eyelids close as Kim softly groomed my hair with her fingers, just as she had as a girl, but my eyes shot open hearing a familiar squeal. Steering my eyes towards the sound, I caught sight of Angie's mass of curls. She was peeping through the window and signal-ling to someone. A sudden gleam of white teeth. She waved as she saw me. I sat up trying to look more alert as she and Neil came rushing in with their wide smiles and arms open. Next all four of us were in an embrace and I heard myself wail before jets of warm tears gushed out of me. My skin must have soaked up half the snow I had lain on, because they wouldn't stop. I hugged them both, thrilled to see them.

'Where are the others?' I managed, grabbing some tissue off the side.

Angie stepped back. 'Neil suggested it might be too much, all of us. And, naturally, we had to keep the back seat free for you two. How are you?'

'Staggered I'm in one piece,' I said. 'But glad I'm alive.'

'And I have a great story to tell you about this heroine,' Kim boasted. 'She literally saved my life.'

'Oh, no I didn't,' I protested. 'I did what any good friend would do.'

Kim gave me an appreciative grin.

'Wow, can't wait to hear all about it,' Angie said.

'You never cease to amaze me,' Neil said, rubbing his hand up my spine.

I flinched. 'Oo-ah! That's sore.'

'Oh, I'm so sorry. What a numbskull I am. I'm not surprised. That snowboarder really whacked you in the back.'

'No, it had gone while we were sitting. I wriggled at the stinging sensation that had momentarily returned at the touch. I wasn't sure exactly what happened.'

'It happened so fast,' said Neil.

'I was thumped in the back and head and all I remember next is hearing Kim's ringtone and waking to find myself half-splayed, face down on a ledge. I think I might have landed on my side, because all this side is bruised. I'm OK internally though, I think. Just waiting for the doctor to dismiss us. They've checked our bones, checked for internal bleeding and organ damage. All that stuff I'm sure Kim could explain far better than I.'

'So, what happened to that boarder?' Kim asked. 'Was he or she down there too? I don't know.'

'I didn't see any of it.' Angie looked at Neil.

'No. I was too busy watching Ginny and then saw Kim in the air, dropping down.'

Angie took my right hand and clenched it into hers, then took Kim's, the caressing of her fingers comforting. 'Whatever! My beautiful Flowers, I'm so glad you're both OK.'

'I know I nearly ran into a child,' I said horrified at the damage I could have done.

'Yes, well, don't ever blame yourself,' Angie said. 'Every adult who takes a child on a ski slope knows the dangers. You were both extremely unlucky. Accidents like those are rare. Just be thankful you both did little damage.'

'Absolutely,' Neil agreed. 'So, have you eaten, had anything to drink?'

Angie gave my hand a squeeze and let go. 'You stay here, Neil. I'll go and find something. We need fuel too. I'll ring Cath and Lou. Let them know you're in one piece.' She gazed at me, tilting her head with a smile, then tapped her pocket as if to check for her purse or phone and strode to the door.

'Actually, I could do with a walk. I'll come with you,' Kim said slipping on her socks.

Neil sat beside me. A caring gleam from his eyes made me warm and my lips curled with his. 'We'll have you back to the chalet soon. Your friends are very worried. Sit back and rest for now. You've had a stressful twenty-four hours.'

Pushing my head back into the pillow, I sighed thinking of the girls. 'I've probably put them all off skiing for life. I can't ski again.'

'They managed to ski back to the six-man chair – even Cathy. She saw what happened.' Neil guffawed.

'Can't say I blame them. I expect I would do the same if I was to go back up.'

Neil's expression turned serious. 'Please don't give up. You've done so well. The trouble is, the slopes are always packed over New Year and school holidays.'

Automatically, hearing New Year, I looked at the clock. 'It's gone four o'clock. It's New Year's Eve. We're supposed to be out celebrating tonight. I can't ruin the Flowers' night. I know I'm not going to be much fun, but I feel I ought to go. It's booked.'

Neil peered out towards the corridor. 'I will look for a nurse or the doctor, shortly. There's something I just wanted to say before the girls return or the doctor comes in.' He licked his lips, nervously. 'What would you say to coming back here on a quieter week, when your back feels better? I've two spare rooms if you and the girls ever want to return. You could squeeze in, or if you ever find yourself alone and at a loose end, you're more than welcome to stay. That's if you feel as I do.' His eyes lowered momentarily. 'I was so scared earlier ... when ...' His voice choked. 'Let's just say, I had a beautiful evening with you last night. I'm sorry that you have so much to deal with, but if there's anything I can do, let me help you. I won't change my mind. You are special and I'd rather like you to return so that we can spend more time together.'

I felt a gasp escape my lungs. 'That's extremely kind of you. And flattering.'

'And we could work at building your confidence back up on the slopes. I promise it will return. I've been skiing for over twenty years and I've never witnessed anything like today.' He sighed, smiling. That adorable expression, just creasing those sparkly blue eyes and that sultry grin as he tilted his cheek towards me, soared to my core every time. Had I really fallen for him or was it the romance of the mountains and village and everything good that's happened this week?

'Neil, I don't know. I really do need some time to think about things. I like you very much but ... I just don't feel in the best place to make decisions, or judgements at the moment. I'm still trying to come to terms with discovering Mike's betrayal, and Kim's, come to that. Now this has happened. I'm sorry I can't give you something more positive.'

Neil took both my hands, lowering his eyes. 'You do, and the last thing you need is pressure.' He met my eyes again. 'Ginny, like your friends, and that includes Kim, as I believe her intentions were sincere, I care a lot, and have all the time in the world for you.' His lips tightened, then curled, his eyes gleaming with excitement. 'In, what? Three or four days since I set eyes on you, I've been a different man. That in itself has given me so much faith. I mean, discovering my heart is capable of feeling has been a revelation.' He chuckled lightly and raised his eyebrows, then looked over his shoulder lowering his voice. 'It's getting the opportunity to speak to you alone that's been challenging. So, I wanted to let you know how much of a difference your presence has made.'

Trying to hide my blush, I shook my head in awe of his honesty. I couldn't imagine admitting the same to him. I lifted his chin mindlessly and brushed his lips. 'I'm pleased to hear I've managed to do something cheerful. Thank you for telling me.'

We gazed at one another for several seconds, both resisting, before I turned my head. Instantly, he brought it back with his finger on my chin. 'I'll give you my phone number, if that's OK; you can ring me if you want to.' He waited for my approval, which I gave as a nod before I smiled, then he checked his watch. 'OK.' He winked. 'I'll go and hunt down this doctor. Get you back for the New Year celebrations.'

'Neil,' I said as he jumped up. 'I er … can't thank you enough. You've been so kind.' I watched him go but I didn't want him to. I wanted him to hold me, tell me everything was all right. I liked that I could talk to him, bounce my worries off him. I wanted to understand his reasons for believing in Kim. Express my thoughts about Mike even, my hurt, my feelings for him, my yearning for him. The things that friends, however special, cannot give to one another. But he was right. He could leave me his number. It was early days. Whether I could ever bring myself to trust a man again was certainly something I would have to think about.

'I expect this coffee is cold by now,' Angie said sashaying through the door as Neil got there. She held takeaway cups on a cardboard tray in one hand and a small brown-paper bag with sandwiches in the other. 'You two seriously need to get a room, not a hospital one either.'

Chapter 21

Ginny

Kim and I received a delightful cheer arriving back at the chalet. As soon as our boots were off, Lou and Cathy rushed to us with open arms as though we had been gone a week, rather than hours. And the place sparkled. They had evidently been busy cleaning. The entrance, kitchen and living room were all spotless and smelled as fresh as a mountain meadow; candles were littered on tables and shelves, the log fire radiated its heat with an amber glow. I was so grateful to be alive and among them. Removing our coats, Kim and I were ushered in and sank into the sofas. Filled Champagne flutes were handed round and as I downed a glass of Prosecco, Kim relayed our injuries and our story – with, embarrassingly, my 'life-saving' episode.

'She's my hero,' Kim cheered.

I sighed. 'OK, I accept my heroine-worship on one condition,' I told them. 'That you are not to mention it again.'

Cathy clapped her hands as she rushed over and hugged me. 'That's impossible, and a story that has to be in my next novel. Darling, I'm so proud of you.'

305

'Me too,' Angie said, giving me a light squeeze. 'Although you didn't need to throw yourselves down a mountain just to make up. It would have been much easier sitting in the bar.' Bubbles of laughter floated around the room.

'No, but I'm so glad we did,' Kim said, with a snort. 'It was so worth it.'

Lou kissed my cheek. 'What a relief. So, we can dispose of the eggshells.'

'I think so,' I said.

Cathy hugged herself. 'What a day. I'm so happy. And, if it's any consolation, Ginny, I might have done the same as Kim, the state you were in.'

I smiled and conceded, 'Well, maybe I would have too.' I watched as their brows almost collided with their hairlines. 'Anyway, how's Anthony?' I asked Cathy.

'Oh, it's very exciting, darling. I spoke to him just before you came in. He's booked us a lovely cottage in the Cotswolds for a few days next week so that we can talk without any distractions. Apparently, the boys have given him a good talking-to and his head is filled with possibilities for the future. I've not heard him this enthusiastic for ages.'

'I'm stoked, Cath,' Kim said.

'That's lovely news.' I smiled approvingly. 'Well, time I had a bath and got ready.'

'Yes, me too,' Kim and Angie echoed.

'Well, we're done, so our bathroom's free,' Lou said. 'Just don't leave a mess.'

Cathy almost choked on her bubbles.

My skin was lobster pink and the bathroom hot and steamy. I could barely breathe as Kim expertly saw me safely out of the bath, her eyes stationed on the floor.

'Leave the water,' she said as I leaned towards the bath plug. 'I'll jump in yours,' she said handing me the large white fluffy towel she had hung on the radiator to keep warm. I rubbed it over my arms and torso drying myself off as I left, closing the door after me.

'Thank you. I would have gone in after you,' I told her.

'No, heroes get priority treatment in my book.'

I rolled my eyes and finished drying off my glowing limbs. As my muscles had soaked and relaxed in the water, my mind had been whirling. Wondering. Would I ever know if my dearest friend had been protecting me? Her own blood, Paula, must really hate us. Why, when we had put up with her silly, sometimes nasty antics when she was young, seeking attention and certainly drawing attention to herself? Quite the bully, so like her father, Kim had often reminded us. We had all tolerated her childish ways, her flirting, scheming, even her lying.

I tossed the towel over my head to my back, but my movement was limited. I rubbed it as best I could, then wiped my buttocks and the tops of my legs. A notion was forming. Had Paula sensed that mocking, along with Kim's neglect, and channelled it into revenge? In her eyes, I had won Mike and I had taken her sister away. The big sister who had always been there to care for and protect her; who continued to protect her younger brothers, more so than her mother who was forced to work and find her own way of healing.

Angie was finishing her make-up, still in her bra when I entered the bedroom.

'You OK?' she asked, zipping up her make-up bag and laying it on the side.

'Thanks yes, better. I think the bath has eased it.'

'I'm glad you and Kim had a chance to talk,' she said, pulling down a lovely purple tunic from its hanger in the wardrobe and spinning around. 'You seem much happier. Neil thought so too. He's such a sweetie. Let me bang on about all my plans for the centre.'

'He is. I wish I had time to get to know him better but …'

'Make it happen,' Angie said, removing her dressing gown and sliding into her top.

'I love that top,' I said. 'It's about time I found something a bit brighter.'

'Thanks. Well, we could have a day out together at Bluewater. Ask Lou and Cathy and make a day of it.'

'Yes, I'd like that,' I replied, finding myself looking forward to joining the human race and, in particular, my friends again. I took my body oil from the shelf and sprayed my arms.

'Do you need any help?' she asked, slipping on black leggings.

'I think I can manage actually. I've loosened up a bit.' I then went to spray my legs but thought better of it. I wasn't going to push my luck. I added deodorant under my arms.

'OK,' she said, smoothing her top in the mirror, which looked more beautiful on. Then spraying herself with perfume, she said, 'Just shout if you need us, sweetie. I'll go down and get you another glass of wine.'

'No more wine for me, yet. Thanks. But I'd appreciate a nice cool glass of water when I come down. I won't be long.'

I dressed as fast as my movement allowed, choosing a silky sequin-embellished black top I'd kept in my wardrobe for years. I brought it with New Year's Eve in mind. As I wriggled slowly into it, my head was still awash with intrusive thoughts. I picked up the hairdryer and with my fingers, scrunched the wet edges of my hair. I had forgotten to wash it. 'Attractive,' I muttered to myself, thinking of Neil. I gave it a quick blow-dry on top and ran my fingers through it in the mirror.

Seeing the pallid skin and sunken eyes, I quickly smoothed in some moisturiser followed by some liquid foundation and brushed it in, blending it around my hairline and neck. After applying some eye make-up and lipstick, I squeezed some perfume onto my wrists, grabbing socks from the drawer, found my coat, shoes and filled my evening bag. I headed downstairs. It was hard to imagine just a few hours ago, I'd been hanging off the side of a mountain. Tonight, however, I was going to forget the disasters and dance into my new destiny.

The girls were ready and waiting as I marched with noticeable agility down the stairs. I drunk the cool water thirstily, and after helping me with my shoes and socks, Kim and Angie accompanied me back up the steep slippery path to La Poste. Music blared along with flood lighting as we passed the small square beside it. A few small groups gathered, drinking from steaming cups. The spicy aroma of mulled wine brandished the air. The evening sky had turned from a velvety navy to charcoal black. Dark clouds masked the stars, threatening over our heads.

'I wouldn't be surprised if we have snow,' Angie said as she and Kim slowed at the restaurant steps.

'Not such a bad thing for New Year's Eve,' I said, turning to Kim. She seemed quiet. Perhaps like me, she had found the whole Mike and Paula debacle draining. She had carried it for a long time.

'Are you OK?' I asked.

She forced a smile. 'Yes, just chilled after that bath – it made me sleepy. I barely slept last night.'

I felt a stab of guilt. Kim, more than anyone, had travelled the furthest to make this happen for me and I'd given her nothing but grief in the last twenty-four hours.

'And,' she continued, 'I was disappointed I couldn't get hold of Will to wish him Happy New Year. So, feeling a bit blah!' Her tired eyes widened. 'I'll perk up in a bit.'

'Oh, of course, the time zone. He would be asleep.'

'Yeah, I forgot to ring him. My phone was here with Cathy and I missed his call. He was probably out celebrating with the guys, no doubt a bit seedy.'

'The Rose', Kim's signature tune on my phone, played in my head reminding me of the strength it gave me whilst on that ledge. My instincts kicked in. Kim's energy had always been kind and soothing. She had never had a nasty streak in her bones and it was highly likely that, in my stunned state, I had misjudged her motives. I cradled her waist as we climbed the steps. 'I'm so sorry, Kim. Don't let it get you down. Blame me. I'm the one who is responsible for keeping you awake. Besides, he will understand when you explain you were two thousand metres up, hanging off a tree.'

Kim's snort took me by surprise. 'Yeah, course he will.'

We both laughed. I let out a sigh. 'Would it help if I told you my soreness with you is evaporating? Kim, I do believe you had my interests at heart, and I don't want to ruin your New Year celebrations.'

'Gin, of course you aren't responsible. Gosh, you were in shock. You needed a scapegoat anyway! Don't we all? No, I'll get back and sort things with Will. It's just that I wanted to start the New Year on the right foot. In my head, I'd planned to make more of an effort with him, especially hearing everyone's stories this week. But—' Kim squeezed me '—thanks for that. Knowing you understand why I didn't tell you is absolutely brilliant. It means a lot, and I can finally sleep. She smirked and snuggled in to me. 'Ginny, I'm so pleased. That's the second time you've thrown me a lifeline today.'

'Oh, you're going to start me off,' I whimpered as we hugged by the front entrance.

'No, we're going to all make hay while the snow falls. Well, with all this inspiration I thought I might try a different tack with Will, try understanding him better and confront things in a different way. I thought, maybe we can work out a compromise. Let's go and enjoy. I'll try him in a few hours.'

I thought about all the effort the Flowers had made this week, these last few months, all year, in fact, and beyond, throughout Mike's treatment and suffering. A constant stream of love and support. I really had to stop harbouring my insecurity issues and try to forget about the last twenty-four hours. Make it a memorable evening. It was the beginning of a New Year, after all.

Kim opened the first door to the restaurant and Angie led me into the porch opening. Straight away I saw Neil, even though the room was squeezed with tables and bodies. He was dressed in mid-grey jeans, a navy sweater and a beaming white smile. My heart flickered like a candle and emanated as much warmth. He appeared about ten years younger, his skin rosy and relaxed. He was talking animatedly to a rather glamorous-looking young lady. Then seeing me, he slid behind her, excusing himself. He came towards me, his glistening eyes not leaving mine. It was then I heard shouting.

'Three cheers for Ginny – the woman who saved her friend today. Hip-Hip,' the room roared. I covered my face listening to the noise. Kim's hand was under my elbow, keeping me straight.

'Hooray.'

'Hip-Hip.'

'Hooray.'

Neil kissed my cheeks and I brought my hands down.

'Hip-Hip,' the man continued, and then I saw it was Stefano, the owner. He held both his thumbs up to me.

'Hooray.'

Then, as I went to step forward, a loud chorus erupted.

'For she's a jolly good woman ... and so say all of us.'

Waving my palm at my hot face, I grabbed Kim, showed her off to my audience and hugged her.

'Really, anyone would have done the same.' I sniffled as tissues were offered, then like a bursting raincloud, I couldn't stop and blubbered all over Kim's shoulder.

'Let's sit you down, honey,' I heard Kim say, sniffing herself. 'It's all been such an emotional turmoil.'

Stefano led us like royalty across the room and halted by our favourite round table. 'We are very proud. Tonight, you are special guest, Ginny.'

Blushing with all the unwarranted attention, I dabbed my cheeks with a tissue and air-kissed Stefano with gratitude.

'You are the sweetest,' I said. 'Thank you.' I glanced at Neil who was smiling at me with pride and rubbing his clean-shaven chin.

'Well, we leave you to enjoy your evening,' Stefano said. 'I'm sure you want some peace before you're bombarded.'

'Yes, there's something else you should know,' Neil said lifting his chest. 'Some footage of your rescue has been released and in the last half hour it's got a lot of media attention. On Twitter apparently.' Neil glanced at Christoff for confirmation.

Christoff shrugged. 'It's true. I don't know how, everyone has phones, skiers, helicopter crew? I just saw it on Twitter an hour ago.'

'You may find you are in demand for interviews,' Neil added.

I gasped. 'Oh, my God.'

Chapter 22

Kim

Witnessing this magnanimous scene, I was totally shocked, in awe and wonderfully proud of Ginny. She deserved the attention, of course. She had been extremely brave, but I had no idea how I could ever thank her for the risk she took. Being her friend again, however, was the best feeling in the world.

Lou came up from behind us and gave Ginny a quick hug as we huddled at the table. 'Incredible, let you out of our sight for a few minutes and you're up to all sorts. Our hero. I'm so proud of you, my gorgeous girl,' she chanted before kissing her on the cheek.

'Our star pupil,' Cathy chimed. 'And, darling, karma will repay you; be sure.'

Angie, unable to reach us through the bustle, blew Ginny a kiss. 'It was all that fitness training. You see, it paid off.'

'It must have,' Ginny said. 'I could never imagine having that kind of confidence six months ago.'

'So true,' I said.

Christoff, who was stood by the table now beside Neil, shook his head in dismay. 'I can see headline, "Wonder Woman comes to the rescue in Swiss Alps".'

Ginny chuckled and then crossed her brows at Neil. 'I can only assume you had a hand in all this?'

His mouth crooked to one side, like a naughty child. 'Credit goes where credit's due.'

Ginny smiled. 'I'm not upset, I promise. I'm surprised, that's all. I hadn't given it much thought, to be honest.' Then she mumbled. 'I feel quite guilty that I've been so consumed with such trivia.'

I admired her modesty. A real hero. 'Discovering your husband was cheating on you is hardly trivial, sweetie,' I whispered in her ear.

'No, but I think I've got my head around it a bit more.'

'With all that was going on in your head, it's amazing you could think on your feet and make such a difficult judgement call. I'm in awe.' The girls nodded in agreement.

'Me too,' Neil said. 'It was a huge sacrifice. You should be proud. When Kim told us, I wanted to grab you and hug you. I don't know how I managed to control my jubilation. Honestly, you are one amazing woman.'

'Well, I'm so glad you didn't,' Ginny guffawed.

Neil rubbed Ginny's arm. 'I didn't think you'd appreciate it.'

Ginny crossed her arms. 'You would all help someone in need,' she insisted.

I jabbed her rib. 'I'd like to think I had your gumption,' I said, seeing the waiters head our way. My mouth salivated watching our first course arrive. 'We'd better sit down.'

Angie peered up at the men. 'Time for food. We could squeeze you two in,' Angie said. 'Where are Tom and Florian?'

'No, really,' Neil said. 'Tom and Florian are with their families. We have our seats over there, but we'll come along after our food.'

I peered at Ginny, her mouth dropping as Neil strode off down the aisle with Christoff.

'Don't be sad, you'll see him again later,' I said as we shuffled around the circular bench to our table.

'No, I'm fine,' Ginny said, shuffling in beside me. 'More than fine, actually. After our chat earlier, I was thinking.' She chuckled to herself, in much better spirits. 'I know, it happens occasionally. Anyway, it occurred to me, and correct me if I am way off the scent here, but my theory is that Paula may have built up resentment.'

I crossed my eyebrows. 'I'm not sure I follow ...'

Ginny had barely touched her salad, but our plates were collected and replaced with the next course. A delicious foie gras. I grabbed my fork and looked across to Angie and Cathy's plates of delicious-looking garlic mushrooms.

Focusing again, I said. 'That's interesting?'

Ginny straightened her back and tucked into the duck pâté. I tasted mine; the smooth creamy texture satiated my tongue. 'Mm.'

Ginny leaned towards me. 'Lovely, isn't it. So, the basis to this theory is: when we, you and me, first became friends and began to spend more time together, we became very close, and gradually, not intentionally, we left her out.'

'Well, we were the same age and in the same class,' I said, but I was getting the gist.

'Yes,' Ginny continued. 'And you as her sister, guardian almost, with all that was happening between your parents, were paying her less attention. In her eyes, as we became closer, and with Cathy and Lou as we were all friends around the same age, I think she may have felt neglected, become bitter. I think this could be her retribution. For both of us.'

I stared at Ginny.

Ginny tilted her head as she explained further. 'It all makes sense really, sweetheart. I know she hated being excluded whenever we did things together, and even – I believe – to the extent that she created ways to stop us. Do you remember the cinema that time, she said she was sick, and you had to stay home and look after her? Ice-skating in London, that day she followed us to the station, telling you that she wouldn't be able to find her way back. Oh, and that day she said she was attacked in an alley and we couldn't go to the youth club. Do you see the pattern? I believe she resented me because, unwittingly, I took you away from her. You were her rock.'

'Oh, we're not responsible. She just takes after my dad,' I protested, but I realised Ginny may have spotted something I hadn't.

'No, not directly, but she was always a loner, flighty with her friends. And later when I started going out with Mike, who she became obsessed with, I think she had even more reason to feel bitter towards me. Not only had I taken her sister away from her, but the boy she had fallen in love with as well.'

I stared, raising my eyebrows at her. 'Jeez, Gin, you could be right. I don't know. Sounds plausible. So, by splitting you and Mike, then you and me, she's got her revenge? But how would she have known I hadn't told you?'

'Oh, I don't know. I'm not that clever. It's only a theory. I don't pretend to know how her mind works.' Ginny put her fork down onto her clean plate. 'Perhaps she knows how your mind works. Like I said, it's a theory.'

'And so like you to analyse everything. It could explain why. But she's a grown woman and should have known better. You can't make excuses for her.'

'No, but I can reason to myself. Pity her in my own way. And after what happened to me today, well, it's put things into perspective. Mike's behaviour shouldn't affect our relationship. It was Paula and Mike who were in the wrong. Not you. The thing is, she knows you were more concerned for me and that got to her. Maybe hearing that we were all on holiday together, it made her see red. You have friends when she has so few; she could no longer have Mike. Don't you see? I had everything she ever wanted, and in her eyes, you abandoned her. She's making us both pay.'

'Why did I never see that?'

'She's your sister, maybe you don't want to.'

316

I shook my head. 'To entice Mike … I'm so sorry.'

'Don't be sorry, Kim. I feel a bit sorry for Mike now. He was the real victim in this. He would be embarrassed.'

'Why feel sorry for him?'

Ginny laughed, sticking her fork into the crusted salmon now in front of her. 'Him being lured so easily. I really don't know. I find it a bit pathetic now.'

I smiled, relieved and impressed that she could deal with it so quickly. 'Perhaps you had already moved on. This year I mean. It's possible that the time you spent worrying over Mike's words, you had mentally got it out of your system.'

'Possibly.' Ginny slapped her hands against my thighs. 'I've been pathetic. What was the point of wasting twelve months of my life worrying about it? He's gone. I'm moving forward, shedding Mike out of my skin, my bones, my head, everything.'

I was worried this was all going so fast. It had been a crazy twenty-four hours, but Ginny seemed resolute. I placed my fork back on my plate. The salmon was lovely, but there were more courses to come and I needed to pace myself. I pushed my plate to one side.

'Now then, lovely, you have to stop fretting about me. I'm going to be fine. This accident today has at least knocked some sense into me and shifted my psyche. It's time I left Mike behind and started living.'

Ginny

Taking the flute of bubbling Champagne, I placed it in front of me. With all the exhilaration bubbling around me, I felt drunk already. But with all the attention now off me and the last year erased from my mind, I wanted to share a wonderful evening with my friends.

I stood up and raised my glass along with my voice. 'Let's have a toast.' I paused as they gathered their glasses and got to their feet. I then held my glass in the centre of the table. 'Here's to my gorgeous friends. My beautiful Flowers. I want to thank you for arranging this trip. I love you all. *Santé!*'

'*Santé*,' they chorused.

'And—' I glanced at Kim '—one more for the friend I misunderstood. I'm sorry I accused her because I should have known her heart was in the right place all along, so now I fully appreciate how much she was trying to protect me. I'd like more than anything to raise a toast to Kim. *Santé*, Kim.'

We sat back in our seats pouring the bubbles down our throats when Cathy commented.

'Such a relief you two are friends again.'

Angie placed her glass down. 'Yes, it was getting tense.'

I rested my elbows on the table, just as my mother forbade me to do, and proffered a smile. 'I think it's time I began to appreciate what you've all tried to do for me these last few years. I know I've shut you all out, so this is the perfect opportunity to let you know, in future, I will open up and let you all in.'

'That's music to our ears,' Lou crooned. 'I'm sure they'll all agree,' she said, her moist eyes searching our smiling faces – my besties and me sitting like petals around a pistil. Our reproductive years may have been over but to me, that pistil represented a belly overflowing with seeds of future potential.

Lou lifted her flute and chinked glasses again. 'To our friendship,' she said.

As we munched through our course of crispy fried courgettes, Cathy pushed half to the side of her plate. 'This week you have all shown me precisely what Fun Loving, Older Women Embracing Life with a Renaissance of Spirit is all about. I'm going home with renewed vigour having learned my situation isn't so bad; like you, Gin, I'm not going to shut myself away so much. I'll limit my time in my study and organise time with Anthony and plan some fitness events with you girls.'

'Oh, I've learned so much from you all for sure. I'll tell you now, dangling on that ledge, I felt so helpless. Then seeing just one boot and leg, as I turned to look down the crevice, I was really scared. I imagined a corpse hanging near me. It was so eerie. Luckily, when my phone stopped, I heard a whimper and a surge of relief swept through me. Though weirdly, "The Rose" tune that played between those silences really soothed me. It was like a signal from my Flowers.' I gurgled. 'It was actually Kim's tune on my ringtone, but I found it so comforting. Like some mystic messages, and I ...'

The aroma and sight of beef bourguignon under my nose momentarily distracted me. I began chopping the succulent pieces of meat.

'Anyway,' I continued, as I let my dish cool, 'I felt that you were all urging me on. Encouraging me. I lay there reflecting on everything that had happened this week; all your stories ran through my mind, the struggles you're still dealing with – I was dealing with. The risks. Like the risk you took when you asked that guy to help you by fathering your child, Kim. The desperation you must have gone through, the tension with Will then, and now.'

'And jeopardising our friendship,' Kim added. 'But, I've taken everything on board and not only have I learned to face conflict head-on in the future, but I've realised it's the compromises in a relationship that count. I'm determined to find a workable solution for Will and I.'

'Aww, I hope so, in fact I'm sure you'll find that fighting spirit that I still can't believe came to me earlier.'

'God only knows where that strength came from.' Kim blew out a large sigh, then laughed. 'I was literally bowled over.'

The girls laughed. 'Well, I will have to take some credit, for that,' Angie said. 'You don't get to grab, carry and throw your own weight without physical preparation.'

'I know. And thank God you motivated us to put the work in.

'I would never have had the confidence if I wasn't physically strong,' I said. 'But, your strength has come in a different guise, Ang. You and Lou. Both of you battled with temptation.'

Angie sat up straight. 'Yes, in fact it's done me a big favour. I've discovered a fighting spirit side to me I didn't know I had. I'm determined to focus on my dream instead.'

'Me, too,' Lou said. 'It's time I began getting to know Terry again. I've vowed to myself to communicate with him more and enjoy the great relationship we have. He's a real romantic at heart and I've spent too long comparing him with Jimmy, the tough charmer who really is an absolute knob.'

We sniggered. 'All those years you idolised him,' Angie spluttered.

Lou waved her hand. 'I know. What a waste of time, eh? I'm so glad I chose not to meet him the first time he contacted me. No, I love and appreciate Terry so much, we have a great lifestyle, and of course, great friends. I'm so looking forward to planning our retirement together.'

'That's what I'm looking forward to, too,' Cathy said with shining eyes.

'Yes, well, we'll know to balance our time, won't we, Cath?' Lou jibed, poking her in the ribs.

'Darling, I'm going to take that in the spirit I intend to maintain.' Cath sniggered. 'I know you all think I need a humour transplant.'

'I'll come and get one with you too, Cath,' I said. 'Mine's disappeared.'

'No, you've been great this week,' Angie said. 'You've changed considerably.'

Lou cupped her hands. 'What we need is a little pot of each of our strengths so that we can dip into them when we need them.'

'Great idea, Lou,' I agreed. 'I'll have some of your brave spirit. It helped me this afternoon. Your gumption. Look how you told

Jimmy straight. Got on with it. You know, I really thought you were going to melt into Jimmy's arms when you saw him. Honestly the heat, the chemistry.'

'Yes, I think we were all warming our hands in that fire,' Kim said.

'It's out, I can assure you,' Lou stated categorically.

'Well,' I said, 'my aim is to get braver from now on. Assert myself. Try new things. I don't know anyone who trusts in their own judgement as you do, Lou. You have such an instinct, a quiet confidence. You just threw yourself into the skiing. All these skills I need to learn or reacquaint myself with if I'm to cope better on my own.'

Kim reached for my hand. 'But you're not alone. You have friends. Why don't we set up a WhatsApp group where we can all let off steam or share any news?'

'Yes, why didn't we think of that before?' Cath said shifting another half-empty plate to one side.

'I can keep up to date with your writing, Cathy,' Kim said.

'Sounds perfect,' I said. 'But I intend to get out more, make time to call in to you all from time to time. And like you, Cathy, I want to create a new sense of purpose in my life. I think it's great that you're now following your passion. Maybe I was on that ledge for a reason. To make me question things and test my courage. Maybe a fusion of everything I've learned from you, Flowers.'

I felt all eyes on me. 'It was a massive test.' Kim chuckled.

'Well, there'll be more of those to come,' Angie declared. 'We're not Flowers without a reason.'

I looked at my plate, still half full of bourguignon. 'I'm rattling on, aren't I? So, shall we open another bottle and start celebrations?'

Soon, five Champagne flutes were raised in the air, with an explosion of different cheers. I gulped a large mouthful to quench my thirst. I raised my glass. 'To us Flowers – let's celebrate!'

321

'And—' Angie winked '—here's a toast to your long bright future. Did I mention there's a fabulous opening with my company if you …'

'Really? I hadn't heard.' I laughed. 'But I'd be delighted to be part of that amazing company.'

'I've got plans to expand to Nordic walking too.' Angie clapped. 'Yes, I've been making lots of notes from all your input. We'll be the fittest and healthiest Flowers and certainly won't be growing old gracefully! Not in Nepal!'

'Or Machu Picchu,' I said. We laughed, chinking glasses again, and Kim squeezed my hand. 'To a wonderful future, sweetheart.'

'Thank you. I've got the best friends in the world,' I said nibbling at my delicious bourguignon and sipping more bubbles.

* * *

'Let me top these glasses up,' Neil said, popping the cork on a cool bottle of Champagne.

'Oh, hi Neil,' Kim said, rising from her seat and shuffling along the bench. 'Yes please, I'll shuffle round, and you can sit with Ginny.'

'Oh, apologies, you haven't finished your food.'

'Oh, we've had plenty, so sit down,' Lou said, shuffling along to allow Christoff to sit the other side of the circle beside her. 'Gorgeous food, but waaay too much.'

Neil topped up our bubbles. 'Thank you, Kim. Yes, as ever, Stefano, in true Italian style, loves to fatten us up. I don't think Weight Watchers would survive up here.'

'Not a chance.' Cath giggled.

'Whoa, I was going to cancel my personal trainer but, even with the skiing, I've blown up,' Kim said.

'It's not just the flab. We'll be fighting for this lady's attention, won't we, Kim, as you'll be heading back to Oz,' Neil said, sitting snugly beside me, my skin tingling as I smelt his familiar scent.

He immediately wrapped an arm around me and kissed my cheek, swiftly reminding me of what it was like to be loved.

'You are an enigma, beautiful lady,' he said. 'In less than a week you've got me hooked trying to work you out. From your first stumble to your heroic but self-effacing charm. All I can say is I need more. I want to know what you'll surprise me with tomorrow.'

'It's our last day,' I said puckering my lips and making a sad face, but in a way, I was looking forward to starting my new life. This trip had more than served its purpose even though I would miss having my friends together, and Neil.

'Don't remind me, I'm missing you already,' Neil said lowering his eyes. 'Do you think you'll ski tomorrow?'

My hand flew to my throat. 'No. I won't be getting back on skis, even if my back felt better.'

'What if I took you on to the nursery slope in the morning, if you're feeling up to it? Maybe we could go for an hour, just to get your confidence back; then we could drive down to the lake. Spend the afternoon there.'

I felt a wave of excitement flush through me, but I was wary. 'Neil, I'm not sure I should do either. I've ...'

'You said you were asleep when you passed Lake Geneva. Wouldn't you like to visit Montreux? It's beautiful. You'd love the flowers along the path, particularly lovely in spring but even this time of year, there's the colourful alpines and decorative cabbages. There's a good restaurant by the pier, overlooking the lake.'

Our eyes locked. In those amazing eyes was a yearning, just as my body longed for him. In just a few days we both knew this was something special, but were we kidding ourselves? The distance between us, and the fact that I could never trust a man again, would make it impossible.

'Neil, I ...'

Kim screamed beside me and jumped out of her seat. 'Will! Oh my God, Avril, Mai! And, Tandy! What are you all doing here?'

323

Kim

I scrambled out from the bench and threw my arms out catching Avril first. 'Wow, this a surprise.'

Avril had her arms around my neck. 'We had planned to get here earlier, but Dad's flight was delayed, and we wanted him to be here for the big surprise.'

'Well, you've certainly done that.' I was speechless. 'How lovely, and New Year's Eve too!' Tears welled in my eyes as I grabbed Mai, then Will. Will had come all the way from Australia, Avril from London, and Mai, not so far, from Milan where she was working. And Tandy from Ouchy, near Lausanne.

'Hey, Kimmy, sweet.' Will pulled me into his chest and enveloped me in his arms. 'I didn't think I was going to make it. So pleased we got here. I've missed you.'

I looked at my watch. 'With an hour and a half to spare before the New Year strikes. I've missed you too.'

I heard my daughter Avril calling me. 'Mum, you should meet David.'

I let go of Will and shook a young man's hand. 'Avril has told me she met someone. You've been together a few months, I understand.'

'Very pleased to meet you,' David said politely in broken English. 'Yes, we met in June. I was, am, as you say in English, head over heels in love with her.'

'That's good to hear,' I said, wondering if his accent was Italian. 'Avril's certainly smitten.'

He smiled, then crooked his mouth. I detected the word smitten may have escaped him.

Will was rubbing my shoulder. I turned and pecked him on the lips.

'So how long have you been planning this?'

'Err. Since three days ago.'

324

'What? You're kidding, right?'

'Nope,' Will said shaking his head from side to side. It was so good to see him. He looked a little tired, his clothes creased, but that was understandable. And he must have got last-minute cover at the hospital. This was so out of character for Will, and so unexpected. What a day this had been. I couldn't have been happier. I looked around, straight into wife and mother mode, wondering how I could fit them in and feed them. Stefano was already on the case, however. He was shuffling people along the bench and chairs of the nearest long table and working out what accommodation he could spare at the hotel. I hadn't taken too much notice, but many people were now finished with their meals, and were either up dancing or going out to the square.

'We have plenty of food,' he said to me, shrugging his shoulders. 'I charge them half the price.'

'Thank you so much,' I said hugging Stefano. 'We had better order more Champagne,' I added, then continued to introduce Neil and Christoff to my family. It was then that Tandy's husband, Jean-Pierre walked in.

'He's been to park the cars,' Tandy said hugging me. 'We couldn't get them all in one so we left one just down the road and he's been sorting it all.'

'You don't know how much I appreciate all this, my dear Tandy. They could have hired cars.'

'Yes, but I wouldn't want to miss this. I've never been up here over New Year. We managed to get an apartment for two nights.'

We sat down once the introductions finished and the table was set for the gathering, including one extra.

Mai sat beside me on the bench with Will squeezing on the end and Avril and David opposite, holding hands and gazing adoringly at one another. Tandy and Jean-Pierre wriggled in. Food and drink arrived swiftly and, feeling overwhelmed, I pinched myself. Not only did I have my best friend back today, but my whole family and Tandy. Life really didn't get much better than this.

'So how was skiing, Mum?' Mai asked.

'I'm addicted,' I said honestly. 'I'm not sure if it's the skiing or après-ski I've got addicted to but I think I'll be back for more. In fact, I think we all will. Well, Aunt Ginny and I had a nasty scare earlier. Had to be rescued from the mountain. I'm not sure how we feel about returning yet.'

'Oh, my God, Mum.' Mai leaned back to inspect me. 'Were you hurt?'

'We're fine, sweetie, honest, Ginny was more bruised than me,' I told her. Mai leant forward on her elbows. 'No, really? She looks amazing.'

'Yes. Although, she is also the local hero.'

'Heroine, Mum,' Avril corrected, but was all ears. 'What? Why?'

I glanced over at Ginny, hoping she wouldn't mind but her hand came up covering her face as she listened. I scanned my audience, Will now attentive. 'She saved me. I was caught on a tree branch and she did this amazing stunt to grab me and throw us to a safe spot of snow. Apparently, it's on social media.'

'Oh wow, Auntie Ginny, go you,' Mai said.

'Thank God you're OK, Auntie Ginny. But well done and thank you,' Avril said, already scrolling down her phone. 'Oh, is this it? Is this you on Twitter? Ooh, you're trending on Twitter. Go to hashtag gransrescuealps.' Avril watched as the video played, turning it so we could watch. 'Wow! Wow, how on earth? Oh, ace, Aunt Ginny. I don't know how you managed that. I thought I was fit, but that's amazing! Have you seen it?'

It was a truly amazing scene. I was astounded at Ginny's strength, as were the others.

Ginny wiped her brow. 'No. And I don't need to. It was horrid.'

'Well, it's probably been edited but, that didn't look horrid at all. You should be proud.'

326

'Let me see,' Angie called across and took the phone from Avril.

Lucien arrived with Champagne distracting Avril and David as they whispered. I saw Avril tap Will's arm and whisper in his ear.

As the girls and Neil and Christoff watched the video, Tandy wriggled back out of her seat and watched with Angie, Lou and Cathy.

Will was pouring out Champagne as their first course arrived. He then took what was left in the second bottle and offered it to the other table.

'We have some here,' Christoff said, taking the bottle from the cooler and topping up the flutes.

Avril rose from her chair, chewing her lip. She then took a knife and banged lightly, trying to grab everyone's attention.

'Aunt Tandy, Mum, Dad, Mai and all my other aunties here. David and I have an announcement to make.'

I immediately grabbed my cheeks. They'd come all this way to announce their engagement. It was too soon, but it was comforting to feel she would be looked after in London. My head was swimming in anticipation. I stood and braced myself.

She took David's hand as the noise in our corner died down. 'We are thrilled to tell you – David and I are expecting a baby.'

I gasped with air trapped in my lungs. The corner filled with *ahhs* and congratulations.

Avril looked at me, then Will. 'Mum, Dad, you are going to be grandparents.'

I gazed at Will, my eyes spurting tears. A cocktail of emotion whirled in my head, my stomach. Avril and David were suddenly caught in a mob of embraces. I sat stunned, staring at Will.

'Did you know?' I suddenly voiced accusingly at him.

Will looked sheepish. He shrugged. 'She was desperate to get me here.'

Avril's face appeared beside him. 'Aren't you pleased, Mum?

Sorry, I so wanted to ring you when I found out, but I wanted to wait the twelve weeks. I had to tell Dad otherwise I'd have never got him here. I really wanted it to be a surprise for both of you.'

I started, 'Yes, it is a surprise, poppet, but what about ...' Lou and Cath grabbed her attention. 'Darling, congratulations, David is so lovely,' I heard Cathy say.

Ginny sidled up to me, her arm looping through mine. 'Granny Kim, eh? Congratulations. Face says horrified rather than thrilled though.'

'I don't know how I feel, Gin, if I'm honest. She's so young. She's just finished uni and begun her career. And they haven't been together long.'

I looked at Will across the table. He shrugged. 'I'm with you, love, but what can we do?'

I pinched the skin between my brows. 'She's sharing a flat.'

'Apparently, they're buying a flat in London,' Will said, obviously having checked a few things out. 'Av says she'll keep her job part-time. She seems to have it all worked out. David's a few years older and has a well-paid job. We have to trust them to make the best of it, love.'

Cathy pulled Will to his feet and hugged him.

Ginny rubbed my forearm. 'We all met our husbands when we were young. We managed. I was younger than Avril is now when I gave birth to Ross. Lou, Angie only slightly older. She's a bright girl with a sensible head on her shoulders.'

'But she'll be in London, on her own. A baby. Plus, childcare will cost a fortune,' I protested.

'No one can prepare themselves for children, Kim. Our budget was always tight; but you manage, you have to be creative, but you manage.'

I sighed. I couldn't get the fact that this was still my baby girl. So young. It wouldn't be so bad if I could be closer. Ginny did have a point though. 'Yes, I suppose they'll have to manage. It

328

won't be easy. I can't profess to have scraped by, I didn't have that problem, but, yes, I know you all had financial constraints early on. Maybe we can help out financially at least.'

'They've got one another and presumably David's parents may be able to offer some support.'

I spurted tears again. 'You know how to cheer me up, Gin.'

'Oh, Kim. Sorry, that was meant to comfort you,' Ginny said stroking my wrist.

'Ginny, I'm sure it was.'

We laughed. 'Yes, well, we know how easy it is to feel you're helping someone, don't we?'

I squeezed Ginny's hand and met her warm caring eyes. 'I have to get on with it, don't I?' She peered at me with a tight-lipped smile and I raised my brows. 'I suppose it will give me further ammunition in my armour when I tackle Will.' I looked up to see Will and Cathy looking down on me.

'You'll work something out, I'm sure,' Ginny said. 'Embrace it and enjoy it.'

'Darling, congratulations, you'll get used to the idea,' Cathy said, reading the situation and holding out her arms.

'Sorry, Cath, I haven't congratulated Avril and David.'

I rushed round to the other side of the table to my daughter who was stood grinning from ear to ear beside her tall handsome partner. I held out my arms. 'Congratulations to you both. I squeezed her tight, then hugged David. 'It took a minute to soak in but I'm very happy for you both. And you have to promise me you'll look after my little girl.'

'Mrs Anderson. I still can't believe my luck. Avril's more than I ever dreamed I would ever meet. I'm not even sorry we've done things slightly askew; we'll make it work, I promise. We have a lifetime to put the rest in place.'

Will's hand rested on my shoulder and he kissed my cheek. His chest protruded proudly, and I felt his arm slip around my waist. I admired him for his handling of the news, despite having a few days to digest it all. I would never have expected him to stay so calm. We stood united, watching as my friends – my twins' 'aunties' – rushing around fussing and congratulating them. Tandy, I then noticed, was snapping photos with her phone. Both Will and I obliged with a proud smile and Avril and David joined us glistening with happiness.

'Is there going to be a wedding?' Will asked. I nearly choked. He sounded so like a proper father – nothing like my own.

Avril was being fussed over, but David turned, hearing Will's question.

'We are in the process of getting a mortgage for a flat in South London. We are waiting to hear. If we can save once we have our own home, we will get married as soon as we can.'

Will held up his palm. 'No, I am Avril's father. I insist – or rather we insist. I know it's old-fashioned, but Kim and I will be happy to pay for your wedding. When you're , of course.'

'But, Dad, we want to get married in London. I know you'll be disappointed but …'

Will interrupted. 'London is fine,' he said ruffling up my top as he squeezed my waist. 'I've had your mother nagging me these last few years to come back, so guess who's going to lose the argument now there's a grandchild on the way.'

Will's head locked to mine for a few seconds and, wondering if my ears were fooling me, I asked, 'You mean that?'

'You think you're the only one who wants to be near our girls and grandchildren? I can work here too.'

I'd never squeezed him so tight. 'Oh, Will,' I sang peering at Avril, and for the first time, spotting a roundness in her frame.

Ginny spun from her seat, charging up to me and making every effort to lift her arms to hug me. 'Oh, sweetheart, wishes can come true,' she said. 'My hugest congratulations. I'm so thrilled for you all.' In seconds it seemed midnight had struck early as hugs and kisses spread like wildfire around our corner. Food and Champagne was snatched from our plates as we nattered loudly and excitedly. Then Stefano turned on the TV for the New Year countdown.

'This is going to be the best year ever,' I said to those around me, which was everyone, Will, Avril and David, Mai, Ginny, Neil, and the girls, Tandy, Jean-Pierre. 'Five, Four, Three, Two, One … Happy New Year!'

Chapter 23

Ginny

'Happy New Year, darling Kim. I can't wait for you to get home to England,' I said, hugging her and then Will. 'You must all come and stay whilst you're searching for a place,' I said as Will and the girls kissed her. Then Lou, Cathy and Angie came and grabbed us, tossing us our coats and inserting a flute into each of our hands as we raced outside to the square. Everyone followed. Neil helped me get my coat on. Large droplets of snow wet my hair and face as I stepped out to the terrace, but I didn't care. I felt my heart racing with sheer joy. This place had a real air of magic and I wanted to savour every particle.

As the last dong of the bell chimed, we linked arms for 'Auld Lang Syne.' I grabbed Neil as Angie pulled Christoff beside her and we all sang as we marched to the music in and out.

Once the dancing stopped, Neil took me in his arms. His lips gently brushing mine at first, then he whispered, 'Happy New Year, Ginny.' Before I could say it back, his lips pressed on mine, exploring every angle slowly until it touched the nucleus of a magical bubble. Neil pierced my core. But my heart and head were tectonic plates, grinding in opposite directions. He was special, my heart was certain, but my instinct and head screamed otherwise. Not only had I only known him a few days, but also mentally, I had a way to go. The sediments of my life with Mike needed draining and a new rock needed to form. I needed to operate as Ginny. How could I entertain a stranger in my home? Or go to a strange man's?

It would take another year to recover, regain my composure. How could I consider a relationship? Music began playing and I recognised the opening. We ended the kiss with a peck, a snow-flake in between. We both laughed. As I stepped back for air, Neil steadied me, holding me close. The Flowers cheered behind us, clapping their hands, the words to 'Waterloo' fusing in my ears. I felt myself blush and hearing the song I knew so well, I had to let Neil know, I hadn't met my Waterloo.

'Let's have a gentle dance,' Neil said, his hand wrapping around mine. We were all then in a circle, dancing to Abba.

'I think we've all met our Waterloo this week,' Kim yelled as the song played. I continued with the dance, but when it finished, I steeled my lips.

Above the noise of the music I shouted. 'Neil, we have to talk.'

The cheerful expression on his face collapsed. 'OK,' he said but I sensed an altered energy.

'Can we go back inside?'

'Erm, yes. Of course,' he said holding out a hand for me to lead.

I saw Lou and Cathy frown at one another as I began to follow Neil. Angie scowled, curious, and Kim yelled, 'Is everything OK? You guys look …'

Determined, I pushed on, threading my way through the body of the partying crowd. Inside, looking for a quiet spot, we found only waiters racing around with trays of soiled plates and half-empty glasses. I chose a long table that was cleared, not too far from the door, and sat at one end. Neil sat opposite me on the wooden bench, placing an elbow on the corner.

I sat upright, both elbows on the table and hands clasped for support. I rested my chin on my hands. 'Neil, I don't want you to take this personally,' I started, 'because I do have feelings for you. But, I can't do this. Not yet, and maybe not for a long time. It's all happened too fast.'

He took one of my hands. 'Ginny, if the feelings are there, that gives me hope. I realise it's early for you, but allow yourself to be, give yourself permission to live in the moment. Enjoy the now while you can.'

'I have. I've enjoyed this week, your company, the skiing, the mountains, the sunshine, my friends, après-ski, every part of it, very much; everything about it has exceeded my expectations, bar the fall, naturally. But in so many ways, this week has been a huge challenge. Who I am here is not who I am at home. My issue is that I haven't even begun to begin, or plan to begin my new life. I'm not in that place that I can commit to someone. And I don't want to.'

'That doesn't sound like you at all,' Neil responded. 'Although, an enigma is what attracts me to you. You are complex.'

'No, Neil. Not necessarily complex, it's very basic in my eyes. I know I'm not ready to take on a relationship. I need to be honest with you. I feel what we have is deep, and I can't deal with it. I won't want to let you down because my normal life, the real life I have to pursue each day, isn't in place. I can't lose the Ginny Watts, the wife, mother that I am. It's difficult to explain.' I tried to find the right words. 'I'm not the single Ginny if that makes sense and I can't just switch. I can't imagine you being in my home or meeting my children or me staying here with you. I don't know if you understand. It's not simple to explain but I feel it could take a long time for me to feel different, so I don't want to stop you meeting someone else.'

Watching Neil swallow, I knew he was hurt, but I also knew that I would hurt him more by committing to him. He licked his lips. 'There won't be anyone else. I'd given up hope of finding you, if I'm honest.'

334

'I never meant to lead you on,' I tried. 'This week, this … it's just happened as far as I'm concerned.'

He shook his head. 'You haven't. Not at all. You've identified your limitations, told me straight and I don't want to deal with them. I'm sorry it is what it is. I accept and respect your honesty.'

I sighed and turned my hand, squeezing his. 'Thank you. Maybe if we do ski again next year, I hope to be in a different place. I couldn't expect you to wait though.'

'Well, anytime you want to come out, no commitment, you're welcome,' Neil said, then let go of my hand. He cupped his chin with both hands. 'But can I ask you something?'

'Of course. I'll forever be your friend, Neil.'

'Theoretical question. If you had fallen off that slope and lost the opportunity to ever feel alive again, even for a few hours, what would you choose to do?'

I shrugged. 'I don't know.'

'OK, if you broke a leg, who would be there to look after you?'

I twisted my mouth. 'No one. My friends … somehow. I don't know.' I got his argument, but I didn't have the answers.

'OK. It's not a test. Just something to think about. If you returned home and missed me, would you ring?'

I shrugged again. 'I really don't know. I haven't thought of all these what-ifs.'

'No. And I never did.' He placed a hand on the table and tapped his fingernails. 'If you get home and find you miss me, would you call me?'

I inhaled. 'Possibly.'

'OK. If I said, while you are sorting everything out in your life, you have a friend who wants to visit, say, in a month, six weeks, someone who will stay in a local hotel, no pressure, but offered to meet up a few times, take you out to lunch, a stroll, or for dinner a few times, maybe in your local, or if you're more comfortable with your friends, how would you feel about it?'

'I'd probably say, it's a good idea. It could be a welcome break.'

'But if you got home and didn't like that idea, what would you do?'

'Cancel.'

'So, would that idea be a compromise to where you are in your plans for the future?'

'Possibly.'

'Would you like to think about this proposal and analyse it?'

I laughed. 'Let me ask you something?'

'OK.'

'Am I really the first woman you have met and had feelings for in six years?'

'Bull's eye!'

We both stood and as his arms opened, I fell into them.

'I think I may have met my Waterloo after all,' I said, finding his lips. 'And, as long as there's no pressure, I might cope with a visit or two.'

'Well, take it one step at a time. Let me come and see you. See how you feel. Think of it as an escape from your daily battles.' Neil grinned.

I squeezed Neil's hand. 'I certainly will,' I said. 'And, I won't be defeated by a mountain either. I can't wait to tell the Flowers. I'll be celebrating my sixtieth end of February too, so maybe we can do something special with *our* friends and their husbands. They're yours too.' I smiled to myself; this was exactly what we were talking about earlier. Making something work. And Neil had just demonstrated to me a great way of approaching it. It was odd because I've always asked questions in my job; they came as second nature. But, this way, Neil had erased any pressure.

Pleased with the outcome, I let out a sigh. 'And, in the morning, I want to get back on the slope and ski again and I hope Kim will come along too.'

'That's the spirit.'

'But then—' I stroked his arm, reaching for his hand '—I'd

336

love to walk and lunch by the lake with you if that's still OK? As long as I can come back for our last après-ski.'

Neil's eyes melted me with their sparkle. 'Ginny. I'm happy with whatever makes you happy. You've brought sunshine into my life this week. I told you, my heart is pumping again, and I'm savvy enough to know I can't have that all year, but you're welcome here anytime; winter, summer if you want to come travelling, or back in the UK when I'm home.'

'That's very kind, Neil. Thank you. Maybe in a few months. Come on,' I said pulling his hand. 'Let's join the ladies on the piste.'

Neil clutched my waist as we wandered towards the door. 'I would love that. Meanwhile, you concentrate on building that fresh start, what passions to follow, choices to make. I have faith you'll do what is right for you.' He pulled out his wallet and took out a piece of paper. 'I've written down my phone and email details. Keep them safe. You send me details of a local hotel and set a date. Not February half-term, I have kids and grandkids out, but a date that suits you. We'll meet and see how you feel. You can decide if and when to come out. Or, you can just ring for a chat.'

The girls rushed up to me as Neil and I joined them in the crowd. 'Is everything all right?' Kim yelled.

I smiled as the music faded. 'I couldn't have imagined a better outcome,' I yelled and immediately froze at the heads turning. I giggled and shrugged, then as the girls stopped laughing I said, 'Girls, I've learned so much this week. Neil and I will take it slow. I've still so much to do and learn, but I couldn't have moved this far without you all; thank you for bringing me.'

Angie held out her arms. 'Group hug,' and the signature sound of Abba's 'Dancing Queen' wailed. Our favourite. We danced for another hour, our coats and jackets, hair and skin soaked by the giant flakes of snow, my body soothed and lifted by the music.

* * *

The following morning, I skied. Slowly at first, on the nursery run with Neil, then we joined the Flowers on that very piste I had slid from. Naturally, I was quivering initially, but as many skiers were still in their rooms nursing hangovers, the slope was clear and I relaxed, carving smoothly down the soft snow of the wide slope, making lovely turns, and even as we got to the dreaded junction, the strength from those around me was palpable. I glided back to the lift easily, their love cheering me on.

Neil and I had a wonderful romantic walk and lunch in Montreux on the shore of Lac Léman, the lake we call Lake Geneva. The sunlight broke through the soft haze swirling around the mountains and glistened on the lake as we strolled along the colourful flower-filled promenade and then sat on the restaurant terrace, enjoying a lovely meal. It was beautiful, and he promised we would return for a paddle steamer ride if I came back to Switzerland in the summer.

As Neil drove along the valley and I looked out to the mountains, it seemed an age since I had taken in that first view. My perspective had spun on its head in just a week. No longer were these great rocks cold and hostile, huge and threatening; instead they were wonderfully warm, sunny and inviting, and open to any challenge. As we wound back up the mountain road and I gazed down, my fears had transformed to respect. Respect for their beauty, respect for their danger. But mostly, respect for how, like my Flowers, and Neil, they had lifted my spirits.

Twelve Months Later

New Year's Eve

Ginny

I hope you enjoyed the Flowers story. Ross, Rachel, their families and I have recently gathered for Mike's second memorial and as it has now been a year since the ski trip with my Flowers, I thought you might be interested to know how this year has panned out.

I'll start with Lou because there haven't been any major changes yet with their business. I will tell you, however, that Lou has been so much happier in her own skin. She has employed someone who she hopes will take over her position. It's allowed her to cut down on her hours and make some time for herself and Terry. I think meeting up with Jimmy finally killed her curiosity. She and Terry have been spending more time together, walking and enjoying pub lunches. They've even bought bikes, so they can go off to the coast and cycle.

And Lou is keeping to her fitness training with Angie four times a week. And, three months ago, she and Terry received an offer from a potential buyer, which they are still considering. The offer is a good one, but they are struggling to let go. They're going to make a decision early in the New Yesar. What is lovely for Lou, however, is she's stopped fretting about the latest expensive designer handbags and even thrown away her lip gloss – she's still beautiful without it.

Then, Cathy and Anthony. Well, Anthony is barely recognisable now. In a good way. Soon after Cathy returned from the ski trip, they went away for a few days and had a good chat. She did, as she promised him, manage her time better, and together they compiled a list of things they felt they were passionate about. Cathy naturally wished to continue writing and has since had another three short stories published. She has also completed and sent her first novel out to agents. Two have shown interest so far, but she's writing her second novel, deciding which of the two are her best fit, and waiting to see whether any more come to the table, so I'll know more in the new year.

She and Anthony have also been making time for one another and taking days out, as well as embarking on a fitness programme with Angie, Cathy is working with us for two sessions and with Anthony for another once a week.

Anthony has been dieting and exercising for ten months now. He's lost two stone and is working towards losing one more. Naturally he's cut right down on the booze. He's done very well and looks so much better. And, during this time, he's got involved with the Prince's Trust, two days a week mentoring young entrepreneurs who have been accepted on the scheme. He loves it and enjoys being around the youngsters, helping them adjust and set their short- and long-term business goals.

As well as that, he's built himself a log cabin in the garden. Yes, his own shed, he says to keep out of Cathy's hair. But with Terry's help, it's turned out so amazing he's keen to build more, and now he's thinking of setting up a local Men's Shed group for men in a similar position to socialise. So more to come on that, I'm sure.

Kim and Will did finally take that huge leap across the ocean. We celebrated their homecoming and her sixtieth the weekend after they returned. They're currently staying with me in the village and Will found a similar position in London. Naturally, Will is still settling in with his work. Kim is concerned and doing everything she can to keep any other stress off his back. They moved back in June just in time for their first grandchild.

Avril and David had a little boy, Jules so, besides house hunting, Kim is now looking after Jules two days a week and has flown to Milan a couple of times to see Mai. It's been great having her close again, and we've managed a stroll or a trip to Bluewater lunching out every week. She has also joined us with the fitness sessions. What she hasn't concentrated on, and I'm sure it's only a matter of time, is getting back to her garden. Once she has her own home, I'm sure she will. They're hoping a suitable house will come onto the market in the spring when the daffodils bloom. So, whilst she's thrilled to be home again and close to her loved ones, Kim's situation is still a work in progress.

Angie has kept to her plan and thrown so much of her energy into her wellbeing campaign. She has upped the ante on the blogs and regular newsletters, as well as running competitions and giveaways for free sessions. The local and national press have helped, featuring her in their Health pages as well as several glossy magazines. She is looking at franchising the business at the moment so I'm looking forward to finding out more in the New Year.

It seems Rob has caught her contagion too. Inspired by Angie's compassion for better education about fitness and health as well as seeing the business flourish, Rob has also got involved. He's been working on new software for monitoring the health and fitness programmes, a new class-booking system as well as the marketing system for the business. He's also started fitness training and keeps Anthony company twice a week. If that isn't enough, he's also considering getting involved in the mentoring at the Prince's Trust. Angie couldn't be happier – Rob's energy is up!

So, it's been a very exciting year for my Flowers. And what have I been up to? Well, when I returned home I was fired up too and began planning a party for my sixtieth, sending out invitations and phoned Neil with a date. He booked his car ferry straight away and I booked him into a hotel. I also tackled the huge pile of paperwork and Mike's belongings, which I hadn't faced up to yet. With Lou, Angie and Cathy's help, we spent an entire Sunday going through paperwork, most of which was binned, but the girls helped me with a filing system, and we also found a share certificate I didn't know about. When I say didn't know, I think Mike had mentioned it, but I hadn't really paid attention.

Anyway, it turned out I still owned twenty-five per cent of his business. When he sold it 'for a song' it had been run down because of his ailing health, so Scott paid what he could afford, but when the girls saw dividends had gone into a bank account, I contacted Mike's old partner to find out more. Scott had taken on two new partners since he bought Mike out and he told me the business was back up and thriving. That twenty-five per cent was now worth five times the amount we took out of the business nearly three years ago. So, I thought it prudent to sell them back as they rang back and offered. It took a lot of pressure off me financially, and Scott and his guys were delighted to have the shares of the company back. Naturally, I handed in my notice at work.

However, the following Sunday when the girls helped with Mick's belongings, it was awful. My emotions really dipped. I set aside some things for Ross and Rachel, but it was a wrench. Watching his favourite shirts, jumpers, trousers, shoes, suits, golf clothes, aftershave, towels, hats, gloves, coats, books – all Mike's life, reduced to black sacks. I couldn't let the girls just take them away. I kept them for a few days and rung Ross and Rachel. They didn't want clothes but said I should keep anything special to him that he would want them to keep. I took the clothes along to the Cancer Research shop. I kept the golf clubs, watches, cufflinks, his football trophies, even though they had tarnished in the loft. I put them in Ross's old room and Ross took most of it when he came down a few weeks later. Leaving some for Rachel, and me with just a wedding ring and, of course, his phone. Not a pleasant task at all. But it made me realise I wanted to make more effort to see Ross and Rachel. So, I've diarised dates for visits and get-togethers once a month.

So, after that little rollercoaster, I managed to collect myself and get back to Angie's gym. As the weeks passed, I gathered momentum and spent time with Angie doing fitness sessions and getting to know her business. In February, I took up her offer of the marketing director position and got started. Three days a week, I sat with Angie getting to know the intricacies of the direction she wanted the company to go, and we discussed immediate strategy and priorities. I then worked with Rob on the software, using what knowledge I had and tapping into some I'd read about it, then set to work.

I'm loving it. Angie has been great to work with and I'm loving getting back to my preferred way of working. The money is great too. Plus, all the perks. Our fitness programmes are working well, and the Nordic walking has taken us up another level. And we Flowers are fundraising to walk the Great Wall of China in the autumn next year for the local hospice and cancer research.

It's been exciting. I have all my Flowers close and we've been adding meetings and events to the diary. I managed to force myself to go out with them as couples for meals, dances, quiz nights. And all the guys seem to like Neil. Neil made his visit at the end of February keeping his promise – no pressure. I was apprehensive at first. I wasn't sure how I'd feel about meeting him on my own territory, but just a few minutes after the initial date, we fell easily back into step. Then it was time for my party.

I had told Ross and Rachel about Neil and was pleased they came along, but I felt the strain. It was difficult for them. The celebration went as well as it could, but I had to give them time. They admitted they liked him and enjoyed his company, so it was a good start. After the party Neil and I spent several days together, walking, talking, having lunch, meeting the guys in the pub in the village two evenings.

Then, one night we went to eat at a hotel. A cosy old inn I chose for its Dickensian feel and connection. We ate a light meal, as I ate very little with my training anyway, but with it, we shared a beautiful French wine and held hands, our chemistry building – the moment felt right. Just as it had in Ma Maison before I had checked my phone.

Neil ordered another bottle to take up to his room and we sealed our bond. It was wonderful to feel loved again. Neil made me feel so comfortable, so special. And after that night, I knew we both wanted more.

He returned at the end of April staying again at the same hotel. I stayed with him for three nights and our time together just got better. We spent time with our friends, Neil gaining friendship and respect from the guys. He fitted in with the group very well. Then I got a call from Rachel inviting us to hers. Neil was due to return home to Surrey, but he was accommodating and extended his stay. Ross came too and helped Rachel's husband with the barbecue as the sun was kind.

We had a lovely afternoon and both my children and their families made a great effort to be accepting. My confidence was growing and as Neil was back in the UK, I saw him every other weekend, in Surrey or I booked the hotel close to the village. In June, Neil invited the children to his home in Surrey. It was a small cottage, but the garden was spacious, in a beautiful setting overlooking hills and paddocks. Ross helped Neil with the barbecue and it was heartening to see them gelling; beers and banter rocked back and forth with Rachel's husband joining them when he wasn't entertaining the kids. That was when I found the new Ginny Watts. When I told my friends, we had a girly night to celebrate. Angie insisted I take August off to spend with Neil.

My yearning to see Neil grew but I managed to pace myself. We drove down to Switzerland and spent most of August in Europe visiting Lake Geneva again, then up to the village and Verbier to celebrate Swiss National day. It was all so empty without the snow, but the mountain and forest walks were beautiful. Neil then drove us to the Italian lakes, taking in the sights and boat rides of Lake Como and Lake Garda before a train ride to Venice.

I couldn't believe I could be so happy again. The months have passed so quickly with Neil, my love for him grows daily and my friends and family have grown to love him too. In fact, they are all here in Switzerland with us, to ski. We've just arrived to celebrate the New Year and a quieter week on the slopes. My Flowers can't wait to show their guys how it's done – not Angie of course, but I can't wait to show my children and grandchildren my skills. One thing's for sure, Christoff has plenty of booking for his lessons. And, all importantly, I have so much to thank my beautiful friends for.

Acknowledgements

As always, my love and thanks to my husband Glyn for his constant love and support, and for the hours he spends each night creating delicious dishes for my hearty appetite. I'm resigned to the fact that I'll never be slim again – ever!

Huge appreciation is also overdue to our friends, Lynette and Stephen. This novel would have been impossible to write without the huge inspiration I drew from their passion. Not only did they introduce me and my family to skiing, but have for years so generously accommodated Glyn and I at their bolthole in Switzerland as well as extended that same generosity with their efforts and patience with our skiing. Our lives have been so enriched by those fantastic weeks we have spent with them skiing, along with the warm and wonderful people of La Tzoumaz who served to add to that enjoyment.

And my gratitude extends further to friends, Christine and Nigel, Sally and Pete. Again, their love and support through the years, the skiing and my writing journey have brought an abundance of fun, laughter and tears which has provided much inspiration for this book. Rest assured, my characters and their situations are purely fictional and in no way portray their real lives, but what the novel does reflect is those wonderful aspects that deep, long-lasting friendships can bring.

I also owe a special thank you to my children and grandchildren. Unwittingly, their love and support provide every grain of motivation and every ounce of perspiration I need to complete each book. Huge thanks also to all my readers and the book bloggers who make it their mission to make time to share their passion and introduce other readers to my and other authors novels. Their dedication and energy amaze me.

And, finally, I'm forever grateful to my lovely editor, Nia Beynon and all the team at HQ Digital/HarperCollins. For Nia, for believing in this story and for all the wonderful support in the editorial process. It's been an absolute pleasure working with her. And the team, thank you for all your hard work making it all possible and for my beautiful cover.

Dear Reader,

Thank you so much for reading Five Ladies Go Skiing. It's been a great pleasure to write and I really hope you've enjoyed it. The characters will stay with me for a long time and it's always sad to leave them. I will miss them all greatly, as I hope you will too. The idea for the novel was inspired by my own wonderful friends and that warm glow I feel inside when I'm among them. We have shared many activities and experiences, skiing being one, so the idea to send my ladies skiing was a clear winner for Ginny's recovery. It was a change of scenery for one as she had never been to Switzerland with Mike, and the challenge to learn to ski was quite different to anything she had done before, so my own late experience of skiing provided an impetus.

And a challenge it was. Although my children had skied, I was over forty when I first took the plunge. It was tough to begin with like anything worth doing, but it soon became addictive. Not only was I lucky to have great friends and mentors, but it was an activity that our whole family could enjoy. We returned to Switzerland, the French Alps or the Italian Dolomites at every opportunity, and I was even fortunate to ski at Lake Tahoe in the USA. What I find even more amazing is that I can now enjoy skiing with my grandchildren too. They love it!

And who couldn't fall in love with the setting? Switzerland has it all. The mountains, the snow, rivers and lakes are stunning, and each season offers something new and different. From skiing to mountain climbing, walking, cycling, whitewater rafting, and sailing not to mention the mountain food and wine. I can't wait to return, and hopefully the Flowers, the five ladies, have inspired you to visit the Swiss Alps too.

Wishing you all a very Happy New Year.

Love

Karen x

Dear Reader,

Thank you so much for taking the time to read this book – we hope you enjoyed it! If you did, we'd be so appreciative if you left a review.

Here at HQ Digital we are dedicated to publishing fiction that will keep you turning the pages into the early hours. We publish a variety of genres, from heartwarming romance, to thrilling crime and sweeping historical fiction.

To find out more about our books, enter competitions and discover exclusive content, please join our community of readers by following us at:

🐦 *@HQDigitalUK*

f *facebook.com/HQDigitalUK*

Are you a budding writer? We're also looking for authors to join the HQ Digital family! Please submit your manuscript to:

HQDigital@harpercollins.co.uk.

Hope to hear from you soon!

Turn the page for an extract from Karen Aldous's
brilliantly uplifting read *Under a Tuscan Sky* …

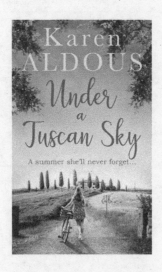

Turn the page for an extract from Karen Almond's brilliantly uplifting read Dancing Through the Sky...

Chapter 1

It was so much more than an image. Olivia Montague's finger stroked the ageing photograph of the elderly couple gazing, not at the camera, but intensely at one another even after all those years. And even in sepia tones, glints of love and passion sparkled in their eyes. Olivia's skin prickled looking at them standing huddled among the vines, their chemistry radiating from the now dulled, once glossy paper almost as if it were present in her Bermondsey sitting room.

More significantly for Olivia, her Italian grandparents represented family – solid, the roots of her being, an impenetrable foundation. Nonna Elena and Nonno Angelo had such adoration for each other, just like her mother and father in those brief years before her father's death.

She picked up the other photograph her mum had given her just before Nonna's funeral. The one in colour, two sunburned hippies blazoning sun-bleached hair against a lapis blue sky and pink sand, eyes lost in one another. So much longing and love dazzling between them. Sadness gripped Olivia's throat. Was it real or was she imagining it? Was it an Italian gene that had by-passed her? Why couldn't she have that love? She and Will Parks had never looked at one another like that.

Lowering the image, she glanced up, her eyes seemingly fixed on wooden shutters encasing the bay window, but they stared vacantly, imagining the inscription on her headstone.

'Sadly, she was never loved, nor could ever love.'

In her mind a sinkhole appeared, a huge void spreading fifty feet or more on a wild meadow splashed with blue crocuses and daisies. Sliding into it was Nonna, Nonno, her mum and dad, her gran, grandad, Will. Then her. She lurched violently forward then quickly grabbed a long twine, then clutching tufts of long grass and a thread of tangleweed, she scrambled on her knees to save herself.

On her knees on the bank, she twisted herself reaching out in the hope one of them would be close enough to pull her to safety. Instead she watched each slowly sink into the blackness, tumbling in different directions, not one of them reaching for her. It was a nightmare imitating life, reinforcing the abandonment she constantly felt: that hollow space she'd locked inside her that no one could or would want to fill. Even Will.

The image played repeatedly during the night and the following morning whilst she was on her run. As she was drinking cold water and black coffee in Starbucks afterwards, her phone pinged. A message from Will saying he would be back from football about seven. A sigh escaped her as she slid the screen back and stuffed the phone back in her pocket. At the tables surrounding her, young couples and family groups seemed to be looking on with pity.

'Of course I have a life,' she screeched under her breath, pulling out her phone again and willing it to ring and hitting Chiara's number when it didn't. It went straight to voicemail.

The problem was, the only people she could talk to about the photos just weren't available. Like most Saturdays, there was no Will to hang out with until later, much later, and when he was still likely to be in his football coma. Her friend Chiara would be taxiing Sophia to some activity or other.

Olivia felt she would really value another opinion right now. But no other friends knew her as well as Chiara. It was times like these when she really wished she had someone else close, particularly family, but unless she counted a runaway hippy mother somewhere in northern Italy, she was on her own.

Their last tête-à-tête ended in tears after she'd asked for help with – and invited her mother to – her Granny Nora's funeral. Not only did the inebriated Roz tell her to pull herself together, but she also refused to come on the grounds that she'd barely known her, and couldn't even bring herself to send a spray of flowers. Sometimes she just wished her mum could be a proper mum and at least offer a friendly ear when she needed one. She swore the woman didn't have a heart. Olivia's mood was sinking.

She folded her arms, hugging them in to support herself. Maybe staying at Nonna's villa in Tuscany without Will would give her some space, a proper chance to deal with her grief, and maybe, clearing out the villa would give her the opportunity to discover more about her nonna and her mum. It was their home, and the place where her mother grew up. An insight into a woman who could abandon a child and then thrust responsibility for both grandmothers' funerals and property on that child could prove interesting.

Trying to muster up enthusiasm for the dreaded task of sorting through Nonna's things, Olivia opened her phone and tapped on to the newly created schedule for 'Trip to Italy', on her Diary app. There was so much to fit into eleven days and if Will was adamant he couldn't make it, she had double the workload.

Already listed was her meeting with Signor Ricci, the real-estate agent, at four o'clock on the Friday afternoon she arrived at the villa. Being the pragmatist she was, she added a scheduled stop at two-thirty at the co-op supermarket in the village on the way – just to gather supplies; although she was sure Gabriella would leave a few essentials.

She then blanked the first two days specifically for cleaning the three-storey villa, in preparation for a viewing booked in already on the Monday, possibly two. It would be hard work and it had crossed her mind to employ cleaners and house clearers even, but she figured it was better to assess what was important first.

Her thoughts were interrupted when a woman approached asking her if the chair beside her was taken.

'No, take it,' she said.

The woman lifted it across to the table close by and Olivia observed as the woman was joined by a younger woman carrying coffee. Probably mother and daughter, she thought with a sigh of envy. How nice to just call your mum and meet up for a coffee or shopping. Even have an adult conversation with her. Why was her mother so different, so distant and cold? Maybe when she cleared the villa she would uncover something about her. She figured there must be some remnants of her mum's childhood within its walls.

Thinking she was sounding like a detective, hunting clues as to why her mother was so estranged, she chuckled to herself. Although she saw her two or three times a year, she was still curious about her and her elusiveness. It was possible there were personal journals she kept as a child, or diaries. Somewhere she wrote down her thoughts – schoolbooks, even.

In her teenage years, she had discovered quite a collection of her father's schoolwork when she had helped her gran clear out the loft. In fact, growing up in his home in Bermondsey had given her some comfort at least. Her grandma Nora had everything neatly boxed and took great pleasure in talking about her son. Unlike Nonna Elena in Italy who seemed to close down when she asked questions and treated Olivia's mum with contempt.

As a little girl, Olivia remembered crying on occasions when she visited her nonna's Tuscan villa, because her mum could only stay a day or two. Each time she said she had to get back to work. It made sense as an adult, but as a child, Olivia resented it and now she was more curious as to why her mother was like she was and why they never spent much time together. She could only hope there would be something to give her more of an insight into the woman; maybe she could even find out where her mother lived now.

As they had always stayed at Nonna's to see one another, Olivia was now eager to discover where her mother currently called home. Was she living in some hippy commune or moving from one to another? It was never discussed, although she was sure she had enquired on a few occasions but was told only that she lived north of Tuscany. Regardless, once the villa and farm were sold, she would still want to visit her mother and needed to know her address. Yes, this could be her raison d'être.

She opened another heading on her app, the one with her 'To do' and 'Lists'. She added a new heading: 'Mum's history'. There were several she used constantly, the 'House', the 'Work', the 'Italy' the 'favs', the 'wish' list, all the daily functional stuff, then there was the 'Wilting Will' list she'd begun in the early hours this morning when she had woken up, the images from the photos stamped on her mind. The list of cons on this far outweighed the pros. The top one being no great love or passion.

Why was she still with him? she had asked herself. He didn't exactly cut the mustard. The only two things on her list in his favour were his pretty face and barbecuing skills. Like those before him, any spark that she may have once imagined had undoubtedly failed to ignite. Love just didn't seem to feature in her genetic make-up. And to add insult to injury, Will – knowing how necessary it was for her to go to Italy next week – was as ever too wrapped up in his all-consuming football and job to accompany and support her.

Should she blame herself for buying him the season ticket? Probably. The mortgage on his London flat was extortionate; but then, the choice was his, and he could at least be there when she needed him. He clearly didn't give a damn and, if she was totally honest with herself, neither did she.

Life could be far more exciting as a forty-year-old singleton. She needed to widen her circle of friends perhaps. At least she would get out of the habit of sitting around weekends waiting for Will to turn up in his football-induced drunken stupor, only to watch him splayed across the sofa, snoring it off.

'Best to speak to Chiara and get her opinion, then go with it,' she muttered to herself. 'Bloody well set myself free.' In a determined frame of mind, she ordered another coffee and, seeing some people leave, curled her feet up on the comfy two-seater sofa, which was still warm. At least if she stayed here she would be among company rather than home alone.

She unlocked her phone and began a 'New Olivia' list. The possibilities were endless, she thought, entering ideas of places she wanted to travel and the goal of learning to salsa. She was sure she was doing the right thing. If only Chiara would ring back. It was always comforting when her friend approved; besides, she knew that if she didn't act soon, she would talk herself out of it. She needed Will out of her life.

At seven-thirty, Chiara still hadn't rung back, and after looking at the photos again and adding to her 'Wilting Will' list, Olivia was convinced the time to ring him was now, before doubts crept back again. Taking a deep breath, she punched her finger on Will's avatar, straightening her back, ready to jump up when he answered. There would be no more wasted weekends or listening to him and his pathetic mates drivel over every second of a game she had no interest in.

How grateful she was to her mother for once, as it was Roz who had insisted she squeeze those few photos into her cabin-sized baggage. It felt like the wake-up call she needed. She just hoped she wouldn't live to regret it. Her hand hovered over the call-end button.

If you enjoyed *Five Ladies Go Skiing*, then why not try another delightful read from HQ Digital?